Outstanding praise for the novels of Daniel Palmer!

Desperate

"Fans of well-crafted Hitchcock-like thrillers will enjoy *Desperate*."
—Associated Press

"Palmer's best book to date."
—BookReporter.com

"Palmer has a way of telling the story and making it fresh."
—*Winston-Salem Journal*

Stolen

"Unrelentingly suspenseful."
—*Publishers Weekly*

"He already exhibits the skills of a master craftsman. Fans of Harlan Coben or Lisa Gardner will adore his look into the lives of an everyday couple."
—*RT Book Reviews*

"A twisting, suspenseful chiller of a book."
—William Landay, *New York Times* bestselling author of *Defending Jacob*

Helpless

"Warning: Once you start reading this novel, you will not stop! Palmer has concocted an adrenaline-fueled thriller."
—Lisa Gardner, *New York Times* bestselling author

"Slam-dunk readable, scarily real, and emotionally satisfying. If you're looking for a hero to root for, an innocent man charged with unspeakable crimes, an everyday town riddled with secrets, and a desperate father with everything on the line, look no farther than *Helpless*."
—Andrew Gross, *New York Times* bestselling author

"A high-speed thriller . . . *Helpless* is edge-of-your-seat reading."
—Lisa Scottoline, *New York Times* bestselling author

Delirious

"Smart, sophisticated, and unsettling . . . not just a great thriller debut, but a great thriller, period."
—Lee Child, #1 *New York Times* bestselling author

"A solid, well-constructed thriller, nicely convoluted and definitely suspenseful."
—*Booklist*

"A debut that is satisfying as a psychological thriller and as an ultramodern techno-thriller."
—*The Sun-Sentinel*

Books by Daniel Palmer

DELIRIOUS

HELPLESS

STOLEN

DESPERATE

CONSTANT FEAR

Published by Kensington Publishing Corporation

DESPERATE

DANIEL
PALMER

PINNACLE BOOKS
Kensington Publishing Corp.
www.kensingtonbooks.com

PINNACLE BOOKS are published by

Kensington Publishing Corp.
119 West 40th Street
New York, NY 10018

All Kensington titles, imprints, and distributed lines are available at special quantity discounts for bulk purchases for sales promotions, premiums, fund-raising, educational, or institutional use.
Special book excerpts or customized printings can also be created to fit specific needs. For details, write or phone the office of the Kensington sales manager: Kensington Publishing Corp., 119 West 40th Street, New York, NY 10018, attn: Sales Department; phone 1-800-221-2647.

ISBN-13: 978-0-7860-3381-2
ISBN-10: 0-7860-3381-9

First mass market paperback printing: May 2015

10 9 8 7 6 5 4 3 2 1

Printed in the United States of America

First electronic edition: May 2015

ISBN-13: 978-0-7860-3382-9
ISBN-10: 0-7860-3382-7

Dedicated to Marjorie and Stephen.
Thank you for raising such a wonderful daughter.

and

In loving memory of my father, Michael Palmer.
I sure do miss you, Pop.

CHAPTER 1

The only thing unusual about the bus stop was the crying woman sitting on the yellow-painted curb. Her hands were covering her mouth, and even with all the traffic whizzing down Massachusetts Avenue, I could still hear the muffled sobs. It was the beginning of August, and a warm breeze carried with it the sweet scent of marigolds mixed with pine. I was carrying a brown paper bag with a carton of General Tso's chicken steaming inside. Stapled to the front of the bag was an order slip with just my name, Gage Dekker. No phone number or address supplied; the gang at Lilac Blossoms and I were that close. In fairness to my heart, the bag also contained a carton of steamed broccoli, brown rice (not white), egg drop soup, and some vegetable medley thing that came with the squishy tofu Anna loved.

It was Anna, my wife, who stopped, stooped to the crying woman's level, and asked, "Are you all right?" What Anna was really asking was, "Do you want our help?"

The woman looked up at Anna, her eyes veined as though layered with bloody spiderwebs. She was breathtakingly beautiful, like a runway model: high cheekbones, a translucent complexion, and almond-shaped brown eyes perched below two perfectly arched eyebrows. Her face was a delicate oval, framed by dirty-blond hair, which hung limply over her shoulders in long, straight strands. As for her age, I'd have said late twenties—a decade my junior—but her denim jeans, ripped at the knees, along with the accompanying jean jacket, suggested a younger woman. A girl, really.

"Are you okay?" Anna asked again.

The young woman sucked in a heavy breath, pushed a thick band of hair away from her eyes. She sniffed twice, rubbing the underside of her nose with the back of her hand, flashing me her chipped (and chewed) fingernails.

"Yeah, I'll be all right," she said. "Thanks."

Anna sat on the curb beside her. I kept standing, marveling at the depth of my wife's strength and compassion. She connected while I just watched like a spectator in the stands. It didn't surprise me; Anna had done the same for me.

"Are you sure you're okay?" Anna asked, reaching out to touch the woman's shoulder with her well-manicured hand.

"I'm fine, really," she said.

"Do you want to talk about it?"

"You're not from Planned Parenthood, are you?"

Anna looked up at me. The flicker in her eyes registered something important, or the possibility of something important.

"I'm sorry, I don't understand," Anna replied.

The woman exhaled a weighty breath and shook her head. "Sorry, bad joke. Look, since you asked, I just told my boyfriend that I'm pregnant and he went nuts, made this big scene, and just drove off. I guess he left me stranded."

Something passed between Anna and me, a look we'd shared on any number of occasions. It was the look she gave me every time we saw a pregnant woman or a mother with her baby, the look that said: *Why can't we have what they have?*

"How come your boyfriend was so upset?" Anna asked.

The crying woman's laugh was spiked with anguish. "I guess 'cause I don't know if it's his," she said.

I studied Anna carefully, gauging her gestures and mannerisms to get a lock on her emotions. In the six months we'd been married, we already had been to couples therapy. In fact, everything about our union was accelerated, but that wasn't uncommon in extreme situations like ours, the marriage counselor had explained. In those half-dozen sessions, I'd learned all about active listening. About checking in. Making sure Anna knew I was there for her. In truth, we had gone to therapy proactively, before we had any major issue to address. Figured it was a bad idea for two grieving parents to join their lives without having the tools to make the marriage work. Anna likened it to moving into a house without checking to see if there was a roof.

"Do you have any place to go?" Anna asked.

"I'm going home, unless that asshole won't let me back in."

Anna stood, brushing bits of sand and gravel from the back of her skirt. She found her wallet from within her purse, took out a business card, and hesitated before offering it to the young woman. Anna was a management consultant. She worked out of the house and traveled a lot on business. She was accustomed to passing out her card with our home address on it to strangers, but with this young lady she had hesitated. This wasn't about business. No, this was a personal matter, and Anna knew giving out her card was as much about Anna trying to remediate her own troubles as about offering to help this young woman.

"Please take my card," Anna said. "My name is Anna Miller and this is my husband, Gage. If you ever need to talk to someone, you can give me a call. Okay?"

I knew what Anna really wanted to say. I could read between the lines, no different than learning a new language. Anna's eyes spoke of hope; her hands, each trembling slightly, spoke of desire; her skin color, flush with a rush of blood to the head, spoke of divine intervention. Our hopes and dreams could be answered in the form of this girl.

"Thanks," she said, taking the card from Anna. "My name is Lily."

Lily.

She'd always be the crying woman to me.

CHAPTER 2

We didn't intend to grow our family through adoption. We weren't even planning to get married or have kids, at least not right away. But I knew from past experience that plans and reality were not always one and the same. On our wedding day, Anna and I laughed, and said we'd had a five-year relationship in less than one year's time.

We went out on six dates before we made love. Six months later we were essentially living together. Three months after that, we got married in a private civil ceremony. No family, no friends were in attendance. It was a mutual decision. We wanted to celebrate each other but didn't want to explain our reasons for rushing into matrimony. A few months before our wedding, a few days after Anna missed her period, she had gone to CVS in Arlington Center, bought an EPT, peed on the stick, and showed me the word PREGNANT. We were going to become parents again. It was both terrifying and elating, and we needed to experience those feelings in private.

I held Anna in my arms, the two of us kneeling on the tiled bathroom floor. Even though I was happy, I felt a stab of guilt. I didn't share this with Anna. This was a time for us to celebrate. But secretly, I felt I had betrayed the memory of my son, and wondered if Anna felt anything similar in regard to her son, Kevin.

How quickly did our elation come and go? Two weeks and seven hours. That was when Anna, her voice strangled by tears, called me from a hospital in Seattle. Anna, a self-employed and highly sought-after management consultant, was traveling on business, finalizing a significant new contract, when the bleeding started. I didn't get all the words, but enough to paint a vivid picture in my mind. Alone in a hotel bathroom, trying to breathe away the throbbing pain in her abdomen, reaching down between her legs and having her hands come away covered in blood. I found out later she took a cab to the hospital. I was crushed to think of her desperate, panicked, and so alone.

When Anna came home, everything was different. I could see it in her eyes. We wouldn't try again, even though her doctor in Seattle said we could give it a go as soon as Anna felt emotionally ready. But Anna wasn't ever going to be emotionally ready. That was what her eyes told me. But the experience had awakened in her a strong desire to become a parent again, as it had with me. It also brought us closer together as a couple and made me realize this was the woman I wanted to marry.

The day Anna decided she wanted to adopt was early springtime, a cool and crisp morning with a blanket of fog low enough to kiss the ground. She had emerged from the shower, towel-drying her shoulder-length dark brown hair. She flopped down on the bed in her plush and fuzzy bathrobe and looked up at the ceiling.

"I've had enough loss, Gage. I can't risk getting

pregnant again," she said. Tears lined the bottom of her eyes.

I climbed onto the bed and lay down beside her. Our eyes met. My mind flashed on an image of my first wife, Karen. Anna looked nothing like Karen. My therapist told me this was all intentional on the part of my subconscious. I said it wasn't subconscious at all. I couldn't be with a woman if every day she reminded me of my first great love.

In truth, I hadn't noticed Anna right away. She was new to our grief group, which met on Tuesdays in the basement of a nearby Unitarian church. Her blank and unreadable face didn't draw me to her, but she was clearly attractive—later I'd say gorgeous—tall and long-limbed, athletically built, with alluring brown eyes, a prominent nose, and a beautiful olive complexion. Unlike most of us at group therapy, Anna kept to herself. But one evening while filling our Styrofoam cups with coffee, Anna had smiled at something I said and I felt my heart quicken.

Was it attraction? Could I be interested in another woman? It had been four years since the accident that had claimed the lives of my wife and son. *Was it too soon to have this feeling?* But I felt it—a powerful tug on my heart from just one simple smile.

Hope.

Attraction.

Desire.

Anna had experienced a similar loss with the death of her son, Kevin. After this new loss we agreed on two things: we wanted to parent a child, and we wanted to adopt. A few days after we made the major decision Anna said, "I don't want to use an agency in the traditional sense."

Again, we were in bed and I propped myself up on elbows to look at her. "How else do you adopt a child?" I asked.

"I've been doing a lot of research," Anna said.

I wasn't surprised. Anna was on a mission to have a baby, and I was in lockstep on the journey with her. She was also very practical and methodical in her business dealings, and these attributes carried over into our new quest. She felt her age, thirty-eight, and wanted to have a baby as soon as possible. It was like a thirst that had to be quenched.

"We can skip the agency and do a direct adoption with a birth mother. Technically direct adoptions aren't legal in Massachusetts, so we'll eventually have to hire an agency to facilitate, assuming we find a willing birth mother."

"Why go that route?" I asked.

"Direct adoptions are much faster than agency adoptions. At least, that's what I've read online. But it does require a lot of extra effort. We'll have to use our enthusiasm and initiative to find a birth mother. It might take some luck, but from what I've read it'll definitely take a lot of work."

"Do we take an ad out on birthmotherswanted.com?" I asked, smiling.

Anna gave me a funny look. "Actually, you're right about taking out an ad, sort of," she said. "We have to make a profile on a website that birth mothers search to select potential parents."

"So we make a profile and then the birth mothers contact us?"

"Like I said, it's faster than going through an agency. I want this, Gage. I need it," Anna's eyes were wide with exuberance, her hands wringing mine like they were dishrags. "My heart hurts. It literally aches with this longing."

We both lay quiet on the bed. "Do you think I'm turning my back on Max?" I asked. It surprised me to hear myself voice this fear aloud, but relieved me too.

"You mean by adopting?" Anna asked.

"Yeah," I said. "Do you think I'm betraying his memory?"

Anna nestled into my chest.

"I think we'll never heal," she said. "But I don't want to give up my dream to become a mother again. I want to raise a baby. I want to see my child grow up, play sports, have friends, learn an instrument, go to a dance or on vacation. These are all the things I can't do with Kevin anymore, but it doesn't mean I can't ever do those things again."

"The obligation of the living is to live," I said.

Anna sat up, looking impressed. "Did you just make that up?"

"No," I said with a little laugh. "My therapist did."

For the next few weeks Anna and I were on a mission to make the greatest, most compelling, most desirable profile on ParentHorizon.com, the largest registry of parents seeking to adopt.

This was, I soon discovered, a very competitive process. Yes, it's all about giving a child your complete and total unconditional love. And yes, it's also about expressing sincere gratitude for the gift, the true blessing of the birth mother who makes possible the completion of a family. But at the end of the day it's also about being picked from tens of thousands of would-be adoptive parents, so you've got to put your best foot forward. Anna and I wrote draft after draft of the birth mother letter until every single word conveyed the spirit of our family and the reasons we've decided to adopt. I'd learned that this letter was extremely important in the adoption process, not unlike a cover letter from a job applicant. It set the tone for the rest of the profile.

After the letter, we completed the profile information. We listed our education (BA for me, MS for Anna), occupations (Director of Quality Assurance at Lithio Systems for me, self-employed management consultant for Anna), ethnicity (Caucasian for us both), religion (Unitarian for me, Presbyterian for Anna), smoking (no for both), years married (one), preference for a child (baby), and special considerations. Were we willing to consider an adoption with an open grandparenting arrangement? I said sure, but Anna said not so sure, so we decided not to list any special considerations.

The process of creating our profile offered us both the opportunity for some serious self-reflection, something neither of us did much of since we stopped attending grief group. For Anna, it rekindled a desire to start painting again. Prior to Kevin's death, Anna would paint murals in the hospital rooms of extremely sick children near her former home in Los Angeles. Soon after we started dating, she showed me samples of her work—pictures the parents of the children had posted on social media—and it was truly breathtaking. She could paint a jungle, a moonscape, or an underwater scene with such vivid detail, it was like being transported there.

Her passion to paint, inspired by her mother's artistic streak, was partially responsible for her becoming a business consultant to top retail clothing brands. Anna had graduated with honors from San Diego State University, carrying a dual major in art history and business. After graduation, she moved to LA on a whim and got involved in the world of high fashion as a PR flack and quickly climbed the ranks. From there, the jump into running a successful retail consulting business was ten years and various jobs away. Uniquely skilled for her line of work, Anna could critique a balance sheet as cleverly as she could a window display.

It took nearly a week of steady effort to complete our profile. We identified our favorite things from a preset list of categories. Mine included sweet tea, Twix, Rock'Em Sock'Em Robots. Some of the items Anna had selected were Dr Pepper, Skittles (never liked them myself), and her Strawberry Shortcake doll.

Pictures for the photo album section of the profile presented us both with a bit of a conundrum. Prospective birth mothers would want to know what we looked like. Anna and I had a few photographs of the two of us together to share, but most of my pictures included Max or Karen. Most of Anna's pictures, what she had on her smartphone, included both Kevin and her ex-husband, Edward. Soon after we started dating, I'd given Anna a surprise gift. I'd used Photoshop to take Edward out of one of the pictures with Kevin and had the doctored image framed so Anna could hang it up in her office. I was more than happy to delete her ex from the photograph, but I'd rather have him deleted from the planet.

Edward was good-looking in a California businessman kind of way; I had no trouble seeing Anna's attraction to him. Perpetually tan skin, dark hair, strong jaw line and teeth whiter than the whitecaps off the coast of Santa Monica where they used to live. He didn't look like a rapist, but that was what he was. Six months after Kevin's death, Edward forced himself on Anna because she was too depressed to have sex with him. The bastard raped his own grieving wife.

Anna never reported the crime. She was mourning the loss of her only child to a rare blood disease and couldn't endure more pain and emotional turmoil. Instead of charging Edward with rape, Anna left him in the dead of night—along with the home computer containing all of their family photographs. She hadn't been in touch with Edward since and, despite my urging to at least get more pictures of Kevin, showed no desire to revisit that part of her past.

So we made our profile with the photos we had, and Anna kept an online journal to show we were active on the site. When we met the crying woman, the profile had been a part of our lives for two months, our version of Geppetto's wooden puppet before it turned into a real little boy. Anna had a few contacts via the site, e-mail exchanges with prospective birth mothers, but nothing that led to a face-to-face meeting.

This was our life, playing the waiting game. I went to work at Lithio Systems, a manufacturer of lithium ion batteries located in Waltham. Anna went to work in her home office, or she'd travel on client business. She was working hard to reestablish client relationships neglected in the aftermath of all she had endured. Each morning brought renewed hope that we'd find a willing birth mother, and each night we went to bed with a hole in our hearts that could be filled only by the presence of a child. And so we waited and wondered when he or she was going to come home. Meanwhile, we did that thing living people were obliged to do. We lived.

On the day everything changed, the Red Sox were playing a day game at Fenway, but I was watching a rerun of *Pawn Stars*. I can't watch the Sox anymore. Can't read the sports section, either. Our air conditioner was doing what it could to keep the apartment cool. My beer was doing what it could to numb my thoughts. It had been a long week at work. Too many meetings collided with too little time. The doorbell rang.

Anna called from her office, “Babe, can you answer that?”

“Who is it?” I called back to her.

“If I knew without opening the door, I would have a superpower, love. I’m busy in here. Can you please get the door?”

The doorbell rang again.

I groaned as I got up from my beloved green armchair. I was too young to be groaning when I stood up. We lived in Arlington, on a street with lots of two-family houses and nice landscaping and not a lot of crime. It didn’t occur to me to check outside before I opened the door. But when I saw that woman standing there, my jaw came unhinged.

“Hi,” the woman said. “My name is Lily. I hope you remember me.”

CHAPTER 3

"Lily," I said. Some quick mental math: it had been two weeks since we'd seen her crying on the curb. "What can I do for you?"

She was wearing an aqua green jersey tank top sporting a peace sign shaped into a heart. Her light denim jeans, again ripped at the knees, partially concealed a pair of scuffed black lace boots. A waiflike nymph dressed in hipster clothing, Lily tilted at the waist, attempting to look past me and into the apartment.

"I was wondering if I could talk to you and your wife for a moment," Lily said.

I stepped aside, motioning her in.

"Yeah, yeah," I said. "Please, come on in. Anna, honey," I called. "It's Lily, the girl from the bus stop. She wants to talk to us."

I tried to quiet the shake in my voice, but I'm pretty sure Lily picked up on it. I heard commotion from the back room, Anna shuffling her papers, then the sound of footsteps rushing. I loved seeing my wife in her Saturday garb, hair askew and in a loose ponytail, gray baggy sweatpants, purple tank top, and bunny slippers still on her feet in the afternoon. She looked every bit the frantic mom, with one notable exception. Anna tightened her ponytail and smoothed her hands nervously down the front of her sweatpants.

"Lily," Anna said. "What a nice surprise. Please, come in, sit down. Can I get you something? Something to drink?"

I picked up the anxiety in Anna's voice and, if I'd tuned my ears right, could have heard her heartbeat tick up a few notches, too. What was Lily doing here? What did she want from us? Was this related to her pregnancy?

Lily took a few tentative steps inside and made a quick inspection of our home. "No, I'm fine. Nice place you have," Lily said, following Anna into our living room.

We lived in a modest two-bedroom apartment. The baby's room, or what would be the baby's room, was Anna's office. The living room was small but nicely decorated. Anna and I bought all new furniture after we got married. We had black bookcases from Boston Interior, a nice oriental rug covering part of our hardwood floor, a plush new couch, lots of houseplants, and some artwork—oils and watercolor landscapes that Karen had collected. Anna could have painted something as good, if not better, but she was not emotionally ready to break out the brushes and paints just yet. I had kept the paintings Karen had bought in the attic of our upstairs rental unit, but Anna insisted we hang them on the walls.

"She was your wife, Gage," Anna had said. "She'll always be a part of our lives. I think it's unhealthy if you try to hide the past. We need to celebrate her."

This was Anna. She wasn't threatened by my past.

She embraced it. That was why she never asked me to remove the silver chain with a heart-shaped locket that hung on a corner of the wall-mounted medicine cabinet in our bathroom. I had bought the piece of jewelry for Karen's birthday. Inside the locket, I had placed a picture of Karen, Max, and me, small as can be, but somehow we all fit. Every morning Anna sees that locket while she's getting ready for the day. Brushing her teeth. Combing her hair. Putting on her makeup. She's never asked me to move it, because she knows I need them there while I'm getting ready for my day. It comforts me. Anna understands that it doesn't take away from the life we're building together. The chain has been in the same spot day after day.

Lily peered into the dining room, which was connected to the living room by a wall-length pass-through. She paused to study the mess on the dining room table: cardboard tubes of various sizes, smaller cylinders that functioned as engines, launchpads, glue, tape, and a small toolbox.

"What's all that?" she asked.

"Oh, Gage builds model rockets for the kids at St Luke's Hospital," Anna said. "There's a field out back, so if children are too sick to come outside to see the launch, they can watch it from a window."

Lily's face brightened. "Oh, that's so sweet. What made you decide to do that?"

Like a fog drifting in, a weighty and uncomfortable silence filled the room. "Gage and his son, Max, used to build model rockets," Anna said, her voice lowering. "He wanted to do something that would honor Max's memory and help other children as well."

That Anna and I both did work with sick children—her painted murals and my model rockets—was one reason our bond had developed so quickly. Lily broke eye contact, and I got a sense she was familiar with our background. Based on her reaction, I knew better than to show her the rocket in a box I kept under my bed, the one I couldn't bring myself to launch. It was an Estes Cosmic Explorer Flying Model Rocket with laser-cut fins and waterslide decals. The oversized body tube made for precision fin alignment, and the E engine could propel the rocket some 900 feet in the air. It had one of the biggest blow-molded nose cones of any flying model rocket. It was the rocket Max and I were building before he died.

Lily and Anna each took a seat on the couch, while I shut off *Pawn Stars* and returned to my perch on the green armchair.

"So," Anna said, flashing me a nervous look. "What can we do for you?"

Lily was still looking around, as if she'd never seen how two adults lived.

"I can't get over this place," Lily said. "It feels so . . . homey."

"Gage and I are very happy here," Anna said. "Lily, do you need something?"

Again Lily looked around—stalling, or at least that was my interpretation. She kept massaging her interlocked hands. I noticed that she hadn't repaired her chipped manicure since our last meeting. Lily's mannerisms were that of a forest creature, eyes darting about, legs bouncing, a bundle of nervous energy.

"I need some help," Lily began.

"Help," Anna said.

"I decided I don't want to get an abortion," Lily said. She dropped that piece of news as if we had been a part of her decision making from the very start. "I mean, I could. I could afford it, that's what I'm saying. But I don't want to. I want to give my baby up for adoption."

Anna and I looked to each other and then back to Lily.

If Lily picked up on our shocked expressions, it didn't register in her eyes. "I didn't know what to do," she continued. "I went to the library and did a Google search thing for adoptive parents. Anyway, it took me to this website with a bunch of people looking for birth mothers. I did search by state because I thought maybe I could still see my baby, you know. Not take care of it, but see it." Lily laughed, uncomfortably. "I mean, him or her. I don't know the baby's sex yet. But anyway, I thought if the parents were at least in Massachusetts I'd be able to see my baby—well, not *my* baby, but *the* baby. You know what I mean. I'm sorry. I'm really nervous, and I don't know how all this works."

"Go on," Anna said, reassuringly.

"Anyway, I started clicking through all these profiles and seeing all these different families looking to adopt, and it really made me happy. I mean, I could actually help complete somebody's family. Really, it was amazing for me to think that I could do this. I haven't done much good for anybody, but here I am in a position to do something really great for somebody. And then I saw your profile on the site. I remembered you right away. You guys were so nice to me."

Anna was nice, I thought. I didn't do or say much of anything.

"Lily," Anna said. "Are you asking if we would be willing to adopt your baby? Is that what you came here to find out?" Anna's voice lifted. Her eyes welled.

Lily nodded as she bit at her lower lip—revealing, at

least to my eyes, the girl within a woman's body. Scared, confused, but also hopeful and excited.

Anna was elated, her eyes beaming. But there was another side to her as well. She was already guarded, fearful of getting her hopes up. *Is this really happening?* she seemed to be asking herself.

"You want us to adopt your baby?" Anna asked again. She needed Lily to say the words.

"That's what I'm here for," Lily answered, still massaging her hands. "I want to pick you guys, but I don't really know how."

Anna did a laugh/cry thing, inhaling a breath while swallowing a sob. I got up from my chair, went over to Anna, and sat myself down on the arm of the couch. I put an arm around her shoulder.

"Lily, this is a huge decision," I said. "We're incredibly grateful, but are you sure this is what you want?"

Lily looked around the apartment, as though searching for anything that might change her mind.

"Yeah, I'm sure," she said. "I mean, I read your story on the website, so I know that you both . . . you both . . . you know."

"We both lost a child," I said. "It's okay, Lily. We can talk about it."

"I'm really sorry," Lily said. "I hope this helps, you know, with . . . stuff."

With stuff.

Goodness, Lily was a child herself, I thought, completely inexperienced.

Anna leaned forward and wrapped her arms around Lily's neck, her hug it seemed matching the force of a python's embrace.

"There's so many details to work out," Anna said as she let go, excited, which meant she was using her hands. "We'll need to get the home study done right away, and of course I'll have to find a new place for my office, then there's the matter of a lawyer. I've got one, but we need to call her ASAP. What about medical? Are you okay with the medical care?"

Lily made several nervous glances, first to me and then back to Anna. Lily had a look about her that I couldn't quite fathom. Panic, perhaps? Anna's own eyes were widening with panic. Was it the word "medical"? Could something be wrong with the baby? In the span of a few short minutes, Anna had begun bonding with Lily's unborn child and brooding over an uncertain future. I found myself worrying as well.

Lily clarified her predicament. "I don't have any medical insurance," she said. "I know I'm supposed to have it, but whatever. I work as a cocktail waitress at Jillian's Pool Hall. They don't have great benefits, but hey, at least I make good tips. So I haven't really been to a doctor, but I can tell you that I'm probably close to three months along." Lily looked down at her stomach. "I know I'm not showing much, but my clothes are definitely tighter. I Googled it just to make sure everything was okay, at the library when I found you guys, and a lot of people don't show until like four months or something."

"So what's wrong?" Anna asked, her voice steeped with concern.

"Nothing," Lily said. "Look, I'd love to get a checkup. You know, one of those picture things."

"Sonogram," I said. "An ultrasound is the procedure, a sonogram is the picture."

Anna's look wondered how I knew the distinction. My look said I remembered it from when Karen got her sonogram of Max.

"Yeah. One of those," Lily replied.

"We can help with that," Anna said. "We'll get the lawyer to include your medical costs in the agreement. That's not so unusual in these situations." Anna was talking in her management consulting voice, direct and authoritative.

"Yeah, that's great," Lily said, evidently still unsettled about something. "While you're at it, can your lawyer work up a place for me to live?"

Anna and I exchanged worried looks.

"What's going on?" Anna asked.

"Remember my asshole boyfriend?" Lily said.

"Yeah," I said.

"Well, he's changed the locks on the apartment. Says he doesn't want to see me no more."

"Did he threaten you?" I asked. "Did he try to hurt you?"

At this point in the conversation, somebody else, somebody other than Anna or me, might have stopped these proceedings. Despite my personal tragedy, I was pretty much leading a normal life. I went to work at Lithio Systems each and every weekday. I was married to a woman I loved. I liked watching shows on Nat Geo, the Discovery and History channels, and fixing stuff around the house. I built model rockets for sick kids. I grew up in Rhode Island, the only child of two loving parents, and I've never been much except for a good husband, good father, and a good employee. I've always done my best to do the right thing. This was my existence. It wasn't about pool halls, medical insurance issues, homelessness, financial troubles, and angry ex-boyfriends with potentially violent tempers. I had been, to that point, on a steady course, my true north.

With the decision to adopt, however, my comfort

zone shifted far from that northerly direction, and I was more than happy to adopt other people's problems along with the gift of their unborn child.

"He hasn't hurt me, if that's what you're asking," Lily said. "But he might. I don't trust him. I can't stay there."

"Where have you been sleeping?" Anna asked.

"With friends," Lily said. "Couches and stuff."

"What about your parents?" I asked.

"What about them," Lily said with a snap of venom.

Evidently that would be a conversation for another time.

Anna looked over at me. I knew exactly what she was going to say.

"We might have a solution to that problem, too. Gage and I need to discuss it first."

"Wow, that's amazing. Talk about our fates aligning," Lily said.

Anna's expression appeared equally enthralled, while mine remained somewhat guarded.

Maybe that's because I was thinking about Max.

CHAPTER 4

Lily left the premises. Where she went, I didn't know. Our lives were not closely tethered yet, and I wasn't certain they would be, so I didn't think it appropriate to ask. I met back up with Anna in the living room. Her eyes were dancing, drunk on this nectar of possibility. Anna undid her ponytail, and I took a moment to appreciate the way the afternoon sun lit her wavy brown curls. She seemed to be glowing with happiness, and I felt something stirring inside me as well. I was confronting the very real possibility of having a child to parent.

Anna sat cross-legged on the couch, biting her finger and staring at me anxiously.

"What do you think?" she asked.

"I think I know what you wanted to offer Lily," I said.

"Gage, the apartment is empty. She could move right in."

I couldn't argue. I'd bought this white clapboard two-family home about a month after Karen and Max died, four years before I met Anna. Prior to that, I'd been living as a family with Karen and Max in Swampscott, a lovely town on the north shore of Massachusetts. In hindsight, those were near perfect years, but I didn't always think so. Every desire I had for more money, a nicer house, fancier vacations, all of Max's frustrating behaviors (too many video games/too few books, not sitting still at the table, no concept of the inside voice) used to bother me. I wasted a lot of time and energy sweating the small stuff. Death, I'd discovered, had a cruel way of magnifying my regrets as both a husband and a father.

Anyway, not a single friend or family member questioned my decision to put the house on the market. They understood that memories could become monsters if not given the proper distance. So I bought in East Arlington, figuring I didn't need as much space. Aside from the change in locale, the added rental income from the upstairs unit would help out at a time when I wasn't so sure I could keep on working. I had taken six months off after the accident and spent most of it in therapy or self-medicated on the couch.

Until a few weeks before Lily's visit, the rental unit had been a zero hassle and a highly beneficial part of my life. Sure, sometimes it took a while to find a suitable tenant, but I always managed to find someone who paid the rent on time and kept the place in reasonably decent shape. But at the moment nobody was living there

My previous tenant, a guy named Will Gaines, had planned to spend another year in the upstairs unit while he finished pharmacy school. But about a month before, he'd changed his mind and given us two weeks' notice, forfeiting his security deposit in the process. Will never did explain his reasoning. Anna had been advertising for a new tenant, but as with our online profile on ParentHorizon, we'd gotten only a few nibbles—no quality bites.

"It's furnished," Anna said. "Between both our jobs, we've got money to cover the rent for a year."

I got up from the couch to stretch and yawn, something Anna said I did anytime I'm uncomfortable about something, which aptly described my current condition.

"I don't know, honey," I said. "We really don't know anything about her."

"What did we know about Will? Or your tenant before him?" Anna asked.

I shrugged. Anna, as usual, had a point.

"I mean, what did we know about each other before we got married?"

"I knew that I loved you," I said.

"And I you. I'm just saying that knowing all the details about somebody doesn't mean that you really know the person. I'd want to help this girl anyway, especially because she could be our baby's birth mother."

"Anna, you're already counting on this, aren't you?"

"I feel it in my heart, Gage."

Anna came over to me and burrowed her face against my chest. I felt my resolve weakening, my arguments ringing less potent in my head. She had that effect on me. Maybe I was being overly cautious.

"This is what we want, Gage. We can make it happen now."

I broke from Anna.

"We've got to do more," I said.

"Like what more?"

"Like who is she, Anna? Who are her parents? Where is she from? How about we get some of those questions answered first."

"I'll talk to her," Anna offered. "I'll get whatever information we can get, okay? I want to give Lily the apartment, and I need to hear from you that we're in this together. I need to know that we're a team, or nothing is going to happen."

I broke from Anna, wanting to make sure she could see my eyes. In addition to my yawning habit, I apparently blinked a lot whenever I fibbed. "I want this," I said. I tried to keep from blinking. Really, I did.

Anna turned from me, arms folded.

"Gage, I don't know what to say. I thought you were on board. What's the trouble?"

I grabbed her shoulders, turning her to face me.

"I am on board. I'm just . . . I guess maybe I'm just scared."

"I know you're scared. I am, too. But we're entering a new phase in our lives. It's been five years since you lost Max and four since Kevin died. It's so hard for me to think about becoming a mom again, and I have a lot of guilt about it, too, but I also know that we're ready for this. We've talked about becoming parents again. We both want it."

"Sweetheart, I know, I know," I said, keeping a grip on Anna's well-muscled shoulders. "Everything just happened so fast that I think I'm reeling a little bit."

"I understand," Anna said. Her look broke my heart, which softened my stance.

"Let's do this," I said. "You check up on Lily, like you said, okay? See what you can learn about her. If you think this is all on the up-and-up, we'll offer her the apartment. It'll be your call and I'll back you a hundred percent. Sound like a plan?"

Anna nodded. I let go of her shoulders and collected

my keys from the basket on a table in the foyer. Before Anna, my keys could have been anywhere.

"Where are you going?" Anna asked. "Oh, let me guess. You're going to touch base with Brad."

Anna knew me better than anyone.

CHAPTER 5

My circle of friends had grown smaller since the accident. According to my therapist, this wasn't uncommon. I kept in touch with my closest friends from college, but they didn't know what to say. Post-graduation we talked about dating and careers. Then it was marriage and kids. But one missed traffic light later and they didn't know what they could or couldn't say. If it weren't for Facebook, I doubted we'd have any regular contact at all.

I saw my parents on occasion. Probably should see them more considering I'm their only child. They were still married—forty years, bless them—and living a quiet life in a small town just outside of Providence, Rhode Island. Dad had a tough go of it, having worked his whole life for RIDOT only to spend the last twenty years on disability. Money was tight for them, so I funneled some of my rental income to them to help pay the bills. My work buds were solid, but let's be honest: after spending the week together doing battle in the trenches, I wasn't up for much after-hours hanging.

So basically I had friends I saw on occasion, but for

the most part they existed on the periphery of my life. Anna had become my safe harbor. She needed me and I needed her, and yes, I realized we had a codependency thing happening. Anna, too, felt alienated from her circle of happy friends with healthy children. If that was what made us initially compatible, so be it. For the moment, at least, I didn't need friends to keep me grounded. I needed Anna.

And Brad.

I drove my red Dodge Charger, a sporty little compact sedan, along the leafy and quaint streets of Bedford, Massachusetts. Brad didn't know I was headed his way. If I had called in advance, he might have ducked out. Yeah, we were that close.

The view through my car window showed people doing what people did on Saturday afternoons. They were mowing their lawns, pulling up weeds, laying down mulch, or watching their kids play. The sound of children laughing tore at my heart and made me ache for Max in a way I could only describe as suffocating. It hit me like a massive wave, dragging me to the depths of my sorrow, my ocean's sandy bottom, violently tossing me about. Still, I drove on. Living with a chronic condition made me adept at managing the pain.

Brad's cargo van was parked out front of his colonial-style house. The sides of the white van displayed black lettering that read LOMBARDI PLUMBING, the words positioned next to a colorful graphic of a strong hand gripping a durable, rust-colored wrench. Brad's twin daughters were away at college, and I didn't see Janice's Corolla in the driveway, which meant Brad was probably home and alone. Good.

I strode up the front walk, past the ceramic garden gnomes hiding in Brad's well-tended and richly colored flower garden. With each step my heart beat faster with anticipation. I rang the doorbell and listened to the pleasant chimes. Brad was smiling until he saw who rang his doorbell.

"No," he said to me.

"Hey, Brad," I replied.

I slipped into the house without being invited. I knew to leave my shoes in the mudroom so as to not mark up the new pinewood floor in the kitchen.

"I'm still saying no," Brad said, following me inside. He was dressed in his Saturday casual outfit: untucked navy polo shirt and dungarees.

"I brought food," I said, not turning around. I held up a bag so Brad could see the Ken's NY Deli logo. He would know a roast beef sandwich was inside. I got two sandwiches on my drive over, having anticipated the need to soften Brad up a bit.

"The answer is still no," Brad said to my back.

I headed straight for the kitchen without needing to be guided, but I stopped at the doorway into the living room.

"Did you guys get a new couch?" I asked, not remembering the white sofa with blue piping from my last visit.

"Same couch, I just reupholstered it," Brad said.

"Well, it looks great," I said, marveling at Brad's handiwork from afar. In addition to his talents as a master plumber, Brad could grow a colorful garden, cook gourmet meals, build furniture, and evidently reupholster it. But Brad had another talent, a special talent, and that was what had brought me here.

Judging by appearances, Brad looked every bit the guy who could make an upper-middle-class living with his hands. He wasn't a giant of a man, five eight with a stretch (I had four inches on him), but he was slender at the waist and well muscled up top, more fit than most college wrestlers. He sported a full head of jet black hair, deeply set dark eyes, and a pronounced nose that called attention to his Mediterranean heritage. Brad's most distinguishing characteristic, a bushy black mustache, evoked constant comparisons to Freddie Mercury, the late front man of the rock band Queen.

My socks glided across the new kitchen flooring as if it were covered with ice. Afternoon sunlight streamed in through the bank of windows overlooking a lush, green backyard. Surrounding me were gleaming stainless steel appliances and sunny artwork of fruits and vegetables. I set the bag of sandwiches down on the kitchen island, running my hands along the expensive, greenish colored granite surface. As Brad would tell you, plumbing was a recession-proof business.

It was a habit of mine to check the fridge whenever I came to visit, which was usually once a month. I'd come more often but figured Brad would get a restraining order at some point. Brad didn't use Facebook, so I followed what was happening with the twins by checking the new photos Janice had on the fridge. Apparently, Janice hadn't tired of the digital photo printer I bought her for Christmas last year. The girls looked to be doing fine. Sports, friends, travel, all the things Max would never experience. Splayed open on the kitchen table was the book about flower gardening that Brad must have been reading before my intrusion.

"How are the mums?" I asked, absently flipping through the pages of his flower book.

"They're the word," Brad said. He retrieved two place settings from the cupboard and set out two glasses of water for us to drink. I soon joined Brad at the kitchen island and watched as he dove into his sandwich.

"Aren't you going to eat?" he asked, chewing a mouthful of food and savoring the bite.

"I don't have an appetite," I said.

"Why'd you buy yourself a sandwich?"

"I didn't want you to eat alone," I said.

Brad looked at me curiously, and then broke into a smile that arched his mustache like a caterpillar's stretch. Almost immediately, though, that smile dimmed.

"I thought we talked about this," Brad said. "I thought we agreed we were going to take a break for a while. It's not in your best interest."

"Something's come up," I said. "A big something. Anna and I might be adopting a baby. No, scratch that, we *are* adopting a baby."

Brad's expression brightened. "Hey, that's wonderful news," he said.

"I need to tell Max," I said. "I need . . . I don't know . . . I need to know that he's all right with what I'm doing. I need to have his blessing, Brad. Please. I can't move forward without knowing."

Brad looked me hard in the eyes. The sandwich, I realized, was probably overkill. He never needed much prodding to help me out. Brad set aside his food and used a napkin to clear a dab of mustard from his mustache.

"Did you bring anything for me to use?"

From my back pocket I removed a picture of Karen and Max, well worn as a beloved LP. In the background of the photo stood one of the most recognizable landmarks in New England—the famous Motif Number 1, located on Bradley Wharf in the harbor town of Rockport, Massachusetts. Karen's straw-colored hair was lit angelically by the sunset. Max, Red Sox cap slightly askew, gap-toothed, stood smiling in front of his mother. Karen's arms were draped over Max's slender shoulders.

My son wasn't acting silly, as he tended to do whenever a camera was involved. He looked like a little boy who loved his mommy, loved being by the ocean, loved the sunset, and loved his life.

Brad took the picture over to the kitchen table. I sat down across from him.

"Give me your hands," he said.

CHAPTER 6

Give me your hands.

Brad had made this same request of me on the day we first met. I'd heard about Brad from a woman in the neighborhood who told me all about his special ability. He didn't charge for his services, nor did he shy away from discussing it if anybody asked. What he did, and did very well, was plumbing. The other thing was just a part of him, like an arm or a leg.

I was a natural-born skeptic when it came to Bigfoot and UFOs, but I believed in a loving God and had faith that death was not the final chapter. After learning about Brad's unique ability, I decided the upstairs unit would benefit from a new toilet. I started sobbing while Brad did the installation and had to come clean about my ulterior motives.

We'd been friends ever since.

Brad took my hands and closed his eyes. The picture of Max and Karen rested beneath our interlocked fingers. His grip tightened, and he jerked his hands back as though he'd suffered a slight electric shock.

"I'm picking up a game. Is there a game? Something about a game," Brad said, his vocal inflection calm as someone reporting facts and not communing with the spirit world.

"Is that Max? Is it Max asking?"

"It's definitely Max," Brad said, his eyes still closed. "He keeps asking about a game. Something about a game."

My throat closed as an ache of longing rose up within me. This feeling constricted my chest, making every breath futile. My heart seemed to stop beating as if acknowledging this primal urge to be with Max, wherever he was. Speaking to Max through Brad was a drug of a different sort. It made me feel high and low at the same instant. As soon as our conversation ended, I'd want more. It was never enough. It never satisfied. There was no closure, only longing, aching, and a deep yearning to hold him again. I knew the agony these sessions caused me, but after each one I still wanted more, just one more hit.

"It's probably the Red Sox game," I said, swallowing a sob.

Brad nodded. "That's it. It's the Red Sox. He wants you to watch a game."

I couldn't do that, and I wouldn't lie to my son, or the spirit of my son, or whatever I was communing with through Brad. I could never see another Sox game again.

"He says it wasn't your fault. He wants you to stop blaming yourself," Brad said.

Brad had connected me to my son's spirit seven times, four of them occurring only after I begged. He saw how these sessions tore me apart. Max would always say—through Brad—that it wasn't my fault, but he'd never given any specifics. It was a story I'd never shared with Brad. Some things were just too painful to relive.

"I'm getting something about a ticket, or a stub of a ticket. Is there a ticket?"

"A Red Sox ticket," I managed to say.

"He wants you to tear it up. He doesn't want you to have the reminder."

I got the ticket from a friend at work—great seats on the third-base line. *If I hadn't gone to that game . . .*

"Now I'm getting something about a car trip," Brad said, his voice staying even. "You drove. Somebody drove. You didn't need to drive. Something about his mother driving. Something about driving."

This was true. Karen had volunteered to drive Max, but only after throwing a medium-sized tirade about making seven-year-olds travel so far to play a game that only vaguely resembled soccer. I had offered to give my Sox tickets away, but Karen insisted I go. My last words to Karen weren't "I love you." I was so worried she'd blow up at Holly, our volunteer league coordinator, that I said, "Promise me you won't get confrontational." Death and regret were unfortunate companions.

"He's saying it was an accident, just an accident. I'm getting the word *accident*."

True as well, but Max was just a boy when he died. He didn't understand that Karen drove the speed limit and I never did. There was no way I would have been at that intersection when a Honda Accord, driven by a drunk driver, ran a red light at a high rate of speed. The impact crushed the side of Karen's sedan as if it were made out of aluminum foil. Max died at the scene. Karen was in a medically induced coma and died a week later. In my sessions with Brad, I'd only been able to communicate with Max, never Karen. As Brad explained, when a loved one died in a coma they might still be asleep, unable to send a message.

"He wants you to watch the Red Sox again," Brad said. "He says he remembers watching games with you."

I was feeling a longing of a different sort. I wanted the pill bottle stashed inside the glove compartment of my car, the one Anna didn't know about. It was filled with Adderall, a medication used to treat ADHD, which I didn't actually have. Thankfully, shrinks were more than happy to prescribe a solution for their diagnosis, so if you knew how to fake it, you could get it. The pills had become ice for my pain. They focused my thoughts to the point where I could sometimes feel a blip of euphoria, a little hint that happiness could be mine once again. Technically, this made me a drug addict, but not a hard-core one. My crime was taking meds I didn't need to dull a pain I didn't want.

"Is he okay?" I asked Brad. "Is my boy all right?"

I squinted my eyes shut, but those hot tears managed to squeeze out anyway.

"I'm getting the word *happy*, that he's happy, that he wants you to be happy. I'm just getting the word *happy*."

"Should I adopt a baby? Should I become a dad again? Would Max feel like I'm forgetting him?"

Tears carved a snaky path down my cheeks. God, I missed my boy so much. His smell. The silky feel of his hair. The toys. His box of rocks we vowed to categorize. The squeals of joy when he saw me. "Daaaaaddyy." Our rockets. Our life.

Brad got quiet.

"I'm sorry, Gage, but I'm not getting anything now."

I gazed up at the ceiling, pushing the tears back into my eyes and wishing that I could look beyond the physical world into Max's realm.

"Thank you, Brad," I said. "Thank you."

"I guess you'll have to make this decision on your own, buddy."

I'd already made the decision to double my daily dose of Adderall.

"There's something else, Gage," Brad said in a somber and concerned tone.

"Yeah?"

"I'm picking up on something else, a dark energy, something I haven't ever sensed before."

"Is it near Max? Is it threatening him?"

Brad shook his head.

"No, no, I'm not explaining myself. This energy, this darkness, it felt terrestrial."

"What does that mean?"

"It means it's earthbound. It's here in our world, not his. And Gage—whatever this energy is, it's something very dark, a blackness I've never felt before. And it's surrounding you."

CHAPTER 7

I returned home like a soldier shell-shocked from the war and parked my Charger in our narrow driveway. I appreciated not having to deal with my former tenant's car and the constant inconvenience of tandem parking. I wondered if Lily had a car, and if we'd be juggling our vehicles.

Trudging up the front stairs, I found an envelope taped to the outside door with my name written on the front. I had forgotten all about Brad and his strange and ominous warning, although my brief contact with Max continued to cover me like a second skin.

I recognized Anna's handwriting as I opened the envelope. From within, I removed a perfumed sheet of light blue stationery. My head was buzzing. I had taken a double dose of Adderall after leaving Brad's, and it heightened all my senses. I could feel the bumps of the paper's texture while my focused eyes traced each contour of Anna's looping handwriting style.

Gage,

You are my light and inspiration. I would be so lost without you. I love you more than these

words can say. I respect you and support whatever decision we make. I love the life we've built together. We'll work it out together like we always do.
Love,
Your Anna

Anna and I had a rule about fights. Whenever we wanted each other to feel good about returning home after a tiff—big blowouts or smaller disagreements—we'd leave a note tacked to the door. It always cleared the air and made reentry that much easier. The aroma of chocolate chip cookies baking hit me soon as I stepped inside. I followed the savory smell down the hallway like a floating cartoon character hooked by an alluring scent. I found Anna in the kitchen, her apron sprinkled with flour, removing the latest batch of goodies from the oven.

"You're home," Anna said, setting the piping-hot tray on the stovetop. She hugged me with her oven mitts still on. Keeping one arm draped around my neck, Anna let an oven mitt fall to the floor. Bending to reach the counter, she dipped her finger into the bowl of cookie batter and hand-fed me a hefty gob.

"Yummy," I said.

She kissed my lips and I kissed her back with passion.

"Thanks for your note," I said.

"I love you," Anna said.

"I love you, too."

I broke from her embrace and headed for the stove. I grabbed a hot cookie from the tray and bounced it in my palm until it cooled enough to eat. Taking a healthy bite, I savored the melted chocolate swimming about my mouth. Heaven. I even ignored the stab of guilt about my weight. Whenever I declined sweet treats, people said,

"But you're not overweight." To which I'd respond, "Well, there's a reason for that."

"Did you see Brad?" Anna asked.

"I did," I said, contemplating another cookie.

"What did he say, or . . . you know, what did you learn?"

"We're going to have to make this decision on our own."

"Did you talk to him? Was Max there?"

I nodded but couldn't speak through the walnut-sized lump that had materialized in my throat. Anna never wanted Brad to connect her to Kevin. She was worried it would leave her shattered. Knowing what I knew, I couldn't blame her.

My emotions settled. "What did you find out about Lily?" I asked.

"I ran an online criminal check and nothing came back," Anna said. "I also did some Google searches and checked a few people databases, but not much there. Oh, and I did call Jillian's, where Lily works, and asked to speak to a manager."

I perked up at that.

"And?"

"And he said she's a terrific worker, very dependable, never a problem."

"Never a problem," I repeated.

"I got him talking," Anna said. "And he told me she's one of the most levelheaded girls on his staff. She doesn't party, is not into drugs. He wished more of the waitresses were like Lily."

"We have Lily's number," I said.

Anna understood the subtext of my comment. Her eyes began to dance excitedly. I'd never forget that look of pure joy on her face—it was every Christmas rolled into one.

"Do we do this? Should we?" she asked, a slight squeal to her voice.

I ate another cookie. Hard not to. "Lily seems to be a reasonably put-together young woman," I said. "Just in a tough spot. No drugs, not a drinker, she's dependable at work."

"That's all positive."

"But she's not close to her family," I added. "That could be a symptom of other problems."

"That's not so unusual. I don't speak to my father."

"That's because he walked out on you and your mother."

"And my mother doesn't speak to her sisters," Anna pointed out.

"Your mother wouldn't recognize her sisters even if they did come to visit," I said, feeling cruel. "I'm sorry. I shouldn't have said that."

"It's okay, but that doesn't give my aunts any excuse. Her cousin Gladys would come to visit if she could travel, but my aunts don't have any good excuse."

"Speaking of which, we should probably go see your mother."

"Agreed," Anna said. "But let's make this decision first. Do we or don't we?"

Anna's mom, Bessie, was a resident of Carney House, a respectable nursing home in Brookline. At seventy-five, Bessie had late-stage Alzheimer's disease and no memories of the cross-country trip she had made with her daughter four years ago. No recollection of Anna's steady stream of tears as she left one life for another. Bessie lived each day anew, and in many ways I envied her for that.

"So we're doing this, then?" I asked.

"If you think we should, I think we should," Anna

said. "I want this, Gage. It's fate that we met Lily when we did. It was meant to be."

This was the moment of truth. We had reached a decision point. If I said the word *yes*, we essentially were pregnant. I would become a father once again and Anna a mother. We would relive those sleepless nights bottle-feeding a newborn, changing tiny diapers, addressing every need, every cry, and feeling like we were doing something outside ourselves by taking a sacred and cherished vow to nurture and deeply love another life.

I said yes.

CHAPTER 8

Here's the most important thing to know about making a lithium-ion battery: it's hard. The basic science is simple enough. Take two electrodes (the anode—or negative electrode—and the cathode, or positive electrode), combine them with an electrolyte that allows charged ions to flow between the electrodes, and voila, you've got yourself a battery. Well, there's a bit more to it than that, but the essence is there. Putting it all together requires a lot of complex machinery: Automatic Desk-top Grinder with Built-in Agate Mortar, Electrode Cutter, Ultrasonic Welder, Slurry Viscosity Tester, Pouch Cell Case/Cup Forming Machine for Aluminum-Laminated Films, Compact Vacuum Sealer for Preparing the Pouch Cell—oh, this list goes on. The process requires a variety of skill sets. It's a combination of advanced materials science, chemistry, applied mechanics, software, electronics; this list goes on as well.

Lithio Systems, my company, had been in the battery business for the past fifteen years. It was all we did. We made batteries. Might not be the sexiest thing to manufacture, but a lot of essential products don't register high on the sexy scale. The batteries we made went into everything from telecom products to the electric grid, transportation, and all sorts of commercial applications.

I helped make batteries, and I loved my job. The hours could be exhausting, the politics maddening, the pace frenetic, but it was never boring. I always had a new challenge, some unforeseen obstacle to overcome. And we were important, too, at least in the eyes of the government. They ponied up a hefty $250 million grant to help fund several of our R&D initiatives, including the effort that eventually became Olympian. It just so happened that R&D was my division, so I directly benefited from this government funding. Our job was to push the boundaries of battery technology.

And push we did.

Everyone I worked with was in the supersmart stratosphere, even Matt Simons, whose jerkiness was proportional to his intellect. I reported directly to Patrice Skinner, the vice president of R&D for Lithio Systems. Patrice reported to a guy named Roger, who reported to a woman named Sarah, who reported to the CEO. So I was a mere four steps removed from the big boss. They were pretty giant steps, but still, I wasn't on the bottom rung anymore. Lithio Systems had more than two thousand employees and a million and a half square feet of manufacturing facilities in Asia, Europe, and North America.

I was a player there and took a lot of pride in my work. In addition to my regular job responsibilities, I was also part of the highly selective three-member Security Breach Team, like SWAT for data security. All high-tech companies are worried about security, but when our lead scientists developed the first early prototype of Olympian, and it looked like we had something that would leapfrog us over the competition for years to come, Lithio Systems went to great extremes to protect our invention.

Even our IT folks didn't have access to all of Project Olympian's intellectual property. In addition to our daily responsibilities, the Breach Team looked for unusual network activity, followed up on unauthorized data requests, controlled access privileges for project teams, and implemented best practices for safeguarding our sensitive information.

Patrice's universe held about thirty-five engineers, including us quality assurance folks. As the Director of Quality Assurance, I oversaw a team that took all the stuff everybody else had been developing and made sure the manufactured product actually worked.

What made Olympian such a special little battery was the supercharged electrode nanotechnology, more specifically our patent-pending carbon nanotubes. These tubes were about one ten-thousandth the size of a human hair, but harness a few billion of them in the proper way and a new generation of long-lasting, more powerful, superfast-charging battery was born. The secret to building these nanotubes was locked up and secured in our electronic vaults, safeguarded by the Security Breach Team as fervently as Google's algorithms.

Not a big deal? Imagine if every cell phone manufacturer had to offer their customers the longest-lasting, fastest-charging battery just to stay competitive. Who would they buy their battery from? Well, it would be us, Lithio Systems, because we had the goods to sell.

Others had ventured into this territory, but thanks to those nanotubes, Lithio was the only company with a manufacturing process that wouldn't be prohibitively expensive for commercial production. And first-mover advantage was the key to success. Some research wonks had predicted that the next generation of lithium ion batteries would become a $50 billion industry in just a few short years. Fifty billion! With all the products lithium ion batteries power—smartphones, wearable devices, electric vehicles, medical equipment, and more—it was a wonder that number wasn't even larger. So it was a big deal, and my company was laps ahead of the competition in the race to develop the technology.

Now that we were in the home stretch of this multi-year project, everybody was on edge, quicker to anger than we were with a smile. The number of meetings rose proportionally with the level of panic. We used to meet with Patrice once a week, but now it was almost every day.

Four of us were sitting at the round conference table in Patrice's spacious corner office. There was Adam Wang, our program manager; Matt Simons, senior scientist; Mamatha Joshi, a Bangalore-trained scientist and saint of a person, who was recently promoted to director of our R&D manufacturing process; and me. Mamatha, along with Matt Simons and me, comprised the three members of the Security Breach Team,

Patrice was a short, stout, Swedish woman with shoulder-length blond hair and bangs cut straight as a ruler's edge. She wore the same style sweater vest to work every day. In our business, expending energy on what to wear was viewed as wasted effort. Like everyone here, she was brilliant: Columbia educated, with a PhD in Mechanical Engineering from McGill University.

As Patrice's trusted advisers, it was our job to present project status and reassure her we were on target for the upcoming big demo. We had just sat down when Patrice went to her desk and came back with some cupcakes.

"It's Mamatha's birthday today," Patrice said as Mamatha blushed. "I thought we'd have a little treat while we went through the status."

What followed was probably the saddest-sounding rendition of "Happy Birthday" ever sung, a tuneless, lifeless dirge that couldn't have ended soon enough. Everyone laughed at how badly we had performed except for me. I hated that song. It made me think about Max's last birthday cake—a soccer ball on a field of green frosting—and how it had seven candles on it, and how it would always have seven candles on it. That's the thing about death—it's permanent. Max and Karen had been frozen in time, while every minute I lived was one more minute I had spent without them.

I had days when it seemed the chasm of my grief would find no bottom. It always hurt to miss them, but the pain turned physical when I thought of my son, and pictured in my mind his tiny body fast asleep on sheets decorated with soccer balls and baseballs. My stomach would cramp, and my legs would begin to ache. I couldn't drive past a playground, or see a school bus, without remembering him.

The meeting couldn't start soon enough. I needed to focus on something other than my ever-present grief. I wished I had known it was Mamatha's birthday. I might have doubled my usual dose of Adderall just for an added layer of protection.

"So let's get going, shall we?" Patrice said after everyone devoured the cupcakes. "Adam, what's the current status?"

Adam Wang checked his notes and returned a reassuring nod. "We're looking good here. I think we're on track. No major issues right now," he said.

"What about my thoughts on the constant current threshold of the higher density nanotubes?" Simons asked. "I believe we can improve the degradation above our performance standards, and I've recommended several adjustments. Have those been integrated into your plans?"

Matt Simons worked on one of the largest teams in our division but rarely did anyone hear him use the pronoun "we." In fact, his nickname was IMM, short for I, Me, Mine (also a well-known Beatles song).

Wang looked uncomfortable in his chair. "I saw your e-mail."

"Which one?" Simons asked. "The one from yesterday or the one I sent at three o'clock this morning?"

Oh, give me a break, I thought. Simons *would* have to work in a mention of the time of his e-mail. He was the sort who e-mailed at all hours just to prove he was more dedicated than everybody else. He was also the sort of officious jerk who would make sure everyone knew about his great sacrifice.

"I'm not sure," Wang said, shifting in his seat. "But I did see it."

"Well, I got the idea from one of Patrice's papers on thermal conductivity in nanotubes. I practically have it memorized."

Patrice perked up at the mention of her name (or the flattery), and Simons, arms crossed, looked impatiently at Wang.

Wang launched into all the reasons why we shouldn't integrate Simons's enhancement to try to increase conductivity. Simons rolled his eyes and laughed at most of Wang's reasons in a mocking way. This went on for some time.

I tuned out, thinking about Max and Lily and becoming a father again. Would my new son or daughter be into soccer, like Max? Or would it be ballet, or horses, or art? I was daydreaming about having a yard with a play structure in it again, and it was at that moment I realized I wanted this as much as Anna.

"What do you think, Gage?"

Patrice's voice only sort of pulled me out of my fog.

"I think it's a great idea," I said.

Wang looked appalled.

"That means you'll have to redo all of your production tests before the demo?"

I shook my head. Obviously I was not fully engaged. "What? Oh, I'm sorry, guys. I guess I let my thoughts wander. I don't think we should do anything different right now. We're stable, and it's too close to the demo to be fiddling with any formulas. No offense, Matt. But I say it's an emphatic no, now is not the time."

Mamatha agreed but looked curious about something.

"What's a good idea then?" she asked.

I laughed at myself, embarrassed.

"My wife and I are going to adopt a baby," I announced. "I was thinking about how excited I am, and well, it just sort of slipped out."

Everyone broke into broad smiles—except for Simons, who apparently was still seething about not getting his way.

"That's wonderful news," said Patrice, who knew my history.

"Yeah," I said. "It really is wonderful."

CHAPTER 9

As soon as the yellow cab made the turn onto our street, Anna and I raced down the porch stairs to greet Lily curbside. I had offered to pick Lily up at her friend's house, where apparently she'd been couch crashing, but she insisted on taking a cab.

"She doesn't want to be an inconvenience," Anna explained after I protested. "Let her do whatever makes her feel most comfortable. If she wants to take a cab here, then she should take a cab."

The hours leading up to Lily's arrival passed slowly and with much anticipation. I felt like I was about to meet a long lost relative. Even though I'd seen Lily twice before, this encounter had the feeling of being a first, and a significant one at that. The moment the cab door opened and Lily stepped out, our lives would be interlocked like a ball of twine, its string unable to be unraveled.

Anna clutched my hand, leaning on me for support. We stood curbside, beneath a cloudless sky, while a soft and warm breeze pushed fragrant air through Anna's long and wavy hair. Our pleasant street bustled with the usual Sunday activities, and our neighbors busied themselves with their business.

We were dressed for an occasion: Anna in a purple, sleeveless cowl-neck top with dark jeans, and me in a short-sleeved button-down shirt. Clutching my hand tighter, Anna whispered, "I'm so nervous, Gage."

"Everything will be great," I whispered back, not sure why I whispered.

The world appeared brighter to me that day, the sky, the trees, the grass, everything, and I realized this heightened awareness came without the benefit of Adderall. My own excitement had turned palpable, a drug unto itself. Anna's skin looked to be glowing, her joy equaling, if not surpassing, my own.

"I can't believe this is actually happening," Anna said.

No sooner had Anna voiced her enthusiasm than Karen and Max came to mind, casting a cloud across an otherwise glorious day. A part of me would always long for them, for my wife and son, but that didn't dampen my enthusiasm for Lily's pending arrival.

The realization that Anna and I would soon become parents created a seismic shift in my perspective and thinking. My marriage to Anna could not close the door to the past. But waiting for Lily, for the first time since the accident I had a profound sense of truly moving on with my life.

The cab pulled to a stop. Lily emerged wearing a gray hooded sweatshirt, jeans with holes, and those black-laced boots she seemed to favor. Shielding her face from the sun's glare, Lily assessed our neighborhood anew with a guileless, childlike wonder. After a moment's pause, Anna and Lily embraced—not for long, but more than a friendly hello. Meanwhile, I hefted Lily's green suitcase out of the cab's trunk, brought it over to the curb, and paid the fare.

"I can get that," Lily said to me. "I had a good night, tips-wise."

"Nonsense," I said while giving the cabbie a hefty tip. His smile back at me said he just got away with something.

Lily had packed her life inside a piece of green hardcase luggage with silver tone latches and white stitching on the sides. It looked like something from the 1970s, retro in design, and also lighter in weight than I anticipated.

"Do you have enough in here?" I asked, lifting the suitcase with no more effort than curling a five-pound weight.

"I don't own much," Lily said. Her eyes widened as the cabbie started to pull away. "Oh, wait, there's another bag in the trunk!"

I whirled right and smacked the cab twice with the palm of my hand. The cabbie popped the trunk when he saw me in his side mirror. The brown paper bag I had missed was tucked to the side by the spare tire. In the dim light I saw the end of a wrapped present sticking out. I showed the bag to Lily, who confirmed with a nod that I'd retrieved the forgotten item.

"Those are for you guys," Lily said, pointing to the bag. "It's nothing much. Just a couple presents, but I'd have hated to leave 'em behind."

Anna looked touched. "You shouldn't have gone to the trouble."

"It was no trouble at all," Lily said. "I'm just so excited to be here. I guess I can't believe this is really happening."

With Lily's suitcase and brown bag of presents in

hand, I climbed the porch stairs, opening the door to what now was Lily's new rent-free home—at least until the baby was born. Anna and I hadn't discussed plans for Lily after the baby's arrival. We'd probably give her a few months to rest and recuperate, but after that I thought it would be best if we had a bit of distance from each other. Lily's constant presence might inhibit Anna and me from bonding with the new baby. I wasn't sure if that would be so. It was just a thought I had. We hadn't even talked about how "open" this adoption would be. Those were details still to be worked out. This was all new territory. To accommodate Lily's need for a speedy decision, we'd made one of our own.

We were advised by the lawyer Anna hired to draft a postadoption contract agreement as a written commitment to the level of openness. The lawyer would prepare all the required documents as the process went along, but this agreement, we were told, would help to dispel any fears about each party's role in the child's life. Would Lily see pictures of the baby? If so, how often would they be supplied? Could she visit? What role, if any, would she play in the child's life? While it might not be legally binding, it was believed a postadoption contract would establish ground rules that would be important later on. We obviously had much to consider and discuss.

Lily and Anna followed me up the narrow wooden staircase to the second-floor apartment. As soon as Lily stepped inside, her eyes widened with delight. Sunlight spilled in through the large bay windows and bathed the place in a beautiful, natural glow.

"Oh, my goodness," Lily cried, her hands covering her mouth. "I'm going to be living here?"

Lily walked through the small entrance foyer and came to a stop in the center of the living room. She twirled on her heels, taking everything in. We rented our upstairs unit fully furnished because it cut down on the damage from tenants moving in and out. Lily looked around, her hands still covering her mouth. This was a girl who last night had been sleeping on what might have been a ratty sofa. Now, judging by her expression, she was living in a palace.

"This is nicer than anyplace I've ever lived."

Lily brushed her long hair back across her shoulders. Her hair was shiny, freshly washed, and the strands fell together like she was filming a Pantene commercial. I couldn't decide if she was more blond than brown, and that made me wonder what color hair the baby would have. I wondered, too, what the father looked like, but remembered Lily wasn't entirely sure of his identity. Would this man ever come forward? Did he have parental rights? More questions for the lawyer.

Anna began the tour and I followed, noticing Lily's mannerisms more than listening. She kept playing with her fingernails, chipping away at the little bit of polish there.

While she stood still, Lily's fingers always found a strand of hair to twirl, yet another nervous habit. Again, I wondered what mannerisms our child would inherit. Would the baby grow up to be fidgety like Lily, an anxious waiflike child with darting eyes and bouncy feet? Would he or she have Lily's arched eyebrows, high cheekbones, small nose, and hair perfectly suited for twirling? Freckles? Would the baby's skin be creamy white like Lily's? I didn't know the father's race and I didn't care at all. What I wanted most for Anna and myself was what I wanted for Karen and myself before our son was born—a healthy baby to love.

"Now, we keep linens in here," Anna said, opening the door to our (no, make that Lily's) linen closet.

"Oh, my God, sheets," Lily said, as if she'd been waiting for this moment all her life. She ran her hand along the edges of our guest linens and towels from downstairs that we had moved upstairs. "Fluffy towels! Oh, my gosh. Can I take a shower later? I don't want to bad-mouth my girlfriend, but it's been like sleeping in a frat house over there."

"Lily, sweetheart, you can take a shower whenever you'd like. This is your home now."

Lily giggled as she followed Anna into the kitchen.

Questions nipped at the back of my mind, but they could wait. What happened to her boyfriend? Was he going to demand a paternity test? Had she told anybody about what's going on? Did her frat house friend even know? Each minute spent together brought new reminders that we were a living oxymoron—we were intimate strangers.

I heard Lily yell delightedly from inside the kitchen. When I passed through the entranceway I saw her bent over, peering into the refrigerator.

"It's stocked with real food," Lily said, clasping her hands together, still peering inside.

"Now, I didn't know if you've been having nausea," Anna said, "but hopefully you'll be able to eat what's here."

"I want to eat it right now," Lily said. "I'm starving!"

"You want to have a lot of folic acid in your diet," Anna said. "It's really the best for proper brain and nervous system development, so the spinach, kale, broccoli, all of that is really good food for the baby. Ideally you'd get between 600 to 800 micrograms of folic acid a day." Anna stopped speaking, put her hands on her hips, and shook her head, dismissing herself. "I'm sorry," she said. "I got carried away. I shouldn't be putting all this on you right now. I read a bunch of baby blogs before I went food shopping. Please forgive me."

Lily closed the refrigerator door—finally—and approached Anna. I saw a maturity to her that I'd not seen before, as though she had gone from being a twentysomething to a thirtysomething in a matter of steps. She reached out with her arms and embraced Anna in a brief but comforting hug.

"That's so sweet of you," Lily said as they broke apart. "I just want you guys to have a healthy baby. I'll take whatever advice I can get."

Anna seemed to get emotional, dabbing at her eyes with the tips of her fingers.

Lily craned her neck and looked back at me over her shoulder. A secretive, sly little smile creased the corners of her mouth. I was sure the look was meant to say, *I hadn't forgotten about you, Gage,* but something about the exchange disturbed me.

"The bathroom is right down the hall," Anna said, continuing with the tour.

I fell into step behind them, forgetting all about Lily's odd facial expression. While the ladies talked, laughed, and shared with ease, I kept trying to get a read on what we'd just become. I wasn't about to tell Anna that I felt like two future grandparents committing to raise our daughter's unwanted child. Yet that was what we appeared to be. I looked like a guy who took up golfing late in life (which I had), Anna was the businesswoman, and Lily seemed to have mastered the just-got-out-of-bed look.

While I felt weighted by doubt, Anna floated across the floor, breezing in and out of rooms as the tour continued, her expression radiating a joy that could not be contained.

"I'll show you the laundry downstairs soon as we're done," Anna said as we vacated the bedroom.

"I can't tell you how great it's going to be to sleep on a real bed," Lily said. "Say, before you show me the downstairs laundry I want to give you guys your presents."

"You really didn't need to go to the trouble," Anna said. "Gage and I just want you to feel at home here, that's all."

"It was no trouble at all," Lily said. "I want you both to know how much I appreciate your taking me in the way you did." Lily patted her stomach. "Though I guess we're both getting something out of the deal."

I felt like a human trafficker. *I'll trade you an apartment for a kid.* Even Anna's look showed displeasure.

Lily took notice. "Oh, guys, I didn't mean it that way. I just wanted you to know that I'm totally okay with what we're doing. I don't know if you're worried that I'm going to change my mind or anything, but don't be. I'm not. I can tell you're going to be amazing parents. I guess I'm just so sure of this decision that I wasn't being very sensitive. I'm sorry if I sounded like a jerk just now."

Anna brushed aside Lily's apology with a wave of her hand.

"I'm actually glad you said that," Anna said, nodding her head repeatedly as she tended to do whenever broaching uncomfortable territory. "We both want you to feel completely comfortable with us. And please know that you can talk to us about anything. Honestly, anything. Any doubts or concerns you may have. This is obviously an unusual circumstance, and we need to be open and honest about what we're getting ourselves into here. So I'm glad you shared with us."

“Me too,” I said.

That comprised the extent of my contribution to the conversation.

Me too.

In truth, my thoughts were occupied by Lily’s light packing job, wondering how that meshed with her being here for the next two trimesters. Did Lily’s lack of clothing suggest a subconscious worry about getting cold feet? Could it be conscious worry? Did she just need a place to crash, and we were easy marks? I hadn’t considered the ramifications of Lily’s changing her mind midstream until now. One look at Anna, who already loved the baby growing inside Lily’s body, suggested the emotional consequences would indeed be dire. We were in, and we were in deep.

Lily left us to retrieve her bag of presents from the foyer. When she returned, Anna and I were already seated on the couch.

“This is for you,” Lily said, handing Anna a square package wrapped in white paper decorated with dancing elves, snowflakes, and floating Christmas trees. “I’m sorry about the paper,” Lily said. “It was all my friend had in her closet.”

“It’s putting me in the holiday spirit,” I said. “Eggnog, anyone?”

Lily pointed to her belly once again. “Better make mine a virgin.”

Anna laughed warmly as she began unwrapping the present with careful attention, perhaps thinking this tiny scrap of paper should be saved for the baby book.

“It’s obviously a CD,” Lily said, sounding embarrassed by the size and content of the gift.

When Anna finished unwrapping, she squealed with delight.

"Tony Bennett," she said, showing me the package. "I love his voice. Thank you."

Lily shrugged.

"I wanted to get you an iPod shuffle, but they were too expensive. I just figured everybody loves Tony."

"How do you know his music?" I asked. Subtext: *aren't you too young to know about Tony Bennett?*

"He's been on *Ellen* a bunch," Lily said. "With my job I get to watch a lot of daytime TV. I love his music. I'm sort of an oldies fan. In fact, I'd play it all the time—if I had a music player, that is. My boyfriend, my ex-boyfriend, kept mine and he won't give it back. He's such an ass."

"Well, I love Tony Bennett," Anna said, holding up the CD. "And I have an iPod shuffle, but I don't have any of his music on it. So thank you for this."

Anna stood and gave Lily a quick peck on the cheek. From virtual strangers to cheek peckers in under an hour must be a record. For all intents and purposes, we were a family. We hugged. We kissed. We exchanged presents.

Lily handed me a much larger gift, wrapped in the same paper as the Tony Bennett CD.

"Here is yours, Gage. I really hope you like it."

Lily's nervousness came across as endearing. Her excitement proved contagious, and I wanted very much to know what she had picked out for me. I felt bad for considering that she had ulterior motives, plans to live off us and then skip town with the baby. Her sweetness I found truly touching. I ripped the paper, not planning to save it for the baby book.

The first hint of bright yellow packaging meant nothing to me. It looked like something that would catch the eye of a younger person, the kind of bright yellow color that adorned many toy store shelves. I ripped the sides of the package some more, and then my breath caught. A chill ripped through my body. Some sound came out of my mouth, a slight moan perhaps, but my ears buzzed too loudly to hear it. I studied the package with intent, hands shaking, rattling the contents within.

"Gage, what's wrong?"

Anna's voice sounded very far away.

"Are you all right?"

Was that Lily?

My thoughts blurred. I was spinning, falling, reeling.

"Gage, what's wrong? You're scaring me."

I turned and held the box up for Anna to see. Anna's hands covered her mouth and partially hid the look of horror stretched across her face. Lily glanced back and forth between us as though observing a tennis match sped up, confusion and worry shown on her face.

"What is it? What's wrong?" I heard Lily say.

I dropped the box to the floor by my feet, taking in short, sharp breaths that bordered on hyperventilating. My eyes, watery and raw, were transfixed by the top of the box. I reread the flap packaging through a film of gathering tears: Estes Cosmic Explorer Flying Model Rocket. Below that, in smaller type, I could make out the words: *laser-cut fins and waterslide decals*. It was the exact same model rocket as the one still inside its box and pushed underneath my bed. The same rocket Max and I were building just before he died.

CHAPTER 10

My eyes opened while it was still dark outside. Pivoting, my body fought against the stretch and tug of tight muscles. Stress and exhaustion had turned me into a Tin Man of sorts. Eventually, I worked myself into a seated position on the edge of the bed. Anna rolled over onto her side, ever the light sleeper, and exhaled softly.

"Baby, are you all right?" she asked, her croaky voice sluggish.

"Yeah, I'm just going to watch some TV," I said.

My feet felt around in the dark, eventually finding the opening to the nappy black slippers I kept at my bedside.

"What time is it?" Anna asked.

"Two-thirty," I said, glancing at the red glow of the digital clock, dismayed by the hour. I had to go to work in the morning—well, make that in five hours.

"You can't sleep?"

"Not really, but I'm fine," I lied. "I'm all right. Go back to sleep."

Anna propped herself up on one elbow.

"Is it the present from Lily?"

A sliver of moonlight escaped from a passing cloud and lit her face with bluish light.

"Maybe," I said, this time telling a half truth.

"Gage, it was just a coincidence, a horrible coincidence," Anna said, rubbing my back with her warm hand. Her touch was comforting at a time when I needed to be comforted.

"Come here, baby," Anna said, patting at the queen-size mattress. I flopped back down and Anna fit into my body's contours like a puzzle piece. "Lily felt horrible about the gift."

"I know. I know. It just took me by surprise, I guess."

"She feels sick about it, but really she thought you'd like a rocket to build with the kids. She just stumbled on it at a yard sale and thought it would be a good gift for you, that's all."

I didn't respond. I was trying to wrap my head around the likelihood of it happening as Lily had described. There wasn't any cellophane around the box, so it could have been from a yard sale like she had said, but the rocket had never been launched. Other than me, who buys a rocket and lets it sit in a box? The Cosmic Explorer is a Skill Level 4 model, meaning it's the kind experienced builders would buy, build, and let fly a bunch of times. It's also currently out of stock in every local hobby store I called—and I called them all. There were, however, a couple for sale on eBay and some specialty hobby stores farther away, but it took effort for me to find them. My eyes locked on the ceiling where one floor above me I believed Lily to be sleeping.

"I'm making appointments for Lily to see a doctor this week," Anna said. "She's worried that you're mad at her."

"She told you that?"

Anna rubbed my shoulder. Her palms were smooth and without calluses because Anna preferred running to lifting weights.

"We talked after you left," Anna said. "She's worried that the whole thing is in jeopardy now."

"Over a present?" I said with a slight laugh.

"She thinks you'll take it as a sign."

"That would be crazy," I said. "It was just a coincidence."

"That's what I told her."

But I was taking it as a sign, and thinking about Brad and what he saw or felt about a dark energy following me. I began to concoct a scenario of my own—one without coincidences, one where Lily Googled my name and saw the article in *Wicked Local*, a North Shore publication, honoring Max and Karen. There were pictures included with that article, I recalled. Pictures I hadn't looked at in a very long time.

"I know this is going to work out," Anna said. "Lily has a huge heart. I've never felt more certain about a decision in my life. Please don't hold this against her, honey. She already feels bad enough."

"I would never," I said, kissing Anna's forehead. "Get some sleep. I'll come back to bed soon."

Anna smiled sweetly and rolled onto her left side, which I affectionately referred to as her sleep side. Like the speed of our intimacy, it didn't take long to discover each other's behavioral quirks. From past experience we knew we'd have to love 'em and not change 'em. Time had stripped away some memories I had of Karen's idiosyncrasies, but not all. Karen, a fastidious organizer, had carefully arranged everything in the house, including my work area where Max and I built model rockets. Whenever she straightened up, Karen turned the rocket kit boxes so the front of the packaging faced out like it was on display. That included the box for whatever rocket Max and I were building at the time. We kept that box on the plastic foldout table covered with a red-and-white checkered tablecloth, along with all the kit parts. We used the picture on the front of the box as a reference guide. I had given *Wicked Local* a photograph of Max and me building that Estes rocket for a tribute piece, but I couldn't recall if Karen had done her usual OCD routine with our model rocket kit before she snapped that picture.

I knew only one way to find out.

I padded down the hall, my feet cocooned inside slippers. I kept asking myself, What where the chances of Lily coming across an unused, out-of-stock Cosmic Explorer rocket at a yard sale? I settled on it being somewhere just south of winning the Powerball.

Anna's office was neat as usual. That was one way she and Karen were alike—both women loved order and floundered in chaos. I powered up her Mac and soon had the Safari browser open. I typed "Max Dekker" and "Wicked Local" into a Google search box.

It was just a coincidence, I said to myself.

My finger hovered over the return key, shaking.

What would it prove? Something? Nothing?

I recalled the way Lily smiled at me in the kitchen during the tour, a smile with hidden meanings. I hit the button and a web page loaded in a blink—*Thank you, Comcast*. The link to the article I wanted appeared first in a listing of thousands, mostly web pages containing the word "max," the name "Dekker," and the word "wicked" or "wickedly." I clicked the first link and swallowed a breath while waiting for the page to load.

The headline snapped a vise around my heart: TOWN REMEMBERS MOTHER AND SON KILLED BY DRUNK DRIVER. I scrolled down the page, passing the picture of Karen smiling at the camera on a beautiful spring day. I had taken that picture on our front lawn, and thought at the time that nobody had a more perfect smile.

Toward the bottom of the article was another picture, this one of Max and me. My teeth clenched while blood thrummed in my ears. There was Max, smiling at the camera, pleased with our progress, and me, the proud dad, with an arm wrapped around my son. And on the table next to us was the eye-catching yellow packaging, bright as gold.

CHAPTER 11

Soon as morning came, I told Anna about the picture. Without hesitating, she headed straight to her office. No pit stop for that morning cup of joe. That was how I knew she took this seriously. She put her face right up close to the computer screen, as if proximity might somehow alter the image. We were looking at the same *Wicked Local* article, but clearly through a different lens. I had doubts about Lily's story, whereas Anna's squinty expression told me she wanted to believe otherwise. The present and the picture were simply two unrelated coincidences. Make that three coincidences—Lily just so happened to come upon a yard sale with an unused, uncommon model rocket for sale; the rocket just so happened to be the Cosmic Explorer; and it just so happens there's a picture of me and Max shown with that rocket easily accessible on the web. Two coincidences (though it's still in Powerball territory) I might be able to buy, but three? The picture changed everything.

"I think you're making something out of nothing," Anna eventually said.

"How can you say that?" I asked, jabbing a finger at the screen.

Anna looked at me with a pained expression.

"You don't want this, do you," she said, her harsh and whispered voice a statement, not a question.

"No," I said, protesting.

"No, you don't?"

"No, I do. Yes, I want this. Of course I do," I said.

Anna shook her head. "No, no, you're looking for a reason to back out. I can tell. I know you are."

"Honey, that's not true."

"Oh, please." Anna brushed me away with a flick of her hand and bolted from the office, tightening the cloth belt around her bathrobe on an angry march to the kitchen.

"Why are you walking away from me?" I called out after her.

"I'm not walking away," she said with her back to me and in a tone that implied the opposite. "I have a meeting this morning and I have to get ready."

From the kitchen doorway, I watched Anna pour hot coffee from the freshly brewed pot into a blue ceramic mug. Anna drank mocha-flavored coffee, which I couldn't stand, so we had two automatic drip brewers occupying our limited counter space. Some things in life were not subject to compromise.

"Please, let's just talk about this," I said.

Anna spun on her heels. "Talk about what? That you want to kick Lily out over a present?"

"I want to know if she did that intentionally."

"Gage, what the hell? You really think that about her? You think she'd troll a bunch of hobby stores specifically looking for a Cosmic Explorer rocket? Why would she do that? Can you give me one reason?"

I shook my head. “No,” I said. “I don’t get why. But you have to agree it was strange.”

“It’s nice that she bought you a present.”

“How can you say that? It is strange. You at least have to admit that.”

Anna’s brown eyes smoldered, arms folding across her chest, the coffee mug somehow kept in balance. Her mouth tilted into a frown while her body went rigid. I knew the signs of the coming storm.

“What do you want me to do?” Anna asked. “Confront her?”

“I’ll ask her,” I said, feeling my own anger start to bubble.

“That’s just great. You’ll scare her.”

“What is that supposed to mean?”

“It means you’re angry about this and I’m not sure you’re the best person to ask her about the picture.”

Every word Anna said just made me angrier.

“We are in this together,” I said. “Don’t paint me as the bad guy here.”

“I don’t really think we are in this together. I’m not sure you’re ready.”

“You think I’m being paranoid about Lily?”

“You don’t? Weird things do happen, you know.”

“I think we should ask her and gauge her reaction.”

“You can’t do it,” Anna said.

“You don’t trust me?”

“Honestly, no. I don’t.”

Her tone implied that she didn’t believe I wanted to adopt a baby, that I hadn’t let go of my past life and that any excuse was a good excuse to keep from moving forward.

“Then you do it,” I said.

“Ask Lily if she Googled your name and bought

you that present as a way of hurting you? Honestly, you want me to have that conversation?" She shook her head slightly, as if the sight of me sickened her. "If that's really what you want, then I'll do it. But should I have that conversation before or after her ultrasound?"

"Jeez, Anna . . . I just . . ."

"No, I'm serious, Gage. If this is really important to you, when should I ask? Because if I see that picture of the baby, I'm not going to be able to let go." Anna covered her mouth, but not in time to silence her sob. Her eyes squeezed closed and she turned away from me. Her shoulders shook in reaction to the sudden surge of emotion.

I stopped being angry and felt like a bigger jerk with each step I took crossing our kitchen's white linoleum floor. I wrapped my arms around Anna's shaking shoulders and tried to comfort her with an embrace.

"I'm sorry, babe," I said.

Anna kept her back to me.

"Please just tell me you want this," she said in a soft voice. "Please. I just need to know that you really, really want this the way that I do."

"I want this," I said. "I honestly do."

"Then we'll go speak to Lily together, because that's how we're in this."

CHAPTER 12

On her second day of living with us, Lily dressed much like her first. She seemed to favor that gray hooded sweatshirt with a white tee underneath, but that day she wore baggy sweatpants instead of the ripped pair of jeans I'd seen her in before. By contrast, Anna and I were both dressed for work. The morning sun, already strong, suggested a warm day ahead. The apartment would remain shady for a few more hours, though. Perhaps that explained the chill in the air. Or perhaps it was the way Lily kept looking at me.

Lily sat on the sofa, body leaning forward, only occasionally making eye contact. *What was this all about?* her expression asked. Why did we want to talk to her so urgently? Lily's interlocked hands nervously massaged her long fingers. Anna came back from the kitchen with a glass of water, no ice per Lily's request. Lily worked nights and our phone call had awakened her, or so Anna had said. I felt bad about interrupting her sleep, but this had to be discussed.

I repositioned two chairs in front of the sofa while Anna set the water glass down on a wicker coaster. We took our seats, facing Lily, and once again I thought of us as two parents. This time we were preparing for a knockdown confrontation with our insolent teenage daughter. Lily's nervousness was evident again with those darting eyes, tapping feet, fidgety legs. She seemed young to me, and even though our age gap was only twelve years, those were significant years developmentally. When I was twenty-seven, Lily's age, she was only fifteen. I was building my career while Lily was learning how to drive. Sweat beaded up on the back of my neck. *Why?* Doubt, I thought. I doubted my earlier suspicions. Lily was barely an adult. Her anxiousness gave me pause and forced me to mull over Anna's earlier question. *What motive would Lily have to hurt me?* I came up with nothing. She needed a place to live and we were able to provide. She wanted a loving couple to adopt her unborn baby and we were more than willing. Why would she sabotage her safety net? What gain could she possibly achieve? I could conjure up only two answers for those questions: she wouldn't, and none.

"Lily," Anna began, her voice calm, designed to allay any concern. "Gage and I want to speak with you about the present you gave him."

Lily cringed. Her pained expression conveyed that she continued to blame herself for the incident.

"You guys want me to go," Lily said, making a soft sigh of finality.

With that we went from having a discussion to standing on the edge. Anna's hand went to her chest, a shocked look came to her face, blindsided by Lily's reaction. Anna had wanted this discussion to be a slow build, but Lily had just slammed her foot down on the accelerator.

"No, no, that's not it at all," said Anna.

Lily did not seem convinced. Her eyes glanced toward her bedroom where she would need only minutes to pack that one small suitcase.

Anna continued, "We just have a question, that's all."

"What question?" Lily asked. "I told you I feel horrible about it. I don't know what else I can say."

Anna's expression begged me to facilitate the discussion. This was my doing and therefore my responsibility. I cleared my throat, prepping it for words I wasn't sure would come out.

"I just want to ask you some questions about it," I said. "I'm not angry, I'm just a little confused about something."

Lily gazed at me as though I were speaking in a foreign tongue. More sweat on the back of my neck. My heart fluttered with anxious little spasms. *Was I making a bigger deal out of this for nothing? Was it all just an improbable set of unrelated coincidences?*

"What?" Lily asked, looking to Anna for the answer. She didn't trust me, and I hadn't given her reason to. I was the one hurt by the present, so her allegiance naturally went over to Anna, where she felt safe. Couldn't blame her. "What do you want to ask?"

"Where was the yard sale where you bought the rocket? Do you remember?"

Lily shrugged.

"I don't know. I'm not even sure what town it was in. I was just driving around in my friend's car, doing some errands and I saw a big yard sale, so I stopped, and that's where I found the rocket."

"Did you Google my name before you came to see us?"

"Did I what?"

"Google, or do some other web search. Did you look into my past before you came to us about adopting your baby?"

Lily's top lip curled in disgust. I was calling into question her motives and true intent.

"I told you guys, I found you on that ParentHorizon website and I recognized you from that day you saw me crying at the bus stop. That's all."

"So you never checked into my past. You didn't see the picture of me and Max?"

"What picture?" Lily directed her question to Anna.

"There is a photograph in a local newspaper that shows Gage and Max building the same model rocket that you bought for him," Anna explained.

Looking utterly bewildered, Lily bolted from her seat. Her body shook with outrage.

"You think I found that picture and intentionally bought you that rocket as a gift? Why would I do that?"

"I don't know, Lily," I said. "I just want to understand. It's not a commonly sold rocket and it was unused."

"It was a freakin' accident! A mistake! Look, I'm sorry I hurt your feelings. I'm sorry I brought up the past. But it wasn't intentional. I feel horrible about what happened. But I don't need this. I can't live here knowing you guys think so little of me. I'm . . . I'm sorry."

Lily lowered her head as she raced out of the living room. Seconds later I heard the door to her bedroom slam shut.

Panic overcame Anna. She gave me a distressed, heartbroken look.

"Go speak with her," she said. "Make this right. You fix this, Gage."

Her words left no room for compromise. Anna would never forgive me if Lily walked out of our lives. Hell, I'd never forgive myself. I got out of my chair, my stomach in knots. I had forced this confrontation. But was I misguided? Everything about Lily's reaction told me that I had thrown a grenade into the middle of a peaceful gathering. Strange things do happen. Maybe these coincidences were a sign from the universe, or Max, or something, that this was meant to be. Maybe the signs were there but I was reading them all wrong.

I rapped my knuckles softly against Lily's bedroom door.

"Lily, please, can we talk about this?"

I heard noises coming from the room. Drawers opening. I knocked again and waited. Eventually, the door opened fast enough to create a little gust of wind, and Lily came barging out. She pushed right by me, making no eye contact, head down, green suitcase in hand. Without a word, Lily marched on down the hall, feet clomping in those heavy boots as she crossed right in front of the threshold to the living room where Anna sat waiting for me to fix this.

"Gage!" Anna cried out as Lily bounded down the stairs. "Do something!"

I vaulted down the stairs after her, calling Lily's name over and over again. Not paying enough attention, I lost my concentration, followed by my footing. My feet began tripping over nothing, and I would have gone for a nasty tumble had my arms not gone into reflex mode, extending outward to brace myself against the stairwell walls. By the time I got outside, Lily was marching up the street, her suitcase swinging back and forth, following the motion of her arm.

"Lily, wait!"

I went chasing after her as if she had dropped a twenty on the ground.

"Lily, please!"

Lily came to a stop, her back still to me, in front of the house belonging to my eighty-three-year-old neighbor, Mrs. Trumbull. A curtain in Mrs. Trumbull's home parted ever so slightly, enough for me to notice. We must have looked like we were having a lovers' quarrel. Great, now Mrs. Trumbull—who knew Anna, who gave us Tupperware containers of homemade applesauce—would think we were swingers.

I came up behind Lily, feeling ashamed. "Lily, I know you're upset with me."

No response. Lily kept her back to me, but at least she wasn't walking away. I took this as an opportunity to keep talking.

"I was wrong," I said. "The second I saw your reaction, I knew that I was wrong. My love for Max clouded my judgment. I rushed to the wrong conclusion, and for that I'm so very sorry."

"I don't want to be the source of any trouble," Lily said.

She wouldn't turn around. Wouldn't make eye contact. How was I going to reach her if I couldn't get her to look me in the eye?

"I know, Lily."

"I can't be here if you think so little of me. This is hard enough as it is. I don't know what I was thinking."

"I'd like you to think that you'll give me a second chance," I said. I risked placing my hand on her shoulder.

Lily turned her body, ever so slowly, until we faced each other.

"Please accept my apology," I said. "I believe it happened the way you said it did. I don't think you gave me the present with any intention to hurt me."

"Why would I do that?"

Lily's brokenhearted look shattered me. I felt like a bully who had just found his conscience. My throat felt too dry to speak.

"Anna and I are grateful that you've come into our lives," I said. Lily's suitcase hovered inches above the ground, dangling as a signal to me that she had yet to accept the apology. "I'm still grieving for my son, Lily." I felt tightness in my chest, and my stinging eyes began to blur until I cleared away the tears. My breath turned ragged, short, and shallow. "Anything that reminds me of him hits a place so deep in my heart, I can't explain it. It's like attacking my soul, my everything. It's so real. So visceral."

"What's visceral?" Lily asked.

That made me stop, and I managed a weak smile.

"It's an SAT word," I said. A short silence followed, as my mind transitioned from that emotional place where I stored every single thought and memory of Max and Karen, to return to the present, where Lily stood before me, her suitcase swinging back and forth like the pendulum of a grandfather clock. "It means a deep, inward feeling."

"Oh, I just got my GED. Sorry to stop you. I just didn't know what you meant."

"What I mean is that I'm really and truly sorry to have accused you of anything. And that I hope we can put this incident behind us and start over. Please."

I reached for her suitcase, but Lily pulled back.

"I'm a good person," Lily said. "You need to know that."

"I do. I know that."

Lily thrust her suitcase into my hand.

"I need to keep things simple between us. I can't handle a lot of stress," Lily said. "It's bad for the baby."

CHAPTER 13

Anna's mother lived nine miles from our house—a short drive, unless that drive happened to be going from Arlington to Brookline. Traffic was always a problem, and that Saturday morning it seemed exceptionally heavy. As a couple, we went to see Bessie every other week, though Anna visited more often on her own. We'd never brought a visitor with us, but then again we'd never had a visitor who was going to bring a granddaughter into Bessie's life. This wasn't just about making an introduction, either. We had visuals to share.

The air conditioners at Carney House were blasting on high when we arrived. They didn't cool the air so much as push around an overpowering smell of detergents and cleansers that failed to mask the scent of death and dying. Lily dressed in a black skirt, dark leggings, and a hipster top with glittery beads.

It had been one week since she almost stormed out of our lives forever. One week for the baby to grow a little bit bigger. In that time, Anna took care of Lily's medical needs, including getting her an appointment with an OB/GYN in Arlington. The OB, Dr. Andrew Hill, whom I knew only from his picture on the website, would monitor Lily's progress throughout her pregnancy. I had offered to take time off work to be there for the first ultrasound of our baby, but Anna deep-sixed that idea as soon as it had left my lips.

"I just think in light of what happened," Anna said.

"You think I'd make Lily uncomfortable," I said.

As a way of saying yes, Anna said nothing at all.

"Did Lily say something to you?" I asked.

"You're a wonderful husband, a wonderful person, and you'll be a wonderful father to our baby, so please don't take it personally. Lily didn't even want *me* to be in the room with her while they did the ultrasound. She was very worried they might find something wrong with the baby. She asked me to wait in the parking lot."

I knew the subtext of that conversation. Lily wasn't showing very much. Anna tried to minimize Lily's concern (and Anna's) by using the Internet to find plenty of stories with similar situations and good outcomes.

"It's especially common in first pregnancies," Anna said.

Even with this information, there was still much worrying on the day of Lily's appointment. Needless worrying, as it happened. Lily's doctor didn't find anything wrong at all. In fact, everything looked splendidly right. According to Dr. Hill, Lily was eleven weeks pregnant. That meant we were inching ever closer to the second trimester, during which a miscarriage becomes an uncommon 1 to 5 percent possibility. In statistical terms, that put us in the clear to becoming parents. For this alone Anna breathed easier, walked with a lighter load. She hadn't let go of the ultrasound image since we'd gotten out of the car.

As for Lily, she still seemed bewildered by it all. I couldn't blame her. In a span of a few short weeks, she went from getting pregnant, to living with us, to walking the halls of a nursing home. I could see the nurses here who knew Anna and me as a couple eyeing Lily with curiosity. If asked, what would I tell them? "Oh, she's the birth mother, we're the baby's future parents, and we're here for a show-and-tell that Bessie will probably forget before we even leave her room."

Alzheimer's is a horrible, ravaging, savage disease. What's worse, I asked—knowing you're sick or knowing you're sick and constantly forgetting why? It robbed those afflicted with the only meaningful possessions accumulated over the course of a lifetime—memories. In the three-stage Alzheimer's model, Bessie was late two, moving toward early three. Put another way, she had punched her ticket to the next level of Dante's inferno.

Carney House was a Special Care Unit, staffed with people specifically trained to work with Alzheimer's patients. The yellow-sided, two-story complex sat on a quarter acre of land in a secluded section of Brookline not far from the public golf course. It might have looked a little bit like an Embassy Suites from the outside, but inside it was a skilled nursing facility with 124 beds and all the creature comforts of home. From the beige carpeting to the wallpaper decorated with ivy, the interior design of Carney House tried valiantly to distance itself from the facility's true intent.

Anna stopped at the registration desk to check us in, while I followed Lily over to the common area. It was a typical scene inside the large, sun-drenched room with some residents in wheelchairs, some just sitting, some watching TV, some playing games, some chatting with a visiting relative, some just staring out into nothing.

"They seem so lonely," Lily said in a whispered voice.

"It's the best place for them," I said.

"Best place, huh? Not for me. I don't plan to ever grow old," Lily said.

"We all grow old, Lily. I'm sorry, but it's a fact of life."

Lily's look, almost a smirk, was unnerving.

"Some of us don't grow old," she said, brushing past me on her way over to Anna.

I felt my blood pressure spike. Was she referring to Max and Karen? Or was it just a thoughtless remark from a young woman? Was I again making something out of nothing?

After checking us in, Anna led the way down a long, carpeted corridor to room 102, Bessie's home. I followed, doing my best to believe that Lily had meant something else, anything else. Would I mention this to Anna? No good would come from that conversation—more paranoia on my part, more accusations of my looking for a way out of this situation.

Knocking once on Bessie's door, Anna entered without waiting for permission. Bessie Miller was lying in her adjustable bed doing nothing. The TV wasn't on. She wasn't reading, because she couldn't follow the words. She wasn't knitting or painting, because she had forgotten how. Her room was neat because she had nothing to clutter it up. Anna had put some pictures around the room, including some from our wedding, and one of her and Kevin, a copy of the photograph I had doctored to take out Edward, her ex, the rapist.

There wasn't much to look at. The room had a bed, a little side table with paper cups and a pitcher of water, a large armoire, and dresser with more floral-patterned nightgowns in it. Bessie didn't dress in anything else unless she was being taken for a walk outside or wheeled to one of Carney House's many scheduled activities. The activities calendar was tacked to a corkboard hanging on the wall opposite Bessie's bed. Trivia fun. Simon Says. Beauty Hour. Movie Time. Arts & Crafts. She could even do chair yoga, should the spirit move her. Not that Bessie partook in any of those offerings. Late-stage Alzheimer's sucked the fun out of just about everything. It also drained the life from Bessie's face, and any resemblance between mother and daughter would be found only in the photographs Anna had left behind in her late-night escape from Los Angeles. All of those captured moments, every picture from Anna's childhood, every picture of a young mother and her daughter, of whatever family gatherings had been documented, were lost like Bessie's memories.

"Hi, Mom. How are you feeling today?" Anna crossed the room. She pulled open the curtains, letting in a bright swath of sunlight before giving her mother a tender kiss on the forehead. Anna spoke loudly, as if the timbre of her speech might jog loose some recollection of how Bessie really was doing. "It's me, it's Anna. Hi, Mom!"

Nothing.

Not a single response.

No surprise.

Anna noticed a tray and plates with the crumbs of some meal scattered on the roll-away table.

"Did you have lunch?" Anna asked. "What did you have?"

Bessie moved her mouth, her thin lips parting, words forming, but none uttered. Anna's mother had a round face and a full head of wavy silver hair, jowly cheeks, and loose wrinkled skin. Her brown eyes, set by pronounced crow's feet, were dull as if to announce how her world had gone out of focus. For a woman in her seventies, Bessie Miller looked a decade and some older.

As was the routine, Anna pulled up a chair and sat by her mother's bedside, holding her hand. Meanwhile, Lily hovered in a corner of the room, arms folded across her chest. To anybody who didn't know our story, Lily fit the mold of a granddaughter making a reluctant visit.

"Have you been feeling well, Mom?" Anna asked.

"Hi, you're here," Bessie said in a scratchy voice.

"Yeah, Mom, we've come to share some exciting news with you."

We hadn't told my parents yet, but that would come soon enough. Anna held up the manila envelope for Bessie to see.

"You came here," Bessie said. "What day is it?"

"It's Saturday, Mom. We always come to visit you on a Saturday."

"Oh, you came."

I couldn't guess how much our presence here comforted Bessie. The eyes as windows to the soul might be a cliché, but someone came up with the saying for a reason. Judging by Bessie's blank expression, I wasn't entirely sure she even knew we were here. Our visit comforted Anna, and that was what mattered most to me.

Anna took the images out of the oversized envelope and held each up for Bessie to see. I'd seen them already. They showed a distinct baby form—head, belly, leg, arm, and an umbilical cord terminating into the black mass of the uterus. What the image didn't show definitively was the sex of the baby. We decided not to know even if we got a clearer image. Life had so few true surprises.

"Mom, this is the new baby that Gage and I are going to adopt," Anna said.

"Is it Thursday?" Bessie asked. "I'm supposed to be somewhere Thursday."

"No, Bessie, it's Saturday," I said, coming around to the side of the bed to put my hand on her frail and bony shoulder.

Lily kept to the corner of the room, her arms still folded. Watching.

"Gage and I have decided to adopt a baby," Anna said. "We're going to adopt Lily's baby."

Lily looked like she might pass out at the mere mention of her name. Anna beckoned Lily with a slight wave. Lily came forward in reluctant fashion, stopping at the foot of Bessie's bed.

"This is Lily, Mom. She's going to be the birth mother. She's going to give you a grandchild."

"Hi," Lily said in a weak voice. "It's nice to meet you."

Inwardly, I felt myself shrinking at Lily's evident discomfort. It was my harebrained idea to bring her here in the first place. I'd wanted to show Lily that I harbored no ill will, and more important, that I considered her to be a part of the family now. Lily seemed unsure of the idea, and yet I persisted. Perhaps I should have listened to Anna, who had voiced some concern.

Bessie looked up at Lily. I'd never seen Bessie make eye contact so quickly before. The two locked gazes, and Bessie's mouth began to twitch. The side of her pale and cracked lip moved up and down, as though she were trying to figure out how to smile. Lily seemed more than a little unsure how to react.

"I'm glad you got to see the ultrasound . . . I mean sonogram," Lily said, remembering the distinction I had told her between the two. "We're very excited about the baby."

Something in Bessie's eyes changed. It was as though a film covering them had been wiped clean by an invisible hand. I'd never seen her look at someone with such clarity before. It was a bit unsettling, like she'd become a stranger. A flicker. A flash. Something had transpired, and Bessie seemed to come alive. She lifted one thin, frail arm off the bed. It rose as though being pulled by an invisible string. A finger extended, long and bony, shaking, too. It pointed at Lily, accusatory.

"You," Bessie said in a harsh voice, crackling. "You. I know you. I know you."

"Mom!" Anna said.

"You," Bessie went on. "I know you."

"We've never met. My name is Lily. I'm living above Anna and Gage's house now."

Bessie's lips trembled like two rubber bands being stretched and twisted.

"You!" she said again, this time her voice growing louder until it rose to the decibel of a shout. "You! I know you! I know you!"

Lily's color drained. She covered her mouth with her hands, and then turning on her heels, raced out of the room, fleeing Bessie's rants. "You! I know you! You! I know you!"

The fog shrouding Bessie's memories returned. No sooner had Lily bolted from the room than a window shade of sorts descended over Bessie's eyes. Her head went still, followed by her body. The memory was gone.

Just like Lily.

CHAPTER 14

I still hadn't cracked a smile, and we were well into our second beer. That wasn't like me at all. The look on Brad's face said he knew it, too.

We were sitting across from each other in a booth at Not Your Average Joe's, a casual restaurant nestled within a strip of businesses in downtown Arlington. Brad had been talking about his girls, and Janice, and flower gardens, and his plumbing business, and I had done a lot of head nodding and listening.

"You know," Brad said, taking a meaty bite of his *roast beast* (his name for it, not mine) sandwich, "when your friend invites you out to lunch, usually it involves some form of back-and-forth conversation. You know, I say something and then you respond to what I say, and maybe I build on that topic or it leads to a new topic."

"I'm sorry, buddy," I said. "My mind isn't really on small talk."

"What's going on?"

Brad's eyebrows arched, encouraging me to answer.

"It's Lily," I said.

Brad shifted effortlessly from buddy mode to confidant.

"And?"

I told him about the present that Lily had bought me from a yard sale, and the picture on the *Wicked Local* website, the fight I had with Anna, the fight I had with Lily, the reconciliation in front of Mrs. Trumbull's house, and Bessie's odd accusation.

I know you!

Those words had haunted my thoughts from the moment they left Bessie's trembling lips.

I know you!

"Could Bessie know her?" Brad asked.

"Bessie doesn't even know herself," I said. "Honestly, it was the strangest thing I've ever seen."

We stopped chatting when the waitress came over to see how we were doing. I didn't want anything, but Brad ordered a side of fries.

"How do you eat like you do and not get huge?" I asked, envious because a single fry had the power to tip the scales, and not in my favor.

"Good genes," Brad said with a shrug. "Have you started playing handball again? If you did, you could have all the fries you wanted."

I shook my head.

A year after the accident, shortly after I moved to Arlington, I went on a long walk to clear my head and ended up in a tough neighborhood in Cambridge. Instead of getting into trouble, I got invited to join a handball game. I didn't even know what handball was. We played against a graffiti-painted wall that was part of a run-down housing complex. The game was fast paced, physical, and highly aerobic. I was hooked from point one and became a regular with that crew, attending weekly pickup games, but stopped when one of the young kids I played against was killed during a gang-related altercation. After that, every game I played was a reminder of lives taken too soon, including my son's.

"I keep thinking about starting up again," I said to Brad. "But like Anna and her painting, it just isn't in me yet."

Brad took another bite of his sandwich. "I'll join you if you need someone there for added encouragement."

"Much appreciated, amigo. I might just take you up on that. So what do you think about the thing with Bessie?"

"Maybe it's nothing," Brad said.

"I would agree, but there's been a whole lot of nothings making me feel like it's got to be something."

"Have you talked to Anna about it?" Brad asked.

Now I shrugged and flicked a soggy tomato over with my fork. "She's in love with the baby," I said. "Any doubts about Lily sound to Anna like I'm having doubts about the adoption. I get it, honestly I do. Our situation is unbelievably fortunate. Lily is a beautiful girl. She's healthy, no drugs, no drinking, no birth father in jail. There aren't any siblings to adopt, no arcane rules from some foreign country to follow, and from what Lily says there's no family history of mental illness. There are so many more challenging situations we could end up in. Adoption is a wonderful way to create a family, but there are a lot of pitfalls, too. Anna feels like we're very blessed to have Lily come into our lives the way she did, and she's not wrong."

"Only you don't think it's a blessing," Brad said, his eyes narrowing.

"You have a way of getting to the point," I said.

"My line of work is all about clearing the shit away, bullshit included."

"If I tell Anna we shouldn't go ahead with the adoption, it will devastate her. She's fragile as it is from the loss of her son and then the miscarriage. I can't add to her misery."

"What does Anna think about her mother's reaction?"

"I guess when you want something badly enough, it's easy to justify things or explain them away."

"I presume that's what Anna's done in regards to Bessie."

"With everything I'm telling you," I said.

Brad mulled this over. "You've got to know more about Lily," he concluded. "You guys are in too deep to just let this go. I've learned to trust my gut instinct. It's a powerful tool."

"What do you suggest?"

"Maybe I should meet her," he offered. "I could get a read."

"What? Like read her energy?"

"Yeah, something like that."

I sat quiet, ruminating on Brad's offer while sipping my beer.

"Can you really get something from that?" I asked.

"Only if I try."

"Since you brought it up, I've been wanting to ask something for a while now."

"Go ahead," Brad said.

"How did you know you had the gift?"

"Like the first time?"

"Yeah."

The French fries showed up before Brad could answer—a big, heaping plate of golden badness fried to a perfect crisp. Tempted as I was, I resisted the urge. Anna always marveled at my willpower, and I liked giving her things to marvel at.

"I was a kid," Brad said, blowing on a fry before inhaling it. "I was probably ten or eleven, not much older. Anyway, one day I was just hanging out in my room and I slipped into another state of consciousness. I can't explain it any other way." Brad moved his hand upward in a sweeping gesture, pantomiming his metaphysical shift. "It was something between the state of awake and dreaming. It was like being trapped inside my own body. I couldn't move or scream. These episodes were extremely frightening and went on for years. It wasn't until I was much older that I came to realize it was a form of self-hypnosis that allowed me to travel to other realms of existence. I saw people, people I knew from my street and people I knew who weren't part of this world anymore. I found out I could go into this place, really at will." He snapped his fingers—*at will*. "It was peaceful there, beautiful."

"Couldn't it just have been your imagination at work?"

"Do I really strike you as the highly creative type?"

"You're good with flowers."

"That's a different kind of creativity."

"Point taken."

"All I can tell you is what I experienced. I don't try to convince people that I have this gift. I don't charge money for my services. I just help people who are in need of some help."

"People like me," I said.

"Exactly. So what I can tell you is this. We all have guides," Brad said. "Travelers who walk this world with us. They can't be seen, but they can be felt. Their energy is very distinct, and it surrounds us all. My guide is my grandfather. I'd never met him before. He died before I was born. But I saw him from the moment I made that first shift."

"Maybe you were just remembering his picture?" I asked.

I believed in Brad's gift wholeheartedly, but I was a quality assurance guy who by nature went around poking holes into people's claims. If someone told me something worked, I'd do my darndest to prove him wrong. Couldn't help myself. It was a reflex.

"I couldn't have remembered any pictures of my grandfather, because we didn't have any," Brad said with a smile. "Actually, we didn't have many pictures of my family at all."

I thought about Anna and her comparable dearth of photographic memories. It made me feel sad for them both.

"My aunt had some family photos, but we never saw her much. So I told my mom about this man I'd seen with a mustache—like mine now—a well-scrubbed, long face, dark hair raked back and slathered with pomade, close-set eyes, and a snub nose marked by a jagged scar. She dropped the plate she was drying, and it shattered on the floor."

"You described your grandfather to her," I said.

"Right down to the scar he got from a broken bottle in a bar altercation back in thirty-five. If you got rid of the mustache and pomade, my brother is his spitting image," Brad said. "And my grandfather is my guide."

"Could Max be my guide? Karen?"

That trusty old lump wormed its way right back into my throat with the mention of their names.

"I'm not sure who's walking with you," Brad said. "Maybe we could find out."

"Maybe it's somebody famous," I said. "Like John Lennon or something."

"Or maybe it's not."

"What does a guide do?" I asked.

"They do a lot of things. They provide comfort. They can even answer questions." Brad's eyes were dancing.

What I loved about Brad was that he never shied away from talking about his talent. Some people thought he was a crackpot, but in twenty-five years of being in business, Brad had never had to chase a customer down for payment. He read their energy before accepting a job, so he knew which customers to take and which to avoid. Even a persnickety quality assurance engineer like me couldn't argue with that track record. His competitors didn't know how he did it. Brad's answer: "I read people like you read product manuals."

"So these guides talk to us?" I asked.

"Have you ever gone to bed trying to figure something out and when you woke up the next morning, you suddenly had the answer? That's your guide working."

"Where do these answers come from?"

"Do you know the akashic records?"

"No, but if you hum a few bars, I could fake it."

Brad managed an amused look that somehow didn't patronize. In his heart he wanted me to keep pulling from my trusty stable of semifunny jokes.

"The concept for these akashic records is as old as human spirituality. In the Bible it's referenced as the Book of Life."

"So we're talking about a spiritual book here?"

Brad made the "close but not quite" face.

"You can think of it as a book," he said, "but it's really more like an energy. *Akasha* is a Sanskrit term meaning primary substance. It is the energy that makes up the universe. The book metaphor works because these records contain everything that pertains to you—everything that you are and all you'll ever be. It's a detailed accounting of your soul's journey through this life."

"So we're talking God's library, huh? I'd hate to have to pay one of those overdue fines."

Brad laughed. My well of jokes rarely ran dry.

"We all have access to these records. It's that knowing hunch. Your intuition at work, the feeling of déjà vu. You know the answer because you've got a gut instinct."

"You mean the thing that's making me question Lily."

"The answer to Lily will be found within those records. We just have to tap into them."

"Do you think Lily could be evil?"

"There isn't really good or evil," Brad said. "There is only positive and negative energy. The terrible things people do to each other come from negative energy. Some people have a little negative energy and some have a lot. What we want to know is how much negative energy Lily gives off. Remember what I said to you about that dark energy? It could be Lily."

I took a long breath that failed to calm me down. A tingle of anxiety crept up from my toes and filled my throat.

"There's one very big problem with this plan of ours," I said.

Brad dipped a fry in a mini-mountain of ketchup. My willpower fast fading, I reached across the table and took a fry for myself.

"Lay it on me, my brother from another mother," Brad said.

"Don't take offense, but if something really is wrong with Lily, some hidden agenda, I'm going to need a lot more proof to convince Anna than a psychic plumber picking up her negative vibes."

Brad looked about as bothered as a cat lounging in a ray of sunshine.

"At least you'll get to validate your gut instinct," he said.

"One more issue," I said, holding up a finger to match that number. "If it turns out Lily has to go, I can't lose Anna in the process."

This time, Brad leaned back in his seat and looked uncomfortable.

"Like a guide, I can only point you in a direction," Brad said. "The pitfalls and undesired consequences of our choices, nobody can control."

CHAPTER 15

I had one of those days at work that belonged in the annals of those days at work. So I called Anna and asked her to meet me for a stroll down Newbury Street in Boston. Anna and I loved to walk Newbury Street, especially on a warm, pitch-perfect summer afternoon like this one. We thought it felt like a European enclave tucked inside Boston proper. Many of the shops were unique, with specialty boutiques outnumbering the chain stores by at least a two-to-one margin.

Having come directly from a client meeting, Anna wore her hair in a working-girl bun that I thought looked sexy. She was wearing one of my favorite dresses on her, a blue number that just barely scraped the knees, cinched at the waist by a thin black belt that gave a pleasing shout-out to her fit figure. For all my bad fortune, I was a lucky man to have Anna in my life.

Our first shop stop was Dona Flor, a high-end specialty home goods store. Normally we just browsed, but this time we walked out with a set of nickel-plated roller shower curtain rings. Who didn't need nickel-plated roller shower curtain rings?

"Do you want to take the T over to the art museum?" Anna asked. "It's open past nine tonight."

Anna had bought us a membership back in December, and we'd already earned back the value with the frequency of our visits. I liked the Impressionist collection, Degas especially, whereas Anna favored the American Wing. We both gravitated to the Egyptian exhibit. Anna was deep into studying ancient cultures, believing it helped with her consulting businesses by broadening her perspective on human behavior. It was my heartstrings pulling me to the earthy rooms of mummies, and sarcophagi, and ancient hieroglyphics. Max had loved the museum, but he favored the Egyptian Wing most of all. I ached to leave the museum without picking him up a little something from the gift shop. It was the little things I no longer did that often caused the greatest amount of pain.

"No, I think I'd rather just walk," I said.

We hit a few more stores. As usual, Anna had something to say about the quality of the retail window displays we passed, but I was quiet and she noticed.

"Is everything all right?" she asked as we were leaving another store without buying anything.

I took her arm.

"Yeah," I said. I liked how she always checked in on me. We were like two bent arrows learning how to fly straight again. "It's just Matt Simons," I added with a grumble.

"Who is that?"

"He's one of the senior scientists working on the Olympian project," I explained. He was also a big jerk who could pass for Ichabod Crane's twin brother, but I left that part out.

"What's up with him?"

"Now that the project looks like it's going to be a huge success," I said, "he's scrambling to claim a lot of the credit he doesn't deserve."

Anna knew all about how Olympian was going to leapfrog the market for lithium ion batteries.

"What's he doing? Attacking the quality of everyone's work?" she asked.

I returned a surprised look.

"How'd you know?"

Anna gripped my arm and we kept walking.

"Sweetheart, it's my business to know. I see it all the time. Office politics is just a fancy term for bullying. Retailers are some of the biggest bullies around. I've worked with clients whose egos were so big, they'd rather see the business fail than admit they were wrong. What's he doing exactly?"

"I think he wants to be the project's Program Manager," I said.

As Director of Quality Assurance, reporting to the VP of R&D, the Program Manager was technically on my level, but I had a dotted line reporting into that role. Somebody had to be ultimately accountable for the project delivery.

"Isn't that Adam's job?" Anna asked. Adam Wang's numerous assets and few shortcomings had been the topic of many previous conversations.

"It is, and Simons seems to be gunning for it. This guy sniffs out openings to attack the way DEA dogs go hunting cocaine."

"So is he after you, too?"

I gave Anna an approving look. "You *are* good at your job."

"That's why they pay me the big bucks," Anna said, pinching my arm.

"Well, I spent the better part of the day defending

our test matrixes for the upcoming build. Everyone, and I mean everyone, is on edge. So all Matt managed to accomplish was waste time at a bunch of unnecessary meetings."

"Why is everyone so testy?" Anna asked.

"We have a very significant demo tomorrow," I said. "Guess I should have expected some arrow slinging."

"And what about your test matrixes?" Anna asked.

"Our test plans are fine. They're excellent, in fact, but just having Matt call me into question tarnishes my reputation."

"At least you're in the clear."

"Yeah, but just because the test plans are fine doesn't mean the project is going to be a success. A lot is riding on this demo. It really has to work."

Anna pulled herself closer. "I'm sure you'll be just fine, and the demo will go great."

I smiled weakly. "I wish I had your confidence."

For a time, I forgot all about Lily. I didn't know where she was or what she was doing. I hadn't attached a GPS tracker to her ankle. Lily came and went as she pleased, a separate but wholly connected part of our lives.

Neither of us felt in the mood for a big dinner, so we opted instead for cheesecake and coffee at the ever-crowded Trident Booksellers & Cafe. Anna nabbed one of the coveted tables near a window, while I disappeared in search of a book I wanted to buy. When I returned, Anna had our cheesecake, her latte, and my coffee waiting.

"What did you get?" she asked, pointing to the brown bag I now carried.

"A book," I said.

"Cute, wise guy," Anna said. "What, pray tell, book did you purchase?"

I took the book out of the bag and flopped it on the table. Anna's eyes went wide with excitement.

"*The Coolest Baby Names Ever*," she read, her mouth creasing into a breathtaking smile.

"I figured we should start thinking ahead," I said.

Anna leaned across the table and gave me a kiss on the mouth that might have turned a head or two.

"Baby, thank you," Anna said.

"The book didn't cost *that* much," I said.

Anna leaned over the table once again, but this time to deliver a playful slug on my arm.

"I don't care what the book cost," she said. "I care what it represents."

"It represents that I'm in this with you, all the way," I said.

We kissed again, more a peck this time around.

"You know, Lily is still very shaken by what happened with my mom," Anna said while leafing through the book. "We spoke about it this morning after you left for work."

"So I'm guessing she's going to want to delay her visit with my folks for just a bit."

Anna made a little noise, so she didn't have to say that was an understatement. Searching for a change of subject, I asked to see the book and flipped to a random page.

"What about Bay?" I suggested.

Anna made a face.

"As a name, or something we should do at the moon?" she asked.

"Cosimo," I offered.

"Is that even a real name?"

"It's in the book," I said, pointing.

Anna ripped the book from my hands.

"How about Saffron?" she asked.

"Too spicy," I said.

"Trudy?"

"Wasn't she on *The Facts of Life*?" I asked.

"Notice how I'm picking out the girls' names," Anna said.

"Notice that I don't care what we have, as long as he or she is healthy and ours."

"Cheers to that," Anna said, with a sip of her latte.

I took the book from her.

"How about Thelonious?" I asked.

"How about it's not tickling my ivories," she said.

"Oh, do you want your ivories tickled?" I asked.

"Maybe," she answered, returning a knowing smirk.

I stood, took Anna by the hand, ready to usher her out of the coffee shop, quick as could be, but she pulled back and held her ground.

"Let me buy a sandwich," Anna said. "Just in case."

I nodded, because she did this most every time we went out for lunch. Anna purchased a chicken panini with tomato, avocado, and cheddar cheese from the fresh-faced young woman working behind the counter. It did not take long before we came upon a derelict-looking man, with a filthy gray beard, wearing a ratty sports coat and soiled pants, sitting on a metal grating in the shade of a tall building. His hands were extended as we passed.

"Can you spare a dollar?" he asked in a raspy voice.

"I don't have a dollar," Anna said, "but I do have a meal."

Anna was loath to give money to those who begged for fear they would use it to buy alcohol or drugs, but she had no qualms about feeding the hungry. As she knelt down to hand over the sandwich, I thought back to the day she crouched before a girl who sat crying on the curbside of a bus stop. It occurred to me then how one simple act of kindness really did have the power to alter lives.

We arrived home in separate cars. I parked on the street so that Anna could pull into the driveway. We walked up the front stairs holding hands. At some point in our marriage, Karen and I had stopped holding hands while traipsing through the basic rhythms of life. I can't say when that happened exactly, but I only know that it did because I had Anna. I suspected that down the road, Anna and I would stop holding hands when we walked into the house together. It wouldn't mean our love for each other had lessened, just that it would grow and change with the years.

Anna wasted no time getting down to business. Standing in our narrow hallway, she began to undress before I closed the front door behind me. We were kissing now, our mouths locked together, tongues exploring. Anna pushed me away, only to undo her belt. I slipped my hands around her slender waist, pulling up the fabric of her dress, feeling the firmness of her body and silky brush of her leggings. I hiked her dress up higher and higher until the slippery fabric rested above her hips. A groan escaped Anna's mouth as I caressed her hair while kissing her neck. My other hand was still working to touch whatever body parts had been concealed by her clothes. She turned herself around, hands pressed firmly against the hall wall, pushing herself into me, grinding her hips to feel my excitement build.

Pivoting her body, Anna met my gaze. "We're going to be able to do this less and less once the baby is born," she said, breathing hard while working to unbutton my pants. She ran her hand up and down the front of my zipper, getting me even more ready than I was before. We stumbled into the bedroom, kissing and caressing, tugging at our clothes, growing hungrier by the second. Locked in an embrace, we fell onto the bed and peeled away what little remained of our clothing. When I entered her, Anna cried out softly, as though the immense pleasure still came as a surprise. The more Anna moaned, the more I wanted to please her. My body tingled as I began to increase the speed of my rhythm. We were breathless now, sweaty, our appetite for each other insatiable until we climaxed together. Anna cried out as her whole body tensed. I felt her shudder in my arms.

I lay on my back, with Anna nestled snugly against me. She traced the contours of my chest with her long finger, her body completely spent and relaxed. I was home.

I slid out of bed feeling lighter than I had in weeks. Anna looked over my naked body, pleased with what she saw. I took off the condom I had worn and wrapped it in a couple of tissues. Anna was terrified of another failed pregnancy and didn't want to take the pill because it messed up her hormones. I had volunteered to wear protection. It didn't lessen our pleasure any.

"Are you hungry?" I asked.

"For more of that," Anna said, playfully slapping my behind.

"Takeout? Italian? Chinese?"

"You decide."

"Chinese," I said, thinking about the first time we met Lily.

"We need to do this more often," Anna said to my back as I ambled out the bedroom.

"Most definitely," I answered.

I made a bathroom pit stop, did my business, and casually tossed the condom in the trash. I turned the handles on the sink to get some warm water flowing. Steam from the water clung to the mirror on the medicine cabinet, fogging away my reflection. I threw two handfuls of water on my face and thought about what Anna and I could watch on TV while we ate. We had a bunch of stuff on DVR if we couldn't agree on a show. Maybe *Shameless*. Maybe *Californication*. Doubtful she'd be game for *The Walking Dead*.

I was shutting off the water when something caught my eye. To be more specific, it was something that wasn't there that had grabbed my attention.

It should have been hanging on the upper left corner of the medicine cabinet. It had been there every single day. For the first time since I'd moved into this place, the necklace—a silver chain and tiny heart-shaped locket with a miniaturized picture of my family inside—wasn't there.

And I knew just who had taken it.

CHAPTER 16

Before I did anything, before I called out to Anna, before I put my hand through a wall, I went for my bottle of Adderall. I kept the bottle in my Dopp kit, which I stored in the cabinet beneath the sink. It wasn't something Anna would go rifling through, so it was a relatively safe place to hide my illicit drug of choice. Anna didn't know about it and I didn't want her to know.

I hadn't planned to become an Adderall addict. I picked up the med after stumbling on an article about how college students were taking ADHD drugs recreationally. At the time, it seemed the perfect solution to my ongoing problem at work. I read up on the science behind Adderall before ingesting the first pill. Most of my research focused on people who took Adderall and *didn't* have ADHD, people like me. I was curious about potential side effects. It seemed to be the drug of choice for those of us who needed to do it all and do it fast.

I started popping pills six months after the car accident, at a critical time for the Olympian project. I needed the distraction of work to help combat my deepening depression. At least that was what I told myself. I couldn't do my job. I couldn't focus. If my performance at work didn't improve, I figured at some point HR would have no choice but to let me go. This was my thinking, anyway.

Adderall, from what I'd read, would stimulate the dopamine production in my frontal cortex to improve my concentration and focus. It's a blend of various drugs, including amphetamine salts, which technically makes it speed, and yes, it's a controlled substance as far as the FDA is concerned. The neurobiology was pretty straightforward. With the increased dopamine flow, an ADHD brain could carry on its executive functions as a normal brain would. For those without ADHD, it's like being an athlete and taking steroids.

My concentration went from fleeting to superglued on every task. Motivation? That got jacked up, too. Thinking and focus came in sharper and clearer than any HD broadcast. I felt like I could do the job they were paying me to do and then some.

That was how I got hooked.

Adderall gave me the focus I needed and let me forget my pain. Without it, I concentrated on all the wrong things. I desperately wanted something, anything, to numb my shattered soul. That had been five years ago. I should have weaned myself off it; I should have been able to work without Adderall. But I couldn't, which made me an addict, and Adderall my secret.

I popped two pills, double the prescribed dosage. If I weren't careful, I'd go through my allotted quantity before the month was up. But sometimes I skipped days, so I had accumulated a stash for those extra-needy periods. My blood was already pumping like a steam engine on overdrive. For a moment I feared the accelerant would stop my racing heart midbeat. In some ways, I wished it would. To be with them again, to be with my son in the place that only Brad could connect us.

The drug was in me. I wanted it inside me so I could think clearly. Think . . . *what was I going to do about Lily?* I pictured how it all went down. While Anna and I were at work, Lily took the key from under the flowerpot—we'd shown it to her—and let herself right in. She was looking for something to take—to sell, maybe. Why? Drugs? Cash to pay a debt?

I couldn't answer that question, but the necklace wasn't worth much money. What I could do (and did) was to call out for Anna.

A few minutes later, Anna was sitting cross-legged on the sofa, wearing a satin, floral-patterned bathrobe, watching me pace about our living room.

"It's gone. That's all we need to know," I said, changing direction like a duck in a shooting gallery.

"I agree, it's gone," Anna replied, looking rather perplexed.

Together we had scoured every inch of the bathroom floor but had come up empty-handed.

"So, we're going to have to talk to Lily again," I said.

"Are you sure it was there?" Anna asked.

"Yes, I'm sure. It's been there. It's always there."

"But did you notice it, is what I'm asking? Did you actually *see* it there yesterday? The day before?"

I thought back. Did I recall having seen the necklace? Could I pinpoint a specific moment where I was fully aware of it? No, it wasn't like that. The necklace was just there. It was like any object that became so rooted in the familiar. Only through its absence did it become noticeable.

"No, I don't remember seeing it," I admitted.

"Why would Lily have taken your necklace?" Anna asked.

"I don't know," I said, tossing my hands into the air. "Let's ask her."

"She isn't home," Anna said. "I knocked and then I called."

"We'll use the key and go in there and look for it," I said, still pacing the room while running my hands through my hair. My heart was thumping now. *Whap. Whap. Whap.* When I wasn't moving, I was grinding my teeth. *Thank you, Adderall*. Anything might have set me off. My tension could have been harnessed and used as model rocket fuel.

"Gage, are you all right?" Anna eyed me with concern.

A knock on the door, and we both whirled our heads in that direction.

"Hello?" Lily's soft and plaintive voice called. "Are you guys at home?"

Anna stood, rubbing the palms of her hands against the shimmery fabric of her robe. Had my erratic behavior made her so nervous that her palms got sweaty? Maybe so, but this felt like a changing day around here—*Thank you, Dr. Phil*. It was time for Anna to see the truth about Lily.

CHAPTER 17

Anna opened the front door to let Lily enter, along with a thread of humid air that was immediately absorbed by the air conditioning. Lily was wearing a short black skirt, dark leggings, knee-high boots, and a low-cut, black T-shirt with the Jillian's logo emblazoned on the front. Her long, straight hair looked shiny, newly washed. She no longer had the appearance of a wayward forest nymph. She looked confident, like she was going to hustle for tips.

"I was in the bathroom getting ready for work and saw that you called," Lily said. "Is everything all right?"

"No, it's not all right, Lily," I said, glowering.

Anna gave me a look—that look. I swallowed my anger, but it was tough to get down with all the Adderall kicking about my system.

Lily shot Anna a worried glance. "What's going on?" she asked, a quaver to her voice.

I saw Lily's hands rest across her belly and wondered if she was sending a message of sorts: *you can't be upset with me because I'm pregnant.*

"Come on in," Anna said. "There's been an incident."

"Understatement," I snapped, with teeth clenched.

Again, Anna glared. "Knock it off, Gage," she said.

"What is going on?" Lily demanded.

"The necklace," I said.

Lily looked perplexed.

"Where is it?" I asked. "It's very important to me, Lily. It has a lot of sentimental value. I need it back."

The Adderall was doing its thing. My eyes were locked on Lily like heat-seeking missiles. I doubt I even blinked.

"I don't know what you're talking about."

"Come here and I'll show you," I said.

We moved down the narrow hallway and stopped at the bathroom. I went inside, Lily paused at the doorway, and Anna kept to the hallway with her back pressed up against the wall, arms folded across her chest. Standing in front of the bathroom sink, I pointed to the spot on the medicine cabinet where the necklace should have been.

"I've been living here for four years. The necklace that is *missing* has been hanging in this spot," I said, tapping the top left corner of the medicine cabinet several times for emphasis. "I used to look at the necklace every single morning, every morning, because it brought me a lot of comfort. There's a picture in the locket of Karen, Max, and me and it's very sentimental to me. I don't always look at the necklace, but I always know it's there. Do you see what's wrong with this picture?" My voice was thick with sarcasm.

"Gage, please, don't be nasty," I heard Anna say.

Lily looked stunned.

"I . . . I don't . . ."

"There is no necklace with a locket here anymore."

Lily put her hand to her chest as the first flutter of indignation. "Are you suggesting that I took it?"

She took a cautious step back, moving away from me—the threat—and toward Anna—the ally.

"I'm suggesting it didn't take itself," I said.

"Maybe you were robbed," Lily blurted out.

"And all they stole was a single sentimental necklace? Anna has jewelry here. We have a nice TV, computers. If we were robbed, why would the robbers take a necklace and a locket?"

"I don't know!"

Lily's voice trembled. I saw her lower lip quivering, too. Perhaps that was what she did before she started to cry. I didn't know, because I didn't really know Lily. All I'd done was invite this perfect stranger into my home because she gave Anna and me hope for a happier future. Some hope. What I got from Lily was a world of doubt.

"Check the floor, Lily. Check all around," I said, motioning for her to come closer. "It's gone."

"And you think I took it?"

"Give me another explanation," I said, glaring.

"This is because of the present, isn't it?" Lily said. "You're still angry about that."

"I'm not," I said. Adderall might help me with focus, but it does nothing for lying. *Now if they could make a drug for that. . . .*

"Yes, you are," Lily said. "You're upset about the present and about what happened with Anna's mother. Look, do you want me to go? Leave you guys? I thought you wanted this."

"We do," Anna said, alarmed. "Gage, you stop this right now. Stop threatening her."

I could hear rage in Anna's voice—spitfire anger spoken through clenched teeth.

"I'm not threatening anyone," I said. "I just want my necklace back."

"I didn't take it," Lily said. Her eyes had gone moist.

Anna put her hands on Lily's shoulders to calm her. The touch worked. Lily's resolve returned as the gathering tears retreated.

"Gage is just upset, Lily," Anna said. "He doesn't mean to take it out on you."

Lily gave me a look as if to say, *Yes, he does.*

Without my prodding, Lily entered the bathroom. She walked in a slow, purposeful way, like a detective entering a crime scene. Her eyes scoured the pink tiled floor, scanning, probing, as if I had missed a spot. Then, she fixed her gaze on the medicine cabinet itself, studied it awhile, head tilting, looking and looking some more, before moving in closer for a more detailed inspection. I watched her run her hands along the edges of the cabinet, feeling the wall. I think I saw what she was noticing. Plastic anchors had been used to secure the cabinet to the wall and over time they had loosened some, creating a small gap between the back of the cabinet and the wall where it was hanging.

"Get me a screwdriver," Lily said. "I think I know what happened."

I huffed. "You sound like Encyclopedia Brown," I said, thinking I'd muttered that under my breath.

"Gage!" Anna snapped.

"Who is that?" Lily asked.

"Never mind," I said, bending down to get underneath the sink where I happen to keep a screwdriver for the occasional plumbing project. I handed the tool to Lily.

"What do you have in mind, Lily?" I asked.

"Well, something like this happened to me before," Lily said. "Not with something so sentimental, but it was a chain."

"You think my necklace is behind the medicine cabinet?" I asked.

Lily nodded.

"Yeah, a flick of a towel, you move your hands, brush against it, something, and it comes off the corner, but instead of falling to the floor it gets stuck between the back of the medicine cabinet and the wall."

"Then let me help you take it down," I said. "It's got slots on the back where it's attached to the wall anchors. We just need to lift it."

I had to admit that Lily was good, damn good. Of course there wasn't going to be any necklace behind the medicine cabinet. She was a clever girl, though, making a clever smoke screen. I'm sure if Anna and I went looking (and not very hard) through her apartment (really my apartment, as she hadn't signed any official lease) we would find the necklace among her belongings. Maybe I'd have to do a little B&E of my own.

I held one side of the medicine cabinet while Lily held the other.

"Okay, ready to lift?" I said. "It's not light."

Anna's expression became worried. "Lily, should you be lifting anything heavy?" she asked. She took a few steps toward Lily, ready to take her place. Lily raised a hand to stop her.

"It's fine," she said. "It's just a medicine cabinet."

Lily leaned her body away from the wall to look at me from behind the side of the medicine cabinet and I saw something in her eyes—perhaps a little glimmer of delight. It was an inscrutable look, whatever it was.

"So you're ready?" I asked again.

"I'm ready," Lily said, her pitch-perfect girly voice layered with sweetness.

I counted to three and we pulled together. The medicine cabinet came off the wall along with a few bits of plaster as the fasteners loosened as well.

Something dropped from behind the cabinet—the necklace! Only it had fallen into the sink, and the drain had been left wide open. The necklace spun around in a wide circle, following the contours of the sink on its way to the open drain. My eyes went wide as panic set in. I wanted to reach for it, but I was holding on to a pretty heavy medicine cabinet at the time, so I fought the urge.

Lily wasn't as concerned. She let go of her end and made a desperate grab for the necklace, grasping it a millisecond before it vanished down the drain. Off balance, the medicine cabinet tumbled from my hands and smashed onto the tile floor with a thunderous crash. Bits of shattered mirror spread out in all directions like shrapnel from a bomb. Anna gasped as she covered her ears. I yelled, too, and not something I should have shouted at the woman pregnant with my future child.

The medicine cabinet lay on its side. Our toiletries had all spilled out: toothpaste, prescription pills (thankfully not my Adderall), dental floss, makeup (not mine), lotion (okay, mine), Afrin (mine as well), Q-tips, a razor, and my night guard (my dentist claims I grind my teeth when I sleep). It was a smorgasbord of our personal stuff, not that Lily took any notice. Instead, she held up the necklace with a proud and satisfied look. The chain swayed back and forth in her hand, like something a hypnotist might use, with the heart-shaped pendant containing the tiny family portrait still attached.

"I got it!" Lily said, her voice triumphant.

I looked down at the floor and Lily's eyes followed mine. Only then did she seem to take notice of the resulting devastation. She gave me a sheepish look and turned to give Anna the same.

"Oh, my God, I am so sorry, guys," she said, laughing with embarrassment. Lily leaned over and handed me the necklace. "Well, at least it didn't go down the drain."

"Gage," Anna said, entering the bathroom. "I think you owe Lily an apology."

"I'll clean this up," Lily said. "I'm so super-sorry for the mess."

"Don't worry about it," Anna said, setting both hands on Lily's slender shoulders.

"No really, I insist. It's my bad. I let go of my side."

How convenient, I thought. Not the medicine cabinet, but how convenient that it was Lily who found the missing necklace. I felt like a total fool and couldn't help but wonder if that was the intention.

"Look, I'm sorry, Lily," I said, clutching the necklace in my hand. "I'm sorry that I accused you. I was wrong."

"No need to apologize," Lily said, brushing me aside, but in a way that did not seem at all genuine. Her eyes demanded a lot more than an apology from me. She looked as though she had just tasted a few drops of my blood and hungered for more. She wasn't at all done with me. "I understand you were upset, and I seriously insist on cleaning all this up. I'll even pay for a new one."

"Nonsense," Anna said. "We'll clean it up together, and you don't owe us a thing."

Anna and Lily embraced, sweetly and with much tenderness. It was then I began to realize just what was happening. Something else was at work here, something I was just beginning to see and comprehend. An alliance was forming between Lily and Anna, and it was clear that I was the odd man out.

CHAPTER 18

When I arrived at work the morning after the necklace incident, I wasn't thinking about the big milestone demo we had scheduled for the afternoon. I was thinking about Anna and Lily and how they were laughing and giggling like schoolgirls as they cleaned up the bathroom mess.

Anna asked me to get us something for dinner. Her request had a subtext: leave her alone with Lily to complete the cleanup and repair the emotional damage. I could feel Lily wedging herself between Anna and me. What I couldn't figure out was why.

Grumbling under my breath, I left to get the Chinese food. When I returned, the bathroom was cleaned up and Lily was gone. Anna and I didn't speak about the incident again, not even the next morning. I was left to wonder if I had overreacted, misread Lily once again. I battled self-doubt all morning, and might have completely forgotten about the demo if Lee Chang hadn't stopped by my office.

By the time Lee and I arrived at the demo lab, it seemed that everyone in R&D had already gathered for the showcase event of the season. The demo lab was a huge uncluttered room with white linoleum flooring cleaner than any hospital ward. It was here we featured all of Olympian's real-world applications. Mannequins were spaced throughout, many of them holding cell phones, some wearing portable music players. We even had the front half of an automobile in one corner of the room to demonstrate how our next-generation hybrid car battery would look inside the engine of an actual car. There were computers, cameras, and all sorts of gizmos and gadgets representing the full spectrum of products our batteries one day would power.

That day, we were going to turn on a cell phone powered by what we all believed to be Olympian's first prototype battery stable enough to present to our CEO. Olympian had been years in the making, and Patrice liked to make a big celebratory deal of our progress along the way. Then again, she also liked to make a big celebratory deal of her twins' birthdays, so it must have been in her DNA. She'd ordered a couple cases of beer and bottles of soda, brought in pizza from Sal's, and had her assistant decorate the demo lab with streamers and balloons. I had to admit, the balloons and streamers made me feel kind of special.

Even though this demo was mostly pomp and circumstance, tension was in the air. Adam Wang, our program manager, looked especially nervous. I might have certified the battery, but it was still Adam's project to succeed or fail. We were waiting for Patrice to show, making small talk, discussing the next phase in our endeavors, sipping beers but not really drinking them. I went over to Adam to offer my assurances.

"Relax," I said. "All Patrice is going to do is power on the phone, we'll start the countdown, finish a beer, eat a slice, and then get back to work."

Adam looked hopefully at the mannequin holding

the cell phone powered by the Olympian battery in one hand and the digital timer in the other. The timer would start as soon as Patrice powered on the phone and would stop when the battery ran out of juice. Our calculations predicted the battery would hold more than three times the energy of our competitor's longest-lasting battery. The subsequent recharge test would complete in less than ten minutes.

My confidence did not reassure Adam. He still came across terribly anxious.

"Why does Matt look so smug?" Adam asked.

I glanced at Matt Simons. He was talking with a group of scientists, his posse, the ones he'd turned against Adam. They believed Adam was leading Olympian down the wrong path. I could understand why Adam was on edge. It was no fun being Matt Simons's target. Still, I had tested and retested and believed that everything would work perfectly.

"Just ignore Matt," I said. "He's all bluster and bravado, but the proof is in our product. We'll be fine."

As if on cue, Patrice Skinner entered the lab. We greeted her with polite cheers and clapping. Patrice marched to the center of the room and we formed a circle around her and Amber, our mannequin.

"Greetings and salutations," Patrice said, her face broadening into a cheery smile. "I can't tell you how happy I am to be here today. I spoke with Peter a little while ago, and he's planning to stop by the lab tomorrow to see the battery in action."

Peter George was our fearless CEO. We expected that he would come to the demo lab, see Amber the Mannequin holding the cell phone, take note of how much time had ticked on the timer, and praise how long the battery was lasting. For a battery manufacturer, that constituted serious action.

While Patrice was talking, showering us with accolades, I noticed Adam was paying no attention, focusing instead on Matt. Indeed, Matt did look smug, as though all Adam's dire predictions about Olympian were about to come true. As Patrice's speech went on, Matt might as well have been licking his chops like a cartoon coyote and Adam the plump sheep of his desires.

"So let us all toast," Patrice said, "to the future success of our Olympian battery!"

We raised our beers (or sodas, or glasses of water) in unison. Patrice went over to Amber and turned on the phone, and the timer began ticking off the seconds and milliseconds of battery power used. Adam looked relieved. Matt, however, didn't look any less smug. Patrice came over to my side.

"Thanks again for everything, Gage," she said. "I know these past few years have been very difficult for you, but your leadership has played a huge role in getting us to this point."

"It's been the hardest time of my life," I said, surprised at how quickly I felt heaviness build up in my chest. "But I'm glad to be here with you today."

"I just want you to know how much we appreciate your commitment."

"Thanks," I said. "It's been a blessing for me to have my work. I don't know—"

My words got cut short by a sudden and startled shout. "It's on fire!" somebody yelled.

Bright orange flames flashed from within a plume of thick black smoke that billowed up from Amber's hand. The overpowering stench of burning plastic overtook the lab. Each poisoned breath battered my lungs. I heard people start to cough and gag, and saw Patrice doing the same as she covered her eyes to keep out the sting of smoke. Everything was happening fast. People were shouting, rushing for the door, confused, unsure of what to do.

I heard a loud *swoosh* as a white spray began to overpower the dark smoke. Thick smoke still clung to the air, but it was no longer fanning out across the ceiling.

Matt stood at poor Amber's side, clutching the fire extinguisher he had used to put out the blaze. Amber's hand had melted along with the phone used for our demo. Powerful fans kicked in, working on overdrive to suck out the sickening air. Fire alarms were blaring—a deafening sound coupled with bright, flashing strobes. Patrice gave me a look that shattered my heart. She was crestfallen, visibly dismayed. I could read her eyes: *How could a build I sanctioned catch fire minutes after the phone powered on? Didn't I test this?*

Matt wasn't looking at me, but I was looking at him. The commotion and chaos continued all around us, but he didn't seem affected by it in the least. Rather, he looked like a guy who knew he'd need a fire extinguisher before the first puff of smoke ever appeared.

CHAPTER 19

Anna and I had one of those dinners where the forks and the knives made the loudest sound in the room. A heavy silence weighted us down, the kind that spoke volumes. I knew Anna was still upset with me when she didn't so much as break a smile after I waltzed in carrying a brand-new medicine cabinet from Home Depot. It was a lot nicer than the one we had before, but still not nice enough to break the ice.

I started to talk about work, hoping that would lighten the mood. I told Anna all about Matt Simons and my suspicion that he intentionally caused the fire.

"I think he did it to get Adam fired, but of course that makes me look bad, too, because now the quality of the product is suspect," I said, finishing the story even though Anna wasn't really listening. I was grateful for any conversation, even if it was just my own voice talking. "I think he sabotaged the build, if you ask me," I continued, taking a bite of the garlic-flavored tilapia Anna had cooked for dinner.

She didn't ask any questions, but I went on. "We've got a very complex configuration management system in place," I said. "So I think Matt did something to that system that substituted an older build of the product, not the one I approved. Of course, now Adam is a total wreck. He thinks they're going to fire him. Heck, they might fire me, too."

That got Anna's attention.

"Why would they do that?" Anna asked, showing interest in the crazy events of the day for the first time.

"It's a quality issue," I said between bites. "I'm the guy who gave this battery the seal of approval."

"But you said yourself that Matt Simons might have sabotaged the project to get Adam fired."

I smiled while stabbing a nicely oiled chunk of butternut squash with my fork.

"So you *were* listening."

Anna's hard edge softened a bit.

"Honey, of course I was listening. Just because I'm pissed at you doesn't mean I've stopped caring."

"Understood."

Anna shook her head. "No, I'm not certain you do. So tell me, is your job really in jeopardy?"

"Hard to say," I said. "It's not good either way. The CEO was expecting to see a demo of Olympian, and what we gave him instead was a one-alarm fire. I told Patrice we should reverse engineer the battery that malfunctioned and see if it matches the build I approved for the demo. If it doesn't, then I'd say my job is safe."

"For now," Anna said, "but this Matt Simons character isn't going away. Sounds to me like you need to be very careful. Trust me, Gage, people can be ruthless when it comes to getting ahead. I should know. Managing personalities is a big part of my consulting business."

"Well, if I do end up losing my job, at least we've got yours to fall back on."

Anna said nothing, while breaking the eye contact we'd finally achieved. Her only response was to take another bite of fish.

"What?" I asked. "Did I say something wrong?"

"No, nothing," Anna said, but in a way that said yes, something.

"Okay," I said. "Let's pull. Active listening. Seriously, what is wrong, honey? I love you, I care about you, and I want to know what's bothering you. Are you still mad about what happened with Lily last night?"

"Yes," Anna said, flatly. "But that's not why I'm being quiet."

Truth be told, I wasn't in the greatest mood myself. The double whammy of the necklace incident followed by the exploding battery was taxing enough. Add my suspicions about Lily, and I deserved to be downright ornery.

"Why don't you tell me why you've gone silent?" I said, making eye contact, feeling genuine, remembering what I'd learned from our therapist, Dr. Small.

"I want to stop working when the baby comes," Anna said. "Maybe for a year."

"And you're worried I'm going to lose my job," I said, following her train of thought, or so I believed.

"It's important to me to be home with the baby for that first year."

"But how are you going to build your business back up?"

"I've got a great reputation with my clients. I'll outsource some of the work and postpone some bigger projects. Also, I have a very big opportunity with Humboldt coming up. I'm traveling to Minneapolis in a couple of weeks for the final presentation. If I get this job it'll be a game changer for me. It would allow me to take the year off, assuming you still have a job."

"I won't get fired."

"I'm just saying, for your wife and your future child, please do everything you can to make it all right."

"Of course," I said, getting up to come around the table and give Anna a tender kiss. "I'll go see Patrice in the morning. I'll find out what started the fire."

Anna looked up at me and I saw a twinkle in her eyes. "This active listening stuff works great, huh?" I said. "We fixed that problem without even a spit of anger."

"Oh, I'm still angry. Gage, you're risking this amazing situation of ours."

"By this situation, you mean Lily?"

"Yes, Lily."

Here I swallowed, resisting the urge to say more.

"You don't think it's even a little bit weird?" I said. "Lily being the one to find the necklace?"

"I think you're being paranoid."

"Think about all the fights we've had lately," I said. "They've all been because of Lily."

"Oh, you think Lily is trying to come between us?"

That was as good a time as any to retake my seat. I could feel the rumblings of a major fight coming on. I needed to dig deep and show some restraint, because I had a plan. I wanted to say, "Yes, I think she's trying to turn you against me." But if I so much as hinted at what I was thinking, Anna would explode. I could see the anger smoldering. To go after Lily would be like using a backhoe to unearth a gas pipe. I'd be attacking Anna's soul, her maternal desires, and the child Lily promised to us.

Still, I couldn't stop my thoughts. What could Lily be after? I tried to guess at her agenda, come up with some logical explanation for these strange series of events, but nothing held together. The model rocket gift and the missing necklace pitted me against Lily while leaving Anna stuck in the middle. Was that Lily's intention, and if so, to what purpose? Were those the reasons for Brad's warning about some dark energy? And what about the strange encounter with Anna's mother?

Soon enough, I'd get some answers. Soon enough.

"A lot of strange things have been happening lately," I said. "Maybe the strain is getting to me."

"Adoption is no easier than pregnancy. In fact, in a lot of ways, it's harder. So I have a lot of strain, too, you know."

"I do. I'm sorry. I know I haven't been easy."

"What is it that you need, Gage? I just have this feeling you're looking for excuses to keep this from happening."

I need to know if I can trust Lily.

I need some kind of a sign.

Instead of voicing my concerns, I said, "I'll try to be better. Look, I'm sorry if my behavior has upset or worried you. I'll do everything I can to make sure my job is secure and I'll back off on questioning Lily."

For now.

"I could use a little more support from you."

"I promise."

"You know we have the home study orientation coming up? It's the night before my trip to Humboldt. You haven't forgotten, have you?"

"Yes, I remember."

It was then I caught a flash of something bright yellow inside the built-in china cabinet directly behind Anna. Looking closer, I could see it was a mug shaped like Pac-Man, painted the same banana-yellow color as the arcade game character. A vase stood next to the mug. Its blue and purple hues were a lot more fitting with Anna's tastes than the Pac-Man mug.

"What's up with Pac-Man?" I asked.

Anna glanced over her shoulder to where I pointed.

"Oh," she said. "Lily and I painted pottery today. She painted it for a friend who likes the game."

I said nothing as a sick feeling swept through me.

"I'm guessing you forgot today is Kevin's birthday," Anna said.

I lowered my gaze. Every year on her son's birthday, Anna painted a single piece of pottery as a way of honoring his memory. It was the only painting she did these days, because painting pottery was one of his favorite things to do, she had told me.

"You're so focused on Lily," Anna said, standing, turning her back to me, "that you're forgetting your wife."

"Anna, please . . . I'm sorry. I wasn't thinking. Why didn't you tell me?"

"Because I thought you would remember."

No time of the year was lonelier or sadder for me than Max's birthday. A parent doesn't forget it. Some years I wanted to crawl into a hole and hide, wait for it to pass, but I always celebrated Max's life by doing things on that day that remind me of him. Even though it was hard and I was left gutted, I worked on model rockets, drank extrachocolaty chocolate milk, took a drive to the beach and gazed out at the sea. Some day, when I felt ready, when the time was right, I would finish the model rocket we were building together. I'd tuck a message inside the rocket's tubular body just for Max to read and send it off to the heavens with a big blast from its E engine.

But today, I was just the husband who forgot that my wife's pain equaled my own; she had spent her day with Lily and not me, honoring Kevin's memory.

You're so focused on Lily . . .

I got up from the table, crossed the room, and

hugged Anna, who broke from my embrace quicker than usual.

"I'm so sorry, sweetie," I said, feeling like a giant jerk. "What can I do to make it up to you?"

"Just remember next year, I guess," Anna said, but her smile was forced and strained.

I could see she was bitterly disappointed in me, as I was in myself. Opening the china cabinet, Anna moved other pieces of PYOP made on other birthdays aside. She retrieved the new vase, along with a mug painted blue and decorated with green circles. She set both pieces on the table in front of me.

"I was debating about painting a mug for you or a vase for me, and Sally, the girl who owns the place, convinced me I should go for the vase. She's thinking about opening another studio in Southborough or Shrewsbury—she's not sure which one yet—and I told her I'd be happy to consult with her on the business plan if she'd like. She was so excited, she gave me a free mug to paint and a promise to call—so I might get a new client, and you get a mug."

I admired both the mug and the vase, not at all surprised by the craftsmanship.

"These are fantastic," I said, and I meant it. "Thanks for my mug."

"Thanks for the compliment," Anna said, not sounding at all appeased. "I used acrylic paints on clay that's been fired to bisque. Sprayed them with a matte finish after I was done. Never tried the technique before, but I didn't feel like waiting to get the kiln-fired pieces back and now I think I'm hooked. I really like how they came out."

"Lily did the same?"

"No, she's going back to get her mug next week. Sally gave Lily the store display Pac-Man because she liked it so much. I'm keeping it here so it'll be a surprise when she gives it to her friend."

I wondered who this friend was and when he or she traipsed around Lily's apartment, but I asked a different question instead.

"So how'd you end up going with Lily?"

"She called to talk about last night's events," Anna said, her eyes turning cold. "I told her I was on my way out the door, and she asked where I was going. I told her and she wanted to come along."

"That's great."

"Honestly, it was great," Anna said. "I've never shared that moment before with anybody, and it was incredible to have Lily there. She represents so much positive change in our lives. I came home and probably cried a good hour, but it was worth every second."

"I'm sorry I wasn't there for you." I gave Anna a big hug, this time holding. "What did you girls talk about?"

Part of me was uncomfortable with the idea of Anna and Lily having a life separate from me. If I trusted Lily, I'd certainly feel different.

Tread carefully, Gage . . .

"We talked about last night, for sure, and some other things I'd rather keep private."

Or Lily asked you to keep private, I thought.

Anna broke from my embrace to give a sad little smile—as if to say, thanks for trying to comfort me, close but not quite close enough. But I could tell she was glad Lily had been there for her, to share in Anna's painful past, to celebrate her future joy, and to reveal >secrets I couldn't know.

Anna pulled away and vanished into the dark hallway of our home. I heard our bedroom door close shut.

I knocked softly on the door.

"Anna, please. Are you all right?"

"Gage, I just need to be alone for a while," came her muffled reply. I retreated to the dining room table, where I sat alone with my thoughts, pushing the food around my plate.

Some time had passed, fifteen minutes, maybe as much as a half an hour. I hadn't moved from the table when the phone rang. Anna answered it on the third ring. A few moments later, she emerged from the bedroom. Her eyes looked red, but otherwise Anna seemed perfectly composed.

"That was Lily," Anna said. "She said she doesn't have any running water."

I looked up at Anna. The sliver of a smile creased my lips and squinted my eyes. I hoped it wasn't a "tell," a clue to Anna that the water loss was no accident.

"Okay," I said, rising from the table, and headed for where I stored my toolbox. "If it's not something I can fix myself, I might have to call Brad."

CHAPTER 20

An hour and a half later the doorbell rang. There was Brad, standing on our front porch in a work shirt, work boots, and faded dungarees. I invited him inside as Anna emerged from the bedroom to join us in the hall. Whatever anger she'd carried seemed to be gone. Her face was cheery, eyes sparkling. Brad brought along his hefty toolbox, though all he would need to fix this little problem was his hand, to twist a knob clockwise.

"Heard you might be needing some water," Brad said. His voice held a lilt, as if nothing fazed him. We could have roused him from a sound slumber on a frigid cold morning, begged him to fix a problem he wouldn't make much money fixing, and that lilt would still be there. When you had a glimpse into the beyond, and saw something there, everyday problems lost their power to annoy.

"It's in the upstairs unit where Lily, our . . . our tenant lives," Anna said.

Anna and I exchanged looks. Brad and I did the same. *Lily, our tenant. Lily, our birth mother. Lily, the source of the growing animosity between Anna and me.*

Lily, the woman whose aura I suspected would be black, like the strange force following me.

If Lily were headed out for work, she'd have left by now. I knew a little bit about her schedule. After Anna had vanished into the bedroom, I'd waited a while, listening for footfalls, making sure Lily was sticking around the apartment before texting Brad to come over.

"Well, let me go downstairs and have a look," Brad said.

The door to the basement was in the kitchen. I escorted Brad through the apartment and soon we were headed downstairs. We did the perfunctory, "How is everything?" chat, covering Brad's girls, wife, flower garden, and latest cooking experiment all in a two-minute span. Our voices downstairs might carry upstairs so Brad's visit needed to maintain the authenticity of being a real house call.

"Looks like I got the problem fixed," Brad said as he turned the knob controlling water flow to the upstairs unit, which I had earlier turned counterclockwise. *Righty tighty, lefty loosey.* "Let's go upstairs and see if that fixed the problem," Brad said.

I was half expecting Brad to break character, whisper something about our plan. *Is Lily home? Do you think Anna suspects?* He surprised me with his commitment to the role of jovial and capable plumber.

Soon we were headed to Lily's apartment, traveling up a narrow, twisting stairwell to the second floor. We made a brief pit stop at my place to ask Anna to call Lily so she could open the door for us. We came out into Lily's kitchen.

Lily was dressed all in black. I wondered if her color choice in clothing would match her aura. Brad smiled at Lily and she smiled back, showing respectful appreciation for her knight in grungy dungarees.

I couldn't help but take a look around the kitchen—looking for what, I couldn't really say. Maybe I thought she'd have accidentally left her plans for me tacked up on the refrigerator with fruit-shaped magnets. Week 1: give him the present. Week 2: recover from crazy mama making crazy accusations about me. Week 3: take his necklace. Week 4: who knew what?

What I saw instead was a very clean kitchen, some containers from Whole Foods set about the counter in an orderly fashion, and Lily looking a little bit bigger in the belly than she had the day before. Maybe she was wearing looser clothing the night she dropped the medicine cabinet. I couldn't remember.

"Thanks for coming out so quickly," Lily said, bending at the hip in an oddly flirtatious manner as she tucked her hair behind her ears, giving us a first peek at the jangly earrings set on delicate lobes. Her unblemished skin looked white as fresh snow—a by-product, I was sure she'd say, of working nights and sleeping days.

She reached out and touched Brad's arm, smiling at him as though the presence of a male was enough motivation to turn on the charm. Maybe it was the instinct of working for tips, or maybe she was just a touchy-feely person. She'd never been that way with me. Brad didn't seem to mind, which made me wonder if he was still in character or pleased that an attractive and much younger woman was touchy-feely with him. Not that Janice had anything to be worried about. When it came to marriage and fidelity, Brad had the loyalty of a swan.

"I just want to take a look around, make sure the water is running all the places the water should run and none of the places it shouldn't," Brad said.

With toolbox in hand, Brad let Lily lead him on a

quick tour of the apartment on her way to the bathroom—the only other place aside from the kitchen with running water.

For some reason, I expected the place to be in some disarray, a bit like Lily herself. I was looking for piles of clothes, food left out, anything messy (except, of course, for bottles of booze and cigarette butts, since that would be bad for baby). What I saw instead was a home. Lily had hung three framed posters up (one of Cirque du Soleil, an Ansel Adams print, and a framed movie poster for the film *The African Queen*). Who knew she liked *The African Queen*?

"That's one of my favorite movies," Brad said, stopping to admire the colorful representation of scenes from the film along with Bogart and Hepburn's likenesses.

"Mine too," Lily said, her voice rising excitedly, again touching his arm. "I got it at the COOP in Harvard Square. I'm a total old movie fanatic. I know, it's so weird, but that's me." Lily smiled and shrugged. Once again she was the innocent and shy tree nymph from Greek mythology, unsure of each step, a sweet little fawn of a thing, too innocent to do me any harm. Brad gave me an over-the-shoulder glance, but his eyes cast no meaning.

"What other old films do you like?" I asked.

Our eyes met and Lily held my gaze, but not my elbow as she'd done with Brad. No, ours was apparently a deeper bond that required no physical contact to make a profound and very clear statement. She knew, from the moment we locked eyes, this was a test. What might have been the hint of a smile, a crease of sorts, just barely teased the edges of her mouth without ever fully materializing.

"Why, that's a great question," she said. "I guess when push comes to shove I'm *Gone with the Wind* all the way. But then there's Brando—*On the Waterfront*, of course—and *Casablanca*, or *Grand Hotel*. How about Greta Garbo and Joan Crawford? My goodness, now *they* are movie stars! Oh, and can't forget John Barrymore. Do you know him? I have a little crush on him. Believe me when I tell you there are no men like Barrymore shooting pool at Jillian's, that's for sure. You know something? You and Anna should come up and we'll have a classic film marathon. I watch them all the time." Here Lily set her hands upon her belly. "I wonder"—her voice trailing off—"if it'll be good for the baby because of all the music in the soundtrack."

She was good, but I didn't believe her for a moment, and she knew it. Had she and Anna talked about old movies while they painted pottery, I wondered. I remembered her suitcase, the antique-looking green luggage carrier; it was sort of fitting with this old movie fanatic person. But there were incongruities as well: how she dressed, where she worked, those were truly modern designs. The mystery of Lily only deepened, and, as if she possessed hypnotic powers, Brad, it seemed, had fallen completely under her spell. Not one iota of concern registered in his eyes.

We finished checking the apartment and found the water was running just fine (surprise, surprise). Lily thanked Brad. She shook his hand and of course touched his arm again. *When did she become so touchy?*

I walked Brad downstairs. He stopped to say goodbye to Anna. I had told him in the basement that today was Kevin's birthday. On his way out, he gave Anna a hug, a quick kiss on the cheek, and a standing invitation to come over to his house for dinner.

"I wish I could connect you to him," Brad said, pausing at the door. "Just so you knew he was in a good place."

Anna put her hand to her heart.

"I know he is," she said.

The night was pleasantly cool. I walked Brad over to his van, eager to hear his assessment. My Vegas line favored Lily's aura being some shade of gray—something lurking below the surface.

"Well?" I asked. "What do you think?"

"Gage, I got nothing."

"Nothing as in no blackness, no something following me?"

"Nothing as in nothing. I don't know what it means, but it was like she was warm water. Not too hot, not too cold. She seemed just right to me. In fact, she seems really great, Gage."

"What about Anna's mother?"

"Late-stage Alzheimer's is very unpredictable."

"So you're saying it's all just a series of coincidences? The present, the necklace, the strange dark force, Anna's mother, nothing is connected, no paths back to Lily, no hidden agenda here."

"I'm saying, I couldn't read Lily's aura. That's it. But as a friend I'd say you should let yourself relax and enjoy this experience. I think you and Anna are two very lucky people."

Brad drove off, leaving me alone to wonder why I didn't feel lucky in the least. I glanced up and saw Lily standing in the window, looking down at me from her vantage point above.

This time, I had no trouble seeing her smile.

CHAPTER 21

Much transpired in the weeks following Brad's visit, most of it at work. For reasons of great complexity, we were unable to reverse engineer the exploding battery. We did root cause analysis, but no one could figure out why it had caught fire. Subsequent builds of the battery, we found, worked fine. Something had happened to the big demo build, and my only conclusion was sabotage.

"Who would want to sabotage Olympian?" Patrice asked me in a private meeting after I'd flung my accusation.

I should have said "Matt Simons," but thanks to Lily, who seemed to have wormed her way into my office life as well as my home life, I was gun-shy about making unsubstantiated accusations. So when Patrice asked the question, I gave no answer and the discussion ended as quickly as our big battery demo.

Meetings followed, many meetings, some in Patrice's office, some in the large conference room, some in the demo lab, but none with the CEO. Apparently he was too busy visiting projects that actually worked. Even with all the uproar and chaos surrounding this significant setback, Adam kept his job, at least for the time being. However, it was clear to all that his tenure on the project was tenuous at best. Matt Simons was no longer shouting for his dismissal, probably because he'd already fired the bullet that would eventually be fatal.

It was Patrice's job to break the news to upper management. We would need to conduct a full audit of our configuration management systems before we could demo again. These batteries were a big deal, and the testing had to be exhaustive. Bad press from a burning battery (hello, Boeing Dreamliner) could cost a company its fortunes.

While work continued on the battery—not business as usual, not by any means—my home life seemed to smooth out. I stopped doubting Lily, or more accurately stopped voicing my doubts.

Anna and Lily were growing ever closer. A bond had formed between birth mother and adoptive mother that I had inadvertently helped forge. My suspicions, my outbursts, simply drove the two together. There were shopping trips, lunch dates, and such. On one memorable afternoon, I came home from work to find Anna and Lily in the living room chatting like a pair of college roommates. Apparently, they'd just come back from the nail salon and were sitting on the sofa admiring their results.

"How'd you end up there?" I asked, slipping away into the kitchen to grab myself something cold to drink. Anna's voice carried as I fished around for a Diet Coke in one of those pony-sized cans.

"Oh, we were just doing some window shopping and decided to pop in and get one."

I offered them both something to drink, but they turned me down. I returned to the living room with my soda, wondering when, if ever, it would feel natural and normal to have Lily in the home.

"What did you talk about?" I asked. *What secrets did you share?*

"Mostly we talked about shopping and read magazines," Anna said.

"Or we fished our magazines out of the water," Lily said.

They shared a laugh while I wracked my brain in search of the joke. Anna noticed I was on the outside looking in.

"I was getting my pedi done," Anna said, "reading a *Cosmo*, some article about work mistakes to avoid like the plague, and it just slipped out of my hand and landed in the water."

They laughed again, effortless, easy, and genuine. Then they took turns showing me the results of their mani-pedis. Anna went for a more neutral look—no surprise there—while Lily's looked like the flag from some African nation.

"Mine is called Fiji Weejee Fawn," Anna said, showing me the muted brown tones coated with a metallic sheen. "Do you think I should have gone more extreme?"

The subtext of her question was evident: *should mine have been more like Lily's?* That was when I knew for certain they really had grown close. I hadn't become a nonfactor, but clearly my role had been diminished.

Anna and I dropped in at Jillian's to play pool when Lily was working. Naturally, Lily was our waitress, and she took great pleasure serving us fried mozzarella sticks and Diet Cokes. She also demonstrated some remarkable pool skills, sinking what to me was an impossible two-ball combination with fluid ease.

I wanted to change my tune about Lily. I wanted to

embrace her and our future family with joy. But when I let my guard down, into my head popped all the various incidents, including Bessie and her accusatory rant.

You! I know you!

Anna and I visited Bessie again, but this time Lily didn't come along. There were no incidents, no flare-ups, nothing to suggest Bessie had any memory of Lily from that day or before, for that matter. In truth, she had no memory of anything, not our last visit, not the sonogram. Anna broke the news about the baby again and she'd keep on breaking the good news until the baby was born. The other person Anna told was her mother's cousin, Gladys, who resided in California and whom she called every Sunday night without fail. I spoke with Gladys on only a few occasions, and she always ended our brief chats by commenting on how handsome I looked in the pictures Anna had sent. During those calls, Anna would give detailed updates on her life and Bessie's health and well-being along with some harsh words directed at Bessie's errant sisters. If Gladys weren't eighty-five and of bad health herself, she'd have come for a visit.

This was our life for the better part of a week or so. We were halfway through Lily's fourth month of pregnancy: the sixteenth week of gestation. By this point, the uterus should have been around the size of a melon, but Lily's could not have been much bigger than a navel orange. Still, she was rounder in the belly, though not round enough to assuage all of Anna's concerns. There was a frustration for adoptive parents, I read, that had everything to do with control. A pregnant woman decided what she ate, when she slept, how she might exercise, while the mother waiting to adopt could only hope for the best. We were the navigators, guiding our passenger on a pathway to home, but we were not the pilots. Those controls were in another's hands, and so Anna's concern grew in reverse proportion to the size of Lily's belly: the smaller the bump, the bigger the worry—simple math for a complex equation.

Anna showed me a website after we got home from playing pool.

"Do you think Lily's gained five pounds since we met her?"

I read the post on BabyHelp.com. An expectant mother had expressed her concern about not showing at fourteen weeks.

"What did you search to find this thread?" I asked.

"Not showing at fourteen weeks," Anna said.

Sure enough, I typed the words "Not Showing" into the Google search bar and got auto-complete results for not showing at twelve weeks all the way up to twenty weeks.

"If she's gained five pounds, I think we're fine," Anna said, though her voice failed to mask a lingering concern. Anna looked me in the eyes and it broke my heart. "I just want this, Gage. I want this so bad."

I felt her pull toward motherhood. It was strong enough to create its own presence. I remembered Karen's pregnancy more vividly than I recalled Max's infancy. I knew where Karen's stretch marks were, what ointments she would rub on her expanding belly. I could tell Karen when she was hungry before she knew it herself. We did the music thing—little headphones on the belly playing intelligence-boosting classical music—even after reading articles that debunked claims of benefits.

"What if they're wrong?" Karen had said.

Nodding in agreement, I'd turned up the volume on my iPod just a notch.

"They could be wrong," I had said.

Perhaps sleep deprivation played a part in my fuzzy recollections of Max's infancy. Or maybe it was this: a first pregnancy was when all the possibilities of the world drew parents closer, and then, after the birth, reality set in with feeding schedules, fumbling newness, constant uncertainty, and lack of sleep. With no control over the pregnant body, Anna and I were missing a component of this early bonding. Perhaps that was the dark energy surrounding me, pulling us apart.

CHAPTER 22

On the third day of Lily's fifteenth week (yes, that was how we measured time), the doorbell rang. On our porch stood a rather heavy woman wearing a pink paisley blouse and flowing black skirt. She was in her late fifties, I determined, with shoulder-length brown hair parted down the middle. Her glasses were wire-rimmed—no fashion statement there—but her jewelry, big and colorful beads, along with the rest of her attire, gave off little echoes of her past. It was easy to imagine her at a Grateful Dead show, twirling in the twilight to "Uncle John's Band." But her dark eyes were kind, and she was the sort who made anyone feel comfortable in her presence. If Brad were here, he'd probably see a yellow aura bordering on a pure white glow.

"You must be Gage," the woman said, extending her hand along with a smile. "I'm Margret Dodd, your social worker." We shook hands, and I noticed the padded folder tucked underneath her arm. I assumed it contained all the paperwork for our home study orientation.

"It's great to meet you, Margret," I said, stepping

aside. "Please come in. Anna is looking forward to meeting you as well."

I escorted Margret (it took all of two seconds) through the living room and into our small dining room. If I hadn't been paying attention, I might not have noticed a slight shift in Margret's eyes. She was searching our home in the subtlest of ways, looking in this understated manner for signs of future trouble. Did we smoke? Was the home clean? Did we live like respectable people? Could we be trusted to care for this precious gift? I knew she was just doing her job, but it was hard not to feel slightly judged.

We were safe, though. The apartment was probably the cleanest it had been in ages, right down to the freshly washed floor. If anything, the place smelled like a Pine-Sol bomb had gone off.

Anna came out of the kitchen carrying a tray with a pot of tea and some milk and sugar. Lily followed on her heels, carrying a tray of cookies neatly arranged in colorful pastry holders.

Lily looked absolutely beautiful. Here was a girl who could be a contestant on *The Bachelor* and receive a rose every single episode, even if she just sat in the corner and sulked. Her hair, freshly washed, shining, flowed with a life force of its own. She wore a long, floral-patterned dress—not her usual black hipster attire—that flattered her narrow shoulders and hips, and she had sandals on her feet. Margret gave me a look as if to say, "Your baby is going to be absolutely gorgeous."

The tea, the cookies—all of it had been carefully chosen by Anna beforehand. Everything here was intentional, well-thought-out, as though this orientation meeting were really a job interview, which in a way it was. Margret had shaken my hand, but she gave Anna a warm embrace. They were somewhat familiar with each other. Anna was in charge of managing communications with the lawyer, the social worker, and adoption agency. It was Anna who was writing the checks. She maintained the big folders of paperwork, all neatly labeled and organized in a file cabinet in her office. This, I'd come to realize, was as close to being in control of the pregnancy as Anna could manage.

I, too, learned a lot about the process. Massachusetts law prohibited the placement of a child for adoption by any person other than a licensed or approved placement agency. Exceptions were made in cases of relations by blood or marriage. Birth mothers were allowed to select the adoptive parents, and such adoptions were referred to as "identified," "designated," or "parent-initiated" adoptions. Margret came to us via the agency Anna hired. As long as Margret felt we were suitable, she would honor Lily's wishes to have us become the adoptive parents.

Lily was a new person to Margret, but they hugged anyway, a quick and friendly little embrace. Anna wanted Lily to be a part of these meetings from the onset so she would be informed each step of the way. Lily didn't seem to mind. In fact, I picked up on a childlike exuberance from Lily in Margret's presence. This meeting, after all, was centered on Lily. Perhaps for the first time in her life, she felt truly important. What did Lily have besides us? She had a job in a pool hall, a louse for a boyfriend, an absent birth father, and a distant relationship with her parents. It seemed to register in Lily's every move that her pregnancy was a very big deal. She wasn't just part of the show, she *was* the show.

We sat at the kitchen table making small talk, drinking tea, and going about the business of becoming parents. Our home had become a fertility clinic of sorts. Instead of hormone injections, we would use a pen. And until we passed the home study, Lily's baby was ours by desire alone.

"So tell me a little bit about yourself, Lily," Margret said.

"Not much to tell," Lily said. "I grew up in Saugus."

"Did you go to high school there?" Margret inquired. "I know some people from the town."

"Oh, yeah," Lily said, her Boston accent coming out now. "I didn't go to college or anything. Is that a problem?" Lily gave Anna a nervous look as Margret laughed warmly.

"Not at all, Lily," Margret said. "I just wanted to learn more about you."

I noticed Margret wasn't taking any notes, so I hoped Lily understood this to be an informal inquiry. Still, she was looking at Anna a bit apprehensively, as if she was failing some sort of test, wanting our approval and worried about disappointing us.

Well, not us, but Anna. Lily hadn't really made eye contact with me. I was a prop in these proceedings more than a participant, as far as Lily was concerned. This was the Lily and Anna hour. And even though Brad had cleared her aura, it was hard for me not to think that this had been Lily's intention from the start.

"What do you like to do?" Margret asked. "Do you have any hobbies?"

"Mostly I just work," Lily said. "I'm a waitress at Jillian's. I do like to draw."

Draw? I'd never seen Lily so much as pick up a pen or pencil in the time she'd been living here. No drawings of hers hung on the walls.

"Have you always been artistic?" Margret asked.

Lily became shy, reverting into herself.

"I wouldn't say that I'm artistic," she clarified. "I'm not very good."

"What do you like to draw? Do you have a favorite subject matter?" Margret inquired. She took a long sip of tea, eyeing Lily over the rim of her mug. Lily got a pensive look to her, thinking.

"I mostly draw people," Lily said with a shrug. "I like to observe people, watch their mannerisms and stuff. I think everyone has a secret life, you know? Something they want to hide, something they wouldn't want anybody else to know about. That's what I like to draw."

My throat tightened and I felt my palms turn slick. For the first time since Margret's arrival, Lily was looking right at me.

CHAPTER 23

The meeting continued without any hiccups, nothing that would derail our plans. If Lily had some hidden designs, she held out. Margret went through the details of the home study process never bothering to check her notes. I suspected she'd placed so many children in so many homes that the process had been etched into memory.

The point of the home study, she told us, was to educate and prepare the adoptive family. In most cases the social worker gathered information about prospective parents that could help the adoption agency connect the family with a child whose needs they can meet. Since we had a child in waiting, our home study was to evaluate our fitness as parents.

Margret began by getting our story. Why did we want to adopt? What had led us to this moment? How did we connect with Lily?

Oh, but she didn't know the floodgates her questions had opened. As I told her about Max and Karen, Margret went fumbling in her purse to remove a package of tissues. I was sure Margret had heard sad stories before, but ours might have exceeded her emotional threshold. When Anna spoke of Kevin, his sickness, a tear that had been threatening formed fully and fell. Anna left out the part about how her ex-husband, Edward, raped her body and soul—which was for the best, as I was sure Margret would have turned into a fountain.

Anna and I were finishing each other's thoughts as we told Margret how we met at the grief group. Here even Lily looked emotional and Margret was downright heartsick, wetting half the tissues in the package. By the time we told her about how a chance encounter at a bus stop led to Lily finding us on an adoptive parent website, Margret had gone through the entire package of tissues.

"And I thought I'd heard 'em all," she said, making a nervous laugh as she dabbed the corners of her eyes. "You're all so very lucky."

A heavy silence followed until Lily threw open her arms wide and clapped her hands together, snapping the spell of sadness.

"But we're here now and everyone is happy," she said.

Anna and Margret nodded with enthusiasm, while I did my best to pretend to agree.

Over the course of the next hour, we discussed more elements of the home study process. There were training programs we were required to complete, educational seminars designed to help us understand adoption issues and agency requirements.

"How involved will Lily be with the baby?" Margret asked.

"We haven't decided," Anna said. "We're still working out the details of our postadoption agreement with our lawyer. It's in process."

"Well, we have training sessions geared for open, semi-open, and closed adoptions."

"We might have to take all three," Anna suggested.

There would be interviews with Margret, several of them, in which we'd discuss our approach to parenting and strategies for managing stress.

Naturally all this made me think of Max. Did I have regrets in how I parented him in our seven short years together? No, my only regret was not having an eighth year to parent some more. Memories flooded me, washing me with grief anew. I thought of Max in the morning, shuffling over to me as I drank my coffee. He would have, as he had every morning, one nappy fur paw of his stuffed dog clutched in his small hand. He'd lean his body into mine for a quick snuggle and I'd bury my nose in the top of his head, smelling his hair and the sleepiness of his body. I would trade my life for one more day of that smell. Not only had I lost my son, but each day he was gone I also lost a little more of his memory.

"Gage, are you all right?"

Anna's voice drew me out of my fog.

"Yes, I'm fine," I lied.

"Margret asked about the smoke alarms. Do you remember when we changed the batteries?"

"Oh, um, I think we did it during the spring forward."

"That's good," Margret said. "It's just one little item you won't have to take care of before the home study visit."

Margret would have to go through the entire house and make certain it met with state licensing standards (e.g., working smoke alarms, adequate space for a child, free from any hazards, a child-friendly environment). We all nodded; of course we would meet all those requirements and more.

When Margret brought up the health statement, I

got a look from Lily that made me shiver. I caught the hint of something mischievous lurking in her eyes, a warning to be ready. What could she be planning?

Everyone has a secret life . . .

Including me.

"So if you have a medical condition that is under control," Margret said, "high blood pressure or diabetes, that doesn't disqualify you from being approved. It's something a lot of our families are worried about."

"That's not a worry for us," Anna said.

"That's good to know. Mental health care is, just so you know, a big concern for a lot of our adoptive parents. If you've sought counseling or treatment for a mental health condition in the past, you'll want to let us know about those visits."

Blood thrummed in my ears as my breath clogged. At the same time, I fought to clear a tightness gathering in my chest. *They won't find out about the Adderall*, I assured myself. *If I don't tell them, they can't find out*. I'd done some homework. My doctor would be required to fill out medical forms, but like Anna, he knew nothing about my shrink. So if he didn't know, and Anna didn't know, there was no reason for Margret to know.

Out of the corner of my eye, I caught Lily looking at me. Her mouth was lifted upward, a pleased-with-herself smirk. I could feel my breathing accelerate.

"Just to waylay any concerns you may have, our agency views seeking help as a sign of strength. If you've sought any mental health care, it will not preclude you from adoption."

"No worries for us, regardless," Anna said. "Neither Gage nor I are taking any medications for our mental health. We've even stopped going to the grief group where we first met. Honestly, his love and support are really what's gotten me through these very difficult years."

"Yes, that's true," I said, feeling my tight chest constrict even more.

Lily made a surprised "huh" sound.

"What is it?" Margret asked.

"It's really nothing," Lily said. "I'm just a bit surprised Adderall isn't considered mental health medication. I knew some kids at school who used to deal it, so I always thought it did something to the brain, like get you high or something, but I guess it was something else. What do I know? I wasn't into drugs or anything, so I didn't really pay much attention."

"What does Adderall have to do with anything, Lily?" Anna asked.

I felt a red-hot flash curl up from my toes and shoot straight through my spine.

Lily appeared flummoxed.

"I just saw Gage's bottle of Adderall when I was cleaning up from the medicine cabinet disaster. I figured that was, you know, for mental health, but I guess I was wrong."

"What are you talking about? What bottle of Adderall? Gage?"

Anna was looking at me, her eyes two steely daggers. Something unraveled in my gut. Lily cupped her hands over her mouth.

"Oh, my God, I'm so sorry," she said. "I figured it was nothing. I wasn't snooping. It was just underneath the cabinet. I was looking for some paper towels to help me clean up the mess. I . . . I was just thinking out loud. Oh, my gosh, I hope I didn't mess anything up."

"No, no," Margret said, reassuring, brushing aside the concern with a wave of her hand. "Taking Adderall is fine. We just need that information recorded on the medical forms, is all."

Anna kept her gaze locked on me. I'd broken a seal of trust and doubted it could ever be fully restored again.

Lily turned her head. Only I could see her expression. Her eyes were dancing with delight. If they could sing, I'd hear them belt out the refrain, "Everyone has a secret," over and over again.

CHAPTER 24

Judging by her wan expression and pale coloring, Anna was emotionally drained. It wasn't just Margret's visit that had done her in.

After everyone left, we spent a good hour, maybe more, talking about Adderall. Anna packed for her flight the next morning while we discussed things. She had a client meeting with Humboldt in Minneapolis—the big deal, the one that would allow her to quit work for a while and stay home with the baby.

At the moment, however, she had other things on her mind. How long had I been taking the drug? Why hadn't I told her about my—let's call it what it was—addiction? What was I gaining from it? Why hadn't I confided in her?

I did my best to explain my actions in the most simple terms possible. I'd become dependent on the drug to get me through the workday. I needed the steroid-like focus that came from the rush. I didn't have ADHD, but that shouldn't exclude me from getting something to numb my pain.

"And you thought I'd have made you stop taking the drug?"

"Wouldn't you?" I asked. "If we switched places, I would have been worried about you. I would have wanted you to stop taking anything that was a crutch and not a necessity."

"But you've been lying to me, Gage. I'm your wife. I'm on your side, not in your way."

I lowered my head, feeling foolish. The fear of losing my Adderall had kept me from confiding in my wife. I could have, as she said many times during our chat, put some faith and trust in her.

"How'd you get the drugs?" Anna asked, emphasizing the word *drugs*.

"I filled out an eighteen-question survey," I said. I explained how I'd rated various symptoms on a scale of zero to three and scored off the charts for ADHD simply because I'd studied up on the symptoms beforehand. I got a thirty-milligram dose for Concerta, which eventually became a fifty-milligram per day prescription for Adderall as the course of my "treatment" evolved.

"What else? What other secrets are you keeping from me?"

"Nothing," I said. "I'm not keeping any secrets. I swear."

"How am I supposed to believe you?"

"Look in my eyes," I said. "Just look in my eyes."

Anna did as I asked. A shadow crossed her face.

"You blame her," she said.

"Blame who?"

"Lily," Anna said. "You blame Lily for what happened tonight."

"Well, she did bring it up," I said. My voice had the smoothness of sandpaper and was full of anger. Just the mention of Lily's name was enough to quicken my pulse.

"What are you after?" Anna asked. "Are you trying

to undermine what we're doing here? Because that's how it seems."

"Why would Lily even mention it?"

"Because she was confused," Anna said as if the answer should have been obvious to me. "She was thinking out loud. She's a young girl. She's not experienced or worldly. She's just an innocent girl who noticed something and thought to share it, which is what you should have done with me in the first place."

"Lily is not innocent," I said.

Anna's body shook.

"Damn you, Gage," she said. Anna zipped shut her luggage. As a consultant, she had learned to become a quick, efficient packer. "You don't want it. You're dragging me through this and you don't want it like I do."

"Yes, I do. I'm just worried about Lily. You said you wanted honesty from me? Well, I'm being honest."

"No, you don't want it or you wouldn't be behaving this way!" Red splotches like heat marks sprouted up on Anna's face and neck. "I want a baby, Gage. I want to be a mother again, and you're doing everything in your power to turn my dream into a nightmare."

Anna went to the living room, and I followed.

"Don't you get it? Lily brought up the Adderall for a reason," I said. "You didn't see how she was looking at me? She was letting me know, looking forward to making the big reveal. She knew she was going to get the opportunity."

"And what reason can you give me for that?" Anna asked, her voice trembling. "To make sure we don't get approved to become the adoptive parents?"

"No, no," I said, shaking my head. "I think Lily is trying to pit you against me."

"What are you talking about?" Anna looked exasperated, even angry.

"Think about it," I said. "Ever since Lily has come into our lives, we've been at odds."

"No, you've been at odds with us," Anna said.

"That's my point exactly," I said, stabbing the air with my finger. "It's now you and Lily versus me. The present, the necklace, the Adderall—it's all about making me think one thing about Lily and you another."

"Good news. You've now got something real to go talk to your shrink about," Anna said. "Go get yourself a prescription for your paranoia to go along with the Adderall."

That was how the conversation ended: with Anna retreating into the bedroom, leaving me alone to wonder if maybe, just maybe, she was right.

Hours after our "discussion," long after Anna had fallen asleep, well past the midnight hour, as soon as I heard Lily walking upstairs, I snuck out the front door. I couldn't wait a second longer to confront my suspicions. Was I intentionally trying to derail this process? Was it possible my heart was not ready for another child? Could my subconscious be imagining behaviors that simply weren't there? Was my mind the enemy, and not Lily? Brad hadn't detected anything evil from Lily's aura. Everything that had happened was sort of explainable but required eyes that saw through a different lens. The beliefs about Lily that I held certain—certain until my fight with Anna—needed clarity.

We'd told Lily to lock her front door at night. Apparently, she was absentminded. I went up the stairs and paused on the landing. The door to her apartment was closed and I presumed locked. I hoped she was safety conscious enough to lock at least one of her doors. Maybe she'd think it was Anna coming to pay her a visit. Either way, I knocked twice, waited, knocked a third time, and heard footsteps shuffling toward the door.

"Who is it?" Lily asked. Her cloying voice made me think she was expecting me.

"It's Gage," I said to the shuttered door. "I'm sorry it's late, but I heard you come home. I'd like to speak with you for a moment, if you wouldn't mind."

The door opened and there was Lily, still wearing her waitress uniform.

"Hi, Gage," she said. She stood with her hip cocked, like a vintage pinup, with one arm propped against the door frame as a barrier. Her tongue slipped between her ruby-painted lips to wet them just slightly. "You're probably wanting to talk about the home study, aren't you?"

"I think we need to have a little chat," I said.

A man's steely voice called from out of my view, "Who is it?"

Lily lowered her arm and motioned for me to enter.

From the foyer I saw the man standing just down the hall, drinking Budweiser from a can. He was tall and wiry, and though he wore a denim jacket with a black T-shirt underneath, I could tell his body was ripped with muscle. Intricate tattoos were visible on his hands and others snuck out from the collar of his shirt, wrapping around his neck like growing vines. His lean, sharp-featured face was pockmarked and covered in a heavy five o'clock shadow. His hawklike eyes gave the impression he saw every situation as potentially confrontational. He had thick black eyebrows and close-cropped dark hair. He looked like the sort who had come out of the womb with a chip on his shoulder, the world against him, and the fists to fight for his survival.

"Who is this?" the man asked again.

"Roy, this is Gage. He's going to adopt my baby," Lily said. "Gage, this is Roy. He's the baby's father. He's going to live with me for a little while."

CHAPTER 25

"Why don't you come in and have a beer?"

Lily headed toward the kitchen, presumably to get me something to drink, a beer I didn't want. She left me alone in the narrow hallway with Roy, who stood just a few paces away.

Roy took a long, purposeful swig of his Bud, keeping his eyes locked on me as if I might try something—attack, run, who knows what—if he let himself be distracted. Roy finished his beer in one long drink, crinkling the sides of the can with his fingers to show me he was done. He still didn't speak. He just kept eyeing me.

"So, you're the dude who's going to raise my kid," he said.

The word *awkward* popped into my head.

Roy kept eyeing me. I noticed how deeply set his eyes were and I wondered if it gave him a different perspective on the world. He was a hard man who made it hard to tell if I repelled him, amused him, sickened him, or a combination of all three.

"This is a lot to take in," I said. My heart was pounding now, palms gone sweaty. How did we end up here, meeting like this? Lily acted so nonchalant about it all. Didn't she understand the ramifications of the father entering the picture? Other thoughts crossed my mind. Would he be willing to sign off on the adoption? Would he contest Lily's wishes? Would the baby grow up to have the same hard-edged look in his eyes as his father?

"What do you mean, take in?" Roy asked.

I picked up the drawl in his speech and wondered if he came from someplace warm, where people walked slowly, where they weren't used to rushing to get out of the cold. Florida perhaps. His dark complexion could be genetics or the product of the sun.

"It's a big new development, Roy," I said.

I wanted to get his last name, but we hadn't shaken hands, and Roy made no gestures to break the ice. We remained a good distance apart. I saw him run his tongue back and forth along the bottom of his lip. For some reason, I got the feeling this was a habit of his whenever he got to thinking. And I could see Roy was a thinking man. If Lily was the crying woman when we first met, Roy was the thinking man. The way his eyes probed, how he shifted weight from one foot to another, he didn't do anything without having planned for every possible contingency. This was my suspicion, anyway. He knew the exits before he entered a room. He wouldn't talk to you, not really talk, until he knew your angle, your backstory, your weakness, something he could use to his advantage. No movement was wasted, no thought without purpose; everything about him projected the single-mindedness of a predator. He was all about the hunt. One minute you might be hunting by his side, but in a flash he'd turn you into his prey.

Lily came back from the kitchen with two beers.

"Wish I could join you," she said. "But the baby isn't ready to drink."

Lily tossed me the beer. I caught it midair, inverted it with a twist of my wrist, popped the top, and took a long swig, slurping up foam. Roy and I eyed each other as I drank my beer. That was when I saw the first hint of pleasure cross his face.

"So, why don't we go into the living room and hang out," Lily said. "It takes me a while to wind down after a shift."

I wondered what time it was. One in the morning? One-thirty? I wasn't wearing my watch, but it was late, or early morning. Everything told me to get out of there, go downstairs, wake Anna up, have a chat, do something other than what I was doing, which was sitting on the couch in Lily's apartment. But I didn't go anywhere. I sat down and became a part of the moment. Maybe it was Roy. Maybe in a way I was thankful for his sudden arrival.

Here was the shameful part, the thought I couldn't speak aloud: *maybe Roy was the answer to my problem.*

Roy pulled up a chair, spun it around, and sat in it so the chair back was pressed up against his chest. He stretched out his arm and held out his hand, and Lily responded by tossing him a beer. Roy popped the top and Lily raised her bubbling glass of what I guessed was soda water and cranberry juice.

"Well, here's to all of us," Lily said, then took a sip.

A moment of silence expanded. The only thing I could do to settle my unease was to drink. Before I knew it, half my beer was gone and we hadn't spoken a word.

"So, Roy," I said. "Where are you from?"

"Sort of all over," Roy said.

I gave him a chance to join in the small talk, but he preferred to let the conversation die. Instead, he drank more of his beer. I did the same and realized I'd finished all twelve ounces in about three swallows.

"So what brings you to us?" I didn't know what else to say, but that got the hint of a smile from him.

"I needed a place to crash for a while," Roy said. "Lily told me how nice you folks have been to her."

"Were you two living together before?" I asked.

Lily laughed.

"OMG!" she exclaimed, tossing her head back with another laugh. "Yeah, Roy and I were living together when I met you guys. He's the big jerk who locked me out of my own apartment. Jerk!"

Lily flung a couch pillow across the room, and Roy batted it away like some irritating insect.

"I didn't want you to leave, be-yatch," Roy said, giving Lily a hard stare. "I told you I didn't want no baby."

"Yeah, well, you don't have to have no baby, asshole," Lily said, her tone both mocking and mimicking. "We got a family now."

"You could've dealt with it other ways."

Lily set her drink down on the floor so she could use both her hands to flip Roy off. I took a guess about what Roy meant by other ways of dealing with it.

"I told you that wasn't an option. But I took care of it. It's all good now."

I wondered if that was the real reason for their fight. Lily had told me she wasn't sure who the father was, but she seemed sure now.

I watched Lily cross the room and wrap her arms around Roy's wiry neck. She kissed the side of his head and ran her tongue around the outside edges of his ear. I swallowed hard. Who were these people? What were they doing in my apartment? What was I doing here?

Lily stopped kissing Roy and started to massage his shoulders. Roy tilted his head to the side and I heard his neck snap with a pop. First time I'd seen him look happy.

He went back to eyeing me while Lily continued to work his shoulders. I tried to stay relaxed, but the way he was watching me made the hairs on the back of my neck start to rise. I still couldn't figure out what was going to happen. He could get up and start beating me, or come over and give me a bro hug, and neither would have been totally surprising.

"So what happened to your apartment, Roy?" I asked.

"Got kicked out," Roy said.

Again he passed his tongue across his bottom lip. Then he ran it along the inside of his mouth. Next thing I knew, he took a can of Copenhagen chewing tobacco from his jacket pocket and slipped a dip into his bottom lip. He started spitting into his beer. I guess that explained his oral habit.

"Roy got kicked out because he can't get a job," Lily said to me.

"You hush now, Lily," Roy snapped. "Gage here isn't interested in all my business."

"Oh, but I am," I said.

"If you ask me, it ain't fair how they treat convicts. Everyone thinks if you do time, you can't ever be good. But Roy is good. Real good. He just made some bad mistakes, that's all."

"Lily, let's change the subject."

"Do you mind if I ask what you were in for?"

Roy's expression turned dark and serious—menacing, I'd have to say.

"I guess since you're going to be the daddy," Roy began, leaning forward in his chair far enough to lift the two back legs off the floor, "you're going to want me to tell my story. I didn't know my daddy, didn't much care to from what my mamma said. But it would be better if the kid knew a little something about me."

I tried to swallow more beer but forgot I'd already drunk it down. Still, I sucked hard enough to get a few cold drops to take away some of the dryness.

"I did five years for armed robbery. I'm not going to lie to you, Gage, I did the crime and paid with time. Nobody got hurt, but I got caught. Sent me to Walpole. Did my time peaceful, made no trouble, got paroled, and I've been clean ever since."

Again the conversation died and we went back to our heavy silence. Me tapping my feet on the floor, running my hands nervously on my empty beer can, eventually crushing the sides. Lily was rubbing Roy's shoulders and I could see through the doorway a corner of one of her framed movie posters. I tried to imagine Roy and Lily together in bed, munching on popcorn, watching a classic Garbo and commenting on the dresses she wore, the setting, the wonder of cinema from that period. I could more easily picture them watching *The Texas Chainsaw Massacre*. Hell, I could imagine Roy being one of the stars (a star with the chainsaw, that is). How was Anna going to react to this new major development? Would she welcome Roy the ex-con into our home as she did Lily, or would she view him as a threat, someone who might talk Lily out of the adoption? What about the genetics? Would she be worried the baby would grow up to be an armed robber just like Daddy?

Roy spit into the mouth of his beer and swigged from a freshy. He didn't seem to mix the tobacco and alcohol, a skill that took time and practice to perfect.

"So, where did you two meet?" I asked, clawing for conversation when really what I wanted to do was leave.

"Jail," Lily said. She held back a smile until her mouth couldn't contain the joke any longer. "Just kidding. You should have seen your face, Gage."

"We met at Jillian's," Roy said.

"He'd come in and play nine ball a lot," Lily added. "He wasn't a hustler, but he was a good player."

"The way I recall it, I was the best."

"Baby, you are the best," Lily said, and she leaned over his shoulder to kiss him on the mouth.

When Lily pulled away, Roy and I were left looking each other over. I imagined he was wondering what I was good at doing. He knew it wasn't playing pool, and it certainly had nothing to do with crime. Was he thinking I was too soft to raise his kid? Meanwhile, I was left wondering if I could raise a child from such hard stock when my only experience was a son who loved stuffed animals and never spoke an unkind word in his too-few years.

Lily left Roy and returned to the couch.

"Want me to put on some music?" she asked. "I play it at night, but softly. I hope it's never been a bother."

"It's never bothered me," I said, standing up. "But I really should get going. Roy, it's been a pleasure."

I stuck out my hand for the proverbial shake goodbye, but Roy just eyed it with a contemptuous look. He looked away only to spit some dip into his empty beer can.

"What were you doing up here, anyway?" he asked. It sounded like the suspicion in his gut had finally bubbled up to his throat. "You always come check on my girl at this late hour?"

"Roy." Lily stood. She'd seen this before. The way he was eyeing me was a warning sign. "Don't be silly now."

"He's a big boy," Roy said. "He's gonna be my baby's

daddy. He knows how to answer a question all on his own, Lil. Now, you let him answer. Why'd you come up here at this late hour? Do you do that a lot?"

I could see the muscles in Roy's neck start to tighten and coil. His eyes burrowed into mine as he held his gaze unflinching. I was afraid to speak—afraid I'd stutter. An icy chill raked up my body. Nothing I could do but quake just a little. Roy looked ready to pounce. If he was trying to agitate me, it was working. I tried to think of something to say. I couldn't imagine how the truth would sound: "Well, Roy, since you asked, I think Lily here is a cunning individual and I came up here to confront her, but gosh darn it and go figure, she's acting nothing but sweet as honey and peachy as pie and I shouldn't ever have been questioning her intentions, so I'll just be going on my way. Pleasure meeting you and thanks again for letting me raise your child as my own. God bless you both."

The truth wouldn't set me free, it would set me on my ass, with Roy's fists flying in my face. So I needed another story, and by the grace of God it came to me.

"I heard more footsteps upstairs than usual," I said. "Lily always comes home alone, so I got nervous there might be a break-in or something. I checked your front door and it was unlocked." Here I turned my attention to Lily. "I got to tell you again, always lock that door. You can never be too safe."

"Lots of criminals around here, huh?" Roy said, making a slight chuckle somewhere deep in his throat. "You don't know tough neighborhoods."

"It's very nice of you to check up on me," Lily said. "But I'm fine, really."

"Well, then," I said, clearing my throat. I took a step toward Roy and extended my hand again. He gave me the eye, as if he could see right through my deception.

Whatever still troubled him, he managed to shrug it aside.

"Gage, it's a true pleasure," Roy said, swallowing my hand in his viselike grasp. I nearly cried out from the force. I searched Roy's eyes for any sign that he intentionally wanted to hurt me but saw nothing. The fact that Roy was just that strong was no less disconcerting. "And thanks for all your hospitality," Roy continued, "especially with what you're doing for Lily. If it were up to me there wouldn't be no baby, but if there's got to be one, well, I guess you'll be a much better daddy than I'd ever be."

With that parting salvo, he finally let go of my hand.

CHAPTER 26

On my way out, I felt like I was floating down the stairs, like I'd just had an out-of-body experience and was still trying to come back into myself. I entered my home in stealth mode, quiet with the key, careful closing the door, quiet with my steps, even though I had every intention of waking Anna.

Rousing her, I soon discovered, was a job easier said than done. I called her name four or five times, first in a whispered voice and in the end shouting it.

"Anna! Wake up! Wake up!"

I was sitting on the edge of the bed, shaking her shoulder.

"Huh? Gage? What? What's going on?"

She sounded dazed and agitated.

"We need to talk."

Anna fought against the sleep to open her eyes. "I was having the craziest dream," she said in a faraway voice. "I was dreaming about the baby."

I wondered what her baby dreams would be like after she met Roy.

"I just met the father," I said.

Anna sat up fast, as though the bed had become electrified. She pulled the covers to her chest, craving, it seemed, all the comfort and security they could provide.

"What are you talking about, you just met the father?"

"I went upstairs to speak with Lily," I said.

Anna looked over at the dresser, but her jogging clothes were blocking the digital clock.

"What time did you go up there?" she said, shoving her clothes aside. Immediately, she groaned. "What are you doing going up there at this hour? What are you doing going up there at all?"

Ire had supplanted any trace of sleep in her voice.

"Don't be mad at me. I couldn't sleep," I said, in my best soothing tone. "I wanted to ask her about the Adderall. I wanted her to tell me to my face it was an innocent question."

"Won't you just leave her alone?" she said. "It's really starting to get out of control."

"Hear me out," I said. "When I went upstairs, Lily wasn't alone. She was with a guy named Roy. She told me *he's* the baby's father."

Anna shook her head, as if she was trying to force my words into a proper place where they actually made sense.

"This is the same guy who kicked her out of her apartment?" she asked. Her eyes were pleading, desperate to pull every nugget of information.

"I think so," I said. "At least that's what she said."

"Was Lily all right? Was she okay, Gage?"

Worry now. Fear for Lily's safety trumping all else.

"Yes, she seemed more than fine," I said. "She was glad he was there."

"Wow, I mean . . . just wow . . . well, what's he like? Who is he?"

I did my best to describe him. If anything stuck, it was that Roy *Something,* Roy whose last name I didn't get, was a hard man.

"There's more," I said. "He's done time."

"Prison time?" Anna's voice lifted, the situation worsening by the second.

"Armed robbery," I said. "He served five years in Walpole."

"Are you telling me that a felon has just moved in upstairs?"

"A felon who just so happens to be the father of the baby we're going to adopt."

"What are we going to do?" Anna said. She cupped her face with her hands. "I don't know if I'm comfortable with this."

"Do you want to call it off?" I asked.

There it was again, that little rascal of thought that should remain unspoken, a wish for a clean slate, an adoption do-over. I thought Anna might agree, in light of Roy, but she gave me a horrified look.

"God, no!" she said. "I don't want to start over. This is our baby. We just need to figure it out. We need a plan. What else do we know about him? Where is he from? Does he have family here? Did he say anything about the adoption?"

"He said he didn't want the baby," I told her. "He didn't use the word *abortion*, but it was certainly implied. I think that was what was really behind their big blowout. As for his background, I don't know much. I think he's from down south somewhere, Florida maybe, but he said he was from all over."

"Is he going to try to stop the adoption? Do you think he'll sign off?"

"I don't know," I said. "It's a new wrinkle. It's definitely an unusual situation. Maybe we should speak with Margret about it."

I couldn't believe this conversation. I wanted Anna to talk about the nursery we were going to build; maybe we'd debate the color scheme (well, I planned on deferring to her). Maybe Anna would even paint one of her amazing murals on the wall. We should have been reading books about what to expect the first few months (it's been a long time since I parented a newborn), maybe discuss, in a loving way, the latest baby trends. Would Anna want to give the baby milk from a strap-on that mimicked breast-feeding? It was a legitimate question. I'd read about it on some adoption blog, and apparently it helped with bonding.

Would we get the ultra baby monitor, the one with a close view built-in camera and SIDS alarm, or something on the cheap side? What about a stroller, or the best infant formula? How about BPA in bottles? These were all questions I was more than happy to discuss with my wife, but it wasn't working out that way for us. No, we were thinking about a hard-ass guy named Roy, who showed up unexpectedly in the dark of night and might very well decide he didn't want to sign the papers giving up his parental rights. This wasn't what I signed up for when I agreed to adopt, and by the sick and worried look on Anna's face, it wasn't in her plans, either.

Anna nodded. "Yeah, let's call Margret and see what she recommends. Oh, shit," she said.

"What?"

"I'm going to Minneapolis tomorrow."

We'd both forgotten about her flight in the morning.

"We'll wait until you get back to have a chat with her about Roy."

Anna wrapped her arms around me and buried her face in my neck.

"I don't want anything to go wrong," she said. "I'm worried about this. I'm really worried."

"Me too," I said.

And yet, strangely, I was feeling glad about Roy, too. Thanks to him, I felt like I had my wife back.

We were a team again.

CHAPTER 27

It was early morning, and the sun had just begun to paint the sky with a glorious swath of pink, yellow, and blue. The air smelled sweet, birds were already chirping, and there was every indication of a spectacular day to come. It was the perfect day to fly. I waited at curbside with Anna for her taxi to arrive. Her hand rested on the extended handle of her roller suitcase—a black number with lime green handle covers to make it easier to identify hers from all the other black roller suitcases. She'd slung her black canvas computer bag across one shoulder, tilting lopsided. She'd done so much business travel over the years sometimes she stood at a tilt even when the bag wasn't strapped to her shoulder. We had our back to the street, both looking at our house, more specifically the dark windows of the second-floor apartment.

"It's so weird that he's just sleeping up there," Anna said.

I drank more of my coffee and put my free arm around Anna, pulling her in tight.

"We'll figure it out," I said. "Let's not waste our time worrying."

"It's so hard," Anna said, her eyes still locked on those darkened windows. "I just don't want anything to go wrong."

I said nothing. So much, so very much could go wrong. My peripheral vision caught a flash of movement, and I glanced down the street to see an approaching car. Anna's cab.

"Don't worry about a thing," I said as the cab neared. "You're going to get the Humboldt job, so keep your focus sharp and go be your fabulous self. You'll wow them. You always do."

Anna kissed me gently on the lips.

"I love you," she said.

"I love you, too," I answered.

The cab pulled to a stop with a little squeak of the brakes. Anna put her suitcase in the backseat, climbed inside, and shut the door. She rolled down the window before the cab pulled away. She didn't say anything. She just blew me a kiss. I gave her a little smile, toasted her with my coffee mug, and then she was gone: off to Logan, off to Minneapolis, off to closing a deal, off to secure her year's sabbatical to bond with the baby we were no longer sure would be ours.

At work, it was the day Adam Wang got fired. I came into the office as I did every day—sat down at my workstation, powered up my computer, opened Outlook, scanned e-mails, looked at my calendar, did a bit of web surfing, and then got up to get another cup of coffee. This was the routine of my life, and I loved it. I loved my work. I loved being consumed by it. And I loved my Adderall, which made it possible for me to be here and to be effective.

The morning Adam Wang was fired was a one-pill

day—just a regular run-of-the-mill trip at the office. I walked into the kitchen for my cup o' joe and found a somber gathering of engineers. They were talking in hushed tones, which was saying something because these engineers weren't loud to begin with.

"What's going on?" I asked.

They told me and we all got quiet, as if Adam Wang had died and deserved a moment of respect.

"Patrice?" I asked.

My question was understood: did Patrice make the call, or had she been forced into it? The consensus was that Patrice had no choice, and wasn't happy about it.

Of course it was the demo that did him in. We'd blown a big project milestone and lost the confidence of our CEO, all in one tumultuous afternoon. Someone had to be held accountable, and the only person who didn't seem bent out of shape about it being Adam Wang was Matt Simons.

We'd never been able to figure out what caused the battery fire. Tests were inconclusive; configuration management checklists were double-checked. The battery should have worked as designed, but it had failed.

For Adam's sake, I wished I could have figured out what happened. I wanted to clear his name. But it wasn't my job to build the batteries. I just tested them. Heck, I didn't even understand all the science, not the way Matt Simons did. And the only person I trusted less than Matt Simons was living directly above me.

I was home for about an hour, post work and post gym workout, when Brad called. He was finishing a job in the neighborhood and wanted to stop by to say hello. He had charged the woman for the water heater he had replaced but not for making contact with her departed husband's spirit.

Brad sometimes tapped into his abilities the same way I tapped into breathing—it was just something he did without making it happen. He sensed the presence of the woman's husband while he worked. In a flash, he knew about the man's passion for fishing and even made a reference to the RV trip they'd been planning. She was going to take the trip now. Apparently, it was what her dead husband wanted.

Brad was my good friend, one of my very best, and yet he was a bit like Adderall for me—a pill in human form. Every time we hung out together, I thought about Max. He was my conduit to my son as much as Adderall was my conduit to focus. Over the year I'd gained more control over my impulse to use Brad than I had over the ADHD meds. I went to Brad only when I *really* needed my Max fix. Maybe if Adderall had the same side effects I got from connecting to Max's spirit—depression, heartache, upset stomach, a painful longing—it would be a much easier habit to break. Still, Brad was coming over and it would take all my willpower to restrain from asking for a reading.

Brad showed up in his workday uniform, black polo shirt embroidered with his company logo and jeans. I mixed us two summertime cocktails—Bud Lights poured into chilled glasses. We sat on the front porch like a couple of neighborhood old-timers who could predict the weather by the amount of fluid in our knees.

I'd just finished telling Brad about Roy when the front door to the apartment opened and out stepped Lily. She was dressed in a paisley print sundress that hid the slight swell of her belly and ankle-high boots. She came breezing out the door like she'd been carried along on a gust of wind. She was light and airy on her feet, and I wondered if being with Roy did for Lily what my spiritual contacts with Max did for me. Was she high one minute and down the next? Did Roy know how to manipulate her the way I thought Lily could manipulate me? Was he the architect, the tutor of her deceptive talent? I wanted to smile at Lily, invite her to join us, but she was Anna's girl, and always would be. We were no better than distant relatives with an uncomfortable shared history and a strained relationship.

"Hi, Gage," Lily said before noticing Brad. When she did see him, her smile widened. "Oh, hey," she said, breezy as the summer evening. "I didn't see you here. Nice surprise."

"Hi, Lily," Brad said with a tilt of his glass. "How are you doing?"

"Great, really great," Lily said with a coy (and I'd say trademark) tilt of her hip.

I watched Brad carefully, looking for any indication of some vibe he hadn't picked up before. But Brad appeared even more enchanted by Lily than he had on their first meeting.

"Gage, I was just talking to Anna," Lily began. "She called to talk about Roy." I might have made a little noise because Lily made Roy sound like no big deal. "Anyway, we were talking and I was telling her about Roy and she sounded cool, you know, like you were, but while we were talking she realized she'd left an important folder on her desk. She's going to call you in a minute. She's like totally panicked. There are documents in there she needs for her meeting. She wants you to FedEx them tomorrow. Anyway, that's the message. She's going to call."

"Okay, thanks for letting me know," I said, checking

my cell phone and making sure it was on. I felt terrible for Anna. I knew the horrible, sinking feeling of being at a critical meeting and not having what you need.

I was going to preempt Anna by calling her when the door to Lily's apartment opened again and out stepped Roy. He was wearing a faded red T-shirt with an iron cross design on the front, jeans, and black combat boots. The iron cross was filled in with the graphic design of skulls. Without the denim jacket, I got a better look at Roy's rippling muscles, the envy of any trainer at my gym. I also got to see the tattoos on his arms: tribal designs, mostly. The tats were dark, no color. His eyes were hidden behind dark sunglasses.

"Hey, Gage," he said to me with a nod.

He acted just like one of my tenants—a guy who paid me rent and never expected our conversations to get beyond "How you doing, I'm fine thanks, you?"

"Roy, this is my friend Brad," I said.

"He's the plumber who came over to fix the water," Lily added. I was sort of surprised she had shared that story with Roy. I was so caught up in the ways of Lily that it failed to occur to me she might just be living a normal life, sharing normal everyday things with this man who now shared her apartment.

Roy and Brad shook hands.

"Nice to meet you," Roy said, noticing the beers. "That's what we're out for." Roy looked at me but pointed to my beer. "Going to take a little walk into Cambridge to pick up a six. You need anything?" he asked.

"No, we're good," I said. "Thanks."

"Okay. See you later, then."

Roy and Lily bounded down the front stairs, and I watched them walk up the street headed for Mass Ave. They weren't holding hands, but they walked close to each other, as if they were a couple. Brad took a drink, but he wasn't watching them walk away. He was staring ahead with a distant look in his eyes.

"What's up?" I asked him.

"Do you remember that dark energy I said was surrounding you?"

"Yeah," I said.

"Well, it just walked up the street with Lily to go buy a six-pack of beer."

CHAPTER 28

Anna called the next morning before I got in the shower. I was a bit foggy from a fitful night's sleep plagued by bad dreams. They were all horrible, all somehow related to Roy's dark energy, but one was especially bad. Roy and I were buddies, involved in some crime together, until he turned on me, with no thought, no remorse, no emotion showing in his dead, dark eyes as he plunged a six-inch knife into my gut.

"Hey, baby," she said. "How's it going?"

"Good," I said, wondering again if I should tell Anna about Brad's warning. Yesterday she'd had enough on her plate to worry about.

"You know why I'm calling so early?"

"You're reminding me about the folder?"

"Smart man."

We'd spoken about it last night, after Lily and Roy went off for that six-pack. I'd found the folder on Anna's desk, right where she said it would be. It was a big green folder filled with papers. I'd been instructed to leave it there until Anna came up with a workable plan to get it to her.

"I called FedEx and they can get it here in time for

my meeting, but you have to get it to them before ten. Can you do that?"

"Of course," I said.

"Can you do it from work? I don't want you to have to make an extra stop."

"Yeah, no problem. They can ship FedEx."

"Thanks, honey. So you'll put it in your workbag, you won't forget?"

I didn't carry a briefcase (who does these days?), but I did have a black canvas workbag that looked a lot like a computer bag. When I didn't shuttle my laptop to and from the office, it functioned like a purse without the embarrassment.

"I'll put it in before my shower," I said. "That's a promise."

"Do it while I'm on the phone," Anna said. "Not that I don't trust you, love."

I laughed but complied.

"Remember, you've got to get it to them before ten," Anna said.

"Do you want me to fax you anything so you get it sooner?" I asked.

"No, that's all right. As long as it gets here tomorrow I'll be fine. I'm so stupid for having forgotten it. I never forget anything. You know me. I'm all about the details."

"Well, you have some other things on your mind, sweetie."

"That I do. Anything new about our upstairs companion?"

"Roy," I said, as if Anna needed the reminder. At the mention of his name, I couldn't resist telling Anna the latest developments. Maybe I was pissed about Roy sneaking into my dreams—you know, to kill me. "Brad met him," I said.

"And?"

"And he got the creeps. I mean he got a very bad vibe about this guy."

"Oh, shit. What does that mean?"

I sighed into the phone. "I don't know," I said. "I don't know what else to do, short of telling Lily we're not comfortable with Roy living here."

"No," Anna said. She sounded panicked, as if simply voicing the idea would be enough to derail all our plans. "We can't do that. We'll lose her. We'll lose the baby. We'll lose it all."

"So what do you suggest?" I asked. Her anxiety was contagious.

"I'll run a background check. One of my clients owns a PI agency, so I'll get him to do it for me. We'll see what we can learn. For now, we'll just be careful."

"I didn't get his last name."

"I'll get it from Lily," Anna said.

Of course that made the most sense. Anna and Lily were tight, while I was the guy questioning our birth mother's motives.

"Sounds like a plan," I said. "Now go get us that big, new client."

"I will as long as you mail me that folder."

I pictured Anna smiling on the other end of the phone, and it made me miss her. We each took a turn saying, "I love you," and the conversation ended.

On my own, I'd learned about CORI, Criminal Offender Record Information. It was a process to request a criminal record, and I was glad Anna had the resources to get that done. We'd both sleep better knowing more about who was sleeping above us.

The rest of the morning was rather uneventful. I was still foggy, but perked up a bit after my shower and coffee. I dressed in the usual khaki pants and polo shirt, took my workbag out to the car, drove off, grabbed a bagel at Bruegger's, ate it in my Charger, and listened to NPR all the way to work.

I went straight to my desk before heading to the postal center. Before I got there I bumped into Matt Simons. Adam Wang had only been gone a day, so Olympian was down a program manager. Since nature abhors a vacuum, even in the workplace, Simons had stepped in as de facto leader. I didn't much care for our new boss and Simons knew it. That didn't stop him from acting like Wang's anointed successor.

"The new battery is ready to test," he said. "I hope there won't be a repeat of the last time."

"There won't be if you don't dick around with the formula for this build like you did the last one."

I didn't know what had gotten into me. Maybe it was Roy. Or Lily. Or it could have been the dark energy overcoming my better judgment. Whatever it was, it felt good to be the bad guy, the hard-ass guy, to inject a little Royness into my personality.

Simons took a step back. His eyes widened. He started to speak, but stammered. His words got snared in a prickly thicket of whatever lies he was preparing. Maybe Roy *was* rubbing off on me, because I knew I'd nailed it. Just watching how Simons shifted his weight from his right foot to his left, off balance, and how he moved back a step, and how he couldn't find his voice, I knew I had him dead to rights.

"What . . . what are you talking about?" Simons managed to say.

I patted Simons on the shoulder.

"That's the best you could come up with? You should stick to sabotage. You're much better at it."

Simons looked like a guy who'd been sucker punched. His panic-stricken face made me smile.

"See you at the standup meeting." My tone was intentionally patronizing. I had no proof that Simons did it, but fear lingered in his eyes. Simons would spend the rest of the day wondering if I had evidence against him. We were both on the Security Breach Team, so I was sure he felt confident about how he covered his tracks. Still, I was going on a hunting expedition when I had the time. I owed it to Wang. He was a good guy who got a raw deal. If Simons had left a digital trail, I'd do my best to find it.

After a quick stop at my desk, I went to the company mailroom near the building's main entrance. Abby, a stout woman with a haircut bordering on a mullet, was working behind the counter. She greeted me with a warm smile and a friendly hello. I was still on a high from my run-in with Simons. I'd been the victim for so long, the suffering widower, the grieving father, and Lily's punching bag, that it felt amazing, utterly empowering, to be the aggressor at last.

"Well, somebody is in a good mood this morning."

I didn't even realize I'd been smiling.

I set my workbag on the counter, trying to force my expression back to center. It was hard while savoring the terrified look on Simons's face.

"What can I do for you this morning?" Abby asked.

"I need to FedEx something to my wife in Minneapolis." I undid the latches of my workbag. "If it doesn't go out before ten I'm going to be setting up permanent residence in the doghouse."

"Well, we wouldn't want that," Abby said.

I opened my bag and reached inside. I brushed up against some loose papers, a paperback book, and a spiral-bound notebook, but no folder. Dread overcame me. It was a sick feeling—a reply to all when the e-mail conversation should have gone private, forgetting a term paper on the day it was due, rear-ending the car stopped at a traffic light, not having the critical folder I needed to FedEx before ten o'clock—that kind of dread.

Abby eyed me with increasing concern. My stomach did loops as my palms turned sweaty. I'm sure I looked pale. I checked again, turning my bag upside down, dumping the contents on the mailroom counter, tearing through the pile like a crazed person.

Abby took a step back, her concern for me shifting slightly into concern for her own safety. Was this guy about to go postal?

"What the hell?" I said out loud. I knew how important the folder was to Anna and her Humboldt deal. If I couldn't get this done for her, I'd be the object of her lingering resentment, the reason she couldn't take a year off to bond with the baby. I pushed most of the contents off the counter and onto the floor in one big, sweeping motion.

"Hey! Gage, are you all right?" Abby asked.

"No," I said, breathing hard. "No, I'm not all right. I put the folder in my bag right before my shower."

I was in a bit of a trance, retracing my steps from the morning, squeezing my eyes shut to force out every drip of concentration. I could picture myself putting the folder inside the bag, and it felt right. It felt like something that had happened, something real. Or had it? Wasn't I in a fog from a bad night's sleep? Could I have imagined putting the folder in my bag? Maybe it was the side effects of Adderall. Maybe I was starting to hallucinate.

A new thought: perhaps it had fallen out of my bag on the way to work. Maybe the latches had come undone. It was a possibility, an outside chance at best. Finally I had another thought—a little bug of a thought with a nasty stinger, a thought that left me panicked, confused, and angry all at once. And I could sum it up in a single word, too.

Lily.

CHAPTER 29

The missing folder wasn't on the floor of my car. It hadn't shifted under the seat, either. I drove home with a black rage swirling through my head, a gathering storm, whirling and twisting my thoughts. I kept fantasizing about my upcoming confrontation with Lily, and none of the pictures were pretty. My hands gripped the steering wheel hard. I was grinding my teeth enough to chip away at the enamel. At some point, I glanced at the speedometer and cringed at the number that would have amounted to a four hundred dollar speeding ticket.

To calm myself, I thought of another possible outcome. One where I entered my home, went into Anna's office, and saw the folder on her desk. I checked the time on the Charger's dashboard. It was 9:30. I'd canceled my meetings for the day and informed Patrice I had to go home to deal with a personal matter. There was still an outside chance I could get the folder off to Minneapolis in time for Anna's meeting—assuming, of course, the folder was even in the house.

And that was a big IF.

I made it home in record time. Walking up the front steps, I tried to stay positive.

It'll be on the desk . . . it'll be on the desk . . .

Inside now, marching down the hall.

I'm upset for no reason . . . I know it's there . . . it'll be there.

I went straight to Anna's office. All was quiet—a different sort of quiet. It was a "nobody is supposed to be here right now" kind of silence, and it made me feel, for a moment at least, like an intruder in my own home.

My eyes went first to the desk. No folder. I started shuffling through stacks of Anna's papers. Nothing. Still no folder. I stormed outside, walked across the front porch, and came to a stop in front of the door to the upstairs apartment. I could have knocked or rang the doorbell. Instead, I grabbed my master key to open the door to Lily's apartment.

Each stair groaned a bit from my weight. At the top of the landing, I squeezed my eyes shut. I contemplated backing down, returning to my condo and calling Anna with the bad news about the folder. But I didn't. It was a cloudless day. Sun spilled inside, forming columns of bright rays that shone through the bank of windows overlooking the street. It was the sort of light that gets apartments rented on a very first showing.

I stood in the foyer, perhaps a foot beyond the front door, and looked around the apartment. The place appeared normal, peaceful even, with the lights turned off. The movie posters were still hanging on the walls in the hallway. The little vase of silk flowers was there on the end table near the bathroom door, same as always.

Glancing through the entranceway into the living

room, I saw the silhouette of a figure seated on the sofa. Her body was backlit from the sun, but it was Lily. She kept her body facing forward, while her head was turned to the side, looking at me. She made no effort to stand, offered no greetings, and didn't even question what I was doing in her home. It was as though she'd been awaiting my arrival all along.

I took a step toward her. Just a single step.

"Hi, Gage," Lily said in a soft and playful voice, flirty even. She kept her body perfectly still, hands resting on her knees, back rigid. I could see she was wearing a black skirt and pink tank top. Her gaze was fixed on me, but her face remained cast in shadows, and though I couldn't see her expression, I imagined she was smiling. "What brings you here? Aren't you supposed to be at work?"

I took another step, drawn into the apartment like a moth lured to an irresistible purple light.

"Where is it, Lily?" I asked.

Force of will, I guess, but somehow my low voice managed to stay calm.

"Where is what, Gage?"

Lily said my name with hint of menace, lengthening it, mocking the way I had spoken hers, her voice lilting just a bit.

Gaaaagee.

"You know damn well what I'm talking about," I said.

Another step. I was standing at the threshold to the living room. One more step and into the cage with the purple light I would go.

"I'm bored. I was going to watch a movie. Do you want to watch with me?"

The television was turned off.

I took another step—several, in fact.

Lily's face was visible. The smile I envisioned was there—a teasing little lift to her mouth. The way she sat accentuated the swell of her breasts and exposed part of her rounded belly. She had her hair pulled back into a ponytail, calling attention to her long and slender neck. As furious as I was, it was impossible to ignore her beauty.

"Where is the folder? Don't lie to me, Lily. I know you have it. You snuck into my condo while I was in the shower and you took it out of my workbag. You knew it was important. You had a conversation with Anna on the phone, so you knew damn well I needed to get it to her. You took it from me, and I want it back."

My phone rang. I checked the number. Of course it was Anna calling.

I answered the call, but curtly. "Yeah."

"Yeah? That's how you're greeting me these days? How nice. I'm just checking to make sure you got the folder off to FedEx."

"There's a problem," I said.

"What are you talking about? What problem?"

"I don't have the folder."

Lily was just on the couch, watching my meltdown, delighting in it.

"Gage, are you kidding me? Please tell me that you're kidding me."

"No," I said, rather calmly. "I'm not kidding. I don't have it because Lily took it from the house."

Lily touched a hand to her chest and made an insincere face—*Moi?*

Anna made an angry noise. "This is out of control with you and Lily. It has got to stop. Where is the folder?" I could hear desperation in Anna's voice.

"I told you, Lily took it."

"Enough!" Anna shouted. "Enough blaming Lily! Gage, find my goddamn folder and get it to me now! Do you hear me? There is a lot riding on this! I can't take it anymore! I can't. Honestly, I don't know what's gotten into you, but it has got to stop. You've got to stop blaming Lily."

"Here," I said. "If you're so convinced she has nothing to do with this, then you talk to her. Ask her for yourself and see if you believe her."

I handed my phone to Lily. She took it in a nonchalant manner.

"Hello?"

Of course I could only hear one half of the conversation.

"My apartment," Lily said. "He just came up here looking for the folder. No." She lengthened the word *no* as if to emphasize the impossibility of whatever question Anna had asked. I assumed that question was, Did you take the folder?

Lily said "No" again, and then, "I'm not worried. No, I'm fine, really. He's not being threatening."

My pulse dropped. Was Anna really worried I'd get violent with Lily?

Lily finished with a volley of short responses—okay, sure, all right, and no problem—and handed the phone back to me. It felt hot to the touch, but that was just my imagination. I put the phone to my ear with some trepidation.

"You get out of that apartment right now, right this instant, and go find wherever you put my folder," Anna said. "And don't tell me that Lily took it. Like she did the necklace? I don't know what the Adderall is doing to your brain, but something is seriously wrong with you."

"I'm not making this up."

"You listen to me, and listen very, very carefully," Anna said, seething. "I'm not going to give up the baby. I'm not going to do it. I want to be a mother again. I need this. I need it like I need air. With or without you, I'm raising this child. So go figure out what happened to the folder, turn over every piece of furniture in the house if that's what you have to do. But you will get the hell out of Lily's apartment, right now. You have no business being there. None!"

Blood thrummed in my ears. My mouth had gone cotton dry.

That's when I saw Roy was standing in the entranceway to the living room with a grin on his face. And that was also when I got it. I knew what was happening. And I knew what I had to do.

"Anna, sweetie, you're right," I said. "Maybe it is the Adderall messing me up. I'll look harder. I'm sure I'll find it and I'll call you back."

I hung up before she could respond.

"How much?" I asked, looking at Roy. "How much money will it take to get you two leeches to leave my life forever?"

"Now we're finally getting someplace," Roy said.

CHAPTER 30

Roy sauntered into the living room, chewing on a toothpick. His thumbs were tucked inside his belt, and he walked noiselessly from heel to toe. He was wearing a faded blue T-shirt, lightweight jacket, and dungarees. His deep-set eyes took in everything.

"Give me your phone," he said.

I hesitated until Roy lifted his jeans, offering me a flash of the large hunting knife sheathed to his ankle.

"You can't record this conversation, Gage," Roy said. He paused, Roy the thinking man. "So," he said. "We've got ourselves a little situation here. Something we can address like adults. Are you ready to talk?"

"How long?" I asked.

"Excuse me?" Roy said.

I was looking at Lily, addressing my question to her. She'd gone back to sitting on the edge of the sofa. Her skirt rode up her legs, but I got the feeling she would have been equally comfortable naked. She didn't care. If there ever was a girl named Lily who loved old movies and drew portraits to uncover hidden secrets about people, she was gone. In her place was the new Lily, the one who didn't care about our dreams.

Roy stood to my right, with his thumbs tucked back in his belt, the knife still in its sheath. He was eyeing me the way a prison guard might stare down an insubordinate inmate.

"How long have you been planning to coerce me into giving you a payoff? Was it before or after you moved into my home? I want to know."

Lily looked over to Roy. *Permission to speak freely?* her eyes said. Roy gave a near imperceptible nod of his head.

"Things just sort of evolved," Lily said. She sounded relieved, like this was a confession of sorts, a weight finally lifted. "I was pregnant and pissed at Roy when I met you guys, but Roy really didn't want me to get an abortion. He was just pissed because I told him the kid wasn't his."

I remembered Lily telling us the same story on the curb. My eyes met Roy's.

"And is it?" I asked.

A flash of anger crossed his face.

"Yeah," Lily said. "I just made up that story because he wasn't happy about the baby."

"So what then?"

"Then I was like, well, fuck you if you don't want this baby. I'll give it to someone who does," Lily said. She looked at Roy again.

Roy seemed to accept Lily's admonition, acknowledging with an indifferent shrug that, yes, he probably could have been more supportive in the beginning. Strange to say, but I felt a bit like a couples therapist closing in on a breakthrough. Here I was, moments from being forced into making a payout, helping the happy couple work through an issue. It was too surreal even for Dali.

"What then?" I asked.

"Then I found you guys on the website. Just like I said. And when you invited me to live with you, well, that was just about the nicest thing anyone has ever done for me."

"And you repaid our kindness by playing games with me, pitting me against my wife."

Lily shrugged. Anna and I were a means to an end, a source of cash. No hard feelings. *Sorry for making you a chump*. That was what her shrug said to me.

"Well, it might have gone another way, but a few nights before I moved in with you guys, Roy and I were hanging out. He was being sweet because he wanted us to be together again. I was going to move back in with him and break the bad news that we were going to keep the baby. But before I did, I decided to torture Roy by making him watch an old movie with me."

I looked surprised. "You really are an old movie fan?"

Lily appeared to be offended by my insinuation. "What? Did you think I was lying about that?"

"Well, the thought did cross my mind," I said.

"He watched *Gaslight* with me," Lily said, thumbing over to Roy. "You know the film?"

"I think so," I said. "It's about a guy who makes his beautiful wife think she's going crazy."

"Charles Boyer gaslights Ingrid Bergman," Lily said, almost reverently—lovingly, I might say. "Roy hates almost every movie I've made him watch, but he loved this one. He got to thinking, could we gaslight you? Not in the same way, but could we, you know, make it so hard on you that you'd pay us to leave?"

"And here we are," Roy said.

"Yeah, here we are."

"So you knew about the rocket before you bought me that present?"

Lily reverted into herself, a girlish retreat, as if she were too embarrassed to acknowledge the truth. *My bad*, her body language said, without feeling bad about it at all.

"Lily told me about your model rocket hobby, and then I found the photo. Figured it would bug you out," Roy said. "It actually wasn't easy to find. I had to call a bunch of hobby stores and then drove to New Hampshire to get it. Sorry 'bout using your boy, but we needed something good to kick things off. The rest of the stuff we did to you we just sort of improvised. Nothing personal." Roy's grimace, the way his cold eyes squinted, the deep creases on his face, like Clint Eastwood staring into the sun, didn't convey any real sympathy for me. No, it was more like he suffered in life, so everyone else should, and tough shit for that. "But I also read your story, so I knew some drunk driver took your wife and kid from you. That sort of accident is going to get you a lot of cash from the insurance company. A lot."

"So what's the number?" I asked. "What will it cost me to make you disappear?"

"Well," Roy said, spitting his toothpick onto the floor, "how much you got?"

CHAPTER 31

This next part was going to disappoint Roy. Sure, he read about the drunk driver, but nowhere in the article did it mention the guy was uninsured. So these two clowns were coercing a quality assurance guy, a middle-income earner who needed the mortgage deduction and rental income from his upstairs unit to balance out the rest of his finances.

"If I pay you five thousand dollars, will you go away?" I asked. I felt the strength return to my voice. There was a way out—we just needed to settle on a price.

Unfortunately, judging by the looks Roy and Lily exchanged, I could see he wasn't going to bite.

"That's a joke, right?" Roy said, approaching me, closing our gap. His shoulders went back, chest pushed outward, a fighter's posture. He got right up into my face, close enough for me to feel his hot breath.

"Roy!" Lily said, sounding alarmed. "Don't hurt him."

"Then he'd better play nice," Roy said.

Lily kept to her seat on the edge of the couch. "Listen, Gage, I like you and Anna a whole lot, and I'm really sorry about all of this," she said, speaking sweetly. "But

Roy here is being serious. He wants a payday. He needs it. I can't get into it with you, but he's got some obligations and he needs the money. So let's try again."

"Yeah," Roy said, replacing his discarded toothpick with another. "Let's try again."

I was nervous, but I wasn't completely scared or intimidated. Perhaps I should have been overcome by rage, shaking furiously. And yet, to my surprise, I wasn't even feeling a flicker of anger, because I was about to get a thorn named Lily taken out of my foot. What we were engaged in carried all the emotion of a business transaction.

Of course, when the deed was done I'd be burdened with a terrible secret. Lily would have to vanish and Anna could never know the reason why. The guilt would carry an additional cost above and beyond what I was about to pay, but it was the price of freedom.

I'd make up for it, no doubt. Once these two parasites were gone, I'd redouble my efforts on the adoption front. No matter what, however, I wasn't going to try to work a deal where we could still end up with Lily's baby. First of all, it was borderline human trafficking. Second, even though the baby was not responsible for Lily's wicked ways, I doubted I could forgive my tormentors enough to give their child the upbringing he or she deserved. Unpleasant and indelible memories would always be lurking just below the surface, getting in the way of all the love I had to give. Once we moved on from this experience, Anna would see how committed I was to our future. Without Lily to get in the way, my wife would never again have reason to doubt my desire to become some child's adoptive father.

"Why don't you tell me a figure," I said to Roy.

Roy propped his foot up on the edge of the coffee

table. He wore black hiking boots, the kind that could easily break my ribs if he kicked me there. He was looking at me as if that was how this might end up.

"Two hundred grand," Roy said. "That's the price."

I swallowed hard. My heart rate climbed until I could feel it beating in my throat. I thought we'd come up with a reasonable number and put a stop to the madness. It was going down a different way. I briefly contemplated charging Roy, but if I did make this a physical confrontation, I'd probably be beaten into a coma and stabbed with his knife.

Instead of fighting, I asked, "Are you serious?"

Roy cocked his head to the side as if I'd confused him somehow.

"You don't have a clue how serious I am. Two hundred grand."

He took his foot off the coffee table and I could see him ball his fists.

Lily noticed as well. "Roy," she said. "Take it easy now. We're gonna work something out."

I'd been frozen in the same spot for a while, but something made me take a step back. Maybe it was the death stare Roy was giving me. Max had taken karate lessons starting at age six. In the dojo, at his very first class, he learned to stand in a horse stance, one leg forward the other back, improving leverage. This was the same stance I took—a fighting stance.

"Roy," I said. "I don't have that kind of cash."

Why? Where was all my money? Roy was eyeing me, asking those same questions. What happened to the payout from the accident? What about my job? My savings?

In truth, I'd been diligent about saving money since entering the workforce. I always contributed the max to my 401k, skimped on vacations, didn't overextend with the home, drove cars until they'd go no more, did a lot of repairs myself, basically lived a modest existence on a modest salary. Then my world ended—my wife and son were gone—and with them went my reason to care about cash. What little money the lawyers managed to get from the driver's family I gave to charities Karen supported and causes Max would have championed. I didn't want it in my bank account. It was tainted with the worst of all memories.

World Wildlife Federation? Yeah, here's twenty grand in Max's name. Save a whale. Save a lot of whales, because I can't save my son. Red Cross? Karen was a trained nurse, so I reasoned she'd want them to have all the money I should have been putting into my retirement savings. But what was I saving for? Myself? My future? The accident took both from me.

When I did finally start paying attention to money again, I made some risky bets on some rancid stock tips. In hindsight, I would have been better off tossing half the money I put into stocks out the window of a moving car. By the time Anna came into my life, I'd managed to pull myself out of the financial kamikaze dive, but the damage had already been done. My savings were pretty depleted. I had enough to scrape together a mortgage on this place only because I'd sold my home in Swampscott. Roy could threaten me all he'd like, but unless he was also an adept money manager, he'd get only what I could give.

"What kind of cash are we talking about?"

I didn't hesitate. "Fifty grand," I said. "That's what I can afford. Fifty grand and that's stretching it for me."

"Fifty grand to make us go away?" Roy said.

"Yes," I said. "Fifty grand and you two disappear. You'll go away and you'll never come back."

"You must really want Lily gone," Roy said, cracking a fractured smile. He gave Lily eyes that gave me the shivers.

"I hope Anna won't be too upset about this offer of yours," Lily said in her lilting voice. "I really like her a lot. She's been really nice to me."

My anger sputtered to life.

"She's not to know. You'll say nothing to her about this. You take the money and you're gone. That's the deal."

"It isn't enough," Roy said. For a second, his defenses came down, giving me a glimpse into his private world. I saw fear in Roy's eyes, an emotion I didn't think he could feel.

"Isn't enough for what?" I asked.

"Roy," Lily said. "Don't."

Roy flashed Lily an angry look. With a burst of movement he charged her. Red-faced now, Roy grabbed Lily's arm with force and yanked her off the couch.

"You said they had money!" Spit came out of Roy's mouth. Lily flinched, but it hit her in the face anyway.

Lily said, shaking, "I'm sorry. I thought he had more."

Roy held Lily's arm as she writhed to pry it free. A look of terror stretched across her face. She knew to fear his rage.

Without warning, Roy let go of Lily's arm and lunged for me. He seized hold of my throat. Digging in with my heels wasn't much help. Roy pushed me back until I crashed hard against the wall. My breath left me. Roy's hands tightened, constricting my windpipe. My eyes went wide as my feet began to kick.

"Roy! Stop it! Stop it now!" Lily shrieked.

Lily had come to my rescue. Through my fading vision I could see her pounding her fists against Roy's back. But she was a gnat on the hide of a bull, insignificant. He spun around to face her without releasing his crushing grip. My vision began to dim and soon my skin felt hot and cold, tingling all over. I heard Lily scream, pleading with Roy, but her voice sounded like it was coming from inside a seashell, distant and muted. I was struggling, kicking to break free of Roy's grasp.

I'm going to die here, I thought. *This is where it ends.*

I was overcome by what I can only describe as an incredible feeling of peace. I'm sure I was still kicking, still clawing at Roy's wrist, while he had me pinned to the wall by his powerful arm. But I also saw Max's face, like a light, a guide, letting me know he'd be waiting. I wanted to reach for him, but the air came back into my lungs, the pressure on my throat went away. I sank to the floor, chest heaving, very much alive, and not sure I was grateful.

"You'll pay me the fifty grand," Roy said. "But you're going to do something else for me to make up the difference." To Lily, he said, "He'll do the Nicky Stacks job."

I was slumped on the floor, rubbing my aching throat and shaking my head to clear away the cobwebs. I didn't think I could speak even if I tried.

Roy crouched down in a squat, getting to my level, staring me right in the eyes. "You might not have all the money I need," he said, patting me on the cheek. His touch was meant to rouse or patronize me. "But you're going to pay me another way," he said. "You see, now I have to make a delivery. Something I didn't want to do, but I got no choice in the matter. So I'm going to need someone to help me with this exchange—a lookout of sorts—only you won't be getting any cut of the action."

"You want me to be a lookout on a drug deal?"

"I need to make more cash," Roy said. "It's no biggie. You're just the eyes and ears."

"I'm not a drug dealer, asshole," I said.

"I think you should reconsider that position."

"Why?"

"Things could get worse for you here," Roy said.

"Worse? How so?"

"Well, let's start with a phone call to Anna," Roy said. Then he mimicked Lily's voice, high pitched and girlish. "Hey Anna, it's Lily. I don't know how to tell you this, but something happened between me and Gage. I didn't mean for it to happen, it just sort of did."

"You sick bastard," I said. "She'll never believe you."

Lily stood, giving me a glimpse of her body, as if to say, of course she'd believe.

"Even if you do manage to convince her otherwise," Roy said, "there will always be a trace of doubt. It's hard living when your wife doesn't really trust you. But there's more."

"More?" I said.

Roy reached into his jacket pocket and took out a small plastic bag. The bag held something inside it, but I couldn't make out what it was. Then Roy held it up, and the shape of the object was clearly unmistakable.

It was a condom. And I was certain it was full of my DNA.

"Maybe Lily will tell Anna how you two are really in love. Heck, she might even give her this little baggie here as some added proof. Go get the DNA tested, she'll say, because it's got your man written all over it."

No need to ask him where he got it. Obviously, it was fished out of my trash.

The adrenaline rush made me light-headed. I felt unsteady on my feet. I thought about charging Roy. Maybe I could wrestle the bag out of his hand. But then I saw the knife he was holding. A long and thick blade, just like he used in my dream to stab me.

"And once Anna's left you, all heartbroken, you'll be stuck with us. You know how hard it is to get a pregnant woman evicted?" Roy asked.

My anxiety spiked at the thought.

"We'll have this place so trashed it'll be condemned," Roy said. "And all that's just the start. By the time we're through with you, you'll be out of a marriage and out of a home."

I let this sink in. I could fight this, I was sure I could, or I could just get it over with. Roy was right. If Lily told Anna we'd slept together, she might never believe me, especially with the physical evidence. She already didn't believe me when it came to anything having to do with Lily.

"If I do this one thing for you . . . this . . . lookout job, whatever it is, then you'll be gone?"

"Plus the fifty," Roy said.

"Jesus, you two really are a pestilence."

"What's that?" Lily asked.

I laughed bitterly, remembering the last time I hit her with an SAT word. Judging by Roy's expression he wasn't coming to her rescue.

"It's a contagious or infectious disease," I said, "like the bubonic plague."

"Jeez," Lily said. "We're really that bad?"

"Maybe worse," I replied. "Look, I won't do it. I'll tell Anna that you're lying. I'm not saying it's going to be easy, but eventually, she'll come to believe me."

"Then we've got a serious problem on our hands."

"Yours, not mine."

"No, it's yours and Anna's, too. She needs that missing folder for her job, don'tcha think?"

"What do you mean?"

Roy sauntered over to the sofa. I watched him reach underneath the cushion and pull out a large green folder with Anna's papers inside.

"If you want these papers, then you're coming with me to meet Nicky Stacks. He's got to see that I have a partner on this deal, even if you don't do the drop."

Inside I was seething, but somehow I kept all the anger just below the surface.

"Just a meeting?"

"That's it. All you have to do is pretend you're going to be there for the drop. Nicky needs to see I have it all worked out before he'll authorize me."

"Why me? Why not one of your other buddies."

"It's complicated. Normally, he'd want me to use a guy from his crew, but for reasons you don't need to know, I can't do that. Look, do you want Anna's folder and do you want us to keep our mouths shut about you screwing Lily or not? If you do, you'll give me the fifty large and just come with me to this meeting and then we skedaddle. Deal?"

I thought about this for a moment. If I went and had a sit-down with some drug dealer, I'd get Anna's folder while getting rid of Lily and Roy in the process. It seemed like a workable exchange, but with one caveat.

"No cash. The meeting for a folder."

Roy shook his head.

"Lily will call Anna and I'll take this to a shredder."

"Then, I'll pay you twenty. I need some money in my account, too, you know. But you won't get a cent from me, not one single cent, until you're out of here. Gone. When that happens, I'll make arrangements to get you the money. Is that understood?"

I needed that folder, and it looked like meeting with Nicky Stacks was the only way that was going to happen. Roy ruminated on my offer. The difference in price didn't seem to bother him any.

Roy tucked the folder behind his back and reached out to shake my hand. "Understood," he said.

CHAPTER 32

Instead of returning to work, getting back to the business of battery testing, I was riding shotgun in the passenger seat of a red 2000 Chevy Camaro Z28 coupe, driving through a neighborhood of East Boston I knew existed but had never seen.

Roy was doing the driving. I didn't even realize the Camaro parked on our street was his until he put the key in the ignition and fired the engine. Until then, I was thinking Roy could be stealing the car. Drug dealer, car thief—in for a penny, in for a pound, as the old saying goes. He wore dark shades and never glanced down at the stick shift when he changed gears. The toothpick in his mouth switched from the right side to the left synchronously, it seemed, with each turn he took. I hadn't seen him pop in a dip of chewing tobacco since the first night we met. Maybe he was trying to kick the habit.

Roy took great pleasure in driving and enjoyed showing off his skills. He'd speed up to the car in front of him, braking hard only when I thought we were going to crash. Then he'd tailgate like a true urban asshole, accelerate around every turn, and hug the corners with his wheels screeching. The air freshener dangling from his rearview mirror swayed to the chaotic rhythm of his driving.

"Do you have any questions?" Roy asked.

He had briefed me on Nicky Stacks, so I knew the rules. Roy had been very specific. It was a laundry list of "don'ts" that we'd gone over multiple times already.

If I had to make eye contact, don't make it last long.

Don't fidget. If I fidget, it'll make Nicky nervous.

Don't ask any questions.

Don't order anything. If Nicky wants us to eat, he'll order for us.

Don't rush. If I eat too fast, he'll think I'm being rude.

Don't get anything alcoholic to drink unless he's the one to suggest it.

I could use my first name, but not my last.

"Let's go over our story again," Roy said.

We'd just made the turn off Cambridge Street onto the Longfellow Bridge. It wouldn't be long now until we were at Nicky's restaurant. The closer we got, the edgier Roy became. We didn't know each other well, but judging by Roy's behavior, I guessed Nicky Stacks could put the fear into the fearless.

"We're cousins," I said. "I live in Key West. You got a place down there. We hang out sometimes. You wanted someone you can trust on this job and I was your first choice. I got a clean record, never did time, but I can handle myself."

"Good," Roy said, nodding. "Good job." I could see in his eyes that he wasn't convinced.

I wasn't with Roy when he had called Nicky Stacks. I was downstairs changing my clothes at Roy's request, because he had anticipated correctly how Nicky would want a meeting right away. Evidently, the deal had to go down soon. Roy had me wearing a black T-shirt and the darkest jeans I owned. I didn't have boots like his, and my work shoes didn't exactly scream "tough guy," but we made do with what we had.

Guess I didn't look quite like Gage the quality assurance manager anymore, but I didn't look nearly as tough as Roy, either. Roy kept eyeing me, like he wanted to tussle my hair, fix me with a fresh scar, something to harden my exterior. I used to say to Max, "You get what you get and you don't get upset." I thought about saying the same to Roy, but instead posed a more practical question. "What if he asks me about us? Personal details or something."

"If I say you're a cousin, Nicky will think you're a cousin," Roy said. "He trusts me. I worked for his crew when I was on the inside. And I've been working for him on and off ever since I got out."

"But you didn't want to do this job," I said.

Roy kept his eyes on me long enough for me to think they should be watching the road.

"I was trying to come up with another way to get the cash I needed so I wouldn't have to do what I have to do, but you screwed up that plan. And now here we are. Working together."

"Here we are," I repeated, staring out my window. "But we aren't working together. I get Anna's folder after we finish the meeting. That's the deal."

Roy didn't respond.

"Say it," I demanded.

"You get the folder after we finish the meeting."

I went back to looking out the window, silent, until Roy pulled up in front of a restaurant called Nicky's.

CHAPTER 33

Nicky's was not a classy joint. A tired-looking roof sat atop a battered red brick exterior. I saw a dilapidated satellite dish held to the roof by a pair of rusty-looking brackets. Closer to street level, a blue awning was suspended above the entrance, and the signage on the front read NICKY'S RESTAURANT FINE ITALIAN CUISINE, with a phone number below the words.

The location itself wasn't all too appealing, which could explain Nicky's worn aesthetic. It wasn't a "lock 'em up" hood—as in, roll up the car windows and lock the doors—but it was close. Maybe there had been a time when this section of town was a city jewel, but I'm pretty sure prohibition was the law back then. The two- and three-family homes were nestled close together and not lovingly maintained. The lawns were the size of postage stamps, and several had more rusty junk than plants. Shades were drawn in most of the windows I could see. There was trash in the gutter, trash overflowing from the wastebaskets, and the street itself looked like it had gone fifteen rounds with Apollo Creed. The sickly hum of air conditioners could barely be heard above the rumbling noise of cars and buses.

Across from Nicky's was a Laundromat called Dollar-A-Wash, but the way the stencils were displayed in the windows it read: DOLLA R A WASH. I wouldn't want to live here, and I sure as heck didn't want to be here.

Roy, by contrast, appeared to be in his element. He'd fortified his shell. Nicky Stacks wouldn't see any of the nervousness I'd witnessed on the ride over. To quell my nerves, I repeated a mantra in my head: it's just a meeting . . . it's only a meeting.

It was dark inside the restaurant. The bar area was somewhat crowded, but the seating areas were not. A few patrons were being served by a single waitress who was tall and thin and as weathered as the neighborhood where she worked.

What Nicky's lacked in ambience, it more than made up in aroma. All the sweet smells and familiar spices of Italian cooking were on full display. Nicky's had to have something that kept it in business.

I followed Roy to the back of the restaurant. I could tell I was being watched. I didn't belong here. I belonged at work. I was a stranger in a strange land, and everyone eyeing me knew it, too. Something made me glance over at the bar. The bartender, a stocky guy with hunched shoulders wearing a tweed cap, gave me a long stare. It was like he knew where I was headed and felt sorry for me.

We ascended a short flight of stairs to another seating area. It was a smaller space, perfect for a private dinner party or function. Cast iron wall sconces with low-wattage bulbs lit the room with a yellowish glow. A row of booths with red vinyl seats lined one wood-paneled wall. A few tables were scattered throughout, each covered with a red-and-white-checked tablecloth.

I noticed candles tucked inside small glass jars centered on each table, but none were lit, as if to say this section of the restaurant was reserved for Nicky and his business and nobody else. Framed color photos of Tuscany tried to fancy up the joint, but I wasn't fooled: we were still in East Boston.

A husky man with broad shoulders sat in the dining area's last booth. He looked up from his *Herald*, saw us approach, but didn't wave. We went over to the booth and sat across from him. Nicky Stacks, I assumed. Roy made me go in first. No getting out. No slinking away. I was there and there I'd stay.

Eventually Stacks lowered his paper, giving me my first proper glimpse. Stacks had a disconcertingly pale complexion, as if he were allergic to the sun, or the sun to him. He kept his fine, straw-colored hair cut short and combed back. He had the thick neck of a football player and the round head of a battering ram, and I figured his forehead was massive enough to be branded a lethal weapon.

As for his eyes, those were slits, set close together and deep in the sockets, and probably accustomed to seeing violence. The right nostril of his prominent nose appeared misshapen, set that way by a fist or a bat, most likely—and if that weren't tough enough, his lips were fixed in a permanent sneer. Just his presence made me shudder. I imagined most every picture of him came out looking like a mug shot.

"Who the fuck is this?" Stacks asked Roy. He was looking right through me with those slits for eyes, like I didn't exist, like it didn't matter if I ever existed.

"Nicky, this is my cousin, Gage," Roy said. "He's going to help me with the Moreno brothers job."

No, I'm not, I thought.

Stacks shifted his eyes over to Roy. He might have

been looking through me, but Stacks was definitely seeing Roy, and he did not seem pleased.

"What are you talking about?" Stacks said. "What cousin? What the fuck is this?"

"I'm not bringing Johnny on this job," Roy said.

I didn't know who Johnny was, but apparently Stacks did.

"Before you called, I didn't even think you were even doing this job," Stacks said. "You said you were out. Then you call me and you say you want back in. Now you're telling me you're bringing in a new guy. Someone I don't know. Someone I ain't never met. You're telling me Johnny is out. This is all very unusual."

Stacks's manner, the tone of his speech, walked the line between peremptory and bellicose. One wrong word or misinterpreted gesture could tip the scale toward his more volatile side. I had a strong suspicion it was a side of him few people saw without next seeing their blood.

"I *need* to do the job," Roy said, his tone almost apologetic. "At first I thought I didn't, but now I do."

"Who do you owe?" Stacks asked.

Roy popped a toothpick into his mouth. His whole demeanor shifted slightly, like he was disappointed to admit his failings to Stacks.

"Some guys in D.C. You don't know them."

"I doubt that," Stacks said matter-of-factly. "But either way, I can't help you down there. How much?"

"A hundred grand," Roy said, fully shamefaced. Before I met Nicky Stacks I never imagined Roy toadying to anybody. Couldn't very well blame him, though. If Brad were here, he'd see an aura around Nicky blacker than any ink.

"You're into some guys for a hundred grand?" Stacks said, shaking his head. "What were you thinking? What the hell were you dealing?"

Roy grimaced.

"Cigarettes," he said.

Stacks did not look surprised. I wasn't either. I also wasn't about to say that I'd read an article in the *Wall Street Journal* not too long ago about an increase in cigarette smuggling. We weren't drinking beers and swapping stories, but still I knew something about the topic.

Cigarette trafficking is one of the most lucrative businesses for organized crime and drug smugglers. The profit margin on illegally trafficked cigarettes exceeds that of heroin, cocaine, and most guns, and it's all because of the discrepancy in state tax rates. Thanks to my weird memory for useless numbers I recalled from the article that Virginia had one of the lowest tax rates in the country, at thirty cents per pack. Every state to the north has a higher tax per pack, especially New York, where the tax runs over four dollars.

Again the numbers: 1,500 cartons could net a profit of a hundred grand. A car could hold six hundred cartons. Rent a U-Haul and you're moving hundreds of cases, worth more than half a million dollars. Something like 30 percent of all cigarettes in New York City are sold on the black market, and more than 70 percent of those come from Virginia. No fancy equipment needed. No laboratory required. All it took for a criminal to make a few hundred grand in a day was a supply chain, the smokes, and a working vehicle.

"Who's smurfing the smokes?" Stacks asked.

I knew from the article that Stacks wasn't talking about diminutive blue people rolling smokes in their mushroom houses. Smurfing is the criminal practice of buying large quantities of cigarettes legally to then sell illegally on the black market for a hefty profit. Sad to think that newspapers are struggling to stay in business when you can learn so much from reading them.

"Like I said, some guys from D.C.," Roy said. "You don't know them."

"You had to ditch your ride?"

"I got jumped when I stopped for gas," Roy explained, sounding disgusted with himself, embarrassed by his failure. "These three guys must have been following me for miles. Pulled a gun on me soon as I got out of the U-Haul. One guy drove the truck and the other two put me in the car. I had a gun on me the whole time. They brought me to some neighborhood miles away and just left me there. Cops found the U-Haul, but the product was gone. Now I'm in for a hundred grand of missing smokes and if I don't get the money to my boys in D.C. soon, I'm going to be a dead man. I'd do some more smoke smuggling, but I'm shut off now. Unreliable, they say. So I need the cash and I need it soon."

"You haven't done a job for me in a while, and now you're bringing me a new guy?" Stacks said, looking over at me, seeing me the way Brad sees spirits. Something was there, but not anything concrete—nothing important, anyway.

"You can trust Gage. I'm vouching for him."

"So you're cutting Johnny out because you need the extra cash to pay off your smoke buddies, is that it?"

"Something like that," Roy said, snapping the toothpick in half with his tongue and replacing it with a fresh one.

"Okay," Stacks said. "We'll do it. But just remember

this. If my deal goes south like your smoke run, I ain't gonna wait weeks to take your fucking head off." Stacks was looking at me, seeing me for the first time as a physical presence in the room. "And I'll fuckin' take your head off too," he said, pointing his index finger at me like it was the barrel of a loaded gun.

CHAPTER 34

Roy asked about the details of the transaction. All Nicky offered was a single word that meant nothing to me: "Eagle." That was it. End of discussion, time for us to go, or so his glowering eyes conveyed.

Needless to say, Nicky Stacks didn't order us any food. He didn't buy us any drinks, either. Not that I could have swallowed a bite. My throat had gone dry, my heart was racing, and the palms of my hands had turned slick with sweat. It was like a triple dose of Adderall. I was beyond jittery. My body was like radar warning me of an enemy on approach, advising me to seek shelter from Roy, from Lily, from Nicky Stacks and his drug dealing ways immediately.

I followed a silent and sullen Roy back to his Camaro, got into the passenger seat, buckled my seat belt.

"Okay, the meeting is over. Give me the folder."

"No, not yet. There's something else you need to do."

"That's not the deal."

"Tough titty. It's the reality. I've got to go check out Eagle right now. Then I'll give you your stupid folder."

"What does Eagle mean anyway?"

"It means don't worry about it," Roy said, firing up the car's engine.

I glanced over at Roy, studying him for a moment. Though he told me not to worry, the same instruction did not appear to apply to him. The car rumbled back to life, sounding angry for having been left dormant for even a minute. Roy pulled the Camaro out into traffic, making a little squelch of the tires that seemed to please him. Next he turned on the radio, classic rock, and upped the volume when the Stones came on. The tune was "Sympathy for the Devil."

"Ironic," I said to Roy.

"What is?" Roy asked.

"Never mind," I said.

Roy shot me a look.

I'd seen how our meeting with Nicky Stacks had left Roy shaken. Maybe it was just a flash, but in the course of our meeting with Nicky I saw the boy hiding out inside the hard man's body. It made me feel sad and sorry for Roy—just a bit, a pinch perhaps. Somehow, God help me, I sympathized with his plight. He was a guy desperate for money to survive, who came up with a twisted plan to extend his life—at the expense of my own.

"It's ironic that I'm helping you out and this song is on the radio," I finally said.

"What does that mean?" Roy slipped a toothpick to the left side of his mouth as he made a left-hand turn.

"It means I can partly understand why you're doing what you're doing," I said.

Roy got quiet for a moment, evidently mulling this over. Then he got a look on his face like he'd just figured something out.

"Does that mean you're calling me the devil?" he asked.

I hesitated. "Yeah, I guess it does."

Roy appeared pleased as he turned up the volume on the radio and punched the accelerator.

"Where are we going?" I asked.

Roy turned to look at me. He lowered his shades until they rested on the bridge of his nose. He winked, gave me a devilish grin, but didn't answer my question.

When Roy pulled the car to a stop, we were at Logan Airport. Well, we were *near* the airport—maybe a mile from the runways. A short distance to the north was the Chelsea River and if we crossed that we'd be in Chelsea, a city next to Boston. Gray clouds, ugly as this concrete landscape, hung low in the sky and seemed to soak up the diesel fuel scenting the humid air. I heard the plaintive cry of seagulls stalking the murky river for a meal. It sounded like they wished to be elsewhere as well.

I knew we were in Eagle Square only because that was what Roy had told me. I figured that was what Eagle meant but didn't ask for confirmation. Oil tanks to my left poked out over some squat concrete buildings, and closer to where we parked was a large, single-story red brick building with an attached loading zone. The loading zone had three truck bays, each big enough for an eighteen-wheeler. An alley separated the loading zone from a fenced-off enclosure that held a dozen decommissioned school buses. The side of the alley with the fencing was lined with trees, while on the other side was the warehouse itself, a massive structure several hundred feet long, storing whatever got loaded through those big bay doors.

As for Eagle Square, that was a bit of a misnomer. It was more like Eagle Triangle, made up of Eagle Square, East Eagle Street, and Chelsea Street. What I could say for Eagle Square was that it was busy with working folk, but at night I could imagine this was one very deserted locale, and I figured, even with my limited knowledge of criminality, it would make for a fine ol' place to host a drug deal. I followed Roy to the entrance to the alley.

"This is where it's going to go down," Roy said. "This is what Nicky meant when he said Eagle. It's one of his chosen drop sites."

Roy, hands on his hips, surveyed his surroundings the way a master craftsman might study a block of marble before making cut number one.

"Come here." Roy motioned for me to stand closer. I'd been in the workforce long enough to tell an order from a request. For Roy, this was all in a day's work. It was business to him and I was just a resource allocated to his project. Not a pretty feeling, but it was a relief compared to the near crippling anxiety I felt in the presence of Nicky Stacks. Judging by Roy's more relaxed posture, I suspected he felt the same.

I got to Roy just as a white truck, an eighteen-wheeler, began to back up into the loading zone.

"Too bad the truck's not delivering cigarettes," I said. "Then you could just knock it over and solve your money problem."

"Is that a joke?" Roy asked. I couldn't read his eyes behind the dark glasses.

"Sort of," I said.

"Yeah, well, I almost laughed." Roy lowered his shades, allowing me to see the smile in his eyes. "Look, Gage," Roy said, setting his hand on my shoulder. I didn't flinch. There was nothing menacing about his touch. "I got to be honest here, I feel really bad about all this. I mean, to use your hopes about adopting a baby and everything to get some cash out of you, well, it's a damn shitty thing we've done. But I'm a desperate man and this is all just business. But I want you to know, I like you."

"You have a funny way of showing it," I said.

"This." Roy motioned to the alley. "This was not supposed to be. If you could have paid me what I needed in the first place, we'd be gone already, but you couldn't, and so here we are."

"Yeah, here we are," I said, a bit wistfully. Roy and I were standing shoulder to shoulder, staring down this dark, empty alley like there was actually something to see. "We're not a *we*, Roy," I said, feeling the need to clarify. "You're doing the deal alone. Remember?"

"I will say I think you're being very cool about all this," Roy said.

"I'm hardly cool," I answered. "What I want to do is take your friggin' head off with that metal bar."

I pointed to the ground at a rusty piece of rebar lying next to a crumbling concrete brick.

"I'd kill you if you tried," Roy said as though it was a known fact, like water was wet and the sky was blue. I gave him a half smile. "Look, I know you hate me. I know that I'm the worst thing that's ever happened to you."

"You're not the worst," I said. "You're not even close."

Roy seemed to appreciate my point, as if he could read my thoughts and saw in them something much darker kicking about, the worst of the worst, the kind of pain that guys like him and Nicky Stacks, hard guys with hard hearts, couldn't ever dream of feeling.

"Let's just get this over with," Roy said. "I've got a lot to teach you before the deal goes down."

"Teach me? What are you talking about? This is over. Done. I did what you wanted. I met with Nicky Stacks, now you've got to give me Anna's folder and go away."

"It's not going to be dangerous, Gage. All you have to do is be my lookout. You just have to be a presence and nothing more."

"It's still no."

"Nothing will go wrong."

"I'm not going to help you and that's final. Now give me Anna's folder like we agreed!"

Instead of the folder, Roy made a strange look and then let out an exasperated sigh, as if to say he was growing tired of my continued protests. From his back pocket, he took out his smartphone, the kind that one day soon would last infinitely longer on a battery powered by Olympian, tapped on the phone's display, and pressed the speaker against my ear.

I deflated on the spot, crinkled up just like the sides of the discarded soda can at my feet. I heard Roy's recorded voice in my ear. It was from the conversation we had in Lily's apartment, the conversation I had no idea had been recorded.

Roy: "What kind of cash are we talking about?"

Me: "Fifty grand. That's what I can afford. Fifty grand and that's stretching it for me."

Roy: "Fifty grand to make us go away?"

Me: "Yes. Fifty grand and you two disappear. You'll go away and you'll never come back."

Roy: "You must really want Lily gone."

Lily: "I hope Anna's not too upset about this offer

of yours. I really like her a lot. She's been really nice to me."

Me: "She's not to know. You'll say nothing to her about this. You take the money and you're gone. That's the deal."

Roy pulled the phone away from my ear and said, "Lily's got a copy, too, so don't try to break my phone or anything. Why'd you offer us a bribe? Easy. You and Lily slept together and I was going to tell Anna. Normally, I'd beat the crap out of you for sleeping with my girl, but I couldn't risk going back to prison. So the payout was my revenge. Only, you reneged on the deal, so Anna hears the recording, and I show her the evidence. Gage, I can screw you longer and harder than a porn star. I need a lookout on this drop and you're my man for the job, like it or not."

CHAPTER 35

The recording changed everything. I could talk until I was blue in the face and Anna would believe, and rightly so, that I had offered Lily and Roy a bribe to disappear. The reason? I slept with Lily. The evidence? Plenty. I seriously doubted our marriage could survive this revelation, and it wasn't a chance I was willing to take.

While I was still reeling with this sick feeling in my gut, Roy went back to teacher mode. He asked me this question: "What don't you see?"

Was this a test? If I got it wrong he might think I was a liability, take my twenty grand, and be on his merry little way. "I don't see a blimp," I said.

Roy knew I was playing games and was none too pleased.

"No more jokes, funny man." He poked my arm hard with his long finger. "Why here? What's good about this location for the drop?"

I took the test more seriously, looking up and all around and did notice something useful.

"Security cameras," I said.

Now Roy seemed pleased. "What about 'em?"

"There aren't any."

Cameras were mounted to the roof of the warehouse closer to the loading dock, but none of those were focused on the alley. There was no need to survey a school bus graveyard. Roy appeared duly impressed.

"That's right. Nicky has a map in his head of all the places in Boston, Everett, Revere, Charlestown, you name it, where we can make drops without being recorded. Each place is coded by the name of the nearest cross street. Eagle. Burbank. Mill. Whatever. So he sent us to Eagle."

"Is that bad?" I asked, thinking it was.

"It's not my favorite," Roy said. "Sight lines down the alley aren't great. How many guys are really coming? It'll be hard to tell. Is it an ambush or just a deal?"

"Why would somebody ambush you?"

"Us," Roy reminded.

I rephrased the question. "Why would somebody ambush us? I thought you said this was a no-brainer job, nothing dangerous, just a straight drop."

"Nobody is going to ambush us, and it is a nothing job."

"Then why bother sending two of us at all?"

"Because if there's only person, then it might become a temptation for our buyer to take more product than they're paying for. That's why Nicky always insists on having a team. He wouldn't let me do it alone for that very reason."

"You took me to meet Nicky knowing you were going to make me do the drop."

"It obviously wasn't going to be easy to convince you otherwise."

I was curious. "Exactly who are the Moreno brothers?" I asked.

"They're distributors. Some superconnected family

controls this territory, and the Moreno brothers work for them."

"What exactly are you dealing here?"

Again Roy looked at me.

"We," I said, impatiently. "What are we dealing here?"

"You're in this. Like it or not, you're a player now."

"I hate it," I said.

"Yeah, I imagine that you do."

"So what are we dealing?" I asked again.

"Oxycodone," Roy said. "About half a million dollars' worth. We're talking about twenty-five thousand pills."

I swallowed hard. I was thinking of irony again. Here I was, a full-blown, self-confessed Adderall addict, dealing in another form of widely abused prescription medication. It was difficult not to imagine divine intervention at work, the universe punishing me for my forthcoming crime, a reaping of what I'd sowed.

"Where did you get all those pills?" I asked. I was watching a little piece of rubbish roll down the alley like a paper tumbleweed spinning toward the darkness. Since I was involved, I wanted to know as much about the operation as I could. A good quality manager was always on the lookout for potential pitfalls, and knowledge was power here in this alley same as it was at Lithio Systems.

"Nicky has a supplier, a rogue pharmacist up in Canada who siphons off the pills," Roy said. "A middleman trucks them down to Nicky, who uses mules like me to distribute to the buyers. We're the wholesalers. The Moreno brothers will put the pills on the street. They've got distribution to move the product."

"So these drugs will end up where?"

"Everywhere, man," Roy said. "Don't get all righteous on me, Gage." Did he know I was thinking about school-aged kids popping pills I helped put in circulation? "You back out on me and it's a shit storm for you."

Roy looked at me like I had somehow forgotten what he had threatened to do without my cooperation. With or without me, one fact remained—these pills were going to find a home in somebody's bloodstream.

"I get that you're nervous, but good sight lines or bad, this is an easy drop."

Roy sounded very convincing, or at least I wanted to be convinced. Either way, I was looking for the fastest and easiest way out of my predicament. That was what my ears were telling my brain this would be.

"What about the cops?" I asked.

"Between Nicky and the guys the Moreno brothers work for we've got half of the East Boston blues on payroll. We got more to worry about from the bad guys than the good guys. That's just the nature of things in this line of work. Trust me."

"Trust you?" I said. "Yeah, sure. Roy, there's nobody I trust more." Despite my sarcasm, I believed what Roy said about Nicky.

Roy gripped my arm hard as he dragged me deep into the alley.

"Now listen close," he said. "The Moreno brothers are going to enter the alley by boat. We'll get here thirty minutes before the drop and case the place. If we see anything different than what we're seeing now, we walk. Assuming nothing is out of the ordinary, when the brothers show, I'm going to hand them the case. They should just take it and give me the cash. They'll leave by boat and we get back in the car. Simple as that."

"What am I going to do?"

"You're going to stand right here," Roy said, stomping his foot on the ground, making an X with the heel of his big black boot. "Right on this spot."

"What if I just run?" I suggested.

"Then things might get ugly. Let's go. Anna needs those papers."

We walked out of the alley together, and soon enough Roy and I were again seated in his Camaro. Rather than pull out, Roy leaned over and reached for something tucked under my seat. When his hand came free I saw he was holding a gun, a pistol of some sort.

"Ever fire one of these?" Roy asked, flashing me a quick glimpse of the weapon before tucking it back underneath the seat.

"What is it?" I asked.

"It's a gun," Roy said. He wasn't being condescending, even though he had reason to be.

"No, I know it's a gun," I said. "What kind of gun is it?"

"Does it matter?"

"To me."

Brad owned a gun, which he kept in his basement, locked in a gun safe, adhering to all the safety protocols with the same attention to detail that Karen and I used when fussing over the proper installation of Max's car seat. I'd held his gun before but never fired it, though I'd been meaning to take Brad up on his offer to join him for an afternoon of shooting at the gun range. Despite my curiosity, I knew a lot more about lithium ion batteries than I did firearms.

"It's a Glock 17," Roy said. "9x19 caliber."

"9x19? What kind of caliber is that?"

Roy sucked down a breath to keep in his frustration. "Nine is the bullet diameter in millimeters. Nineteen is the case length in millimeters," Roy said.

"Right," I said.

"Shit," Roy said.

"What?"

"You really are clueless."

"Why are you showing it to me?"

"Because I want you to carry it."

"I thought you said this wasn't dangerous."

"It isn't, but I still want you to carry it."

"Why?"

"Just think of it as backup in case something absolutely crazy goes down—which it won't, but I prefer to have my bases covered. If something unforeseen happens you'll want to be able to protect yourself, or me."

"Look," I said, coming up with this suggestion on the spot, "why don't you bring Lily in on this deal as your lookout and don't tell Nicky. Just leave me out of it?"

Roy nixed that plan with a shake of his head. "It has to be you. Trust me, I'd bring Lily along if I could because I trust her a whole lot more than I do you, but Nicky's got a thing against girls and drops, which is why I arranged for him to meet you. If he found out she was there instead of you, I'd be in deep shit. Now I've vouched for you, so he's expecting you'll be a part of this exchange. It's either you do this job, or you're fucked by me. You decide how it goes down."

I nodded, showing my commitment to this plan as much as I was committed to getting rid of Roy and Lily. I got it, really I did. Roy had to bring someone along as a lookout who wouldn't take a cut of the deal—either Lily or me—and thanks to Stacks, who didn't strike me as big into gender equality, we had reached this particular moment.

Roy reached under the seat once more. When his hand emerged, he was holding Anna's folder.

"See," Roy said, dropping the folder in my lap. "I'm a man of my word."

* * *

It didn't take long for Roy to bring me to the FedEx store in Boston. I called Anna on my mobile from the store. Roy was parked across the street, sitting in his car, watching me through the front glass window. At this point, I just wanted them both gone, and I was willing to do whatever it took to get them out of my life. I wasn't going to bail on our agreement and Roy knew it. Trashing my apartment was bad enough, but imagining Lily telling Anna we had slept together, showing her what they had fished out of my trash, and then having them play Anna the tape recording of my bribe was motivation enough. The best path forward, at least for now, was for me to do Roy's bidding.

"Hey, babe," I said when Anna answered my call, "guess what I found?"

She sighed with relief. "Thank God. Where was it?"

"Took forever to find it," I said. I needed to explain what happened in the hours since we last spoke. "I turned the whole apartment upside down looking for it, and then found it in of all places on the dining room table, buried under the manual for the rocket I'm building. I guess I thought I put it in my workbag."

The lie sounded good in my ear, still Anna made a displeased noise.

"You've got to get your head on straight."

"I know. I know."

"Really, do you get what's at stake here?"

"I do. I'm sorry, sweetie. Blame it on the Adderall I forgot to take. I can still get it to you by tomorrow afternoon. Does that help?"

I got the deep sigh again.

"Can you fax me some of the pages right now?" Anna asked in a hard-edged tone. "It's obviously not going to come in time for my meeting tomorrow morning, but I could use some pages for another meeting I have this afternoon."

I looked at the folder, all half a pound of it.

"Sure," I said. "But I have to do it from a store."

"You can do it from my office. I have a fax machine."

"I'm not at home anymore," I explained.

"Where are you?"

I glanced out the window at Roy in the waiting car. "Coming home from a dry run for my first drug deal," I wanted to say. Instead of a confession, I took the safe road. I lied again. "I forgot about your fax at home. I took the folder to FedEx and if I go home I'll be late to meet Brad. I'll just spend the money to have FedEx fax the pages. It's my bad. I'll take the punishment."

Part of me knew I was going to get caught in a lie.

I just didn't know when.

CHAPTER 36

We had full attendance for the morning standup meeting. Patrice seemed to be in an extra-chipper mood because it appeared we were ready to test again. This time there wouldn't be any repeat of the last smoke-filled/fire-tainted demonstration. No, CEO Peter would have nothing to fear. We'd start the timer. Amber II would hold the phone in her unwavering plastic hand like a true champ. CEO Peter, looking distinguished in his signature blue suit, would make his appearance; he'd see time ticking away and he'd smile, not broadly but just enough for us to interpret the look as one of appreciation, like a wink with his mouth. We'd all stand around nervous, waiting for the final nod of approval, and when he announced, "Job well done," we'd break into rousing applause.

This was going to happen because Matt Simons made it so. He was all done sabotaging the Olympian project.

A standup meeting, or standup for short, provided real-time status updates to team members without a lengthy agenda. The meetings were time boxed, five to fifteen minutes, and we stood as a reminder to keep the meeting short and to the point. Three questions were asked at every standup: What did I accomplish yesterday? What will I do today? What obstacles are impeding my progress? With those three questions we could keep the meeting simple, brief, focused, and effective.

This was the leadership group, so we had one member at the meeting to represent each of the six main project disciplines: engineering, manufacturing, quality assurance, documentation, materials science, and program management, with our leader, Patrice, making a surprise guest appearance. We all looked like marathon runners with the finish line coming into view. Our eyes were elated; our bodies ached for the end. Matt Simons stood in the circle directly across from me.

Throughout the meeting, I kept looking at Matt, making brief eye contact and seeing myself in his shoes. We were not all that different, Matt and I. We both had made questionable choices to do what we believed had to be done. For Matt it meant being in charge of Olympian, forcing Adam out of the way, to ensure project success. For me, I needed to rid myself of Lily and Roy to ensure my marriage, my future.

Maybe Matt felt the end justified the means, but in my case I wasn't so sure. My heart was broken for Anna because I knew how she'd react once Lily was gone, while I was sure Simons hadn't lost a breath of sleep over Adam's plight.

I kept thinking about how what I'd done would impact Anna. The runway to having a baby was illuminated full and bright, and yes, it was Lily flying the plane, but Anna was her copilot who believed we'd soon become adoptive parents. She could help navigate the craft, act as a support and guide for Lily, be her friend and confidante throughout the pregnancy, form a bond that would last a lifetime, but a crash was coming and I was the saboteur.

Even though we had different motivations, mine being far less ignoble, I was still Matt Simons in a different disguise.

Patrice kept silent during the standup, but when her turn came to speak, she stepped into the center of the circle, something she'd never done. She looked like a woman relieved of an incredible burden.

"I have a few words to share," Patrice said. She wore the uniform of engineering management—jeans and a polo shirt. The wonks doing the heavy lifting, the hardcore engineers, considered themselves dressy if they wore toe-covered shoes to work. Most preferred loud Hawaiian shirts and cargo shorts during the hot summer months.

"First, I want you to know how much I appreciate all the hard work you've put into the Olympian project," Patrice began. "I know at times it's been unbelievably frustrating, the hours long, the task rather daunting. Now that the end is in sight, and I'm a thousand percent confident we won't see a smoking battery this time around, I want to share a little something with you. This is for your ears only, but as team leaders, Peter wanted you to know what's really at stake here."

The air in the room got saunalike heavy. We waited.

"Lithio Systems is in deep financial trouble," Patrice said.

This came from nowhere—a sucker punch to my gut. I'd assumed the business was healthy. But as a private company, partially funded by government grants, the financials weren't broadcast to us via Yahoo stock quotes. We simply went about our daily tasks believing every day we came to work the doors would be unlocked and we'd be open for business.

"Project Olympian is going to save the company," Patrice said, her voice a little flat in an impartial third party observer kind of way. "I'm not spinning hyperbole here," she continued. "This new product will give us a three-year advantage on the competition at a minimum. We've done the due diligence and nobody is even close to what we've created. Nobody."

Girish, a jovial Indian fellow who happened to be amazing on the tennis court, spoke up first. "What if we didn't deliver on time?" He asked the question I was thinking, the question in everyone's eyes.

"We were on the verge of filing for Chapter 11, and I don't think we could have emerged," Patrice said. "Without Olympian, Peter was considering a wholesale liquidation of the company. Now, because of you and your efforts, we're talking expansion."

I swallowed hard, thinking of twenty-five hundred people suddenly out of work, myself included. Some would find new employment, but I doubted it would be in this industry, not with contraction taking place. A lot of the Lithio Systems employees, especially the techies, were the midlife career types, the kind who were getting squeezed out of the workforce by younger people willing to do more for less. The upheaval would be enormous, in a make-national-news kind of way. The thought of the disaster we'd averted put a lump in my throat.

Patrice gave us more financial information. It was a bit like sitting in the doctor's office, hearing a grim diagnosis for the first time, and wanting to say, "Whoa, Doc, wait a second, that's waaaaaayyy too much information."

We listened intently, each of us pondering possible loose ends in our work, something that might derail the project and send Lithio Systems into an irreversible tailspin.

As Patrice answered questions, my thoughts drifted back to Anna. She had called, tickled about how her Humboldt meeting went, and reaffirmed her commitment to take a year maternity leave assuming the deal closed (which it would, she asserted).

"After all that drama with the missing folder, everything went perfectly," she said.

In the back of my mind, I kept thinking how Roy's recording could wreck everything if I didn't do this one thing for him. But something else was bothering me, too, something all this talk of money had stirred in my brain.

How much would Nicky Stacks pay Roy for the job? Two grand? Five? How much did a drug deal pay? Roy owed these cigarette smugglers more than a hundred thousand dollars, or so he said. I was paying him twenty, plus my cut from the deal. Was Nicky Stacks offering us each forty large to make a drop? If so, no wonder drugs continued to be a major problem in America. Maybe Roy had enough to stave off the D.C. guys he owed for a little bit longer. Still, something wasn't adding up here.

I checked my watch.

Ten in the morning.

In fifteen hours I would know if this new worry amounted to something, or nothing.

CHAPTER 37

Anna came home later that afternoon. It should have been a sweet reunion, but I was edgy and she definitely took notice. I picked her up at Logan. She offered to take a cab, but I couldn't wait to see her. I needed to be close to her, hoping her presence would be enough to ground me. In just a few hours, I was going to commit my first and last drug deal.

No matter where I was—working at Lithio Systems or driving Anna home from the airport—it seemed I was still in the alley with Roy. I'd doubled my dose of Adderall to try to get through my workday, but that didn't help me focus. I was so jacked up on adrenaline, I'd apparently taken in every vivid detail of the alley, memorized each possible escape route with startling clarity, soldering the information into my mind until I couldn't look at a street without seeing where the deal would go down.

"You shouldn't have come to pick me up, sweetie," Anna said. "What time is your train?"

"It's not until nine," I said. "But I've missed you and thought we could get at least a few hours together before I have to go."

Anna believed I was going on a business trip (because that was what I'd told her) and that I'd leave for the train right after we ate dinner (lie number two) and I'd be home by dinner tomorrow night (not a lie; I was going to crash at a downtown hotel after the drop with plans to spend the day sequestered in my room praying for forgiveness).

Ain't I a peach?

Though I wanted to be with Anna, on the drive back to our house I wasn't much of a conversationalist. Anna didn't like the change to our natural rhythm.

"What's wrong?" she asked. "Is something bothering you?"

She gave me a sideways glance with a dimpled smile, and that one look honestly made me stop breathing. She was wearing a dark pants suit with a silk shirt underneath and her long neck was ringed by a gold chain, simple and elegant. I felt like I was seeing her through a different set of eyes, younger eyes, not yet accustomed to her beauty.

I'd seen Karen in the same exact way when we first started dating. In the beginning, my love for her heightened my every sense—the sight, the smell, the taste, the touch, the sound of her breath, and her speech. It was that way with Anna, too, at the start of our relationship. But somewhere along the way, bogged down by the daily grind of life perhaps, dulled by Anna's familiar presence, I lost the sharpness, the augmented reality of us, as we settled into something far more sustainable. They call it the honeymoon phase for a reason. I guess it would be impossible to go for a long period of time feeling that primal excitement, the desire to consume my partner whole because I couldn't get close enough, a desperate yearning to become linked, fall into her arms, lock our lips, join our bodies as we made love.

Anna and I started off as lovers, and became partners somewhere along the way.

For a second, I couldn't figure out why I was seeing her as I used to. Then it came to me: because of Roy and Lily, I was afraid of losing what I had.

"I'm just thinking how lucky I am to have you," I said.

Anna reached out and put her hand on my leg.

"I missed you, too, baby," she said.

I drove us back to Arlington, navigating the heavy afternoon traffic, with Anna's hand resting on my leg, not in a sexual way but in a connecting way, a reminder of how we belonged together.

As we pulled into the driveway, my throat went dry and I felt cold all over. I had a terrible feeling I was being given another sign. Maybe it was Karen, or even Max reaching out, but something was sending me a clear reminder to appreciate Anna in the way I had those very first days.

Anna was in the shower, and I was leafing through menus trying to decide what we should have for dinner. I had just finished reviewing a one pager on an ex-con named Roy Ripson that Anna's PI contact had dug up. Everything in Roy's story matched what he had told me. He did five years in Walpole. A previous residence was listed in Tampa, Florida. He had a few other convictions, but those were misdemeanors. It wasn't the worst criminal record I could have imagined, but this guy was no Pollyanna either. At least now I knew his last name.

The doorbell rang. I marched down the hall and opened the door without asking who it was.

Lily and Roy greeted me on the front porch. Lily wore a lime green sundress that hid the size of her belly and leather cowboy boots. Roy was wearing a thin leather jacket, black tee, and dark jeans. They looked like a cool, hip couple, friends we'd never have, but I knew their true colors, and the colors of their auras, too.

Lily was holding a brown paper bag emanating a familiar odor. I could even smell Anna's favorite tofu dish.

"What are you doing here?" I asked in a low voice.

"We saw you come home and thought we might join you guys for dinner," Lily said, hoisting up the bag of Chinese food. Roy held a smaller bag, showing the pressed outline of a six-pack of beer.

"It's our treat," Lily continued. "I got Anna her favorite, so I'm sure she'll be happy to have us over. Besides, she's never met Roy. Not in any proper way."

The blood rush to my head tingled my skin. My hands became fists, my eyes turned fierce. Lily licked her lips, savoring the encounter. My heart was racing. Roy's sharp-eyed, sly expression told me what they were after. I was going to make them say it, regardless.

"Again, why are you here?"

Roy pushed past me, entering my home uninvited, and Lily followed. My mouth fell open.

"Hey, we don't want your food."

From the bathroom I heard the shower turn off and Anna call out, "Gage, is someone here?"

Roy's eyes narrowed on me, glaring.

"How much did you tell her?" he asked.

I was right. They were here to feel me out. My anger

spiked as I gripped Roy's arm, but somehow I managed to keep my voice down. "You're not welcome here."

Roy looked down at my hand clasped around his bicep, and then he lifted his head slowly until our eyes met. His expression darkened, and I knew to let go without his having to waste the words.

"Gage?" Anna called again.

I cleared my throat. "It's Lily and Roy," I said. "They brought dinner and wanted us to eat together." I unfurled my fingers from Roy's arm one by one.

"Hi, Anna," Lily called out in a sickeningly sweet voice. "Welcome home. I got you your favorite from Lilac Blossoms. I also wanted you to meet Roy. Since he's living with me now, we thought it was only right."

Anna said through the bathroom door, "That's great. Give me five minutes to change and I'll be right out."

Roy's fingers wrapped around my arm, constricting with incredible force. *His turn.* We locked eyes, Roy's look meaning to intimidate. "I'll know if you told her," he said to me. "I'll know it within minutes." He let go of my arm and his expression changed, the way a passing cloud can reveal the beauty of the moonshine it had been concealing. A warm, delighted smile came over his face.

"We'll set the food out," he called to Anna. "I'm really looking forward to meeting you." Like a snake retreating into its hole, the smile slipped back into a sneer. Roy eyed me once again.

"I'll know it," he said. "Remember, Nicky is expecting you're doing the drop. And trust me when I say, you don't want to go against Nicky Stacks."

CHAPTER 38

Anna entered the dining room with her hair still dewy from the shower and the smell of soap lingering. She saw the Chinese food spread first, Lily second, and Roy third. She'd put on a white boat-neck tee and jeans—regular attire, comfortable and relaxed.

I watched as Anna appraised Roy quickly and then looked to me. *Is he all right? Are we in danger of losing the baby? Should we be worried?* She asked all those questions with just a glance. Of course there was more, questions she couldn't know to ask.

Taking an audible breath, Anna approached Roy with her hand extended. "I'm sorry we haven't met before," she said, sounding more than a little uncertain. "I'm Anna. It's really nice to meet you."

Roy took her hand. His eyes focused in an appraising way, studying Anna's body language for any hint of knowing. Perhaps he saw worry in her eyes, but that was just her fear of things unraveling. From what I could tell, Roy seemed satisfied that I'd kept my promise about keeping quiet.

His face lifted slightly into a half grin, bringing

some warmth to his steely expression. It was a look designed to make people like him, but Anna wasn't fooled. She wasn't ready to trust him and wouldn't until she had the baby in her arms, adoption papers signed by the judge, and Roy out of her life forever. But he was here for now, a part of things, and so she'd embrace him, without letting down her guard, though it was clear to me what Anna was thinking. She worried that Roy and Lily would vanish with the baby, while I knew they were already gone.

We sat down to eat. Anna and I faced each other at either end of the table, with Roy and Lily seated between us. Nobody spoke as we spooned food from the piping-hot cartons onto the plates I'd set out. Roy put his six-pack of beer on the table, but I was drinking only water. Figured I'd need my wits about me a few hours from now. I guessed Roy was more seasoned. A couple of beers weren't going to dull his instincts any. I poured glasses of water for Lily and Anna as well, while Roy popped his beer top and drank.

I took a single bite of food, a nibble of Anna's favorite tofu dish, but it felt tasteless on my tongue. My stomach wasn't in a state to take in much food regardless. If the tables were turned, if Anna were the one deceiving me, if she knew I was destined for a brutal fall, a coming pain unlike any other, she'd have a hard time eating, too.

"I really appreciate what you're doing for Lily," Roy said. "For me, too, letting me stay with her and all."

Anna made a grimace, an attempt at a smile.

"It's fine," she said, taking a mouthful of food.

I thought about making a grand confession. I saw myself rising to my feet, pointing an accusatory finger at Lily and Roy.

"They're blackmailers," I wanted to stand up and shout. I tried to imagine how it would go down, picturing myself telling Anna in front of Lily and Roy everything—from the stolen folder, to the threats they had made against me, and predicted it wouldn't go very smoothly. For one thing, there was the little matter of the recording Roy had. That would be tough to explain away. They needed only to say how Lily had grown close to Anna and would never hurt her like that, not for any amount of money. Roy had recorded my bribe just in case I got threatening, they could say. Instead of accepting the payout, they had refused my offer and vowed to work harder to make me feel more comfortable about them—hence the impromptu Chinese dinner. I imagined Anna becoming tearful as well, enraged with me, uncertain what or whom to believe. Was I just desperate to stop the adoption? There was also the little matter of Nicky Stacks to contend with as well. Climbing back out of the hole I had dug appeared to be a lot more difficult than digging through to the other side.

Roy took a swig from the can. He held out the beer in a taunting way and wagged it in front of Lily.

"Sorry, baby, none for you."

He laughed and shoveled a heaping bite of food into his mouth, followed by another long drink. Anna retreated into herself, showing only her uncomfortable smile.

"Roy just likes to tease," Lily said, dismissing him with a wave and several—*that kooky Roy!*—shakes of her head. "To be honest, I don't really miss beer," she went on to say. "Now if we're talking a glass of wine . . ."

Anna hoisted her glass of water in solidarity and, with a look, encouraged me to do the same. "We're all in this together," she said to Lily. "If you abstain, we abstain, right, Gage?"

I shot Lily a strained little smile, finding it hard not to let my disdain show and noting how skillfully she stayed in character.

"Yes, of course," I answered, instead of saying what I was thinking: *you belong on Broadway.*

Anna turned to Roy.

"So, Roy, where are you from? Can you tell me a little about yourself?"

Roy was looking down at his food, shoveling in mouthful after mouthful like he'd gone days without eating. He chewed and at the same time used his beer to wash it all down.

"Not much to tell," Roy said, looking over at me—a warning.

"What do you do for work?" Anna asked with a slight swing to her voice. She wanted to penetrate the impenetrable. Fort Roy.

"Kinda in between jobs at the moment," Roy said. "Mostly I drive."

"Trucks?" Anna asked.

"Yeah, trucks," Roy said as if any additional explanation would sail right over her head.

Meanwhile, my insides shriveled. *Stop these lies! End this charade now!*

Lily entered the conversation: "Roy's always on the road."

And he'll soon be on the road again.

"That must get hard," Anna said, seeking common ground, something relatable. But I knew her real goal. *Are you friend or are you foe?* She was looking for a way in, a crevice through which she could peer into Roy's heart to see his intent.

"It's not so bad," Roy said. He took another swig of beer.

"And where again are you from?" Anna asked.

"Florida," Roy said. "Been there?"

"A few times," Anna said. "It's nice."

It's nice.

Obviously, Anna could give two shits about Florida. She had something else on her mind. Something she was bound to ask. I could feel it like a slight ground tremor announcing the earthquake to come. She was never a big fan of small talk.

"Roy," Anna said. "I know this is a lot for you. I'm hoping you're okay with everything. You're not going to fight the adoption, are you?"

A hush settled over the table. Everyone froze in place; only our eyes moved about the room. Lily looked over at Roy. I looked up at Anna, while Anna looked down at her plate, evidently nervous for having broached this sensitive topic with the subtlety of a brass band.

Meanwhile, Roy held his gaze on Anna until she felt compelled to look up, to look directly at him. A hot collar of sweat circled my neck, red and itchy. Anna shifted in her chair, and it was obvious she felt magnificently uncomfortable. A look from Roy had the power to burn, almost like red laser beams shooting out from his cold, gray eyes.

Everyone else had slipped into something like catatonia, but not Roy, who took in another mouthful of food and made two overly exaggerated chews. He crinkled the sides of the empty beer can with one hand and popped a toothpick into his mouth with the other. He never once broke eye contact with Anna, but Lily evidently had had enough. She looked away.

Eventually, Roy's eyebrows arched and his whole expression reset itself. This guy could terrify with one look and with another ease tension as good as any massage. Roy twisted his head in my direction, allowing his steely stare to linger, and next rotated his head slowly to make eye contact with Lily, waiting a beat or two before returning his gaze to Anna once again. He offered her a wide smile.

"Listen to me, Anna, and listen good," Roy said. I heard a faint drawl in his voice, an echo of his Southern heritage. "I think you and Gage will be the best parents this baby could ever have. Truth is, I just needed a place to stay until I get some work going. I support Lily, her decision, and you guys. You got nothing to worry about from me, Anna. I promise you that. Nothing in the least."

Anna and I made eye contact. The joy I saw on her face, the tears glassing over her eyes, hollowed out my guts.

Anna pushed back from the table. "Please excuse me," she said, dabbing at her eyes. "I need to use the bathroom."

Soon as she was gone, Roy gripped my leg with crushing force.

"Good boy," he said. "You kept your mouth shut."

Digging through is easier than climbing out . . .

Anna returned from the bathroom with a tissue. "Gage, are you all right?" she asked. "You don't look so well."

"He's fine," Roy said, lengthening the word fine—*fiiiinneee*—as if I were more than okay. "I think he just ate a bad shrimp is all."

From under the table, out of Anna's view, Roy kicked

me. I looked down at him flashing his phone, making sure I took special notice of his finger hovering just above the play button on the built-in recorder app.

Digging through . . .

Yeah, the drug deal was going to go down.

Eight hours to go.

CHAPTER 39

Roy and I hadn't said a word in the last ten minutes. He was really working his toothpick, thinking about something. I was thinking about how I'd ended up in East Boston, on the verge of committing a terrible crime, amazed how it all began with meeting Lily, the crying woman. Of course, I was also thinking about Anna, trying to stifle my guilt with thoughts of how my actions were justified. We had to rid ourselves of Lily and Roy. These weren't the sorts of people we'd want in our lives.

The pale blue glow of moonlight spilled into the Camaro, putting a natural spotlight on the muscles of Roy's ropy neck and arms. We were both wearing tight-fitting, long-sleeved compression shirts—black, of course; new purchases Roy had made—as well as our darkest pants and shoes. Roy looked like something out of a Nike commercial, all defined and cut, while I looked a little bit like somebody lying on the couch watching Roy's Nike commercial.

In the trunk of the car was a black case. Just to make a point, to prove to me this was the genuine article,

Roy had popped it open to show me the sock-sized bags of pills—thousands and thousands of pills.

"That's half a million dollars right there," Roy said, picking up one of the bags and bouncing it in his hands. The pills inside rattled like some sort of rhythmic instrument.

I'd already popped some pills of my own, an extra push of Adderall—just a few milligrams more than my usual OD. I was still bothered by the finances of this deal, curious to know if the combined payout, my contributions, plus Roy's cut, would buy him time with the D.C. smoke smugglers, or cover the debt completely. When I brought it up to Roy on the drive back to Eagle Square, he looked at me but didn't answer. I pressed him for a response.

"Just tell me," I said. "How much is Nicky paying us for this job?"

"Enough," Roy said with force, implying two meanings: enough to take care of his problem and enough of my asking questions.

For ten minutes, while we sat parked just south of the floodlights illuminating the warehouse truck bay, I didn't press him for an answer. But my patience ran out.

"I can't believe there's enough cash here," I said, fighting off a shiver of cold even though the night was windless and humid. "Are you telling me Nicky's paying eighty grand?"

"You know what you should be doing?" Roy asked, pointing a finger at me and cocking his head to flash me a sneer. "You should be thinking about this deal." He tapped me multiple times just above my heart with the tip of his finger. It hurt, too. "Picture it in your mind. See it going down, because if it's not clear in your head the way you imagine it should be, it's going to be whatever it wants to be, and that could end up real bad for the both of us."

"I'm going to stand at the end of the alley keeping watch," I said. "How hard can it be?"

Roy moved mongoose quick, grabbing the front of my shirt and pulling closer before I could pull away. He got up in my face, flashing me his angry eyes, jabbing at my skin with his toothpick, bathing me with his hot breath.

"This isn't a game, Gage," he said. "There are no do-overs, here. No second chances. What I need is for you to do your job and do it well."

I detected a slight tremor in Roy's voice, a chink in his personal armor, and there was no doubt something was making him very edgy. The Moreno brothers? Nicky Stacks? Or was it the other something, perhaps related to the unsolved issue of money? As I tried to pinpoint the source of his distress, Roy strengthened his grip on my shirt and bent over to reach for something underneath my seat.

When his hand reappeared he was holding a gun. He shoved the weapon into the palm of my hand, then forced my fingers closed around the handle. Without my having to make any adjustments, my fingers slid into the notches of the grip.

"This is a real gun," Roy said, still keeping hold of my shirt, twisting it some more as if he was helping me wring out some water. "It weighs nine hundred and ten grams loaded. It's a hundred eighty-six millimeters long. It has a mag capacity of seventeen, a trigger pull of five-point-five pounds. That's not a lot of pounds of pressure for something that takes a whole heck of a lot of balls to make happen. Now, listen and listen close." Roy's teeth were clenched, making his pronounced jawline look even more chiseled. "If I'm in trouble out there, I'm counting on you—you, nobody else, Gage, just you—to make five-point-five pounds of pressure happen. Does that make sense? Is that being clear enough? Try this just to be sure: if something happens to me, it's not going to be good for you. If Nicky doesn't get his money, there's no country big enough to hide you. We'll all be dead."

I assumed the weapon was loaded, but that didn't stop Roy from squeezing the hand that held the gun until the bumps on the grip dug into my palm. My mind flashed to Nicky Stacks in his restaurant, to his hateful face. A cold trickle of fear crept up my spine, one vertebra at a time.

Roy held my gaze, boring the seriousness of this moment into my skull as if his eyes were two drill bits. I nodded, but Roy wouldn't let go of my hand. I nodded again, more convincingly I suppose, because he released his grips on my shirt and my hand. The hardness on his face, in his eyes, lingered as he pulled back to study and assess my resolve. Something wasn't right about this. I was even more convinced of it.

"What are you planning, Roy?" I said.

"Five-point-five," Roy repeated.

Without waiting for a reply, he opened the door and got out of the car.

Thirty minutes to go.

CHAPTER 40

Roy was right about Eagle Square at this time of night. It was really quiet. Thanks to the moonlight, I could see the dilapidated school buses parked in the adjacent lot. The top of the oil tanks were just silhouettes, but if I strained my eyes I could make out darker splotches where rust had won out over paint. One white cargo truck, maybe twenty feet long, was parked in the loading zone in front of the red brick building. The leaves on the trees lining the chain-link fence were still as the night. Everything looked familiar but different at this hour. It was eerily quiet, and the air felt thick with menace.

I could hear our footsteps as we entered the alley. Roy walked ahead, swinging the case of pills in his hand. The gun, tucked securely into the waistband of my jeans, felt like a tumor on my skin. I watched as Roy vanished into the darkness of the alley. Following, knowing this was unwise, I kept to the plan. Between my nervousness and the Adderall, I wondered how Roy thought I could hold a gun, let alone fire it straight if I had to. As we walked, I reconfirmed my vow to see this through. To save Anna, to save myself from Lily and Roy, the deal would go down.

Roy strode ahead of me, quickening his pace, moving in a nonchalant manner. Maybe he emboldened himself by acting as though he had nothing to fear. From here I could smell the brackish water of the Chelsea River. I continued down the alley, past the warehouse, into a much wider enclosure.

In front of me were stacks of wooden pallets and a Jenga puzzle of square-shaped containers stacked some fifteen feet high. Farther down were a number of truck trailers, varying in length between twenty and fifty feet or so, and a couple flatbeds with some cargo already loaded. The Dumpster was overflowing with trash, mostly brown paper wrappings and cut-open cardboard boxes. An open-ended storage unit, shaped in a semicircle, was filled with blue plastic barrels. They must not have contained anything valuable, because I couldn't see a single security camera. We were invisible here.

Roy walked to the water's edge. This wasn't the plan. We were supposed to meet the Moreno brothers in the alley, not in this open area. I could hear the small river waves lapping gently against the rocky shoreline. The river itself looked like a thick, black line cut into the earth separating Boston from Chelsea. An L-shaped dock jutted out into the water.

I quickened my steps to catch up with Roy.

"What are we doing here?" I asked, my voice quavering.

"This is where they want to meet," Roy said.

I looked at him, incredulous. "What about the sight lines?" I asked. "What about the quick escape? I thought we had this worked out already."

Roy tossed my concerns aside with an indifferent shrug.

"This is the new drop zone," he said. "Take up position by the storage shed over there." He pointed to a twenty-by-twenty-foot white clapboard shed topped by green shingles.

I wasn't budging—not yet, anyway. The change in plan sent a fresh surge of fear rolling through my gut.

"We didn't talk about this. This wasn't the plan. What about the escape routes? What about all the precautions we reviewed?"

Roy shot me an irritated look. "I got a text. They want to do it by the water. Faster out for them. Everything looks good, so the drop happens here. Get in position. Just stay out of sight unless something goes wrong."

"How will I know it's gone wrong?"

Roy kept his head down, his gaze fixed to his feet, but the arc of a smile creased the sides of his mouth, as though my ignorance amused him.

"Trust me," he said, making eye contact, "you'll know. Now get in position."

Roy pulled out his gun, checking it over. He didn't threaten me with the weapon, but I got the message. I scuttled across the enclosure, feeling diminutive against a backdrop of towering stacks of containers and supersized truck trailers.

I reached the side of the shed feeling like a shipwreck survivor who'd just found the life raft. Here I felt sheltered. I couldn't speak even if I had something to say. My focus was on controlling my breathing. *This will soon be over,* I kept saying to myself, taking in a long breath and letting it out slowly. I concentrated on the sounds, the waves lapping, a car driving somewhere off in the distance, the scramble of Roy's feet scraping on the blacktop. *This will soon be over and Roy and Lily will be gone and Anna and I can start anew. This will soon be over . . .*

Soon, I heard the whine of a small craft's engine on approach.

CHAPTER 41

From the side of the shed it was impossible to see the water, so I leaned my body out just far enough to expose my head but nothing else. The boat glided along the dark water leaving behind a thin wake that lapped against the shoreline. It looked like a Boston Whaler, an open cabin sport fishing boat. I could also see the outline of two shadowy figures with heavy-weight builds. One of them cut the engine, and it sputtered to silence as the boat sailed toward the landing on fast-moving water.

Roy walked the length of the dock with the attaché case of pills in his hand, and caught a mooring rope as it was tossed to him. He slid the looped end of the rope around a wooden piling. My ears picked up the clang of the boat softly smacking against the dock, but I couldn't hear any words exchanged. The tide was high, so the Moreno brothers climbed onto the gunwale and jumped onto the dock without needing to use the ladder. Each brother carried an object. One had a duffel bag that looked to be stuffed with something—money, I suppose. The other carried a steel Halliburton attaché case.

More money?

Roy turned his back to the brothers—*Shoot me if you dare,* or so his gesture conveyed. He displayed no fear or agitation; his movements were lithe and confident, like a panther's. He completed his walk down the dock, never once glancing over his shoulder.

The brothers followed, bags and cases in hand. Football players stuffed in crisply pressed suits, with swarthy complexions, square shoulders, square heads on tree stump necks, and chests threatening to pop the buttons on their white oxford shirts. I didn't know what one normally wore to a major drug deal, but it seemed to me that Roy and I were underdressed.

Stay out of sight, I reminded myself. My job was not to be seen but to be present. Nicky Stacks thought of me as added security, vouched for by Roy as someone who could handle himself in a scuffle, who knew his way around crime, and could recite gun stats off the top of his head. Roy had me pegged as something quite different—his free pass out of a death sentence. He knew my skills were sorely lacking, so he opted to do the deal alone, with me an added measure of protection relegated to the shadows. If Johnny (the guy who I replaced) were here, he'd probably be standing right beside Roy, one itchy hand hovering a wrist snap's length from his gun. My orders were to come out from my hiding place only if needed, like a fire ax with instructions to break glass in case of emergency.

Stay out of sight unless something goes wrong.

My breathing came in shallow bursts.

Nothing will go wrong. This is the right thing to do. There was no way out, no other choice to make.

My mind was a powerful deceiver.

The deal was happening, but nothing was said. This was a sort of dance, no speaking required. Everyone knew the movements, exactly how to hit their marks. Roy raised his case and popped the latches, holding it in such a way to show each brother the contents within. The Moreno brother with the duffel unzipped the bag, and I caught the flash of paper inside as he hefted it up to show Roy. Roy nodded, still no words exchanged, the dance macabre continued.

When Roy reached for the duffel of cash, however, the dance moves turned to the unexpected. The Moreno brother who was literally holding the bag pulled the cash away, out of Roy's reach.

Roy spoke, his first words of the rendezvous.

"What's going on?"

The other Moreno brother set the metal case on the ground. He popped open the latches, each one coming undone with an audible click. From within he took out a device, flat and square. It took me a moment to recognize its form and function.

A scale.

"What the hell are you doing?" Roy asked. I detected deep concern in his voice as it carried across the enclosure.

"We were told to weigh the delivery," the brother with the scale said in a thick Hispanic accent. I watched him set the scale on the ground.

"Lucas," Roy said, "what are you talking about? Who told you to weigh it? Come on, guys. We've done business before. Why waste the time? Let's get this done and get out of here."

The other brother reached into his jacket. His meaty hand momentarily vanished inside a curtain of finely tailored fabric. It came out holding a gun made of black steel. It looked a lot like the weapon Roy had given me.

My heart shot up into my throat.

"Jorge," Lucas said to the man with the duffel. "Ask Roy to hand me the case."

Jorge raised his gun and trained the barrel of the weapon at Roy's head.

"I'm asking," I heard Jorge say, also in a thick accent.

Roy glanced over his shoulder toward the shed where he knew I was hiding out. One look told me all I needed to know: *get ready, Gage, you're going to have to make an appearance.*

I had no intention of coming out from my hiding spot. This was way beyond my pay grade. These two guys, Lucas and Jorge Moreno, were killers, cold souls stuffed inside fancy suits. I was a quality assurance engineer whose only experience firing a gun was limited to playing the arcade game Big Buck Hunter at the local Cineplex. My feet were rooted to the ground and I didn't think I could move them even if I wanted to.

"Put the pills on the scale," Lucas said. "We have the number. We know what this should weigh."

"Come on, guys," Roy said.

Jorge moved fast for such a huge man. In a blink's time, he'd come around behind Roy, locked one beefy arm around his neck, and in the same movement managed to get the gun pressed up against Roy's temple.

"Weigh it," Lucas said. "That's the order."

"Nicky wouldn't stiff you guys," Roy said.

"Nicky isn't who we're concerned with," Lucas said. "Don't you know our network extends way past D.C., hombre? We've got the whole East Coast, asshole, so we've heard things about you, money you owe. We agreed to let Nicky send you on this drop, but let's just say the level of trust here is below our standards."

Again Roy glanced my way. *Get ready,* his eyes

were saying. *This is about to get very ugly.* I imagined Roy's pulse was hammering as fast as mine.

"Okay, okay," Roy answered in a strangled voice. "Tell your boy to let go of my neck and we'll weigh it, no problem."

Lucas nodded, and Jorge slowly uncoiled his arm from around Roy's throat. Roy rubbed at the spot where the pressure had been most constricting. Then, looking deflated, he handed the case to Lucas. From inside the Halliburton case, Lucas removed another duffel bag all crinkled up, along with a pen-sized flashlight.

"I know how much this bag weighs," Lucas said, unfurling the duffel with a flick of his wrists. He dumped the pills from Roy's case into the duffel and then placed it on the scale.

"Get on your knees," Lucas said.

Roy hesitated. Jorge, who had remained standing behind Roy, put one hand on his shoulder. He raised his other arm until the barrel of his gun was pressed up against the back of Roy's head. Roy was shaking violently like a chill he couldn't warm.

"Come on, boys," he said, his voice cracking ever so slightly. "Let's be reasonable here."

"We're just following orders," Lucas said.

Studying his face, I imagined what Lucas was seeing—digital numbers showing on a small display screen, illuminated by the penlight in his hand. Meanwhile, Roy looked like a man aware he was taking the last few breaths of his life.

And that was when I knew the answer to the money question that had been troubling me. Twenty thousand from me, along with whatever Nicky Stacks was paying for this deal, did not equal the debt Roy owed to his smoke-smuggling buddies down in D.C. He needed more money. That was why he was so upset about working for Nicky. He'd never intended to make a clean exchange. He'd brought me along instead of some guy named Johnny because I wouldn't have known better. He knew the risk going in, and was betting the Moreno brothers had no reason to weigh the drop.

But from the get-go, they were on the lookout for the swindle, the cheat, the double cross. Roy was a dead man regardless, so he'd skimmed the pills, accepting the risk, and planned to sell what he siphoned off on his own.

And Lucas and Jorge were about to find out what he'd done.

CHAPTER 42

A yellowish beam shined like a spotlight on the scale's display. Roy was still on his knees with Jorge standing behind him. The gun in Jorge's hand was no longer pressed up against the back of Roy's head, but it was only a few inches away. Roy's shoulders sagged.

"I think we have a problem," Lucas said. He elongated the word *problem* like Ricky Ricardo would if he were scolding Lucy.

Jorge looked over at his brother, while Roy took the opportunity to turn his head and look at me. His pained expression cleaved my heart. He was a hard man, a tough man, a blackmailer, but I felt deep compassion for him. Sympathy for the devil. I didn't approve of Roy. I would never extol his virtues. He was depraved and poisonous, but I didn't want to watch him die.

Something else was happening here. Something I almost didn't pick up on because my thoughts were gummed with terror. He wasn't calling out for me. He wasn't going to make my presence known. Whatever was going to happen, it would be the force of my will, my conscience, my decision to leave these shadows or to stay concealed.

Roy already knew what I had just figured out. My only chance to save him was the element of surprise. If he called for me, Jorge would shoot Roy and surely the two of them would hunt me down and I'd become a one-day news story. I could see the headline now: QUALITY ASSURANCE MANAGER MURDERED IN DRUG DEAL GONE WRONG. For all of Roy's detestable qualities, he was not going to panic. No, he was going to give me the choice. Would I be willing to risk my life to save his?

"Roy," Lucas said, stepping away from the scale. "You're short. You're very short on this delivery."

Roy was shaking his head.

"That's impossible," Roy said. "All I did was bring the case."

Jorge came around front and, with a sweeping motion of his arm, pistol-whipped Roy in the side of the head.

Roy's face contorted as he fell to the ground. When he rose, I saw the gash on his cheek and a thin trickle of blood.

Lucas took two steps toward Roy and hefted him up by his shirt. He got him steady on his knees once more. As he did this, Jorge lifted the back of Roy's shirt and removed the gun from the waistband of his black jeans. He tossed the weapon onto the duffel bag of cash, where it landed with a soft thud. Still kneeling, Roy's head bobbed forward as he fought to stay conscious, and just when I thought he was going to pitch headfirst onto his face, he snapped it violently back. He reminded me of people I'd seen nodding off in a meeting, who for some reason were suddenly jarred awake.

Jorge held onto Roy's shirt to keep him upright, while Lucas holstered his weapon and paced in front.

"Roy, Roy, Roy," Lucas said in an admonishing tone. "Listen to me carefully. I am not going to beat a confession out of you. Do you understand what that means?" He waited for an answer. "No? Let me tell you then. It means I am going to kill you. Those are my intentions. But I will give you one chance. Who knows? Maybe I'll be lenient."

Could I watch a man get murdered in cold blood and do nothing to intervene?

"Where are the drugs you took?"

"I don't know what you're talking about," Roy said. Nobody looked convinced, even Roy. Jorge let go of Roy's shirt and backpedaled a couple steps, as if he wanted to get some distance from the splatter zone. He retrained his weapon on the back of Roy's skull when he felt he'd gone far enough away.

"Let's try again," Lucas said. He squatted in front of Roy, grinning like a happy jack-o'-lantern. "Where are the drugs? Now, we also kill your girl. You understand me? Maybe you have hard time with my English." Lucas pantomimed the action of shooting Roy with his fingers. Then he trained his make-believe weapon on an invisible target—Lily, presumably—and made another gesture of firing a gun, his wrist rising slightly to signify the kick from a discharge. "Product is missing. Where is it?"

"It's . . . it's in my car," Roy said, panting hard, the breath leaving his body to make room for the relief of his confession. "It's in my car . . . it's in my car." He bowed his head, chin to his chest, evidence of his shame.

"And where is your . . . car?" Lucas said without standing, delaying the word *car*, for effect.

"I parked it at the end of the alley," Roy said. "It's a Camaro."

"Good," Lucas said, rising, using his hands to brush clean his suit pants. "Jorge, kill this son of a bitch."

Roy looked up at Lucas, confused and terrorized. He thought he'd bought himself more time.

"I don't care if you're lying to me," Lucas said. "Either we find the pills you took or we don't. Figured I'd at least give it a shot to get back what you stole. But Nicky, Nicky Stacks needs to be sent a message: he needs to hire better help, and you will be a very bloody telegram."

Lucas nodded to Jorge, who stepped back to take better aim. Roy cowered, hands clasped over his head.

My eyes went wide. This was going to happen. I was about to witness an execution-style murder. Everything slowed down. Jorge raised his gun higher. He widened his stance as he readied his hand. Lucas gave Roy a look of resigned remorse.

I don't remember taking those first few steps, coming out of my hiding place, but that's what I did, and I wasn't empty-handed. The gun, all nine hundred and ten grams of it, had the weight of an anvil.

I heard myself shout, "No! Don't!" The echo of my voice carried across the river in the stillness of the early morning hour.

Lucas turned to look at me, his brown eyes cooking with rage.

Jorge looked at me, too, but that wasn't all he did. He moved the barrel of his weapon away from Roy's head and aimed it directly at me. Inch by inch, Jorge raised the gun higher until it became level with my face. Then he came toward me, gun hand outstretched, closing the distance between us with long, quick strides.

Instead of retreating, which my instincts begged me

to do, I came out a bit farther, abandoning the relative safety of the shed for the zero safety of the open area. If I turned, if I ran, Jorge would shoot me in the back. At least this way I had a fighting chance, a little sprig of hope I might see my way out of this calamity alive.

In my peripheral vision I caught sight of Lucas reaching inside his jacket, presumably for his gun. Jorge continued to close the gap, but he wasn't firing. Maybe he couldn't make a kill shot from a distance, or perhaps he was just waiting for Lucas to give the command.

In the meantime we were both on the move, two ships on a collision course. Jorge's steps were assured and practiced, while mine were tentative, like a man walking the ledge of a high-rise building. We got to within twenty feet or so of each other. My gun was pointed at Jorge's chest, but then, because my hand kept shaking so badly, it was pointed at his arm, and then it was his other arm, and then maybe the bullet would have struck him in the leg.

Meanwhile, Jorge's gun was pointed at my face and only my face. I figured I had a breath or two between Jorge firing and me dying.

In that instant, Roy fell sideways, reaching for something as he dropped to the ground. The movement must have caught Jorge's attention. He turned his body to look at Roy. I heard Lucas shout, "Shoot him!" but I didn't know if *him* meant me or Roy.

That answer came quick. To my wide and increasingly horrified eyes, the whole series of movements happened like a scene from a Sam Peckinpah western. Jorge's waist pivoted in super-slow motion as his torso swung back in my direction. His left arm rose above his shoulder to help stabilize his right arm and, more important, the gun in his right hand. I watched the barrel of the weapon travel from my navel, up to my ribs, next to my throat, until it came to a stop between my eyes.

I had one instant to react. One second left to breathe. Five-point-five pounds of pressure needed to save my life.

I didn't think. I reacted. It was fear, the survival instinct kicking in. My finger pulled the trigger mechanism. A flash, bright and blinding, a flare in the dark erupted from the barrel of the gun. My hand lifted skyward from the recoil. The echo of gunfire rang out, creating a fading ghost of what I'd done.

A small hole opened in Jorge's chest right where his heart would be. Blood exploded out from the wound in a quick and violent burst. Jorge's eyes rolled into his head as he fell. The bullet's impact pushed his body backward, but then he came forward again as his weight shifted. The gun dropped from his hand as he crumpled to the ground.

Lucas screamed, "Jorge!"

As this was happening, Roy had reached into his boot and his hand came out wielding a six-inch knife. Lucas didn't see this new threat. He was too busy gaping wide-eyed and horrified at his fallen brother.

Even with my hand shaking—I'd probably just killed this man—somehow I managed to hold onto the weapon. But I wasn't thinking about using it again. Cemented where I stood, my body was frozen except for my quaking hand.

Lucas didn't waste time profiting from my momentary paralysis. He took careful aim with his gun, but never got a chance to set his sights on me. Roy lunged at Lucas like a coiled-up snake making a fast strike. The blade tore through the fabric of Lucas's suit, buried to the hilt at midthigh. The shriek of pain that followed may have echoed at the same decibel level as my gunshot.

Lucas, holding onto his leg and yelping, dropped to his knees at the same instant Roy scrambled back to his feet. The danger wasn't over. Far from it. Lucas still had a gun. He could still shoot me, and that seemed to be his intention as he re-aimed the weapon in my direction. Jorge was no longer a threat, judging by the large swath of crimson spreading from the hole in his chest, but I thought for sure Lucas would get off a shot if he could.

I dropped into a crouch and covered my head with my hands. Obviously, I hadn't done much military training, or I would have known the maneuver wasn't going to stop a bullet from burrowing into my skull.

Before Lucas could fire his weapon, Roy kicked him in the side of the head with his big, heavy boot. Lucas fell sideways and landed hard. I heard a clatter as the gun dropped from his hand and skidded a good distance across the blacktop. The contact created a small opening for Roy to make a dash for the duffel bag of cash, but Lucas was able to move with surprising speed considering his injured leg. He grabbed his gun in a movement best described as a slide into first. Flipping onto his back, Lucas got off three shots at Roy, all in quick succession. Bullets sparked against the blacktop, landing near enough to force Roy into a change of direction.

Lucas was on his feet, charging at Roy, putting himself between the duffel bag of money and the other bag of drugs. If Roy went for either, Lucas would have a clean and easy shot. Roy must have known it, too, because he broke for the alley and screamed at me to run while he sprinted past.

I didn't hesitate. I sprung up from my crouch, still holding the gun, and made a frantic sprint for the alley entrance falling into step behind Roy, who was maybe ten feet in front of me. My arms were flailing and my spindly legs kicked out like a deer venturing onto an ice-covered pond before I finally got some traction. I heard a pop—no, make that two—but didn't feel the sting of any bullets.

Roy gave one last look over his shoulder, and I saw him hesitate. Did he want to go back? He thought about it, but Lucas and his gun must have made him think otherwise.

Sprinting, my arms pumping, I wouldn't dare risk looking behind me as Roy had done. I imagined Lucas on approach, his suit jacket flapping like a cape, his gun hand extended out in front of him and pointed at my back like death's long finger. I raced by the wood pallets and stacked crates and soon I was at the opening to the alley. Roy had already vanished into the darkness in front of me.

I listened for the footfalls, for another pop of gunfire, but everything was silent now. Where had Lucas gone? Did he decide to give up the chase? Was he back trying to triage his brother?

I spilled out of the alley just as Roy was pulling the Camaro away from the curb. I caught up to him in time to slam my hand against the car in frantic, rapid succession. *Don't leave me!* my hand was saying. Then I did the strangest thing. I pointed the gun at the windshield because I worried Roy wasn't going to let me in. But he did. He even leaned over and opened my door.

"Get in!" he yelled.

I clambered into the front seat as Roy pulled away from the curb. The squelch of tires gave off an angry hiss and the sour odor of burning rubber. Roy was looking down the alley as we sped by. His eyes were distant, vacant even. It was as though he could see all the way to the dock, where a duffel bag full of money and another bag full of Oxycodone would be found, along with a dead man I had just murdered.

CHAPTER 43

We drove in silence with Roy going through toothpicks like they were M&M's. He wove in and out of Boston streets, his eyes darting about in a predatory way, clearly on the lookout for the police. This was the quietest hour of the day, two o'clock in the morning. The bars were closed, the commuters were sleeping, no reason to be out on the road.

Unless, of course, you were involved in a drug deal gone wrong.

"Why'd you do it, Roy?" I said. My voice came out shaky, like a kid who had fallen and was doing his best not to cry in front of his friends. "Why didn't you just do the deal straight-up?"

Roy's face turned cherry red. "Because I needed more money!" he screamed, smacking his hand against the steering wheel. "Because you didn't have enough. I never wanted to double-cross the Moreno brothers, but what choice did I have? Your wife and kid got killed by a drunk driver! Didn't you get more money? How could you not have gotten more money from that?" Roy was seething, his face in a snarl.

"So this is my fault?" I shouted back at him. "You

set up some crackerjack blackmail scheme but you didn't even know if I had what you needed? That's insane, Roy! And now I've got blood on my hands! I killed a man tonight. I killed him. Do you get that? I shot him."

I was saying this to myself as much as I was saying it to Roy. The reality was sinking in. I was a murderer, forever and always.

Somehow my ire soothed Roy's. He looked at me with a different kind of understanding. We were brothers.

"He was going to kill you. You did what you had to do."

My hands were trembling as we drove past a shuttered pizza joint. Looking at those darkened windows, I couldn't imagine ever eating food again. My guts were twisted and knotted. I imagined they'd stay that way forever. As we drove aimlessly around the quiet streets of Boston, past empty office buildings and darkened storefronts, I kept seeing Jorge, a bloody corpse flat on his back on the ground only a few feet away from where my gun had discharged. He was the stuff of my new nightmares. My head felt full of sorrow and gloom. This couldn't be undone. There was no going back or making a different choice. I did what I did and would forever live with the consequences of my actions. And I hated myself for it.

"How much product did you siphon off?" I asked Roy. "How much?"

"Enough to cover my debts and get me out of town for a while."

"You didn't think they'd eventually figure it out?"

"I wasn't solving my problem, Gage. I was buying myself some time."

"Now what?"

"Now I've got to drop you off and go see Nicky."

My stomach lurched at the mention of Nicky's name.

I thought back to our meeting and cringed at the memory of those hateful eyes. And then it dawned on me. We had just lost half a million dollars of Nicky's money. Gone. Left on a dock for Lucas to carry away in his Boston Whaler, along with his dead brother.

"What the hell are you going to say to him?" My heart was hammering. I felt cold and hot all at the same time, grossly uncomfortable in my own skin. All I wanted to do was go home. I wanted to crawl into bed with Anna, inhale the familiar scent of her sleep, and feel the cottony fabric of her pajamas pressed against my skin. I wondered if Max and Karen were watching from wherever they could watch. Did they know what I had done? Were their spirits at the dock when I pulled the trigger? Was it Max who'd given me five-point-five pounds of courage to do what had to be done?

"I'm going to lie," Roy said. "I'm going to tell him we were ambushed. That Lucas tried to kill us and so we killed Jorge in self-defense. I'm going to lie to him."

"Will that work?" I asked.

"Will Nicky Stacks forget I owe him half a million dollars?" Roy gave me a sidelong glance. "You have a better chance of being a daddy to Lily's baby than you do of Nicky forgetting his money."

"So what are we going to do?"

"Let me handle it."

"And the police?"

Roy laughed, but not in a way that said I amused him. It was more like he couldn't fathom how little of the underground life I understood.

"There won't be any cops," he said, snapping a toothpick in half. "There's not going to be any reports of a shooting, either. They didn't have any video surveillance back there. Nothing. What happened on the dock never happened. Jorge is going to drop off the face of the earth, and Lucas is going to look for retribution, either in cash or blood. That's how this is going to go down."

"So we go to Nicky for protection?" I couldn't wrap my head around being a part of his world, teammates with Roy, but the blood on my hands was as binding as any legal document.

"I go to Nicky and we take it from there," Roy said. "You lay low. Don't do anything stupid."

"What, like going to the cops?"

Roy took his eyes off the road so he could fix me with a baleful look. "Don't even say that." He wagged a finger. "You do that and we're both good as dead. Is that clear?"

"Yeah," I said, breaking away from his angry stare to look at whatever was zooming past my window.

Roy grabbed my shirt and pulled me toward him. The sudden movement caused the Camaro to weave a bit, but nobody was on the road. "I'm not kidding. Don't you get any whistle-blowing ideas. I'll take you down myself. You're a murderer now. Don't forget that."

"No body," I said. "No cameras. No crime."

"Trust me, if you bring the heat on Lucas Moreno or any of his associates, or me, or Nicky Stacks, we'll produce a body and it'll be yours. Trust me on this. Now where am I dropping you off?"

I gave Roy the address for the Hyatt Harborside hotel, about half a mile from Logan, which I had reserved in advance. Roy didn't speak for the remainder of the drive. He was busy chewing on toothpicks, probably thinking about his next move, what he was going to say to Nicky Stacks. He just stopped talking, turned up the radio—we were listening to classic rock—and followed my directions.

When we reached our destination, Roy followed the

curved driveway and pulled to a stop in front of the hotel entrance. He left the car idling while I grabbed the bag I'd packed from the back seat of the Camaro. I headed to the glass doors, but before I got there, Roy rolled down the window and whistled for me.

"Not a word," he said. "I'll be in touch. Just lay low and we'll get through this together."

We. Together. Like we were a pack now. Roy the alpha dog, and me his bitch.

I nodded, trying to ignore the rush of blood to my head.

We. Yes, Roy. I'll be a good boy. I'll be quiet. I turned my back to Roy and his Camaro, leaving the murder weapon in his possession.

I gave the surprisingly chipper attendant my real name and my real credit card. I wasn't in hiding. The police weren't after me. Following the directions, I took the elevator to the eighth floor, found my room, and went inside. My clothes started to itch and burn. I pulled them off of me, and before I knew it I was naked in the shower, with beads of warm water cascading down my back. But I couldn't stand, my legs wouldn't hold me up, so I sat in the tub, curled in a ball with my back to the water, letting it rain on me, washing my guilt down the drain.

CHAPTER 44

The phone woke me. It took a moment to figure out where I was, and for a second I thought I was in bed with Anna. Then the strange and musty smell of an unfamiliar room hit my senses, along with the feeling of too-tight sheets and a comforter about as comforting as an X-ray room's lead apron.

I was in a hotel room in Boston. It wasn't a dream, and neither was the man I'd gunned down at the waterfront. The last time I'd woken up I wasn't a murderer. It was something I could never say again.

The curtains in my room were drawn, so I couldn't tell if the sun had risen. My eyelids, heavy with the kind of sleep only coming down from a double dose of Adderall can provide, came open with the ease of two rusted hinges. My head throbbed in a hangover way, while my body felt as depleted as my spirit.

8:45 A.M.

Had I scheduled a wake-up call?

The phone kept ringing. I picked up the receiver and said, "Yeah." That syllable encapsulated the extent of my conversational ability. I didn't bother to think about who would be calling, or why.

"Gage, it's Roy. We gotta talk. Can I come up?"

Roy's nervous voice jolted me awake with all the gentleness of a slap across my face. I wanted him to be a bad dream, too, but here we were, the blackmailer and the quality assurance engineer-cum-killer tethered to each other like Siamese twins. His anxiety was my anxiety. His terror was my terror. As far as Nicky Stacks was concerned, we were both involved, a couple of partners in crime, literally, and there was not a thing for me to do but let Roy come on up and tell me about our shared fates.

I gave Roy my room number, something the front desk attendant would not have done. I had just enough time before Roy knocked on my door to rip open one of those complimentary in-room coffee packets using my teeth (a habit I'd sworn to both Karen and Anna I was going to break, knowing I'd continue to break that promise), fill the little coffeepot that probably never got properly washed, and get the brew switch flicked on.

When I heard the knock I checked the peephole first, instinctively, even though I knew who was there. It was the way a murderer might act.

Through the peephole's fish-eye lens, I saw Roy dancing on his feet, calling to mind the old adage *ants in his pants*. Whatever he had to say, he didn't want to waste time. I started to open the door, but someone other than Roy, someone who had been standing in the hall out of my view, pushed it open with a good degree of force. Roy came stumbling into the room, evidently shoved inside by the same individual who threw open the door. Following closely on Roy's heels, and closing the door behind him with a quick click of the lock as he entered, was Nicky Stacks.

Stacks struck an imposing figure in a dark blue suit, lighter blue oxford shirt, and no tie. I hoped Nicky wouldn't want to get his nice clothes covered in my blood, but the smoldering fury in his eyes didn't make me optimistic. Roy worked his way over to the far corner of the hotel room, where a small desk might provide momentary shelter from Stacks if the rhino-sized man decided to charge.

"I'm sorry, Gage," Roy said as he shuffled past me. "Nicky made me bring him to you. He wants to talk."

"I can speak for myself," Stacks said, hovering by the door. It was not lost on me that he was blocking my only way out.

As if Stacks could read my thoughts, he put his finger to his lips in a stay quiet gesture, then pulled open his suit jacket just enough to flash me the gun holstered there. It was an impressive showing and secured my full cooperation. I wouldn't have been surprised if the gun in Stacks's holster hadn't recently been pushed into Roy's face.

"Sit down," Stacks said, pointing first at me and then at the bed.

I caught the aroma of fresh-brewed coffee.

"Do you want a cup of coffee? I have enough for two," I said.

"I don't drink coffee," Stacks said.

"Do you mind if I have one?" I asked. I didn't need the coffee to wake up. I wanted something to do with my hands.

"I think you need to just sit and listen," Stacks said. "You too, Roy. Pull up a chair."

Roy grabbed the wooden desk chair and pulled it over to the bed. Nicky took up roost on the edge of the dresser directly across from the bed and eyed us both. I'd met him only once, but Nicky's massive head appeared to have grown in size since then. It was a boulder stuck on a meaty neck. For a while he just glowered, saying nothing, and then he leaned back slightly. As he did, he touched one of his thick fingers to his eye as if he were trying to make sense of what he saw and couldn't believe people like us actually existed. I could have said the same thing about him. Roy sat beside me as if we were siblings being scolded for some offense. It didn't take an advanced degree in materials science to know that Roy's little talk with Nicky hadn't gone very well.

"Do you want to tell me what happened out there?" Stacks asked.

I looked to Roy, my partner, the leader of the pack. Roy didn't even gesture for me to answer, so I took it upon myself to tell our side of the made-up story.

"We were ambushed." I tried to sound tough, because Nicky still thought I was Roy's ne'er-do-well cousin from Florida, a genetically related badass. To my ears I sounded pretty unconvincing.

"It all happened really fast," I continued. "I shot Jorge and Roy knifed Lucas, and we had to run because otherwise we'd have been killed."

I looked to Roy, but he didn't seem at all pleased, which was alarming. Wasn't I corroborating our story? Roy's body language, chin to his chest, face buried in his hands, implied this was far from over.

"Are you checking with Roy to make sure you two clowns have your story straight?" Stacks asked me. "Because if you are, don't bother. Now, do you feel like telling me what really happened out there?"

I didn't say anything, not sure I could if I tried. Dread constricted my windpipe.

"No? Not the talkative type? Well, that's okay, because I know what happened, so let's just move on."

I continued to remain silent.

"I've been on the phone with my business associates for an hour since you two jackoffs screwed everything up," Stacks said. He pointed a wagging finger first at Roy and then at me. "It would appear we hired four of the stupidest assholes to handle this drop."

I was a bit surprised because Stacks implied the Moreno brothers were at fault as well.

"Here's the thing, Gage," Stacks said, looking directly at me. It felt incredibly unsettling to hear him say my name. "I'm sure Lucas Moreno wants to kill you for killing his brother, but I told my associates, in very clear language, that it wouldn't be right. If what Roy finally confessed to me is true, and I believe it is, then Lucas had no business taking matters into his own hands. If there was a shortage on the drop, it should have been brought to *my* attention. That's the way we do business. He had no authorization to execute anybody. None!" Stacks slapped the dresser with the palm of his hand. It made the mirror on the wall shake.

"The good news is, my associates agree. Lucas should not have threatened Roy, period. We have protocols for this sort of thing, ways of handling problems that don't attract so much attention as an all-out gunfight. It should have been up to me to make the deal whole and decide if I should put a bullet in your stupid heads or not. Do you two understand me?"

We both nodded like a pair of charmed cobras.

"Now, this might sound all well and good to you," Stacks continued, "but there has to be retribution paid for what happened, something to set things right between my associates and me."

"Nicky, I'm sorry," Roy said, shaking his head. He sounded on the verge of tears. "I screwed up, man. I'm sorry. I was desperate."

"Shut up!" Stacks snapped. "Just shut the fuck up!

Don't speak. Don't say a fucking word until I ask you to say something. Let me be very clear about this. Don't interrupt me again." Stacks's voice came out as a low rumble of thunder.

"The retribution I must pay is the money Lucas took from the deal, which means your little gunfight at the O.K. friggin' Corral has cost me five hundred large." Stacks paused. His eyes locked on me, two black beads cold as death, making me feel incredibly small under his gaze. Microscopic, even. "Because of you"—Stacks pointed his thick finger first at Roy, then to me, keeping it steady as an arrow in a bow—"I don't have the pills and I don't have the cash."

Roy again hung his head in shame while I stared blankly ahead. This was my new reality. Thanks to the crying woman, Roy, Nicky, and Lucas Moreno were all part of my life now.

Stacks went silent, pondering how to phrase what he wanted to say to us next.

"The bottom line is that the five hundred grand I should have made from the drop is now the property of my associates. The good news is that I'll continue to do business with them, but not with you two mules. You two are dead to me. No more work, no more deals, no more nothing.

"As I see it, my associates have been made whole for their loss, but me, Nicky Stacks, I'm out five hundred grand. Now, my associates consider this matter closed. They're not going to punish Lucas for going rogue because one dead brother appears to be punishment enough. But they aren't going to make me whole for my loss, either. They're kind enough just to let me keep working in this town. So I've decided you two fuckheads *are* going to make me whole."

"What do you want us to do, Nicky?" Roy asked.

There it was again: us, the proverbial we. We were a pack of two. I was with Roy, and Roy was with me.

"What I want you to do is get me one million dollars," Nicky said. "Let me repeat: you owe me one million dollars."

Roy blanched. His hands came up to his face and froze there, as if Nicky's words were a punch he had to deflect. He tried to speak, but his voice was stuck in his throat.

"I'm going to give you two weeks," Nicky said. "Two weeks to come up with the money. I don't care how you get it. Gamble. Play scratch tickets. Beg, borrow, or steal. You owe me this money. Now, Roy, if you run, I'll find you, and if I can't, as a gesture of goodwill, my associates will help. We're quite resourceful. We'll know where you'd go to get a new identity. We'll know how you'd go about disappearing. We'll know all the underground routes you'd take to drop off the grid. There's no place you can hide from us."

"But . . . but . . . we don't owe you a million, Nicky," Roy stammered. "We only lost half that."

"You owe me for pain and suffering," Stacks said, with just the whisper of a smile.

"How are we supposed to get that kind of money?" Roy asked.

"You should have thought about that before you tried to steal from me."

"And what if we can't get the money?" I asked softly.

Nicky reached inside his suit jacket. I almost jumped to my feet, ready to duck for cover if he came out wielding what I thought he might. But instead of taking out his gun, Nicky withdrew an overstuffed business envelope. I looked at it, puzzled by its contents.

"I don't know what you are all about," Nicky said, slapping the envelope repeatedly against his beefy palm. "But I know you're not cousins. I got that much out of Roy. Shame on me, because I should have done my background check on you before, but I did it after."

Roy and I exchanged anxious glances as Nicky tossed the envelope over to me like a Frisbee. It landed on my lap.

"Go ahead and open it, Gage," Nicky said. "Roy gave me your address. It was all I needed to do my digging."

Nervous as I was, I managed to unseal the envelope without it tearing. I pulled out a stack of trifolded papers from within. My body stiffened.

"That's your wife, Anna, right?" Nicky said. "I printed out her picture from her website. Man, she's beautiful."

"What are you doing?" I asked in a voice steeped with alarm.

"Go ahead and flip through the other pages. I've got your parents' address in there. I know the nursing home where Anna's mother lives. I've got it all. I've also got a gun with your fingerprints on it that will be a match for the bullet inside poor Jorge's chest. So if you run, my buddies with the police, and I do mean my buddies, will find Jorge's body, which we're keeping on ice for now, and they'll come after you. Meanwhile, I'll take a knife to your precious family and carve them up piece by stinking piece." Nicky reached inside his suit jacket pocket once more. This time he removed a six-inch switchblade knife, which he unhinged with the push of a button. The blade shot out like a viper's strike.

"You two clowns have two weeks to save your worthless lives and come up with my money," Nicky said, as he hopped down from his perch on the dresser.

The wood creaked from the release of his weight. "Like I said, if you run, I'll find you. If you screw up, I go after your family. If you don't deliver, you're all dead, and by all, I mean Anna, Lily, and you two assholes."

Nicky walked to the door and paused before opening it. Meanwhile, Roy and I didn't budge. We were frozen where we sat.

Nicky turned his eyes on me once again. "You think losing your wife and kid in a car accident hurts?" he said. "Well, let me tell you something, Gage Dekker. You don't know pain."

He walked out the door, leaving Roy and me just two weeks to come up with one million dollars.

CHAPTER 45

Roy and I were in the hotel bar. It was just after ten in the morning, so we needed to seek out hotel staff to serve us a drink. Roy ordered a double shot of whiskey, and I nodded a request for the same. Roy was really working his toothpick, gnawing at the thin sliver of wood like a starving termite. I was numb, in shock. In the span of a few hours, I'd become nothing I recognized, nothing familiar to me. The old me wouldn't drink whiskey before the sun went down. Now I was drinking it not long after it had come up.

The first swallow passed like a screech of fire, but the second tasted a whole lot better, and before Roy could say a word, I was ordering myself another.

"I'm sorry, Gage," Roy said. He took a long drink for himself. "This wasn't how it was supposed to go down."

My eyes went wide.

"Really? Tell me, Roy, how was it supposed to go down? Was I supposed to have enough in my bank account to cover your cigarette debt?"

The bartender, a twentysomething guy, was polishing some glass bottles for want of something to do. He shot us a curious over-the-shoulder glance and Roy looked at me, worried, so we took our drinks over to a table out of his earshot.

"So what now?" Roy asked.

I wanted to reach across the table and slap Roy across the face. Everything tough about him had been evaporated. Nothing about Roy intimidated me anymore—not a twitch of his sinewy muscle, a flash of his tattoos, or a sneer on his curled lips. It felt like I was pulling apart a matryoshka doll of maladies, with Lily the littlest doll inside Roy, inside the Moreno brothers, inside Nicky Stacks. Roy was no longer the hard man—he was a vulnerable man, same as me. And because of him everything and everyone I loved was in grave danger.

"What now, Roy, is you've got to save your life," I said. "And in the process, you'll save mine. So . . ." I knocked on the table for emphasis. "How are you going to come up with a million dollars? How do you criminals do that?"

Roy looked down at his feet and shook his head.

"You don't get this, do you?" he said. "We're dead. I can't come up with that kind of money. We're dead men. Drink up, because you're not going to have many drinks left."

Roy downed half his whiskey in one long gulp.

"Why didn't Nicky just kill us? Why give us the chance to run away?"

Roy gave a dismissive laugh. He straightened his posture and leaned across the table, pointing a finger at me like it was the tip of Nicky's switchblade targeting my heart. A furious look came over his face, dark and snarling, the kind that can only be perfected behind the walls of a prison. I still wasn't intimidated.

"He gave us a chance to come up with his money," Roy said. "Don't you get it? Nicky wins either way.

He's just hedging his bets and seeing if we get lucky. You ask me, he doesn't think we'll come up with the cash, but if we're dead, we definitely don't get it."

"So we go to the cops," I said.

Roy looked at me like I was an exasperating child who would never learn to ride his bike. "Let's say we do that," Roy said. "We go to the cops with the threat, and Nicky produces evidence that you committed murder. You get grilled, you turn on me, and we both go to jail."

"So, we'll be safe."

"Your family will be dead," Roy said, emphasizing his point by repeatedly stabbing the table with his finger, like Nicky would be stabbing my family. "And so will Lily."

"Not if we warn the cops. They'll be protected."

"There are crooked cops on Nicky's payroll, remember? Besides, if we go inside, Nicky has people there who will put us both in the ground."

I shrugged away my own mortality.

"So be it," I said.

I would be a shell of a person—skin, bones, and soulless—if anything happened to Anna, or to my parents.

Ever since the accident, I'd surrounded myself with memories of the dead or with the dying. I'd talked and shared with other parents who had lost a child, and spent my free time in hospital rooms making model rockets for sick kids, some of whom had no hope of ever breathing fresh air again. I gravitated to the people who hungered for second chances, because I'd learned the hardest way possible how precious those chances really were.

I would sacrifice myself to give Anna the second chance she deserved.

"You might be comfortable getting shanked on your way to lunch, but not me." Roy shook his head, his chiseled face flush. "I ain't going back inside. No way. We're going to get out from this."

"Okay, hotshot," I said, taking another sip of whiskey. "What's your plan?"

"I'm thinking," Roy said, looking at his finger as he traced some design on the table surface.

"I heard on NPR that the average bank robbery nets about twelve thousand."

Roy looked up at me, trying to get a read on my sarcasm.

"Do you still have the Oxy you siphoned off? Maybe we could sell that."

"Shut up, Gage," Roy said, his flush turning a different shade of red.

"Or maybe we could try a kidnapping plot? Extortion? I'm just brainstorming here," I said in a sarcastic tone. "It's a little something I learned at work. You toss out ideas, but remember, no idea is a bad idea."

Roy's dour expression darkened even more.

"Look, Gage, you better start getting creative here," Roy said. "You got a rich family? Because I suggest you call them and start collecting."

"A million dollars? My family doesn't have that kind of money, not even close. My father has been on disability for twenty years. I send them money to help pay the rent. If you know so much about me, you should know that."

"What about Anna?"

"She doesn't have it, either." We fell silent, taking slower sips of our drinks, thinking, thinking.

Eventually, I was the one to break the quiet. "Look," I said. "What if Stacks is just bluffing?"

"Bluffing? Nicky Stacks?"

"Yeah, what if he doesn't want to kill me because it would be too high profile? I'm a white-collar professional, and an investigation into my death might get back to Nicky."

"What does that mean? What does white-collar mean?"

"It's a business term. It means professional, managerial work."

Roy got quiet, thinking, the hard man thinking.

"So, what do you do for a living anyway?"

"I thought you checked up on me," I said.

"Only a little. I didn't friggin' look at your stupid job. What do you do?"

"Why?"

"Just tell me."

"I work for Lithio Systems," I said.

"What's that?"

"We make batteries."

"For flashlights and stuff?"

"No. More like cell phones. Computers. Laptops. Airplanes."

A smile, the first I'd seen from him.

"That sounds fancy," Roy said. He took a sip of his whiskey and his eyes darted. Thoughts were coming to him, something appealing.

"It's high tech," I said.

"Valuable?" he asked.

My throat went dry. *What could he have in mind?*

I told Roy a little about Olympian, not the trade secrets, just a thirty thousand foot overview of the landscape. He seemed to sort of understand what I was saying, but when I told him about the billions in market cap for the battery, his eyes went wide.

"That's a lot of Benjamins," he said, licking his lips.

"What are you getting at?" I asked.

Roy had the look of a guy on speed.

"Nicky's been around," he said. "He knows a lot of different types of people, all fine, upstanding citizens just like him."

"What's your point?"

"What if he can give me a name, somebody who might want to pay a lot of money to know how to make a battery like yours?"

My teeth clenched. "You want me to steal my company's secrets?"

"If I can find us a buyer, why not?"

"No," I said. "No way. I'm not going to do that."

"So, what, you'll just do nothing?"

"For a while, maybe. See what happens."

"In that case, let me offer you some advice," Roy said. "Treat your woman real fine these next couple weeks, because I'm betting they'll be the last you'll ever have."

CHAPTER 46

Home.

It had never looked so good, smelled so inviting, or made me feel so despondent. My fresh pop of Adderall was just starting to kick in when I entered through the front door with my overnight bag, looking just like the guy who'd returned home from a short business trip. I was nothing of the sort, but Anna didn't know that.

I'd spent the day in the hotel room and then just walking around Boston aimlessly, trying to kill enough hours so I could come home from my bogus business trip at a realistic time. Anna was in the kitchen when I showed up, cooking something for dinner. I smelled asparagus and got a faint whiff of the garlic and olive oil she used to baste my favorite vegetable. The important thing was that Anna was cooking my favorite food as a way of welcoming me home. She was being kind, loving, and thoughtful, and all the good things Anna was on a daily basis.

It made me feel hopelessly sad for us, for what we were about to lose, which amounted to everything. I thought about the events leading to this moment, this terrible lie I was living, and asked myself: Could this have played out differently? What if I had refused Roy's offer to assist him on the drop? What if instead he had told Anna that Lily and I had slept together? Or what if Roy had played Anna the recording of me offering them a bribe to leave? I suspect Anna and I would be in therapy, a lot of therapy, or separated, but Jorge Moreno would still be alive, and I wouldn't owe Nicky Stacks a million dollars.

But that wasn't how it played out. I made the deal to save my marriage, and everything else went right into the shitter.

Anna entered the hallway through the dining room. She wrapped her arms around my neck and gave me a passionate kiss on the lips.

"I missed you," she said.

"I was only gone a day."

I hoped my attempt at a smile didn't look as sad as it felt.

Anna took my hand and led me to the kitchen. "Come, darling," she said. "You must be starving."

I didn't think I could get down a bite of food, but for Anna's sake I would try. Besides, I could use something to wash away the harsh bite of whiskey still souring my throat. Thankfully, getting back into the groove of being home was a seamless transition. I made a salad while Anna put the finishing touches on dinner. She seemed light on her feet, pleased with life. I could feel her excitement like it was my pulse.

"So, I've got a date from Margret for our home study," Anna said as she stirred the turkey chili and sampled a bit with a wooden spoon. "It's in two weeks."

I choked on a swallow of air and nearly cut my pinky finger off while chopping a cucumber.

"Two weeks?" I repeated.

Anna gave me a backwards glance along with a smile that touched my heart. Did my eyes give me away? Could she tell I was sweating out my booze-laden morning? Two weeks. In that amount of time I would need to come up with a million dollars to save my life and get approved by the state to become a father once more. It was to be an epic two weeks.

"So what do we have to do to get ready?" My voice came out in a warble.

"We'll start by not using any of the furniture," Anna said. "I'm going to cordon it off with ropes like a museum exhibit."

Anna tried to hold a serious expression but couldn't contain the smile. Then she noticed I didn't think the joke was particularly funny. Normally I would have laughed right along with her, but I kept seeing Nicky Stacks looming above me, twirling the blade of his knife against his fleshy palm, telling me I didn't know the meaning of pain. My tongue felt thick in my mouth. Would Stacks kill me? Worse, would he hurt Anna? Kill her, even? What about my parents? Bessie?

Two weeks . . .

I thought about Roy's suggestion. What if Nicky did have a contact for him? What if it was the only way? I could do it, because I had Security Breach Team access privileges. The question was, would I?

"Honey, are you all right?" Anna asked as she crossed the kitchen floor. She got to me and got her answer all in the same instant. "Gage, you're shaking."

I held it together by biting on the inside of my cheek until tangy droplets of blood filled my mouth.

"I'm fine," I said. "I guess it's all happening and I'm a bit emotional, is all."

"Oh, sweetie." Anna's eyes brimmed with sympathy. She smoothed her hand over my cheek, the one I had been biting, and looked deeply in my eyes, trying to comfort me with the intimacy of our connection. She pulled her hand away, but I could feel her love for me linger. I battled back the tears, trying to hold myself together.

"Baby, I know this is emotional for you. I know how hard it is and what it's bringing up for you."

"No," I wanted to say. You have no idea what's really happening. Why I'm breaking down. You have no idea how much we have to fear. How close we are to death.

"I can't take away the hurt, sweetie," Anna said, pulling me into her arms. I smelled the sweet aroma of her hair, the faint scent of lilacs. I took in several deep breaths, letting her familiar smells ground me. Each breath I took served as a powerful reminder of what I was fighting for. We were two halves of two shattered lives that somehow found each other and fit together like the pieces of the same broken vase. I would do anything to protect her.

And that included getting a million dollars I didn't have.

"Seriously, what do we have to do to get ready?" I asked.

"Well, we really are going to have to keep the house spotless," she said. "I know they say they don't give us grades for housekeeping, but I'm not taking the chance."

"We don't have to baby-proof, right?" I felt sick for leading her on, because I knew how this was going to play out. But it would be better for our future if Anna felt the sting from Lily's betrayal rather than from mine.

"No, baby-proofing is not required. Speaking of

baby, I'm going to call Lily. I invited her to eat with us tonight. She said Roy was away and I didn't want her to eat alone."

Roy was away, all right, I thought. I knew *exactly* where Roy had gone.

Anna went to the kitchen to get the phone while I set the table for three. She was dialing Lily when she returned and took notice of my place settings.

"Before you know it, we're always going to set the table for three," Anna said, putting the cordless phone to her ear. She stood marveling at the three place settings, hands on her hips, looking at it like it brought a warmth all its own.

I cringed, knowing we'd be a table of two for the foreseeable future.

"Lily's not answering," Anna said, ending the call.

"Maybe she went out," I suggested. "She works nights after all." Already I felt a twinge of panic.

Anna went to the front door.

"I'll just ring the bell and make sure. She did accept my invitation."

I followed Anna outside, into a warm summer's eve with the dusk sky draped in a serene amber glow. When Anna reached Lily's apartment door she paused. Something was troubling her. Only when I got closer could I see what it was. The door to Lily's apartment had been left slightly ajar. Anna pushed it open fully and called up the winding wooden staircase.

"Lily, it's Anna! Are you there? We're ready to have dinner."

No response.

Anna took a cautious step inside and again called up into the empty stairwell. She waited at the foot of the stairs and motioned for me to join her inside.

"Maybe something is wrong," Anna said, her tone urgent. "I think we should go upstairs and check."

What could I do? I would agree with her without reservation if I weren't so terrified about what we'd find. Soon though, I found myself following Anna up the stairs. At the landing, I could see the door into the apartment was left slightly ajar as well. Anna pushed it open with the palm of her hand and took a tentative step inside.

"Lily?" Anna called out.

Her voice carried down the long hallway. Anna shot me a nervous look. Something was amiss.

I went into the living room while Anna ventured toward Lily's (and Roy's) bedroom. From down the hall, I could hear Anna calling Lily's name. There was a subtle uptick of worry to her voice each time Lily failed to answer.

Why was the door open? Why wasn't Lily home? She knew we were having dinner together. Where was Lily?

I was heading down the hallway to meet Anna when I heard a soft cry of surprise. My heart leapt to my throat, hairs on my arms straightening as my pace quickened. What could she have found? I passed the entrance to the kitchen and took a quick glance inside, seeing nothing of alarm.

Anna was in the bedroom and I could hear her gasping for breath. When I entered, I saw her standing in front of Lily's bedroom closet, one hand covering her mouth, eyes wide. On the windowsill, I saw the Pac-Man mug Lily had painted for a friend and wondered if that friend had been Roy. Anna stood stock-still, gazing at something in the darkness of the closet. My stomach flipped a dozen ways. I wasn't ready to see what I thought I'd see: Lily's body, bloodied by the steel blade of Nicky's knife, or a bullet hole to the head.

But I saw something else entirely.

The closet was empty. There were no clothes. No shoes. No black outfits or laced boots to be seen anywhere. I didn't see any of Roy's clothes, either. Missing was the vintage green suitcase Lily had carried with her on the day she moved in.

"Gage, Lily is gone," Anna said, tears pricking the corners of her eyes. "I really think she's gone."

I tried my very best to look surprised.

CHAPTER 47

Hours later the sun went down and the moon came up, because even when the future mother of your child vanishes without a word, even when a vicious drug dealer has threatened to carve up your family with a switchblade, these things happen. Anna followed her evening routine. Maybe she thought that by acting normally life would return to normal, or our normal. Maybe, if we stayed positive, if we believed hard enough, we'd have a stranger in our family once again. Without proclamation, without telling me what she was thinking, Anna showed me, by doing her evening stretches, checking e-mail, and then washing up for bed.

"She will come back," Anna said, as she got under the covers. "She will. She's just scared. Or maybe she just had to go away suddenly. There's an explanation. I know it."

Oh yeah, there's an explanation all right.

I knew the specifics of the explanation, too. Not long after we'd left Lily's condo, I got a text message from Roy.

Roy to me: Lily freaked and took off. Trying to

track her down. Thinks she's not safe. We gotta talk. Gotta get the money.

I thought of a lot of responses to Roy's text. None of them would have ended with lol or thx. I wanted to unleash a tirade for all he'd done to me. If there was any way to make him suffer, I wanted him to feel it tenfold.

Instead of barking at him, I kept my reply short and simple. I had made up my mind, and maybe Lily leaving was the impetus for my decision. I was rid of her and now I could be rid of Roy with one simple text message.

Me to Roy: I'm not doing anything. You take care of yourself and I'll take care of my family. Going to the cops in the morning. Don't text me again.

Roy: That's stupid. What about my idea. The battery thing. I can check with Nicky to see if he's got a contact.

Me: That's not going to happen.

Roy: Don't quit on me. I need your help. He's going to kill us.

Me: I'm going to the police in the morning. That's my final decision.

Roy: What about Jorge?

Me: I'm betting it'll get back to Nicky. If he wants me to stay quiet tell him to leave us alone. You give him that message from me.

There was a long pause, no reply from Roy. Minutes passed. What I eventually got back put a fresh spike of fear in me.

Roy: Your funeral.

Hours later, Anna and I were in bed, trying to find our normal. I turned on the ten o'clock news but saw no reports of a dead drug dealer. No mention of a shooting down on the docks by Eagle Square. Lucas must have taken the body and the bullets to the associates Nicky Stacks kept referring to. Word of underground happenings might spread on the underground channels, where people like Lily and Roy got the late-breaking stories and straight guys like me wouldn't even know to look.

Anna was asleep when I turned off the television. For a long while I listened to the gentle rise and fall of her breathing while I gazed at the ceiling. I thought about taking a play from Lily's playbook and vanishing with Anna, but if Nicky wanted to hurt us, he could still get to me through the people we loved. And he would do it, too. I knew it when I first set eyes on him at his restaurant. Here was a guy who would shoot me in the back and then piss on my grave.

I wasn't going to the police, either, despite what I had texted to Roy. I had no real desire to spend my best remaining years in jail for murdering a drug dealer. My goal with Roy was to get a message—call it a threat—to Nicky Stacks and hope he'd agree to a truce: my silence in exchange for my life.

I started to fantasize, because the mind can only handle so much stress. It goes into denial mode, assumes things will work out for the better. It's a primitive carryover buried into our genetics, because if we contemplated the dangers we faced on a daily basis—car accidents, slips in the shower, a falling tree branch, wild animal attack, lightning strikes, and so on, and so on—we'd never leave the house. So our genetics helps to block out those worries, infuse us with denial. It's like Adderall for fear—it won't happen to me—and that's how we can go about our daily business.

In my fantasy, as I drifted off to sleep, I was right

about Stacks. He'd change his tune if he thought I was going to the police. We'd be left alone to live our lives without Roy and Lily. Later, perhaps, when Stacks was a shadow of a memory, Anna and I would try again, after she'd recovered from the loss of Lily and a baby that was never going to be hers. When her spirit was ready, I could once again become the thing I loved most in life—somebody's dad.

I woke up hours later to the sound of Anna screaming.

CHAPTER 48

Anna's scream didn't sound terrified—not like someone was coming after her. I'd characterize it as perplexed, a surprised and shocked-sounding noise made from somewhere deep in the throat.

My eyes snapped open and I was out of bed like the mattress was on fire. A blast of adrenaline zapped all the sleepiness from my body, and I was instantly on red alert.

Anna, wearing her jogging clothes, stood at the edge of the bed looking down at her pillow as if something was wrong with it. The curtains had been parted and the first sprinkles of sunlight filtered into the bedroom. Anna was looking at me, not in an angry way, but concerned, as if I had done something wrong that she couldn't exactly blame me for.

"What is it? What's going on?"

I was unsteady on my feet and struggling to regain my equilibrium.

"What are the side effects of Adderall?" Anna asked me.

"Huh?"

"Adderall. What are the side effects?" she wanted to know, her voice steeped in concern.

I scratched my head, thinking.

"Why are you asking me this? Why did you scream?"

"Just answer the question."

Anna was serious and not at all amused, so I rattled off what I could remember in my current condition: loss of appetite, nervousness, easily angered or annoyed, dry mouth. There were more, but I couldn't think of them on the spot.

"There's no sleepwalking? Night terrors? Anything like that?" Anna asked.

I shook my head. "No," I said. "I don't think so. Why? What's going on? Why did you scream?"

Anna didn't answer right away. She eyed me thoughtfully in her pink and black running outfit, perhaps seeing if a prolonged gaze might bring about an admission of something, a side effect I was intentionally keeping secret.

I lowered my head and rubbed at my tired eyes. To help with balance, I locked my arms and braced my hands against the edge of the mattress for support. "Why did you scream?" I asked again, lifting my head to make eye contact.

"I was getting ready to go out for my jog when I saw this sticking out from under my pillow." Anna removed the pillow in a grand sweeping motion, like a stage magician making a dramatic reveal.

My breath caught when I saw what it was. It had nothing to do with the side effects of Adderall.

"I don't sleepwalk and never have," Anna said. "I'm a thousand percent certain I didn't do this. What's going on, Gage? Are you sure you're all right?"

"No, I wasn't all right. I wasn't all right in the least," I wanted to say, but couldn't get those words out.

My gaze was fixed on our largest kitchen knife, the black handle and shiny silver blade shown in stark contrast against the white of our bedsheets. The blade was at least eight inches long, forged from a single piece of high-carbon steel, resistant to stain and corrosion. The thick blade looked strong enough to cut through muscle and then saw right into bone.

Somebody had snuck into my home, had gone into my kitchen, retrieved the knife from the drawer, and slid it under Anna's pillow while we slept.

Roy had given Nicky Stacks my message.

And Stacks had returned a message of his own.

CHAPTER 49

I was back at work for the first time since becoming a murderer. My access badge functioned fine, but still I felt that my colleagues were looking at me differently, as if I gave off an unfamiliar scent. Probably just my imagination, but it was noticeable to me.

I sat in my cube and powered up my workstation. Same as always, murderer or not, the e-mails were there, gathered in my in-box, awaiting my reply. They'd have to wait. I had other business to attend to. Important business, like making sure I stayed alive.

I had given Anna a vague explanation about the knife before I left for work. It was probably connected to the stress of Lily being gone, I said, and made up some BS about my subconscious putting the knife under her pillow as a way of protecting Anna from being hurt even more.

She didn't seem to buy it. She insisted I stop taking Adderall and consider going to see a different shrink. She also, half jokingly, said she'd be sleeping with one eye open from now on.

"That might be a good idea," I wanted to say, but held my tongue. Instead of obeying Anna's wishes, I popped some Adderall—because that's what addicts do—and called ADT from work to schedule an alarm installation. If Anna asked, I'd say I made the appointment beforehand and the knife and alarm were two unrelated coincidences.

I spent the whole day in my cube, avoiding meetings, trying to figure out my next move. Should we run? Could I hide my parents? Hide Bessie? Who else would Stacks go after if he couldn't get to me? Did he know my friends? My coworkers? Would he go after Brad? His twins? What about Roy's suggestion? Could he even find a buyer? Do I go to the cops? How would I get out of the murder charge if that came up? At that point, I was certain of only one thing: Nicky Stacks was a man who did not and would not forget a debt.

Or a promise.

The day slid away in an Adderall-fueled burn. I'd come up with no good answers, no workable plan. The only thing on my side, as Mick Jagger had once sung, was time. It was a short duration for sure, but at least I had enough days before the big deadline for me to come up with something. With luck, that something would generate one million dollars. Perhaps Roy and I needed each other more than I wanted to believe.

On my drive home I was more focused on my options than I was the road. Maybe that was why I didn't notice the black Cadillac CTS with tinted windows until it was riding my bumper.

I glanced in the rearview mirror, furious—I hate tailgating—and checked the side mirror before switching lanes.

The Cadillac switched right behind me and inched even closer. My body tensed as I anticipated the front of the Cadillac scraping my back bumper—it was a hair's distance away, looming large and threatening in my rearview mirror.

Alarmed and unnerved, I gripped the wheel tight and punched the gas. My Dodge Charger lurched forward, but the Cadillac kept pace, mirroring my every move as I erratically changed lanes. My face turned hot as if I'd just been slapped, and again I checked the rearview. Because of the tinted windows, I couldn't see inside the car, but I knew it was Stacks, or one of his minions behind the wheel. The rest of the world went out of focus with my attention fixated entirely on the black machine behind me.

As I accelerated some more, the dotted dividing lines blurred into a single streak of white, and the trees on the side of the highway became a line of green. I nearly clipped the rear of a burgundy SUV while working my way from the far right lane to the far left. The Cadillac stayed on my tail as though it were attached to my bumper by an invisible cable.

I switched lanes again, no signal, but this time the Caddy pulled up to my left so for a time we were driving next to each other at the same rate of speed. I rolled down my window and screamed, "What do you want? What do you want from me?"

The Cadillac abruptly accelerated, pulled ahead of me, switched lanes, and slowed, forcing me to jam on my brakes to avoid a collision. Fortunately, there wasn't another car behind mine; otherwise it would have been a shower of broken glass and a big crunch of steel. I slammed on my horn, which had all the effect of a BB striking a turtle's shell. My palms were soaked with a stress-induced sweat. We were both going seventy-five, weaving in and out of traffic. Whoever was behind the wheel seemed to anticipate my every move.

I saw an exit ahead, but before I could take it, the Cadillac changed lanes, slowed down, and pulled in right behind me. There was no way I was going to lose this tail, so I did the next best thing. I got off at the exit and came to a slow stop on a wide dirt shoulder. The Cadillac pulled in right behind me and came to a stop as well.

I killed the engine and got out of my car. The Cadillac's engine was still running, with the low hum of a finely tuned machine. My hands were balled into fists, face red with rage. There wasn't much traffic rolling by this weedy stretch of road, but the cars that did pass weren't offering to stop and help. They didn't know what we were all about. Could have been mechanical troubles, road rage, or just two friends trying to follow each other to some destination. Whatever it was, nobody stopped to ask.

I went right up to the driver's side and began banging my fist against the door. The tinted window reflected my rabid expression back at me like a distorted fun-house mirror. I pulled violently on the door handle, but of course it was locked.

"Open the door, Stacks!" I shouted. "Come out and face me! You ever come into my home again and I'll kill you! Open this door right now and show yourself, or are you a coward?"

The Cadillac's V-8 engine revved and roared in response, and the message was clear—back away. I didn't care. I pounded my fist even harder against the glass.

The window rolled down just a few inches, enough room for a gun barrel to stick out and point at my chest. Gazing at the muzzle, I staggered back a step, my open mouth frozen in horror. I pivoted as I went to the ground and heard a faint click behind me—the sound of a gun hammer striking, but there was no follow on explosion, no bright and blinding flash like when I shot Jorge, no stench of gunpowder souring the air.

I crouched on the ground, my hands covering my head, whole body shaking. The Cadillac's engine revved several times as if it was getting ready for a drag race. When it went into reverse, tires screeching, sand and stones went scattering in all directions and a column of dirt lifted skyward as the car skidded off the shoulder, fishtailed twice, and slipped back onto the road.

I stood, imagining how it would have felt to take a bullet in the chest. I thought of Anna, the knife, the gun, the giant mess I'd made of our lives. I waited until I was safely back in my car before I texted Roy. My message was simple and to the point.

Check with Nicky and see if you can find a buyer.

CHAPTER 50

Here's the thing about cybercrime: it looks just like work. I sat alone in my cube, clicking, and mousing, and typing. I didn't need a black balaclava to conceal my identity. No, I would need to modify log files to cover my tracks.

In terms of data security, what we implemented to safeguard Olympian's intellectual property could earn us a CIA triad "best practices" award. CIA in my world has nothing to do with the Central Intelligence Agency. It stands for something else: Confidentiality, Integrity, and Availability. Protecting sensitive information from unauthorized access is what confidentiality is all about. When it comes to safeguarding sensitive data, privacy equals security.

The "I" in CIA, or integrity, means protecting the data from modification. Only those with root access, meaning the three members of the Security Breach Team, Matt Simons included, could access or alter any and all data pertaining to the Olympian project. Which was why the Breach Team was carefully selected and highly trusted, and why we changed all the passwords after Adam Wang was let go.

Ensuring that critical data is available when needed, the "A" in CIA, safeguards against power outages, failover redundancy, or denial of service attacks.

The real CIA could take a lesson from us about safeguarding data. What we had was the Fort Knox of data security. There was no single repository for everything Olympian. The design plans were kept on a physically separate server from the materials plans, which were housed in a different building. The measurement plans, essentially the recipe for making the nanotubes, were in the same building as the materials plans but kept on yet another separate server on its own private network. The process diagrams and assembly instructions were also in that building, but they were on a different floor on a physically distinct machine as well. And each room, where each different server was located, was protected by sophisticated access control and tracking mechanisms.

It wasn't a small amount of data. If I printed out everything, the process to cook up an Olympian battery would fill several boxes of three-ring binders. In addition to the physical separation, we also had a suite of high-end data loss prevention products (or because we computer folks love acronyms, DLP products). Try to e-mail some protected files to your Gmail account, or IM them, or stuff them in a Dropbox folder, and we'd block access using in-motion data protection technology. Stick a USB key into the slot on one of our servers, or a camera cable, or an iPod, and we'd deny the file transfer using endpoint technology. Go after our archives, the artifacts of our failed attempts to build the battery, the plans we'd long ago abandoned, and our data at rest security protocols would make sure the Security Breach Team knew immediately. I had to get through four layers of security on four different physical machines to give Roy what we'd agreed upon.

As it turned out, Nicky gave Roy a couple of names; he went dialing for dollars, and came up lucky. Somebody was willing to pay a million for the Olympian product plans—maybe even more. I didn't care if Roy was skimming on this job like he did the other. I just wanted Nicky Stacks gone from my life forever.

It was time to get to work. Security layer one: Did I have the right biometric authentication and badge permissions to unlock the doors to the server rooms where the machines are located? Answer: yes. My fingerprint had been recorded using a biometric reader and as a member of the Security Breach Team, I could use my badge plus a finger-scan to unlock the server room doors.

Layer two: When I logged into the machine, could I access the files I needed? Answer: yes, again, as long as I used my root log-on.

Layer three: Could I decrypt the data? Answer: Each member of the Security Breach Team had the decryption protocols so we could evaluate the content for any unauthorized changes.

Layer four: Could I disable the monitoring? Answer: You bet. I had the same level of access as Matt Simons when he breached the system to sabotage Adam Wang's career.

The whole theft occurred over many hours, involving four different locations, four different biometric scans, and four different file transfers to my 8GB USB drive. The amazing thing about data theft was how so much of it, reams and reams of it, could be stored on something smaller than my thumb, with lots of room to spare.

Four times I needed to modify the server log files to delete my presence. In addition, I also had to delete the logs for the biometric access control to the server rooms. If they were ever checked, logs showing that I accessed the four separate locations in quick succession might look pretty suspicious. It was akin to erasing video surveillance footage of a traditional B&E job. I had been there, but I wasn't there. I was a phantom, a ghost. The whole time it felt like an out-of-body experience, my stomach doing twists to rival Greg Louganis in his prime. My tapping fingers left behind drops of sweat encoded with my DNA on the keypads. Good thing we didn't detect for that marker.

I was on the fourth log file, standing in the middle of a frigid server room on the second floor of my office building. Air conditioners used to keep the servers cool were blasting on high, while my feet felt bouncy on the raised floor. I was just about to complete the last step in my theft. I had committed the robbery in the light of day, during regular working hours, because after-hours access would have raised questions and left records I could not have erased as easily.

I wasn't kidding myself into thinking my actions were justified. I was scared, sick with worry, but felt cornered and out of options. Go to the cops and Stacks would make sure I went down for Jorge's murder, leaving Anna, my parents, everyone I love unprotected, and me a target for one of Stacks's men to shank while I was in jail. Did I let all those people I love die, or did I take matters into my own hands?

I tried not to think of how this would impact my company. I was standing at a fork in a road where each path would lead me to a different but horrible outcome.

My body quaked. I thought of confiding in Brad, but

worried about dragging him and Janice into my disaster. I had made a decision to reset my moral compass because I saw no other choice.

I had no way out. I'd give Roy the plans and pray he could sell them.

All that changed when I felt a tap on my shoulder.

My heart stopped, and a fresh band of terror raced up my spine.

"Goodness, Gage," Patrice said. "What are you doing here? I've been looking all over for you."

Could Patrice see the fear in my eyes? Caught in the act, caught red-handed, I tried to speak but couldn't find my voice. What was she doing here? What did she want?

"We're supposed to have a meeting in my office before we meet with Peter."

I groaned inwardly. In my haste to get the data for Roy's middleman, I hadn't checked my calendar. I knew we had a meeting scheduled for later in the afternoon, but I'd forgotten Patrice wanted to have a premeeting before we sat down with the CEO.

"I'm just finishing up," I managed to say. "I'm sorry I forgot all about it."

"I tried to text you," Patrice replied, sounding a bit frazzled. I hadn't checked my phone. I must have been concentrating hard because I didn't even feel the vibrations from each new text received. "Mamatha said she saw you come up here."

"I'll be right there," I said, exhaling slowly.

"You look busy, so we'll reschedule. Finish up and come down to my office in an hour," Patrice said. "Does that work?"

I didn't bother to check my calendar. "Will do," I said. "I'm so sorry," I wanted to say.

"What were you doing here, anyway?" Patrice asked.

The lie came out before I realized what I was saying. “Just making sure the configuration files didn’t get corrupted during last night’s backup,” I said. “I don’t want anything to go wrong for the next demo.”

Patrice returned a pleased smile. “Thanks, Gage. Really. You’re one of the reasons the project has turned into a success. I honestly don’t want to think of what would happen if we fail.”

But I was thinking about it. I was thinking about the company going out of business. Thousands left unemployed. Countless lives altered or even halted. Careers would be ended. Marriages would crumple under the strain. Families would be torn apart. Savings accounts depleted, all because I gave Roy the secrets to our success.

I thought about Wendy from my group, whose kid needed major orthodontic work. And Zack in documentation, who needed five more years of steady employment before he could embark on his bucket list dream to travel to Europe as a kickoff to retirement. I thought about Rebecca, who was pregnant and the only one working while her husband finished grad school, and Esther, whose husband just died of a heart attack. The ripple effect from my betrayal would reverberate through so many lives.

Save the people I love or save the company that saved me when I was at my worst, my darkest time?

Patrice turned to go, but something made her turn back around.

“Oh, and while you’re accessing the servers,” she said. “Can you make sure the archive is still online? Gerry finished his forensic analysis and wanted to make sure the configuration of the battery that caught fire went into the proper archives, but he couldn’t do the transfer. Maybe you can do a quick check and figure out why. If you can't, we might have to restore the data from our backups."

"I wonder why that happened," I said, honestly curious.

Patrice just shrugged. "Who knows," she said. "Mamatha thinks it has something to do with the disaster recovery system IT is testing out."

"I didn't know we were testing a new system," I said.

"Neither did we," Patrice said, her tone implying corporate inefficiencies were just a fact of life. "Mamatha just found out about it herself, but whenever something that works stops working, the best place to look for the culprit is usually what changed. This new system is probably what caused the archive to become inaccessible."

"So the backups were taking snapshots of everything?" I asked. "All of our data?"

Patrice nodded. "That's what I was told."

My eyes widened. *Yes, of course*.

"I'll be happy to check on the archive problem," I said. And I meant it, too.

Because what Patrice just said changed everything. I logged out of the server and set off to talk to our IT guys.

I never did make the second meeting with Patrice. I was too busy working with IT. When I had what I needed, I went looking for Matt Simons. I found him in his cubical, working away.

"Why weren't you at Patrice's meeting?" Simons asked.

"I was busy."

"This isn't the time to have your priorities mixed up. The meeting with Patrice should have preempted everything."

"I'm confused. Are you my boss, Matt?" I asked.

He looked offended.

"I'm in charge of this project, like it or not."

I crouched down to get at his level.

"I have proof," I said in a low voice. It was hard to contain my ebullience and I didn't really try.

Simons looked alarmed.

"Proof of what?"

"IT is testing a new archiving system. You didn't know about it. None of us did. Those IT guys. They do things but they don't always tell you. Thanks to this new archiving system they're testing, we have two copies of our files published to the archives each night. The copy you know about, the archive you modified to erase all history of your file tampering, and the one you didn't know about, the one IT was testing. You know what I found in those archives? Proof that you were the one who changed the formula for the build that caught fire. You didn't delete that evidence because you didn't even know it existed. I have the modified files with your log-in information all over them, you jackass."

Simons stammered, unable to speak.

"What do you want from me?" he asked.

And so I told him.

CHAPTER 51

Brad had ordered an iced tea from the slender brunette waitress. I got a glass of water with a lemon slice. We passed on ordering food, and her semi-scowl seemed to anticipate the measly tip to come. Of course that wouldn't be the case, scowl or not.

We were in the outside seating patio area at Not Your Average Joe's in Arlington Center. The bright sun baked the metal table hot to the touch, but I wanted to be outside and in a public place when I made the exchange. I also wanted to have a friend along with me in case things got dicey.

Brad wore a dark blue, short-sleeved polo shirt, dungarees, and aviator-like sunglasses. With his bushy mustache he looked a bit like a spy on a stakeout, and judging by the way he acted—highly alert while making several furtive glances—he was acting like one, too.

"Brad, drink your tea and relax. I'm not worried anything is going to happen."

"Then why'd you want me here?"

"Just as security, extra eyes in case I'm missing something." Something I'd learned from Roy.

"So that's what I'm doing," Brad said a bit defensively. "I'm acting as the eyes."

I nodded, surrendering to his logic.

"It's going to be fine, Brad. That's all I'm saying."

"Are you asking me or telling me? Because I'm pretty sure that's not how you feel."

I returned a grimace. "Hey, are you reading my aura?" I asked.

"No, I'm just being your pal. And I can tell you're pretty nervous."

Of course, Brad was right. Every passing car made me jumpy. I kept thinking the windows would roll down and Lucas would lean out with gun in hand, ready to riddle my body with hot lead. My phone would buzz intermittently with text messages from Anna or with a trivial work-related matter, but of course I'd think it was Patrice, who noticed some unusual activity requiring the immediate attention of the breach team. Maybe I hadn't covered my tracks as carefully as I thought, and I'd soon be investigating the data theft I'd just perpetrated. Or maybe I was overly confident and this plan of mine was going to fail.

As we waited for Roy to show, my uneasiness only grew. I twisted several napkins into shreds while doing battle with my emotions. I thought about asking Brad to take hold of my hands to see if Max was somewhere looking on. I wanted to know if he was proud of my solution.

Max and I had talked a lot about no-win situations after I introduced him to the joys of *Star Trek II: The Wrath of Khan* at the wildly inappropriate age of seven. Had the movie come out two years later, it would have been PG-13, but I didn't share that tidbit with Karen when I got it on Netflix and showed her it was fine for Max to watch because of its PG rating. Max fell completely in love with the movie and Star Trek as a result. At one particularly dramatic moment, he made me hit reverse so we could both yell, "KHAN!" right along with Captain Kirk.

After the viewing, we talked at length about the *Kobayashi Maru*, the training exercise at the Starfleet Academy designed to test the character of potential future starship captains. It was a no-win scenario in which the test taker, Lieutenant Saavik, played by Kirstie Alley, must decide to engage in a suicide mission to rescue the crew of a damaged spaceship, the *Kobayashi Maru*, or take choice number two and abandon the crew of the *Kobayashi Maru*, leaving them to a certain death.

The parallels to my own life weren't lost on me. Give Lithio Systems competitive advantage to Roy and put the company out of business? Or don't give Roy the plans, don't get Nicky Stacks his money, and watch the people I love die? A no-win situation.

When it was revealed in the film that Captain Kirk had altered the program to beat the test, he said he did so because he did not believe in no-win scenarios, and neither do I. In fact, Kirk was my inspiration for finding the one way out of this paradox. To win the game, I had to change the rules.

"Where'd you go?" Brad asked.

His voice pulled me out of my daydream, but the lump in my throat from thinking about Max and the movie he loved remained.

"Sorry, I'm just anxious." The speed at which my feet tapped against the patio flagstone was the combination of Adderall magic and fractured nerves.

"I thought you said there was nothing to be worried about."

"I figured you'd know I was lying."

Brad nodded. "Yeah, of course I did. But I'm glad you called me, anyway."

"And do you think I've done the right thing?"

"I think you were faced with two terrible choices."

I had confided in Brad—full disclosure. He knew this was my personal version of the *Kobayashi Maru*.

"What would you have done?" I asked.

"I probably would have been too scared to think of anything logical. He threatened your family, Gage. You're mixed up with some very dangerous people."

"Which is why I wish you hadn't pressed me for the details."

"Hey, I wasn't coming out on a stakeout without getting the facts first."

"Well, now you've got them." I sounded glum. I checked the time on my phone. Roy would be here in five minutes.

"It's going to work," Brad said. "I have a feeling."

"You don't sound sincere."

"What are you talking about? I'm completely sincere."

"No, you sounded overly sincere. That's not the same thing."

"I'm a plumber. We don't exaggerate unless it has something to do with your bill."

I gave Brad a surprised look. "So you guys do overcharge!"

Brad put his finger to his lips. "Shh," he said. "It's a trade secret." He smiled and winked, and I felt a little bit better, a smidge lighter, until I saw Roy approach.

He came walking down the street with his usual swagger, chewing on a toothpick, thumbs hooked into the loops of his jeans, black boots scraping on the sidewalk, his black T-shirt clinging to his trim physique. Roy sat down, lowered his shades, and appraised Brad with a curious look.

"Is he your protection?" Roy asked, switching the toothpick to the other side of his mouth, while thumbing over to Brad. He pushed his shades back up.

"I'm just a guy enjoying a glass of iced tea on a sunny day," Brad said, lifting his glass to show Roy.

Roy mulled this over.

"Okay, whatever. You got the stuff?"

"Yeah, I got it." I put the USB key down on the table.

Roy cupped the USB key with his hand and slid it across to himself. I watched him examine it carefully, twirling it in his fingers.

"This is it?" he asked.

"That's it."

"It's not much."

"It's worth a lot to the right buyer," I said. "Do you have the right buyer?"

"The guy Nicky hooked me up with says so, and he sounds like he knows what he's talking about."

"And you think this will get enough money to pay back Nicky?" Brad asked.

Roy shot me an irritated look.

"You told Lily, I told Brad," I said.

Roy just shrugged. "Whatever," he said again. Then to Brad Roy said, "Yeah, it better bring in enough scratch. We gotta move quick on this."

"Who is your source?" Brad asked.

Roy looked at me, pointed to Brad, and said, "Who is this guy?"

"I'm his friend," Brad said.

Roy stared at Brad, his eyes unreadable behind those shades. "Aren't you the plumber?"

"Yeah, I'm his friend who happens to be a plumber."

Roy grinned, and his crooked mouth seemed to put the world at a tilt. "Well, plumber friend," he said, showing Brad the USB key, "you better hope that this here is good enough to get us the cash we need, or Nicky is going to flush his body parts right down the drain along with mine." He stood up, pushing his metal chair back with a scraping sound. He put his hands against his hips in a move that made the muscles of his arms tighten and his tattoos flex. He nodded his good-bye to me.

"I'll be in touch," Roy said. "Keep a low profile." He nodded to Brad while slipping the USB key into the front pocket of his jeans. He spit out a toothpick, slid in another, and then left.

I watched my future vanish into the crowd, while I'm sure all Brad saw was a black aura moving steadily away.

A woman emerged from the cover of a store entrance about fifty yards down the street and fell into step with Roy. She kept her back to me, but her long, dirty-brown hair swayed across her back in familiar fashion. I could tell who it was just by her gait.

I stood quickly and raced down the street calling her name: "Lily! Lily!"

I wanted her to contact Anna. I wanted some closure. Anna would hold onto hope as long as she had a finger-width of ledge space to grasp. Lily owed her some sort of explanation, a simple good-bye, something about a change of heart, anything that would allow Anna to let go so she could move on. So we could move on together. I called out Lily's name, but the woman down the street never looked back. They turned the corner and vanished from my view. When I reached the same corner, breathless, hands on my knees, panting from the short sprint, I looked in every direction, but Roy and Lily were gone.

CHAPTER 52

One week later and still no word from Roy. No word from Lily, either. Anna had closed the Humboldt deal, so she could take maternity leave without causing any undue financial strain, but we were missing the one essential ingredient—a baby to mother. Anna continued to prep for the home study, believing Lily might still come back. Margret would show up and do her official thing and we'd be sanctioned to adopt the unborn child who had vanished along with Lily.

"She's seventeen weeks along now," Anna had said to me at dinner. "She'll be showing even more. I hope she's okay. I just wish I could talk to her."

And I wished I had caught up to them before the pair vanished somewhere on the streets of Arlington. I had looked everywhere for them, in every nearby store, but to no avail. It was as if they were spirits who had disappeared into the ether.

While Anna kept busy with her job and getting our place ready for the home study, I was at work, trying to maintain the semblance of a normal routine. Peter George was extremely pleased with our efforts. Matt

Simons was driving everybody crazy with his nutty demands, fiery e-mails, and unrealistic project expectations. Even so, we all fell into lockstep behind him, knowing full well the consequences for failure would be dire for our collective employment. Somehow I managed to concentrate on the work, even though every minute it seemed I was checking for messages from Roy.

I was in a standup meeting, doing the Agile project thing, when my phone buzzed. At the time, I was thinking about Anna, worried about her really, wondering when she'd accept the truth about Lily. I wasn't paying attention to the status update as I should have been.

The phone buzzed again. I thought it was Anna because I was thinking of her, a little bit of the mysterious universe at work. But it wasn't. It was a text message from Roy.

I got the money. Meet me at Nicky's.

Two hours later I was back in East Boston, back at Nicky's restaurant. I canceled my afternoon meetings and called Anna to tell her I'd be coming home a bit late. No questions asked. Roy was in the bar area, waiting for me at a round table, chewing on a toothpick. A captain's case, the kind used by pilots and lawyers, stood on the floor beside him. I sat down.

"Is that what I think it is?" I asked.

Roy nodded.

"You're just hanging around here with a million dollars in cash?"

"Nobody is going to rob me while I'm in Nicky's," Roy said.

I nodded because it made sense.

"So what now?"

"Now we wait. Nicky is finishing up some business."

I didn't say anything for a few minutes. I just sat and watched Roy chew on a chip of ice in the Scotch he ordered. I looked around at the patrons, blue-collar types, probably locals, I'm guessing regulars, painters and electricians, and people who wear a uniform to work, enjoying a meal or a drink. Eventually, I broke the weighty silence.

"I saw you with Lily," I said.

Roy returned a cryptic look.

"She needs to talk to Anna," I said. "Tell Anna she's not coming back. Tell her it's time to forget this and move on."

Roy leaned in.

"Listen to me carefully, Gage," he said. His frosty eyes narrowed into slits, his gravelly voice sank an octave. "Are you listening?"

I nodded.

"Once this money exchanges hands, we are done. There's no contacting us. There's no looking for us. We don't exist to you and you don't exist to us. We're gone. Whatever you need to tell Anna to make it all better is fine by me. That's your life with your wife. But I want to be crystal clear about this: our connection ends today. When Nicky gets this money, you are dead to me. Understand?"

"What if Lucas comes looking for me?"

"Sucks to be you," Roy said.

"Thanks. I feel so much better now."

"Honestly, I don't give a crap how you feel. I'm about to hand over the biggest score of my career to Nicky Stacks. A million friggin' dollars, here one minute and gone the next. You know what that does to me? Do you know how that's tearing me apart?"

"My heart is breaking for you, Roy."

"At least I got enough from this sale, a little extra pocket change to cover my other debts."

I knew it. "So the guy Nicky hooked you up with, who did he sell the plans to?"

"No clue," Roy said. "I think they're some Chinese guys. I'm just the middleman. He had no trouble moving what you gave me, that's for sure. It's big stuff what you do, huh?"

"Big," I concurred.

"Okay, well, we got lucky here. Good thing you didn't work for Applebee's or something."

"Yeah, good thing," I repeated.

Roy looked past me, his gaze locked on something happening over my shoulder.

I turned and saw the massive silhouette of Nicky Stacks looming in the entranceway to the upper-level dining area. Stacks motioned with his finger before he vanished from our view. Roy and I walked to the back of the restaurant. My heart started to race, and each breath came with effort. I was having a PTSD reaction to the sight of Nicky Stacks. But as soon as I entered the dining area, my fear spiked tenfold.

Sitting at a table with Nicky Stacks was Lucas Moreno. He wore a different tailored suit, but I recognized the linebacker's build and swarthy complexion right away. I'd seen people angry with me before—people at work, Anna, a whole host of them—but I'd never seen anybody whose only purpose in life was to kill me.

When he saw me, Lucas stood fast enough to knock over his chair. Stacks rose with him, moving surprisingly quick for such a big man, and set one of his massive hands on Lucas's shoulder to hold him in place.

"Search them both," Nicky instructed.

Lucas patted down Roy, found no weapons or wires.

Then it was my turn. When he touched my body I could feel his desire to snap my ribs. His hands slapped hard against my back, my midsection, my legs and arms, more punch than pat.

"Bring me the case," Stacks said to Roy in a commanding voice that could have stopped an angry dog.

Roy stepped forward, case in hand. I followed. Stacks cleared away the set of plates in front of him. It looked like he was eating spaghetti and chicken parm and enjoying a glass of wine, too, but I noticed only one place setting.

Nicky popped the latches on the case and looked inside. I got a glimpse of the stacks of bills, hundreds it seemed. Nicky took out several stacks of hundreds and examined them. Then he took out five stacks total—I'm guessing a hundred bills per stack—or what probably amounted to fifty thousand dollars. The case was still stuffed full of cash.

Nicky glared at me, then at Lucas.

"This is done," he said, speaking to both of us. He stacked the money on the table into three towers. "Lucas, this is yours. It's tribute for your brother. I've spoken with your boss and we've agreed you're not to touch this man." Stacks pointed at me. "Is that understood? He's to be left alone. We are sorry for what happened to Jorge, but it's done. There's no going back. If you start shooting up people, questions will be asked and it will be bad for business. So this ends now. It's done. Is that understood?"

I nodded, trying to quell the fear. Lucas glared at me, his unblinking eyes expressed deep hatred. He wanted to hurt me.

"Is that understood?" Stacks said to Lucas.

Finally, after what felt like eternity, Lucas gave a reluctant nod.

"I'm sorry about your brother," I said. "I wish it could have been different."

Lucas looked ready to pounce. Stacks took a step forward, putting himself in the middle but facing me.

"No, no," he said, wagging a finger at me. "Don't talk about his brother. You don't get the right. It's done. It's over. Now you don't mention it again."

"So we're good here, Nicky," Roy said. "Right? Nobody gets hurt. I'm gone. I'm going someplace and that's the end of it. Is that right, Nicky?"

Stacks stepped away from the table and approached Roy until the two men were standing toe to toe. Stacks dwarfed Roy, and it was surprising to see how mismatched they were as opponents. Stacks was the Kingpin to Roy's Daredevil, both comic book characters that Max loved.

"You ever show your face around here, Roy, and I'll take it off with a vegetable peeler. Is that understood? I'll remove it piece by rotten piece in thin, long, and bloody strips. Are we clear?"

"Crystal," Roy said, backing away a step.

I took a cue from Roy and moved toward the exit as well. I saw Roy take a glance at the captain's case—a long glance. Every fiber of his being was probably screaming to take the money, but he knew better. Like the Kenny Rogers song, he knew when to walk away and when to run. Soon we were both retreating, neither of us comfortable turning our backs on Nicky or Lucas.

Before I knew it, we were standing outside of Nicky's restaurant in this now-familiar East Boston neighborhood. Roy put in a fresh toothpick and slipped his sunglasses back on.

"Can't say it's been a pleasure knowing you," Roy said.

"I could say the same."

"Thanks, though."

"For what?"

"For having five-point-five pounds of guts to save my life." Roy extended his hand to me.

I stared incredulous at the tattoos and scars marring his skin, the wound to his face where Lucas had pistol-whipped him. I gazed at his hand as if it were a hydra's head. But Roy held it out, strong and unwavering.

"No hard feelings," Roy said.

I took Roy's proffered hand and shook it. I think I did it for closure, because this part of my life needed to come to an end. I did it because a part of me really did have sympathy for the devil.

Roy gave me a crooked smile, turned his back to me, and began his slow march away. Thumbs hooked into the loops of his jeans. Feet scuffing along the broken concrete sidewalk, ambling in a thoughtful way, probably thinking about what he could have done with all that money.

I watched until he turned the corner, and just like that he was out of my pack.

But I wasn't a lone wolf.

I still had Anna.

Brad was still my best friend.

And because of Matt Simons, I hadn't betrayed my company. I wasn't going to be responsible for thousands of lost jobs.

Nicky got his money, Roy got his life, Lily got her man, Lucas got compensation, and I got to keep together the pack I loved with all my heart and soul.

CHAPTER 53

Matt Simons kept glancing over at me, his look begging for reassurance. Maybe he was wondering if I'd set him up the way he had Adam Wang. Or maybe I had engaged in some form of corporate entrapment? Something Patrice Skinner and Peter George were in on. Could I be trusted? Would I honor my side of this nefarious bargain? I'd had the same thoughts about Roy. I'd come full circle, from victim to blackmailer.

If I could have done it another way, I would have. But I was a QA guy. I knew how to test these batteries, not build them. Matt Simons had a different level of smarts. He knew how I could modify the design plans so that they'd be essentially useless to somebody who knew how to build a battery. He knew what key pieces of data needed to be stripped out of the plans like a Porsche in a LA chop shop.

With Matt's help—blackmailing wasn't a proud moment in my personal history—what I gave Roy was the equivalent of Olympian's parts, without any conceivable way of using those plans to re-create the battery.

Everyone was gathered in the demo room once again. The mannequins were again spaced evenly about the room, their plastic hands gripping different real-world products powered by Olympian. I'm sure Matt wasn't feeling entirely jubilant, though he had to be more confident about the demo's chance for success this time than he was the last. This time we'd built the batteries using plans my QA team had tested and approved. There was no modifying the recipe to bake an unstable battery like before. No new Adam Wang stood in Matt's way. He was the head honcho, the man in charge of Olympian, his dream gig, and I was the guy with irrefutable technical evidence that he, and he alone, was responsible for the spectacular flame-out of our last demo.

Sweat beaded up on Matt's furrowed brow. It hadn't been easy to coerce him into helping me, same as it wasn't easy for Roy to get me involved in the Moreno deal. Funny, though: it was Roy who'd showed me how people could be pressured and manipulated. Thanks to Roy, I got a master's class in the art of coercion. Be clear—what I wanted Matt to do. Be precise—what are my threats? Be confident—he needed to know I would take him down. Be committed—we were doing this, there wasn't another choice.

I didn't tell Matt why I needed his help to modify the design plans, why I needed them useless. I just told him to do it. Matt's choice was clear. *Help me and I'll keep quiet about your extracurricular efforts. Don't help me and I'll produce the evidence proving you intentionally sabotaged the initial Olympian demo.*

It ended up taking us many hours and a lot of effort to cover our tracks, but we eventually cobbled together a believable set of plans, sans the secret sauce, minus the revolutionary intellectual property that made Olympian such a technical marvel. It was like giving Roy a masterful forgery of some priceless work of art.

Peter George strode into the crowded room and took a quick survey of the engineers gathered for the big demo. He met up with Patrice in the center of the room and everybody circled around Amber II. Peter gave a quick but inspiring speech that would have motivated any sports team on the brink of defeat to a stunning comeback. The highlights were pretty straightforward: *this product is going to save the company and put Lithio Systems far ahead of the competition, you are responsible for this huge success, you should all feel very proud of what you've accomplished.*

Patrice spoke after Peter. This time no beer was being served. We were all still wounded by the memory of the battery fire, so the revelry was far more subdued. We just wanted the damn thing to work.

Peter had the honor of turning on the phone. Soon as it powered up, the timer marking battery life started ticking away. Everyone cheered.

Except for me.

Except for Matt.

The two of us stood in the back of the room and politely clapped.

"It's going to be fine," I whispered into Matt's ear. "You stay cool and I'll stay cool and we'll just move on with our lives."

We hung out for a while, chatting and back-patting. It was a jovial time, and the release of tension was palpable, as if we'd been holding our collective breaths underwater for far too long. At some point, Patrice whistled loudly and asked everyone to be quiet for a moment. The chatter quickly died down. Peter George came over to stand near Patrice. They were flanking Amber II and her tick-tock timer.

"I have in my hand," Peter said, holding up a manila envelope, "a Certificate of Outstanding Achievement. You know as a company policy we always award this certificate to one individual at the end of every successful project. And this Olympian project is a major success. Now, I could give each of you this award, because you're all outstanding achievers, but for those who don't get a slip of paper today, just know that your reward for a job well done is that you'll continue to stay employed."

This was followed by some chuckles and a lot of nervous laughter because we all knew it was true.

Peter continued, "This time around, I would like to award the certificate to two individuals who best exemplify the culture and philosophy of Lithio Systems. These traits—perseverance, commitment, passion, intelligence, and teamwork—are present in each of you, but these two contributors persevered despite enormous challenges, both personal and professional, and through it all played important leadership roles in guiding this project to this major success. They are both deserving of special recognition, and I'm sure you'll all agree."

I was trying to guess who might get the reward. My money was on Girish, but it could have been any number of folks—Brenda, Mamatha, Larry, Jenitta, Kathleen. The list went on, as did Peter's speech.

"One of these individuals I wish to acknowledge today deserves recognition as much for his accomplishments as for his strength of character. Facing unthinkable adversity, he came to work each day. And through it all, he showed tremendous professionalism, unsurpassed dedication, and true commitment to excellence. The other came into the project at a crucial time, and through his dedication, focus, and technical acumen led us to this very exciting milestone. So I'd like you all to take a moment to acknowledge the special work of these two special individuals as I present Gage Dekker and Matt Simons with these certificates of outstanding achievement and a two hundred dollar Amex gift card."

My neck felt flush where a hot band of sweat appeared. My hands started to tingle. Every head in the room turned in my direction as the tingle crept up my arms and down into my legs. The round of applause was truly thunderous. Everyone from my quality assurance team came over to congratulate me. I smiled, doing my best to seem genuinely appreciative. I was squirming.

If Peter George knew the truth, he'd have put my certificate through the shredder. It wasn't superhuman perseverance that got me through each workday—it was the damn Adderall. On top of that, I was a murderer, justified or not, and almost committed the ultimate act of treason against the company. At that moment, I felt about as worthy of honor as Bernie Madoff. Matt wasn't any better—well, he wasn't a killer. But he was even less deserving. He'd ruined Adam's career and reputation for the sake of his own ego.

Without saying anything, Matt and I exchanged looks once again. Here we were, two outstanding achievers, both saddled with a terrible secret, but I felt sort of good inside. I had saved Anna and myself without crippling the company I loved or ruining the lives of these wonderful people. One day, maybe all of this would end. Maybe the police would come to my house to question me about the murder of a notorious and violent drug dealer named Jorge Moreno. Maybe I'd be let go from Lithio Systems, downsized in the wake of some new corporate financial crisis. Maybe in a wink of time, as unpredictable and unforeseen as meeting a crying woman on the curb by a Chinese restaurant, all this would come to a conclusion. It could happen tomorrow, or some far future date, but it wasn't going to happen right now.

No, right now Lithio Systems was going to conquer the battery world, and nobody was going to find Jorge Moreno's dead body, because Nicky Stacks was paid his share, so this was a moment I could live deeply and fully.

I was jawboning with Patrice when my phone started to buzz. I figured it was Anna trying to reach me. We'd spent the morning talking about next steps in our adoption journey once the home study concluded. The whole process was going to take four to six weeks, and we were in the middle of discussing our criminal and child abuse clearances when I had to leave for work. As for Lily, Anna remained hopeful because she had grown attached, but I also noticed a change. Like Brad reading auras, I got the sense that if the right situation came up, Anna would be ready and willing to move on from Lily. It was a sprig of hope like the first bud on a twig at the end of a long winter.

"Hi, babe," I said. "What's up? I'm just finishing the demo and it went well."

People were still chatting and coming up to me, so I had to move to a quieter corner of the room to hear.

"It's not your babe, Gage," Roy said. "It's me."

"Roy?"

"You screwed me." Roy's voice was brimming with anger. "You screwed me and now I'm going to screw you because I'm in freakin' deep."

"Roy, what's going on here? What are you talking about?" A flood of panic sent my blood rushing and quickened my breath.

"What did you give me? What the hell were those plans?"

"I gave you what you asked for."

I left the room in a hurry and ran toward the building's exit. The hallways were empty as everyone was still at the demo. Sweat poured down my face, and I felt a crushing pressure on my chest.

Anna . . . he's in my home . . . he called me from my home . . . where is Anna?

"You gave me crap, Gage, and you know it. And now the guys who bought the plans know it, so we now have a big fucking problem."

"Anna . . ." I managed to sputter out. "Where is Anna? Where is my wife?"

"I'm going to send you something," Roy said. "You ready to scream?"

My vocal cords felt as if they'd been knotted. I didn't think I could speak, let alone scream, but then I saw the picture. A low, warbling moan escaped my lips.

The picture he sent was of Anna. She was dressed as if she was at work but was sitting on the floor of a room that looked like an empty jail cell—a small space with imposing walls. The floorboards were wide wooden planks, each heavily varnished and scuffed. The walls were chipped and made of worn red bricks. Despite the dim lighting, I could see her hands were tied in front of her using several wrappings of a thick rope. A gag made of a white cloth, maybe a torn-up bedsheet, had been stuffed into her mouth and tied around her head. Her watery eyes were wide with terror, pleading for mercy. The look on her face conveyed fear and betrayal, and I knew why.

Lily was in the picture as well.

It was the same Lily from before: laced black boots, wearing a tight-fitting black T-shirt emblazoned with the label from a Jack Daniel's whiskey bottle that showed the swell of her belly. She knelt beside Anna, holding a knife to her throat. Her other hand was extended out of the frame to take a "selfie," a self-portrait using a cell phone camera.

I almost dropped the phone, my hand was shaking so hard. My eyes boiled with rage.

"Don't you hurt her," I managed to say. "You don't touch her. Do you understand?"

"No, Gage, you need to understand something," Roy said. "You messed everything up. I can't have more people coming after me. A million dollars for shit in return buys somebody a lot of animosity. I'm not living my life looking over my shoulder. These guys who bought your crap files are not happy, not at all. And that makes me a target. No way. That's not how this is going down. You give me the real deal this time around and she lives. I get it verified by my guy, get it checked out, and I'll let her go. But you keep playing games and I'll gut her like a pig. Are we clear, buddy? I'll split her open from her throat to her belly."

I was racing down the hallway at a sprinter's pace. I knew two very disturbing facts in the same instant. Roy was never going to let Anna leave alive. He was going to kill me, too. And I wasn't going to let either of those two things happen.

"When?" I asked.

"How long do you need?"

"To do it right, I need a day."

"You have six hours."

I checked my watch. It was two o'clock in the afternoon.

"Where?" I asked.

"I'll call you with a place to meet."

"Let me talk to Anna. Right now. I need to talk to her. I need to hear her voice and know that she's all right."

"That's not going to happen."

"Then you don't get the files."

Roy screamed, "I'M NOT FUCKING AROUND HERE, GAGE! I WILL GUT YOUR WIFE. DO YOU UNDERSTAND ME? I WILL DO IT AND I WILL BOTTLE UP HER BLOOD AND FUCKING SHIP IT TO YOU UPS. NOW GET ME THOSE FUCKING FILES!"

The phone vibrated in my hand from the force of his bellow.

"Don't you hurt her," I said, paralyzed with fear.

"You go to the police and she dies," Roy said, his voice calm again. "I'm not going back to jail, so they can take me out in a body bag for all I care. And since I can't get to you as easy as I can get to Anna, I'll make sure you go down for Jorge's murder. I've still got that over you. Everything has been arranged. Anything happens to me, something happens to you, and to Anna. And I promise, Gage, I'll show her no mercy. It will be a long and painful death. Understood?"

"Understood," I repeated.

The call disconnected. I looked at the picture of Anna again, tracing the contours of her face with my finger, wishing above all else I could hold her in my arms, take away the fear from her eyes.

Roy ended the call thinking I was going to follow his instructions to the letter. But I didn't head to the server room to download the files. No, this was going to end once and for all. The only solution for me was to rescue Anna and get away from Roy, from Arlington, from Lithio Systems—and not for a little while, but for good.

I raced down the hall to the foyer. The receptionist at her desk said hello to me, but I didn't even think to respond. Instead, I threw open the double doors leading to the outside and dashed across the parking lot to my car, all while dialing Brad's cell.

CHAPTER 54

I waited for Brad on the street with the car engine running. He was on a job, so I picked him up at a residence in Bedford.

While waiting, I had my phone out, looking at the picture of Anna. My eyes were ringed with tears, blurring the image of my wife bound and gagged, a knife held to her throat.

I tried to get a read on Lily. I studied her face, her eyes. Would she hurt Anna? Could she kill? *Yes*, I thought. Yes she could. It was all about money and Roy. Lily would do as Roy commanded. It was the same distant, detached look she'd given me when I confronted her about the missing folder. She was under Roy's spell, and Anna meant nothing to her. If indeed they had a friendship, whatever bond there had been was gone. Lily would do Roy's bidding. It was there in her eyes.

Brad got into the car, but before I could drive, I had to focus. I knew what I was capable of doing under great pressure—I could organize a funeral for my wife and son, I could host family and friends in the days and weeks following their burials, I could pop a pill and go to work each day, and I could damn well stay focused and calm enough to save my wife.

I got quiet for a moment, gathering my center, fortifying my resolve.

"Are you all right?" Brad asked.

"No," I said. "I'm not all right. Not at all." I handed Brad my phone to show him the picture of Anna being held hostage at knifepoint. I watched the color drain from his face.

"My God, Gage," he whispered.

I slammed the car into reverse, burning rubber as I spun out into the road.

"Yeah," I said. "My God."

Brad held onto my phone and was looking at the picture of Anna while I drove at probably too high a rate of speed and glanced at the time on the dashboard clock. I didn't know when I'd drive these roads again, or see my parents, or even Brad for that matter. The road map to my future had transformed into something unrecognizable, a total eclipse into which I could not see past today.

My conviction was strong—I was going to rescue Anna and make sure Roy couldn't hurt anybody I cared about ever again. But first I had to find Anna, and then I needed a plan to set her free. That was why I included Brad. I felt confident I could get Anna away from Lily and Roy, but only if I had help creating a distraction. Brad was the only person I trusted.

"It could be dangerous," I said, giving Brad a chance to back out. We were headed into Boston, fighting our way through the unyielding push of afternoon traffic.

"What if I don't go with you?" Brad countered.

"Then I'll do it alone."

"And you'll probably end up dead."

I shrugged off that distinct possibility with maybe a bit too much nonchalance.

"It'll be what it'll be," I said.

Brad mulled this over.

"You sure we can't go to the cops?"

"He'll kill her. Roy won't go back inside. He said so."

"Bluffing?"

"Not a chance I'm willing to take."

Brad gave this some additional consideration. "Okay," he said, running his fingers across his mustache. "So what's your plan? What's our next step?"

"We need to find where Roy is holding Anna," I said.

"And how do we accomplish that?"

"We go ask the one guy who said he could track Roy down anywhere he'd hide and find out where he might have taken her."

Brad had never been to this section of East Boston before, and he certainly had never heard of a restaurant called Nicky's. We had parked down the street, not far from where Roy parked his Camaro on our first visit here. Waves of heat rose from the scorching sidewalk, and the stench of trash cooking in overflowing barrels sent wafts of foul-smelling air my way. Not that this smell deterred any locals from enjoying a fine meal at Nicky's. I saw people going into the restaurant with scowls and coming out with smiles on their faces.

"So you're just going to go ask this drug dealer to

help you out?" Brad asked, studying the restaurant from a distance. He shielded his eyes from the glare of the late-afternoon sun even though he was wearing his signature aviator shades.

"Yeah," I said. "That's the plan."

"And why do you think he's going to help you?"

"Because I'm going to do what Roy did to me."

"And that is?"

"I'm going to show him my text messages with Roy. They're incriminating enough. I'll threaten to send it out to the police if he doesn't help."

"From what you described, he doesn't seem like a guy who responds well to threats."

"It's the best I've got."

"What if he calls your bluff?"

"We'll improvise."

Brad groaned.

"What?" I asked.

Brad shook his head. "I was afraid you were going to say that." He followed me into the restaurant.

The setting was all too familiar. A waitress was working the front room, and I could hear noises spilling out from the upper-level dining area. I hadn't ever seen it in use during any of my prior visits. It was later in the day, so maybe Nicky waited for the after-work crowd to open that section of his restaurant.

I went right to the bar with Brad close on my heels, glancing briefly at the elevated round table where a week ago Roy and I sat with a million dollars at our feet.

The bartender, the same stocky guy I saw working the first time I came to Nicky's, was at the sink drying glasses with a dishrag. The tweed cap he apparently favored stayed firmly rooted on his round head even with his gaze lowered on the glasses.

I went up to him, trying to look confident while ignoring all the other emotions. I thought of Anna, her picture etched in my mind, her distress embedded in my heart. She would give me the strength I needed to do what had to be done.

"Excuse me," I said. "I'd like to speak with the owner, please. I'd like to see Nicky." I tried to bolster my confidence with a smile, but I'm sure it looked forced. The thought of squaring off with Nicky Stacks was not one I relished.

The bartender looked up at me without a flicker of recognition. He picked up a phone behind the bar and keyed in a number. Next I heard him say, "Yeah, it's me. There's some guy here who wants to see you. Okay."

He turned back to me. "Just a sec, all right? You guys need anything to drink?"

"No, thanks," I said.

Brad leaned into me. "What now?" he whispered in my ear.

"Now we wait."

A few minutes later there was no sign of Nicky Stacks. Did he know I was here? Was he preparing an ambush? Was Roy in contact with him? All these thoughts simultaneously came at me when I saw a short and slight Korean woman exit through the kitchen doors and approach the bar. She was dressed for work, wearing a sauce-stained apron over a blue dress made of heavy fabric. Her graying hair was nested inside a mesh hairnet. The woman walked right up to me while I was looking over her shoulder for Nicky to come out the same door.

"Yes?" she asked. "Can I help you with something?" She spoke with a slight accent.

"Yes," I said. "I'm looking for Nicky."

The woman nodded. "Yeah. That's me. I'm Nicky."

I blinked several times and looked back at Brad, my brain foggy and confused.

"No, I'm sorry," I said. "Let me explain. I'm looking for Nicky Stacks. He's a big guy. Big," I repeated, reaching my hand above my head, thinking for some reason I needed to pantomime the description to make myself clear. "He owns this place."

The woman shrugged and returned my quizzical look with one of her own. "I don't know any Nicky Stacks, but I'm Nicky and I own this restaurant."

I turned my gaze to the bartender, thinking he could vouch for my story.

"You remember me, right? I was here with a guy named Roy Ripson. We met with Nicky Stacks, the owner of this place, right up there." I pointed at the entrance to the upstairs portion of the restaurant.

"A lot of guys come here," the bartender said with a shrug. "But I don't know anybody named Roy. Look, I can't keep track of everybody who comes and goes from here, buddy. Sorry, I can't help."

"I can help," the woman said with confidence. "I've owned this restaurant for fifteen years. I'm Nicky of Nicky's. Well, I'm really Mi-Yun, but who is going to eat Italian food if I called the place Mi-Yun's, huh?" Mi-Yun threw her head back with a roar of laughter as if she'd never told that joke before. "My grandmother and mother wanted me to cook Korean food, but me, I loved the meatballs and sauce." Again she laughed.

"I don't get it," I said. "I've met Nicky Stacks. I've met the owner."

Mi-Yun looked at me with a hint of concern. “Look, mister, I don’t know who you met here,” she said. “But I can tell you one thing for certain.” Mi-Yun held up one finger to emphasize her point. “Whoever you met, he wasn’t the owner of this restaurant.”

CHAPTER 55

My thoughts were spinning. Where was Nicky Stacks? It didn't make any sense. Roy had been clear. Nicky Stacks was the owner of Nicky's. Who was Mi-Yun, and what had become of the bull-headed man who threatened my life?

I rethought my plan. Maybe I should just go back to Lithio Systems and get Roy the real design plans for Olympian. It was the *Kobayashi Maru* test all over again, the test for which there was no good outcome. Destroy Lithio Systems or save Anna?

I drove Brad back to my condo in Arlington. I couldn't think straight in any other setting, and I needed a new plan of attack. We got home just fine, but I wasn't prepared for the profound feeling of despair I encountered upon setting foot inside. My wife was gone, but I could feel her presence. Perhaps it was the negative energy left behind by a terrifying kidnapping, something Brad must have picked up on as well. He looked disturbed and agitated.

I imagined Anna's terror as she raced to get away from Roy. Chairs were tipped over, and an end table too. Had he hurt her? Had he used drugs to render her unconscious?

I swallowed my fear. For Anna's sake, I had to stay lucid. Of course that also meant popping an Adderall, which I did in the bathroom.

"What now?" Brad asked.

I was pacing in the living room, trying to answer that question for myself. *What now?*

"I need to find Anna. I need to find out where Roy is holding her hostage."

"I get that," Brad said. "But how?"

I took out my phone and looked at the image of Anna once again. It was surreal. I internalized her fear and felt it as if it were my own.

Hold it together, Gage. For Anna's sake, pull yourself together.

"The image," I said. "Look at it with me." Brad knew as much about construction as any general contractor. He'd have some good insights. "What can you tell me about the space?"

Brad took the phone, studied the image, and took a moment to get composed.

"Good God, Gage," he said. "Who are these people? Why didn't I see Lily's aura for who she really was?"

"Maybe she's a chameleon," I suggested.

"Or she knew how to guard herself. She knew how to shut it off."

"It's not your fault," I said. "Don't blame yourself. Let's focus on this. What can you tell me about the picture?"

Brad made a careful study.

"The building is old," he said. "Very old, in fact. You can see the wide plank flooring—over eight inches wide, I'd say. Looks like pine. It's a soft wood, easy to handsaw and face nail to a beam or a joist."

"What else?" I asked.

"Look to the sides here," he said. "It looks like she's in an empty room. Can you upload this to a computer? I want to get a closer look."

My eyes went wide as excitement boomed through my chest.

"The image," I said, slapping my forehead because the answer should have been obvious. Guess I needed Brad to make mention of a computer to jog my memory. Having worked with cell phones at Lithio Systems for so long, I knew every feature like I was a walking, talking product manual.

"You can extract location information from an image," I said.

Brad appeared surprised. "Doesn't it have to be tagged on Facebook or Foursquare or something like that? The girls do that a lot. I kept telling them to stop in case a stalker wants to track them down."

"No," I said, feeling the excitement coursing through me now. "It gets stored in an exchangeable image file format, Exif for short. Typically the default setting for this service is turned on and people don't even know it. Using an Exif viewer I can get all sorts of location information from an image, including location data. It may not reveal an exact location," I said, "but it could provide us a general idea."

"A general idea might be good enough," Brad agreed. "We'll know to look for old construction, something with thick concrete walls and what looks like a big metal door. A really heavy door, in fact."

"Okay," I said. "Let me get to work on this."

I checked the time.

Four hours to go.

"What do you want me to do in the meantime? I can

try to search for Nicky Stacks," Brad said. "Make some calls."

The word that caught my attention was *search.*

"Go up to the apartment and look around. Look everywhere. See if maybe they left behind something that might give us some idea where they could have taken Anna." I stood to get my laptop, and Brad headed upstairs.

At this point, my thoughts, lucid and rational thanks to a punch of Adderall, betrayed me. My mind flashed on an image of Anna's corpse, gutted as Roy had promised. A shiver ripped through me, so powerful it nearly sent me to my knees. I calmed myself by pacing a series of rapid circles around the dining room table, head lowered, massaging the base of my neck, and eventually settled enough to get my laptop.

Back at the dining room table where Anna had watched me build model rockets for hours on end, where we ate and fantasized about soon putting out place settings for three instead of two, I powered up my laptop and downloaded a Safari extension that would allow me to view the Exif data.

It took a while, a bit of downloading and clicking, but soon enough I had the image open in the Exif viewer and found the coordinates where the geolocation data were displayed. I pasted those coordinates into Google Earth. With a quick refresh of the screen, Google Earth transported me as if I were free falling from space to an aerial view of North America, and then to Station Street in Brookline Village.

The Village, as it is often referred to, is a very neighborly section of Brookline, the town abutting Boston. Brookline's earliest shops and restaurants started here, and to this day the Village retains a special charm, evoking the feel of a small town within the confines of a city.

Google Maps displayed the names of all identified businesses near the coordinates I had entered, giving me a broad overview of this area. I saw a post office, a coffee shop, a yoga studio, a restaurant, and one especially interesting business: Longview Storage Company, a yellow-brick structure about six stories high.

With a couple of mouse clicks, the website of Longview Storage told me all I needed to know. The About Us section contained an old advertisement for the business when it first opened to the public. It was originally called Brookline Storage Warehouse, and it specialized in storing furniture, pianos, works of art, trunks, carriages, sleighs, and merchandise of all kinds. The old ad ran in the now defunct Brookline Street Directory and it was from the year 1903.

We're looking for an old building . . .

I was about to go trumpet my announcement to Brad when he came into the dining room with a small, colorful cardboard box in his hand. It took a second to recognize the familiar labeling of Alka-Seltzer tablets.

Brad dropped the box onto the dining room table in front of me and said, "I found this in the medicine cabinet upstairs." Something rattled inside.

Reaching for the box I said, "Thanks, buddy. I could use something to calm my stomach."

"That's not why I brought this down," Brad said. "Check out what I found inside the box."

I tipped the box open and out spilled a circular plastic container holding about thirty pills. The center of the case had a movable circle with written instructions to use a coin to set the starting day. Next to each pill was written a day of the week, Monday through Sunday, repeating. The pills were color-coded: red, green, yellow, and white, seven pills in each set, one for every day of the week.

I held the pill container in my hand, trying to make sense of what I was seeing. I steeled myself against a fresh wave of nausea, feeling as if the floor had dropped out from beneath me.

"I'm a plumber, not a doctor," Brad said, "but I do know that a pregnant woman doesn't need to use birth control pills."

CHAPTER 56

Brad was on the phone to his contact at the Brookline building department. Through his plumbing business, Brad knew the town building people in almost every area he serviced, and all of them considered him a friend. He wanted to get detailed building plans of the Longview Storage Company. From there we'd be able to figure out a possible plan of attack.

I wasn't going to change my mind about calling the police. Roy was a desperate man who felt trapped and cornered, and if he felt threatened there was a good chance Anna would die.

My mission might not have changed, but the facts surrounding it were startlingly different. Nicky Stacks didn't own Nicky's restaurant, and Lily apparently wasn't pregnant. I had to assume she had never even been pregnant. If so, that changed everything. It meant she wanted something from us, and I thought I knew what that was.

Before I could confirm my suspicion, I had to check something else out first.

Brad finished his call. "My buddy at town hall is

going to take pictures of the architectural plans and text them to me. I should have them in a little bit."

I nodded as I sucked down a breath fraught with anxiety. My heart was doing cartwheels in my chest, and it wasn't from my most recent Adderall fix.

"If she was never pregnant, that means she targeted us," I said.

"Why you? How would she know you?"

"The ParentHorizon website," I said. "Our profile was on the site with a lot of personal information about us. What if she checked out our profile before she even told us she was pregnant? What if we didn't just stumble on her? What if she had cross-referenced our names to our address? She could have been following us, for days, for weeks, who knows, waiting for the opportunity to strike."

"So she was stalking people who wanted to adopt a baby?" Brad asked.

"Not people who wanted a baby," I said. "She was stalking us."

"But why you guys?" Brad asked.

"I don't know."

"What about her belly? You said she was showing."

"Not much," I said. "Not at first, anyway. And when she did start, it was a little swell. She could have just been gaining weight intentionally."

"And the ultrasound? Didn't you tell me that you saw an ultrasound of the baby?"

My eyes grew wide. I sprinted out of the dining room and returned moments later with the ultrasound image Anna kept in a desk drawer in her office. She'd looked at it, occasionally sneaking glances at the picture of an unborn baby, fantasizing about our future, imagining how it would feel to once again call a baby her own, desperate to become what she treasured above all else—a mother.

"Anna brought Lily to her OB/GYN appointment, but Lily told her to wait in the parking lot. Lily said she was nervous and feeling superstitious and preferred to be alone, which made sense to me at the time, but now I'm thinking she had an ulterior motive."

"Such as?"

"Such as not meeting with Dr. Andrew Hill and not getting an ultrasound from there."

"If that's true, where did the ultrasound come from?" Brad asked.

I pulled the sonogram out of its official-looking manila envelope and studied the grayscale image closely. The lima bean shape of the eleven-week-old fetus encased within the blackness of a uterus was easy to see. The fetus appeared to be reclining, with its head, arms, and legs all clearly defined. I didn't notice anything unusual about the image, no special markings or dates—it was just a picture—which on further consideration I realized was a bit strange. I hadn't had a lot of X-rays, but Max broke his thumb once and I remembered the image was stamped with a date and time and other details, a code that probably made sense to the medical records folks.

The image seemed small, portrait-sized. I wondered if those special markings had been removed by careful image cropping. I turned the image over in my hand and studied the back.

The paper was made from heavy but pliable material, like photo paper used by a printer. I turned it around in my hands, tracing the edges for anything unusual. Using the nail of my thumb, I flicked at the corners until, after a bit of scratching and prying, one edge lifted up. I tugged at the lifted corner until the sticky white paper came free, like an oversized sticker mounted to the back of the ultrasound image. The sticky sheet rolled into a tubular shape in my hand. Someone had wanted to hide something on the back of this image.

I turned the sonogram over and saw words in gold type and set at an angle in a repeating pattern, much like a watermark. My thoughts whirled as I scanned the words Tiny Body Imaging printed at least a dozen times on the back of the sonogram.

"Lily never had an ultrasound done," I said to Brad, handing him the image to examine for himself. "She hid it from me and from Anna."

"What's Tiny Body Imaging?" Brad asked.

I did a quick Google search on my laptop. "It's a retail outfit offering recreational medical imaging," I said. "They're in malls all over the country."

Brad kept his gaze locked on the image of somebody's baby, someone we didn't know. "Why would Lily go through all this trouble? What was she doing?"

"I don't know," I said. "But I'm going to find some answers." I closed my eyes to gather my composure, and a vision came to me.

I could see the drunk driver in an old, rust-colored Toyota weaving his way down an empty two-lane stretch of road, headed on a collision course—not with Max and Karen this time, but with Anna. Anna stood in the middle of the road, frozen in place like a statue as the car accelerated toward her.

"I'm not going to let it happen again," I said to Brad. "This time it's going to be different. I won't let anything happen to her."

Again, I checked the time on my watch.

We had less than three hours remaining on Roy's deadline.

CHAPTER 57

I was packing what I needed from my condo: a couple suitcases of clothes, our passports, my laptop computer, pictures of Max and Karen, the picture of Kevin and Anna (the one with Edward's image Photoshopped out), and the little silver locket that hung on my bathroom medicine cabinet. I had no intention of returning to this house, and even with my outstanding achievement award at work, I had no plans of going back to Lithio Systems either. I had as much business working there as Matt Simons.

Anna would have to let her business go. Maybe she wouldn't. Maybe she'd refuse to come with me. It would be her choice, but my plan (hard to even call it that) was to rescue my wife and disappear—go to New York, and from there, catch a flight to a place where Roy wouldn't have any power over me. Where the murder of a drug dealer couldn't get me extradited to America.

While I packed, Brad kept glancing at his phone, anxiously waiting for the text messages from his contact at the Brookline Building Department. We needed to study the building plans for Longview Storage to know exactly what sort of distraction to create. I kept trying to focus on the packing and not the time, but it was hard. Every tick of the clock, every new minute, brought me closer to a deadline I wasn't going to meet.

"Something keeps bothering me," I said to Brad, zipping my suitcase shut.

"Just one thing?"

I gave him a sideways glance. "On the phone Roy said his middleman was going to come after him because the buyer felt cheated out of a million dollars."

"Makes sense to me," Brad said. "You gave Roy sanitized product plans."

"Exactly," I said. "Whoever it was, the buyer knew enough about making batteries to know they bought nothing useful."

"And your point?"

"I'd really like to know who bought those plans."

Brad was about to respond when the phone buzzed in his hand.

"This is it," he said. "I got the building layout." Brad became quiet as he studied the architectural drawings.

I continued to wrestle with my doubts. Should I risk bringing help in the form of the police, or should Brad and I go at it alone? Would he hurt Anna? Gut her, as he so chillingly threatened? What would happen if the choice I made cost Anna her life? I didn't think I could go on. How could I live with myself if I was once again responsible for the death of someone I loved? My thoughts were a mixed-up mess, a blend of my two lives, the one I lived with Karen and Max and my current life with Anna.

I should never have gone to the Sox game. I should have been the one driving Max to his soccer match. I shouldn't have kept secrets from Anna. I should have told her everything as it was happening. She would have believed me. I should have trusted her.

I had failed Anna. Now she was Roy's hostage, and I was terrified of failing her again.

What should I do?

"I think I can create a diversion," Brad said. "Something that would draw Roy out."

"How?"

"I'll blow up a boiler," Brad said. "Well, not a huge explosion, but enough to get his attention. We'll need to go to Bedford first so I can get my van and tools."

"We can do that," I said. "What about your gun? Can we get that, too?"

Brad took some time to mull this over. His fingers spread out across the hairs on his mustache—his thinking habit. Eventually he said, "Yeah, we can and should do that."

For the next several minutes, Brad showed me the plans on his phone and explained his thinking in more detail. We used Google Earth to get a bird's-eye view of the building.

Longview Storage was actually composed of two buildings, a smaller one constructed of yellow bricks that abutted Station Street, and a larger red brick structure directly behind it. A narrow north–south alley ran between the post office on the corner of Washington and Station Street, and the storage warehouse, and connected with a much larger throughway, something between an alley and a road, probably used as a loading zone, running east–west behind the larger of the two buildings.

Brad switched our focus to the building plans sent to his phone. He zoomed in on the north–south alley, more specifically on a row of basement windows through which he felt we could secretly enter the building.

"If I park my van in front of the alley," Brad said, "it'll block the view of any pedestrians on Station Street who might see us entering the storage warehouse through those windows. I'll keep my hazards on so it'll look like I'll be right back. Worst thing that can happen is I get a ticket for illegal parking."

"Where do we create the distraction?"

Brad zoomed in on a section of the basement where the building plans showed the existence of a boiler.

"The boiler room is in the basement near the front of the building," Brad said. He wasn't acting agitated or anxious but kept his explanations calm and clear. That energy inspired me. Maybe he acted this way intentionally, sensing my aura needed some serious calming.

"Anna is being held either in one of the storage units above the basement in the smaller building," Brad said, "or in the units in the much larger secondary structure. Either way, a slight change in pressure will trigger a small blast, powerful enough to get the attention of anybody inside."

"What about the police? I don't want them coming while we're escaping."

"We'll want to disconnect the link to the fire department in case the sprinklers go off or the smoke alarms sound, which I should be able to do. I'll just have to find the box controlling the sprinkler system. Bottom line is we should have enough time to draw Roy out from his hiding place, take him by surprise, and then get him to lead us to Anna. Once we have Anna, we'll need to secure Roy and Lily inside one of the storage rooms and then vanish out the back. You'll need to park your car on Washington Street. Then I'll go get my van."

If all went according to plan, Anna and I would soon be on our way to New York, outrunning Roy and a potential murder charge.

Brad took hold of my hands, and I pulled them away.

"Relax, Gage," he said. "I'm not going to connect you, I'm trying to tell you something."

I nodded, feeling slightly foolish. Brad reached for my hands again, and this time I let him take hold.

"We're going to have to be strong for Anna," he said, locking eyes with me. "We're going to have to be calm and level-headed, like we're doing a job. Can you handle it, Gage? This is your wife we're talking about. Can you be detached enough to focus and execute? This is a one-shot deal here, and we can't fail."

"I think so," I said.

Brad continued to hold my hands for several seconds, getting his answer not from my mouth but from someplace deeper inside me—a place he could touch and I couldn't.

"Okay," Brad said. "Then we should go."

Before long, Brad and I were driving west on Route 2, headed for Bedford, not Brookline. I was quiet for the first part of the drive, trying to answer a troublesome question. After a mile or so of drawing blanks, I decided to get Brad's opinion on the matter.

"Why did he bring Anna there?" I asked him. "Why is Roy holding Anna in that storage warehouse?"

Brad squinted. "It's safe," he speculated. "A quiet place, not a lot of foot traffic. He doesn't have an apartment, right?"

"No, he got kicked out, or at least that's what Lily said. But why would he go there?"

"Maybe he rented a storage space there?"

"In Brookline? That's pretty far away."

"Could he know the owner?" Brad wondered. "Maybe he once had a job there. Maybe he has the keys."

I nodded because it made some sense.

"Can we check who owns the building?"

"The owner's name is included with the plans. I'll look him up."

"What's the guy's name?" I asked.

"Jack Hutchinson," Brad said.

Using his phone, Brad Googled the name Jack Hutchinson and the keywords Longview Storage Company. It took a bit of digging and searching, because for a few minutes Brad worked his phone and kept his thoughts to himself.

"Got something on this website Corporation Wiki.com," he finally announced.

I looked at him expectantly.

"There's not too much information specifically on Hutchinson," Brad continued, "just some details about when he took ownership of the business and a link to his website, a business address and such, but there is a small portrait picture of him."

"Show me."

Brad held the phone at my eye level. I risked a quick glance. I had to jerk the wheel hard left to pull the car out of the breakdown lane.

"Whoa!" Brad said, his fingers gripping the dash to keep from body slamming into me. "You okay, buddy?"

My breath came in short spurts, my thoughts a whirlpool.

"Gage, you're pale. What's going on?"

"The picture," I said, breathing hard. "I know that guy."

"You know Jack Hutchinson?"

The man in the picture didn't look angry or menacing like the man I knew. He was smiling and wearing a nice suit. Clearly, this was his professional portrait. "I don't know him by the name Jack Hutchinson," I said, my voice ringing distant in my ears. "I know him as Nicky Stacks."

CHAPTER 58

I was on my way to Brookline, lost in thought, trying to piece together a logical explanation by using facts only a bit less revealing than the dark side of the moon.

Nicky Stacks was really a man named Jack Hutchinson. He wasn't the owner of Nicky's restaurant, as I had believed, but rather the owner of a self-storage business where Roy currently had Anna held hostage. I thought Nicky (or Jack) had cut ties with Roy. Could they be in business together again? Allies, even? And now I knew the woman who had miraculously come into our lives, who Anna and I once thought of as the birth mother of our unborn child, was taking birth control pills and got her sonogram from a mall. What did it all mean?

Checking the rearview mirror, I caught a glimpse of Brad in his van following close behind. Even with the air conditioner blasting on high, my sweat-drenched back clung to the leather seat. The palms of my hands turned the steering wheel slick. I needed to strengthen my resolve, so I perched my cell phone on the dash in a way that let me see the picture of Anna.

Anna's wide eyes radiated anxiety, while Lily's veiled

expression said nothing to me. She didn't appear anxious, or excited, or even angry. If anything, she seemed calm and composed—professional, I'd have to say, as if she'd done this before.

Twenty minutes later we arrived in Brookline Village. We got there when the bells of the clock tower on top of the redbrick firehouse rang out six times for six o'clock—two hours before Roy's deadline, and many hours for Anna to have lived in terror.

I turned right on Washington Street, and Brad followed in his plumbing truck. This section of Brookline was an idyllic setting, befitting the village's name. The wide and clean sidewalks were lined with verdant ginkgo trees, all tenderly trimmed and lovingly cared for. This could have been Main Street USA with a charming stretch of redbrick buildings fronted by green storefront awnings on the lower levels and apartments above. I doubted the village looked much different from when the Longview Storage Company had opened for business in 1903.

We stopped at a light, and I rolled down my window. Pedestrians were out in force, some enjoying a leisurely stroll, others venturing in and out of stores, some walking with an ice cream or iced coffee in hand. Birdsong filled the air. Leaning my head out the window, I could see clouds drift across an azure sky. It was a perfect time of day, and nothing suggested the horrific events unfolding inside the Longview Storage Warehouse.

Brad and I cruised down Washington Street, past the loading zone where I planned to exit the storage warehouse with Anna. I didn't see anybody guarding the area, so I pulled my car over and parked in an open space on the adjacent block. Brad pulled over, and I climbed into his van. He drove until he could turn the vehicle around, and we backtracked to Station Street.

I took out my phone again, looking at Anna once more. This time, as I studied her face, I let my anger flow and felt it supercharge my determination. Anna had suffered enough. I wasn't going to let her suffer anymore.

"I'm coming, baby," I said, my eyes on Anna, my thumb blocking out Lily completely. "I'm coming to get you."

Brad waited at a stoplight. When he could, he made the left onto Station Street. He drove a hundred feet or so, made a three-point turn, backtracked some, and parked the van in front of the alleyway between the post office and the storage warehouse. He let the van idle.

"Last chance," he said. "We can go to the police right now."

I mulled this over for all of five seconds.

"I won't risk it," I said. "We got to take Roy by surprise. Otherwise there's no telling what he'll do to Anna."

"And, I guess, to you," Brad said. He reached across my lap to open the glove compartment. "It makes sense that if Roy and this Jack Hutchinson fellow are working together they'd be able to pin the murder charge on you."

"Only they're not setting me up. I actually killed him."

Brad didn't respond. He took a gun from the glove compartment and handed it to me.

I hefted the weapon in my hand, keeping it low, being careful not to let it be visible to anybody passing by.

"It's a Glock 17," I said, inspecting the gun closely.

Brad looked at me with a surprised expression.

My mind flashed to the image of Jorge flailing as he fell, blood spilling from a wound in his chest from a bullet hole created by this exact type of weapon. I spoke softly and slowly, staring at the gun.

"It weighs nine hundred and ten grams fully loaded. It's a hundred eighty-six millimeters long and has a mag capacity of seventeen and a trigger pull of five-point-five pounds."

"Geez, Gage," Brad said. "What's up with that?"

"Let's just say I have a mind for useless numbers."

"Yeah? Well, let's hope we don't have to put any of those numbers to use," Brad added.

I nodded.

After checking to make sure the safety was on before climbing out of the van, I stuffed the gun into the waistband of my jeans, recalling the last time I'd felt the same uncomfortable pressure against the small of my back.

Brad flicked the hazard lights on and got out as well, and I watched as he opened the van's back doors and removed his toolbox. We proceeded down a short flight of stairs that terminated at the mouth of the alley. I did a quick check behind me and saw the van perfectly blocked any pedestrian's view. *Well done, Brad.*

The basement of the warehouse had three windows, each maybe a bit larger than a transom, spaced evenly about ten feet apart. Brad opened his toolbox and removed an instrument the size of a pencil, with three break-out notches, a tapping ball on one end, and a hardened steel cutting wheel on the other. He also took out a suction cup attached to a small plastic handle.

"A good plumber is always prepared," Brad said.

The cutter made a slight scraping sound as Brad worked the tool along the edges of the glass. When he finished cutting around the window's perimeter, Brad pulled on the handle of the suction cup. The window came free without a sound. I watched as Brad carefully wrapped the glass in bubble wrap and put it in his toolbox along with the suction cup and cutter. He slid through the window headfirst and I waited until he reached up before handing him his toolbox.

Then it was my turn. I went through the opening, feeling the rough edge of the windowsill scrape against my belly, aware of the gun against my back. I emerged into a massive concrete basement with floor-to-ceiling support posts spaced throughout. The fluorescent ceiling light fixtures were off, but diffused sunlight spilling in through the basement windows lit the space well enough for me to see. It was a dusty basement, somewhat littered, but it was definitely maintained. It was obvious this was a working business.

Soon enough Brad had his flashlight trained on the oil boiler on the opposite side of the room, directly across from the window through which we had entered. While Brad went to inspect the boiler, I took a look around for the staircase leading to the upper floors. Brad was working at a nearby fuse box when I whistled for him to come join me.

He looked pleased with something. "The sprinkler system and fire alarm won't be a problem," he said in a whisper. "It will buy us more time to get away."

"Good," I said, whispering back. "If we stand on either side of this doorway, we'll be able to surprise Roy when he comes to check on the disturbance."

"It'll be smoky, but this space is big enough that it'll take some time before it becomes unbearable."

I looked around and found a flat piece of wood, big enough to cover the window we broke to gain entry. "I don't want any smoke spilling out to attract someone's attention. We can remove the board once we get Roy," I said. I tried to calm myself, but even my breathing wouldn't settle. My eyes were pinwheeling in their sockets.

"Time to get to work," Brad said. "I'm going to separate the electrodes, which will give us a delayed ignition. It should create a loud-enough boom to get Roy down here. I'll come join you in a minute. Stay on guard."

I knew what Brad meant. I took out the gun and undid the safety.

Moments later, Brad, toolbox at his side, started working on the boiler like he'd been paid to fix a problem, not create one. I was feeling the pressure, like a boiler ready to explode myself.

Would this work? Could we rescue Anna? Could we get away?

In the cracks of my nervous thoughts, I tried to make sense of the Roy and Jack Hutchinson connection. Why would Lily have pretended to be pregnant? Why would Jack Hutchinson pretend to be a guy named Nicky Stacks? Why would he pretend to own a restaurant? What's the common thread? I thought I had the glimmer of an answer, something too nascent for me to grasp, when Brad came running over with his toolbox in hand.

"We've got about a minute," Brad said. He bent down and removed a monkey wrench from inside the toolbox, slapping the heavy metal end against the meatiest part of his palm.

"You sure it's going to be a loud-enough boom?"

Brad glanced at me with a slight twinkle in his eye. I was reminded of the anticipation I felt before the launch of one of my rockets. It was always an exciting moment, those anticipatory few seconds between the fuse igniting and the rocket blasting off, screeching skyward to reach for the stars. My pulse began to pound, and I found myself gripping the gun tighter in my hand. Brad checked his watch.

"Yeah," he said. "It'll be loud enough."

A few seconds later a loud bang, like a dozen cars simultaneously backfiring, shook the floor beneath me. I went flat against the door frame, knocked off balance by the force of the explosion. Almost immediately, an inky black cloud began billowing out from the boiler, enveloping everything it touched.

"Now we wait," Brad said.

We watched as smoke poured out from the ruptured boiler, knowing soon enough we'd be consumed in its wake. Brad checked the time.

"Thirty seconds," he said. "We've got about thirty seconds before it's going to get ugly down here."

I shut my eyes, keeping my back against the door frame to the basement's only exit, and held the gun close to my chest. I started to count.

"One . . . two . . . three . . ." My thoughts went to Anna. I said silent prayers for her safety.

"Fifteen . . . sixteen . . ."

My throat began to close as the first poisoned air seeped into my lungs. Spellbound, I watched the black smoke roll on inch by inch as it consumed more of the basement.

I will not fail you, Anna. I will not fail.

And then I saw Max and Karen, their faces coming to me like angels from the darkness, piercing my heart.

"Twenty-five . . . twenty-six . . ."

The black smoke crept closer.

"Twenty-seven . . ."

I heard footsteps, fast and furious, racing down the stairs. I pressed my body even flatter against the wall and saw Brad do the same. He wielded the wrench in his fist like it was a club. I took a short, sharp breath.

A figure emerged through the doorway and took several steps into the basement. It wasn't Roy, I could tell, even though his back was to me. He was much broader than Roy. He seemed to be dressed up, wearing a suit, but he wasn't the man I knew as Nicky Stacks. This man was much smaller than Stacks. Another figure came racing through the doorway, dressed the same as the first. The two men stood together with their backs to me, surveying the mayhem. Like mirror images, each man put his hands on his knees to seek out purer air while coughing out the bad stuff.

They turned around, the heels of their fine leather shoes spinning and scraping against the concrete floor, getting ready to make a fast exit.

I stepped away from the wall and pointed my gun at them. I was about to shout "Freeze!" but something made me stop.

Behind the two men, impenetrable black smoke billowed and rose like a dark blanket settling across the barren room. With enough light seeping in through the basement windows, I could just make out their faces, more specifically their startled eyes.

Brad is right. The dead do walk among us.

I was staring into the eyes of a ghost: Jorge Moreno, standing next to his brother, Lucas.

CHAPTER 59

The two men charged us as though a starter pistol had gone off. Lucas came roaring at Brad, reaching in his suit jacket for a gun. Jorge mirrored his brother's movements while setting his sights on me. Jorge Moreno—the Jorge I had supposedly killed—had the skin coloring of a healthy man and the speed and agility of a highly conditioned athlete.

I raised my gun as Jorge closed the short gap between us. He was ten feet from me, and the time I had to react could be measured in hundredths of a second, or five-point-five pounds of pressure. Instead of pulling the trigger, I flashed on the memory of blood exploding from Jorge's chest. In that split second, I relived the sickening feeling of becoming a killer. I couldn't take his life again; instead of juicing the trigger, my finger froze.

Jorge had his gun drawn and pointed in the general direction of my head, closing in on me with a final quick burst of speed.

"Get down!" he shouted. "Get on the floor and drop your gun!"

With his heels digging in, Jorge slowed to a stop,

close enough for me to feel his hot breath. The stench of oily smoke burned my nose and lungs. My eyes were watery as the tear reflex kicked in. Soon I'd be gagging on each breath, but the more immediate threat was Jorge and his gun.

I put my hands over my head, moving nice . . . and . . . slow. But I opted to remain standing and I didn't drop my weapon.

To my left, Brad and Lucas had squared off against each other. Brad was still holding onto his wrench and Lucas was still holding onto his gun, not quite even odds, but I had something to tip the balance of power dramatically in our favor. I had the truth.

"You're looking good for a dead man, Jorge," I said.

"Get on the ground," he growled.

The smoke continued to close in on us. Brad's calculation of thirty seconds of good air was a bit off, but not by much. All I needed to do was delay Jorge long enough for the inevitable.

Jorge reached for me and I lowered my weapon and pointed it at his face. Lucas turned his head but kept his gun trained on Brad, who showed no sign of fear. Maybe Brad's window into life after life gave him a sense of peace in the face of mortal terror, or maybe he just had stones the size of grapefruits.

"Go ahead and shoot me, Jorge," I said. "Take me out. Go ahead and do it. I'll be useless to you."

"Get on the ground," Jorge said again.

"How much is it worth to you? Forget how you managed to fake your death. How much do you stand to make?"

I looked over at Brad once more. I hoped he understood my intention. Jorge looked to Lucas, the older brother, the leader of this dynamic duo, his watery eyes seeking guidance. Behind him the black smoke, a moving wall of soupy tar, swarmed and swirled as it occupied all available space. Panic tore through me as I readied myself for the coming collision.

The smoke closed around Jorge's face like two hands reaching out from within the darkness. He coughed at the same instant I kicked. My right ankle locked as my foot lifted higher up between Jorge's legs. I kept my toes pointed down, striking the soft flesh of his groin with the laces of my shoes, just as I had taught Max how to shoot a soccer ball on goal.

Jorge dropped to the floor, clutching between his legs. Lucas shifted his gaze from Brad to Jorge as the black smoke enveloped his head. Brad took advantage and swung the wrench in a wide arc, smashing the steel against Lucas's temple, catching the man completely off guard. I heard a sickening crunch as metal met skull.

Before I could rejoice in our victory, my foot got jerked out from under me. I was falling backward, arms flailing for balance, foot skidding in search of purchase. I slammed onto the concrete floor hard enough to rattle my teeth. Air exploded from my body as the gun bounced out of my hand. I tried to take a breath, but I was like a fish dying on a dock. Nothing was getting into my lungs.

Jorge held onto my leg and began pulling me toward him. I kicked frantically, trying to free myself from his grasp. At least the smoke was thinner down here, so whenever I could finally take in some air, there'd be some air to take in. My vision went dark and my eyes filled with tears. I felt increased pressure on my legs as Jorge began to crawl up my body, grappling me like a wrestler going for the pin.

Air began to tease its way into my lungs, partially fueling my fight, while Jorge continued his crawl up my body. Instead of fists, I made claws with my hands, raking them blindly in search of a target. I heard Jorge grunt. Like a bat seeking its prey by echolocation, my probing fingers connected with his face. Once I hit pay dirt, I dug until the tips of my fingers sank into the fleshiest part of Jorge's eye sockets. He yelped in pain and rolled off my body to get away.

I didn't hesitate or back up. I attacked. From a prone position, inhaling sips of air whenever I could, I rolled across the floor until I came into contact with Jorge, also prone on the floor. I unloaded a furious volley of punches at his head, but punching while lying on the ground was a pretty ineffective way of doing battle. Without any leverage, my blows landed but inflicted little damage.

Though my blurred vision had cleared, it was getting tougher to see by the second. The tar cloud of smoke was descending at a rapid pace. As Jorge and I exchanged feeble blows, I did manage to make out the faint outline of Brad's gun on the floor just a few feet away.

Jorge broke away from me and struggled to get to his knees, mindful to keep his head bent and away from the smoke line above. I could see the clear and distinct boundary between smoky air and the breathable stuff, like oil on water. I could also sense Jorge getting ready to pounce. There was almost no chance I would get to the gun before Jorge got to me. I made a frantic scramble, using my fingers to paw for the weapon as I slid along the floor, shimmying forward like a snake on the move. All the while, oily smoke stung at my eyes and burned my lungs.

Jorge lumbered toward me. I braced myself for the impact when I caught a shimmer of movement flash in front of my eyes. Brad zoomed past me and barreled into Jorge without slowing, knocking him to the floor. As they fought, I crawled the remaining three feet to the gun. With the handle in my grasp, I rolled in their direction. I guessed Lucas was out for the count.

Brad had Jorge in a full nelson hold. Jorge was struggling to break free and gasping for air, but Brad had the better leverage and wasn't letting go.

I shoved the barrel of the gun into Jorge's open mouth. "Stop fighting!"

Jorge went still. I took the gun out of his mouth but kept the barrel pointed at his head. Together Brad and I dragged Jorge to the exit. We made it to the stairwell, where the smoke hadn't yet invaded. Jorge and I both started to cough, but I kept the gun trained on him.

Brad went back into the smoke-filled room. He kept low to the floor and vanished within a few feet. Moments later, he emerged, dragging Lucas. Brad's toolbox was perched on Lucas's barreled chest.

With both men in the stairwell, I put the gun an inch from Jorge's knee.

"This gun doesn't fire blanks," I said. I figured that was how they had staged his death: a gun firing blanks, a remote-controlled blood bag attached to his chest, a first-rate Hollywood-type special effects job. "I don't want to kill you—again—but I won't hesitate to blow off your kneecap. Do you understand me?"

We were all coughing, except for Lucas, who was unconscious but breathing. Brad used some wire from his toolbox to secure Jorge's hands behind his back, forming a makeshift pair of handcuffs, while I kept the gun pointed at Jorge's knee.

"The smoke shouldn't get much worse," Brad said. "We'll call the fire department and an ambulance for this knucklehead once we get Anna out of here." Brad tapped his foot against the ugly red welt already discoloring the side of Lucas's head.

I closed the door to the basement, thinking it would help keep the smoke contained, and waited with Jorge on the stairwell landing while Brad dragged Lucas up to the first level. Brad came down, and together we got Jorge to his feet. I kept the gun against the small of Jorge's back as I escorted him up the basement stairs.

We came out on the first level of the storage warehouse, entering into a narrow hallway. The floor was lined with the green stuff used on minigolf courses. Lucas was facedown on the floor, his hands secured behind his back with wire.

"Where is Anna?" I said.

"Upstairs," Jorge answered.

"Where is the stairwell?"

Jorge nodded to our right, and again we were on the move.

We walked down the narrow hallway with corridors to our left and right. Down those corridors were rows of concrete storage rooms secured by heavy doors. The walls were made from thick concrete. It looked like something out of an old dungeon.

Jorge directed us down one of those corridors, and we came to a stop at a stairwell entrance to the upper levels of the storage warehouse. The corridor was big enough to wheel a cart full of stuff to one of the storage units lining the walls but not wide enough to turn that cart around.

"Call up to Roy," I said.

Jorge looked at me, confused.

"Call up to him and tell him you need help. Tell him to come quick."

Jorge followed my instructions. His voice sounded

raspy from all the smoke, but he spoke loudly and his words were intelligible.

"Roy, we've got a problem," Jorge called. "Come on down here right away." He could have been more convincing. I dug the gun hard into his back. "Hurry, man, I mean it!"

Brad came over and covered Jorge's mouth with a big piece of duct tape so he couldn't issue Roy any warnings.

Footsteps raced down the scuffed wooden stairs in the darkened stairwell. We lined up on the wall beside the stairwell entrance, Jorge sandwiched between Brad and me. Jorge's gun was somewhere in the smoky basement, but Brad had Lucas's weapon, so he could keep Jorge in line while I got ready to take on Roy.

As Roy emerged from the stairwell, I stepped forward and stuck my foot out. Roy tripped over my leg and slammed his face into the wall in front of him. The gun he carried fell from his hand, and I kicked it away. Stunned, kneeling on the floor, Roy turned around slowly.

I stood over him, pointing my gun at his face.

"Hey, shithead," I said. "You have my wife and I want her back."

CHAPTER 60

He was the same Roy I'd come to know: jeans and a black T-shirt, tattoos, rippling muscles, and a hard face. Only now that face was red, from the wall or anger I couldn't say.

"How'd you do it?" I asked him. "How'd you fake his death?" I nodded at Jorge.

Roy didn't answer. I hoisted him to his feet by the front of his shirt.

"I'm guessing you're the leader of this pack, the man in charge. So tell me, where is Nicky Stacks? Oh, I'm sorry, Jack Hutchinson. Is he here?"

Again Roy didn't speak. I prompted him with a quick punch into his side, which dropped Roy to his knees with a grunt. I pulled him back up to standing by his shirt. "Let's try again. Where is Nicky? Where is the owner of this place?" I suspected that Jack Hutchinson also owned a warehouse space down by Eagle Square.

"He's not here," Roy said, panting, breathing hard.

"Anybody else here?"

Roy shook his head. "No, it's just Lily and Anna upstairs."

Brad took a step forward, bringing Jorge with him.

"What's going on here, Gage?" he asked.

"Brad, these guys are con artists of the highest order, all of them—Roy, Lily, Nicky Stacks, the Moreno brothers. They set me up to steal the product plans for Olympian. I'm sure those plans are worth a lot more than the million dollars Roy told me we could get for them."

Brad did the equivalent of a silent film double take.

"It was set up from the very beginning, wasn't it, Roy?" I asked.

Roy kept quiet. I wanted to press him for a confession, but I could smell the smoke down in the basement and figured we didn't have time for lengthy explanations. Besides, I needed to get Anna and we needed to get out of here. I didn't need Roy to tell me what I had already figured out.

"Let's secure him," I said.

I kept a gun on Roy while Brad went to his toolbox and fashioned another pair of wire handcuffs. I took great pleasure seeing Roy's arms wrenched behind his back, those muscles flexing futilely against his restraints.

Brad assessed his handiwork and seemed satisfied. I took the leftover wire, thinking I'd do the same to Lily when the time came.

"Take me to Anna," I said, pushing the gun into Roy's back. "Call up to Lily and tell her not to try anything stupid." I figured Lily would listen to Roy more than she would me.

Brad stayed downstairs to keep watch over the Moreno brothers while I forced Roy upstairs, using the gun as a cattle prod pushed into the small of his back. "Tell Lily not to be stupid," I reminded him. We climbed the darkened stairwell, passing the exit to the second floor on our way up to the third. The stairwell walls were made of thick concrete, constructed during a time when things were built to last, so I wanted Roy to be loud and heard.

"Lily, it's me. I'm with Gage," Roy called. "He's got a gun and he wants Anna. Don't try anything. Okay? He's coming for Anna."

"Repeat it," I said.

"Don't try anything," Roy called out, his voice echoing.

"You did good."

We exited at the third level, which was a replica of the lower levels with the same fake green grass covering the floors, same thick concrete walls, same rows of storage units with heavy steel doors.

"If you try to run, I'll shoot you," I told Roy.

Roy glanced over his shoulder, showing me his distressed look. He stopped walking and turned around. His arms were secured behind his back, so I didn't view him as a threat. I raised the gun and pointed it at his face.

"Take me to Anna," I said.

"I'll cut you in," Roy said. "We're talking big money, Gage. Really big. A Chinese company is paying me over twenty million for those plans. That's a huge score."

"Who are you?" I asked. "Who the hell are you, really? Because your name isn't Roy Ripson, is it?"

"What does it matter?" Roy replied. He leaned toward me, but the gun in my hand kept him at a safe distance. "This is what I do. I get and sell information any way I can, and I'm good at my job. I'm really good at it. We've got a big score here. We can still pull this off."

"You picked me because you had to use someone on the Security Breach Team, didn't you. You needed someone who could access all the data."

"Two million. That's what I'll pay you."

"Why me?"

I needed to get to Anna, but I also needed this answer.

"You were the weakest link," Roy said without any hint of emotion, as if I were a business transaction. "We could get you to do what we needed and there'd be no trace left behind."

"No trace meaning no bribe, no overt blackmail. I would become a willing participant, is that it?"

Roy said nothing, which to me said it all.

I made some conclusions of my own: Matt Simons was too committed to his ego for Roy and his crew to trust him. They'd probably done some serious psychological profiling, using whatever we put out on social media. Maybe they were monitoring his e-mails—or mine, for that matter. They could have hacked into that part of our network far more easily than the parts where we kept the truly sensitive data about Olympian. Roy had probably found nothing he could use about our other member, Mamatha—no leverage, no fulcrum on which she could be pivoted into doing his bidding.

But then there were Anna and me, the newly married couple looking to adopt a baby, with a profile on ParentHorizon.com. I was Roy's perfect target, a guy whose life could be taken over by a crying woman on the curb outside a Chinese restaurant.

A muffled sob came from down the hall.

Anna!

"Let's go," I said, motioning with the gun. My clenched teeth were all I had to hold in my rage. "Bring me to Anna."

"Three million," Roy said.

Something inside me snapped. I smashed the gun into the side of Roy's head, pistol-whipping him like

Lucas did that night in Eagle Square. I wondered if the two of them had practiced how to do it without inflicting much injury, how to make the strike look authentic. I didn't have any practice, and I wanted my blow to hurt. A lot. Maybe it was the memory of Lily holding up the silver necklace and locket with a tiny picture inside, the bits of broken mirror scattered all around, or Roy vowing to mail me vials of Anna's blood via UPS that drove me to violence. Or it could have been Roy's bullshit story about needing money to pay off a cigarette smuggling debt, or the staged murder of Jorge Moreno, or a fake heavy named Nicky Stacks, or any number of the deceits levied on Anna and me.

Whatever it was, I got tremendous satisfaction and a twisted feeling of relief as I watched Roy's head snap sideways and blood spurt from a gash I'd opened on his face.

Roy slammed against the wall. I heard the breath leave him as he slid along the wall, using it to stay upright before he crumpled in a heap onto the floor. In obvious agony, Roy managed to get to his knees, where he remained for a few moments, stunned. Blood poured down his cheek, but I wasn't about to give him a bandage. I felt nothing, not an iota of concern.

"Bring me to my wife," I said.

I hoisted Roy back to his feet. Because he was handcuffed from behind, Roy could only press his cheek to his shoulder to stanch the flow of blood. Still, drops fell everywhere, leaving a crimson trail on the fake grass lining the floor.

"You don't understand who you're screwing," Roy said. "These people will hunt you down. If I don't deliver, they will find you, and they will kill you. They won't leave any loose ends, nothing that can be tied back to the company who hired me. You will be eliminated. We'll all be killed. I'm not lying to you this time. I'm not. You've got to believe me. You won't be safe."

"Yeah, we'll see about that," I said.

We walked the length of a long hallway and I glanced down the corridors branching off either side. Closed storage units lined the walls, and I wondered which one held my wife.

At the hallway's end, Roy turned to his right and I followed. He came to a stop in front of the only storage unit with an open door.

Emotion swelled inside me as I rushed to look inside. On the far wall was a small table with a radio on it, turned off, and some water and food. It looked like Roy and Lily were set up to wait out the six-hour timetable he'd given me.

I saw Anna in the center of the cubicle. Her mouth was gagged and her hands were bound using nylon rope. She was sitting cross-legged with Lily standing behind her. Lily held a knife to Anna's throat. It was a massive, nasty-looking blade, the kind a hunter might use to gut an elk.

I put the gun to Roy's head.

"You tell her to let Anna go," I said. "Tell her!"

The force of my voice made Anna cower. She was beyond terrified, almost catatonic. I pushed the gun hard against Roy's temple. "Tell her," I said with a snarl.

"Do it, Lil," Roy said. "Let her go. We don't have a choice."

"Where are Lucas and Jorge?" Lily asked.

"They got them both. Let her go, Lil. Let Anna go."

Setting down the knife, Lily undid Anna's rope restraints, then her gag.

Anna let out a slight sob while rubbing the red and

raw marks on her wrists. She rose shakily to her feet, stunned, disbelieving she was finally free, before rushing to my side. She clutched my shoulders with trembling hands as though I were a life raft on an otherwise vacant ocean.

"Kick the knife out of the room," I said to Lily. "DO IT!"

Lily booted the knife with her foot. It skidded out the door and came to a stop against the wall behind me. I shoved Roy from behind and he lurched into the storage room. In a fluid motion, I dropped my gun and moved quickly to shut the door. Roy lunged, but I had the advantage of surprise.

"Hold the door," I screamed to Anna. "Hold it with everything you've got."

Anna turned around. Wedging her back against the storage room door, Anna maneuvered her feet until they were pressed up against the wall across from her. Using our combined strength, we kept the door closed, even while Roy and Lily pushed mightily to get it open. It was only a matter of time before Lily figured out how to remove Roy's makeshift cuffs.

"They'll come for you, Gage. I swear it. You're not safe! You need me!"

I ignored Roy while threading the wire I'd brought for Lily's cuffs through the unit's locking latch. I made sure to give it several wraps, enough to hold them for a little while. I checked the durability again before releasing the pressure I'd been applying.

Finally I grabbed Anna by the shoulders and looked her in the eye. "Can you walk?" I asked. "Did they hurt you?"

No response. Her vacant eyes were filled with fear. I stroked her hair and cupped her face with my hands. They had assaulted her. Tormented her. I wanted to kill

Roy. I wanted to open the door and use the knife to kill him. Do to him what he'd threatened to do to Anna. I retrieved Brad's Glock, but left the knife on the ground where it lay. I was too overcome with relief, touching Anna, feeling her skin again, to think about revenge.

"Anna, sweetie, are you all right? We've got to get out of here. Can you walk?"

She nodded, but in a dazed way.

I grabbed her by the hand and together we raced down the hallway. Roy and Lily banged against the door, trying to snap the wire holding it shut—apparently Lily had figured out the cuffs. We sprinted down the stairs, our hands interlocked.

Anna came to a stop at the first-floor exit. "Why?" she asked. "Why did Lily take me? Why did they want to hurt me?"

"Later," I said. "I'll explain it all later."

Brad was waiting at the entrance to the stairwell. From somewhere down the hall, I could hear Lucas groaning where we had left him. Jorge was seated on the floor, his hands secured behind his back, duct tape over his mouth, glowering at me. Anna shuddered at the sight and cowered back a few steps.

"He was there," she said. "This is one of the men who took me."

I steadied her with my hands.

"It's okay, baby," I said. "You're safe now."

Brad and Anna embraced.

"Lily and Roy?" Brad asked.

"Secured," I said. "Let's get out of here."

I gave Brad his gun, but he handed it back to me. "You hold on to this," he said. "Just in case."

I took the firearm and stashed it in the waistband of my jeans. I held onto Anna's hand, and Brad followed us out into the main corridor. From here, I'd go right, out the back of the building, and Brad would go left, out the front door and into his truck. I paused to look at Brad.

"Where are you going to go?" he asked me.

"Away," I said. "I'm going to get Anna away from Roy. I need to figure out our next move."

"You don't have to run now. You're not a murderer."

"No, I'm not," I agreed. "But there may be a new problem."

"What are you talking about?" Anna asked. "Murder? Who did you kill? Gage, what is going on here?"

"What's the new issue?" Brad wanted to know.

"Roy told me we're not safe. Whoever hired him to get the product plans is going to come after us next."

"Do you believe him?" Brad asked.

"I believe I'm not ready to take any chances. I'm going to get us somewhere safe. Someplace I can plan our next move."

Anna was not convinced. "Wait. Are we still in some sort of trouble?" Her voice was full of alarm. "Shouldn't we go to the police? I was kidnapped! They threatened to kill me, Gage!"

"Yes, we should go to the police, but we can't—not yet, anyway. We need to know if we're in any danger. Roy might be lying, but I can't be sure and I won't take any chances. Right now the best thing for us to do is run. Trust me on this, Anna. You've got to trust me."

Anna thought a moment and nodded.

"Okay," Brad said. "Call if you need me."

I hesitated. "I don't know when I'm going to see you again," I said, feeling myself choke up.

"You take care of each other, understand?" Brad said to us both.

I made a strained smile, but it was just to hold back my tears. "You're the best friend I've ever had."

I thought about reaching for Brad's hand. Who knew when I'd be able to make contact again? The thought of not hearing from Max put a sharp ache in my heart. I resisted the urge, and the three of us embraced in a huddle. Behind me I could hear Lucas beginning to stir.

"Go," Brad said, pushing us away. "Hurry. I'll knock down the board from the alley to let the smoke out. Someone will call the fire department, and then they'll find these clowns."

I gripped Anna's hand. Together we raced down the carpeted hallway, speeding through the doorway to the back building. Remembering the building plans Brad had shown me, I was able to lead Anna into a massive open warehouse space filled with pallets and boxes. We exited through a back door, stepping into the loading zone, not once letting go of each other's hands.

Soon I was in my car, with Anna seated beside me. We looked at each other as my hand caressed her face. I fired up the engine and got the car turned around, sneaking a glance at the dashboard clock. The entire assault had lasted less than thirty minutes.

We drove past Station Street, where Brad's van was already gone. A thick trail of smoke billowed from the alley entrance. I accelerated to avoid a red light, and soon we were driving west, away from Brookline and Boston.

Destination?

Unknown.

CHAPTER 61

Battling the glare of the setting sun, we continued west. My body—muscles, heart, bones—were all buzzing from a deluge of adrenaline in a way that put every Adderall rush to shame. Stealing glances at Anna, I felt grateful they hadn't beaten her (the only marks she had were from the nylon rope used to bound her wrists), but I wondered how much damage had been done to her on the inside. Her body trembled while her vacant stare, beyond a thousand yards, canvassed the blur of scenery rolling past her car window. Was she in shock? Did I need to get her to a hospital? I prayed not, because of the risk.

I wondered what was going to happen to Roy, Lily, and the Moreno brothers once the police arrived. Certainly they weren't going to confess to holding a woman hostage. But was there any truth to Roy's threat? Would the people who hired him to get the design plans come looking for me? Would they come after Anna? Forget going to the police; would we be safe going to a hospital? The answers would come, I was sure of it, but not until I put some miles behind us, got us someplace where I could clear my head and think.

Anna turned to look at me, her eyes pale and glassy. "What happened? What's going on? Talk to me, Gage."

Traffic grew heavy as the rush of evening commuters surged home. I didn't know how to begin explaining everything to her, but I thought of something I had stashed inside the glove compartment. I reached across Anna's lap, flipped the latch, and let the door fall open. I took out the circular container of pills and set it on her lap. To properly tell this story, I had to start at the beginning. I had to start with Lily. Anna returned a nervous glance as she turned the pill holder over in her hands.

"These are birth control pills," she said.

"Brad found them in Lily's apartment," I said. "They belong to her, I'm sure of it. She wasn't pregnant. She was playing us, Anna. She and Roy, they're both con artists, part of some crew hired by a Chinese company to go after the Olympian product plans. Somebody was willing to buy those plans for a lot of money—I'm talking millions and millions of dollars—and they needed an inside person to provide them with the goods."

Anna's mouth hung agape. "What? Why?"

"It would have been impossible for anyone to hack through the security layers at Lithio Systems. There were only three people in the entire company who had the ability to get them what they wanted, and they picked the weakest link to go after. They picked me."

"But why you?"

"They researched me. They researched everyone on the Security Breach Team looking for the best mark, someone they could manipulate and control. Blackmail is too messy for these guys, I'm guessing. They wanted to give someone a good reason to steal the plans and never talk about what they'd done. They knew about the car accident, and they must have found our adoption profile. It was all online. It was public record—there for them to see and to find. To manipulate me, they had to infiltrate our lives. Nothing was happenstance. Lily made sure we found her on the curbside crying. And she didn't accidently stumble on our adoption profile, either."

Anna examined the pills, turning them over again and again in her hands. The revelation seemed to overcome her. No longer terrified or confused, Anna's expression turned angry.

"She lied to us," Anna whispered. "She lied."

I grabbed Anna's hand, squeezing it tight, feeling swept over with love and aglow with gratitude that we were safe and together.

"I'm so sorry," I said. "There's more to tell. There's much more to tell you."

Anna didn't seem to hear me.

"I was there," she said, speaking softly to herself. "I was with Lily when she got her ultrasound. I was right there in the waiting room. I watched her go inside to have the imaging done." Anna looked at me through eyes lined with tears.

Something she said tugged at my curiosity. "I thought you told me because she was superstitious she made you wait in the parking lot," I responded.

Anna nodded, remembering. "Yeah, that's right," she said. "I was waiting outside. So much has happened since then."

I had a tingle, a thought, just the germ of an idea. Somewhere in the back of the car, in one of my bags, was an ultrasound taken at Tiny Body Imaging. I would show it to Anna.

After.

"Where are we going, Gage?"

"I need to get us someplace safe. I need to make

sure Roy or the people who were paying him won't come after us. Then we'll go to the police. We'll figure everything out together."

"What about my mother?" Anna asked, her breathing suddenly rushed. "Is she in any danger?"

Our eyes locked.

"No," I said. "I don't believe she is."

My heart slammed inside my chest like a bird fluttering against its cage. Still, I managed to keep calm, my focus shifting between the road in front and what I saw in the rearview mirror. Were we being followed? I didn't think so. For many reasons, I didn't think so. I pulled into a gas station about a mile from the on-ramp to I-95 north.

"I need to use the bathroom," I said. "You need to come inside the mini-mart with me. Look at a magazine. Stay near people."

Anna gripped my hand. "I don't want to be left alone."

I thought about giving Anna my gun but decided against it. Anna wasn't in any shape to use it, so for now it would stay in the glove compartment where I had stashed it.

"You'll be all right," I said, touching her face with my hand.

My Anna . . .

The mini-mart was crowded with shoppers, and Anna went to the magazine rack as we had planned. I got the key from the counter clerk and used it to unlock the men's room door. As soon as I got the door closed, I took out my cell phone and was pleased to see I had a great 4G connection.

I opened my LinkedIn app and searched for the name Edward Daggett. Anna had changed her name back to Miller after the divorce, but I knew Edward's last name from many conversations. I sifted through more than a dozen hits, before finding the one I was looking for. I could tell by the profile picture. I had cast his face into my memory while I was cutting his picture out of Anna's one and only family portrait.

My breathing turned shallow. Out of respect for Anna's wishes, I'd never dug into Edward's life, even though curiosity had more than once made me reconsider that promise. Turned out he was a vice president at Brockhouse Financial Management in Southern California. It was late afternoon California time when I dialed his office number. My fingers turned numb as I worked my phone, and my head pulsed like a drum circle. A hot and damp sweat began to tickle the nape of my neck and soon soaked a small triangle in the front of my shirt.

The phone rang in my ear while I spoke softly to myself. "Please no . . . please no . . . please no."

A receptionist answered in a voice cheery as California sunshine.

"Could I please speak with Edward Daggett?" I asked, trying to contain the quaver in my voice. "It's urgent."

Please no . . . please no . . . please no.

I was put on hold, told to wait a moment please.

Please no . . .

A moment later a voice spoke in a deep and rich baritone.

"This is Edward, how may I help you?"

"You don't know me," I said, talking too quickly. "You don't know me, but I know you."

I know you as a rapist . . . as a careless inhumane pig who deserves no mercy.

"What's this about?" Edward sounded nervous.

"I know Anna. I know your ex-wife."

"Anna?" His voice ascended with surprise. "Where is she? Is she all right?"

The pressure building inside me began a quick and sudden retreat. The relief felt intoxicating as I breathed out in a heavy sigh.

Thank God.

"She's safe. She's with me," I said.

I heard Edward let out a sigh of his own.

"Thank goodness."

The relief I felt continued, waves and waves of it washing through me.

"I just wanted you to know that she's okay."

I also wanted to know that you were real, I thought.

It was that one little slip—the waiting room instead of the parking lot. With everything that had happened, all the lies and deceit, Anna forgetting that she had waited outside in her car (at Lily's request) while Lily pretended to get an ultrasound and not in the waiting room as she told me in the car was a small inaccuracy. But Anna was always so sharp when it came to Lily. She'd shared so many vivid details of their exploits together as their relationship blossomed. She remembered the name of the woman from the paint-your-own-pottery store, even the towns she'd been considering for expansion. She recalled not only the magazine—*Cosmo*—but also the article she was reading when she dropped the whole kit and kaboodle in the water at the nail salon. When she told me she felt foolish about the forgetting her folder I knew it was true, because she never forgot anything.

Except . . . except she had forgotten where she waited for Lily during the ultrasound. It was a small slip, but admittedly big enough to make me momentarily suspicious. With all the deception, it was no wonder. Now, thank God, I could relax, but not too much. There was still the issue of the Chinese buyer to worry about. Would they come after us?

"Can I speak with her?" Edward asked, his voice pleading, wanting. "I've been looking for her. I've been searching."

"No," I said. "I'm afraid that's not possible."

"Who are you? Why are you with her? Where are you calling me from?"

Edward sounded on the verge of tears, and if his emotions weren't authentic, then he was a fraud who could put Roy and Lily to shame.

"I can't tell you anything about me. I'm sorry."

"Please," Edward said. "I must speak with Anna. Let me do that one thing."

"No," I said. "Not after what happened."

"What do you mean what happened? She walked out on me!" Edward said. "No explanation. No word of good-bye. Imagine if it had been your wife who left you that way. You'd have been devastated, just like me."

For all the lies I'd been told these past few weeks, I believed Edward. He couldn't be faking the emotion I was hearing. Even so, if Anna wished to speak with him, it would be her decision, not mine.

I thought of where Anna and I might run to and hide out for a while. For some reason, the Caribbean came to mind. I had a vision of swimming in those aqua blue waters with Anna by my side. What would we do about Bessie? She couldn't travel with us. How would Anna leave her mother alone? We'd work something out. We'd work everything out now. Together.

"I don't know who you are, or why you're calling, but I believe you're with my Anna. Will you at least give her a message for me?" Edward asked.

"Maybe," I said. "What's the message?"

"Will you tell her I still love her? Could you do that

one thing for me? I still don't know why she did it. Why she left me. Why she begged me to sign the divorce papers. She threatened to kill herself if I didn't. Did you know that? If I didn't sign the papers, she told me she would slice open her wrists."

Edward's words came out strangled, his voice choked with emotion. This was shocking news to me, but given Anna's emotional state at the time, I could certainly see how it had come to such a threat.

"I will," I said, lying. "I'll tell her."

I wanted to say, "She left you because it's a crime to rape your wife," but I refrained. He'd already given me all I needed to know.

"Who are you?" he asked again.

Here I hesitated, thinking I might tell him something. "Just someone who knows Anna and knows all about you," I said. "I can't say any more."

I heard breathing only. "Okay," Edward said. It sounded to me like he was fighting back tears. I felt a pang of sympathy burst inside me, like a dam giving way. Compassion overcame my anger. He needed to know something, too. He might have been a rapist, but he was still a father and he needed some closure. Now that I knew the truth—the stress of the ordeal had fogged up Anna's memory of the ultrasound—my heart was free to be with Anna and ready to let go of any anger I held toward Edward. He should know what I knew.

"There's something else I want to tell you before I go, and you might not believe me," I said. "This may sound crazy to you, but I have a friend who can commune with the dead. On a number of occasions he's connected me with my dead son. He's the real deal. No gimmicks. No lies. His special ability has brought me a profound sense of peace."

"I'm sorry for your loss," Edward said. "But why are you telling me this?"

"I just wanted you to know that your son isn't suffering or lost. He's somewhere else. His spirit lives on somewhere else, and he's happy. I just thought you'd find comfort in that."

Edward made confused noises, struggling to find some words.

"I'm not sure what you're talking about," he said. "I don't have any children. Anna and I were married all right, but we never had any kids."

CHAPTER 62

How quickly can a person fall out of love? A second? A few minutes? My emotions were a speeding train, zooming through different stages of grief in a matter of moments not years. I went from shock, to bewilderment, to recognition, and finally to rage all in the time it took to walk from the bathroom in a gas station mini-mart to the magazine rack.

Anna saw none of this—she wasn't in tune with my aura. Her eyes lit up when she saw me approach. I was still her knight in shining armor, the man who had rescued her from grave peril.

Anna and I were married, but we never had any kids.

We never had any kids . . .

Edward was the only person I believed. His emotion was real. It made sense to me, too. Anna left, demanded the divorce, threatened him even. She needed to be free of one marriage so she could enter another. But I still had so many questions to be answered, so much I still didn't know. Anna came toward me and grabbed my arm.

"Baby, are you all right?" she asked. "You look pale."

Our eyes locked. For a second I heard the faint echo of the love we once shared. For a moment, lasting no longer than the flutter of a butterfly wing, I forgot about my call with Edward and saw only Anna. I saw the woman I met at my grief group, the person who brought me out of my abyss, the lover who shared my bed, the friend I thought I had. But before I could even begin to embrace the past, it was gone. Our life together was a woven tapestry of lies. How could I have been betrayed like this? Played like this? Who was this person who shared my bed and my life?

"I'm fine," I said. "Let's drive."

At some point on the trip west Anna broke the lengthy and painful silence.

"You haven't spoken since we left, Gage. Are you sure you're all right?"

The radio was turned off, so all we had for a soundtrack was the rumble of my car wheels rolling along the Mass Pike.

"I'm just thinking," I said.

And I was. I was thinking about what I was going to do. However, my feelings were numb. I was driving through a mist; nothing looked clear. My world was tilted and entirely out of focus. I waited, and drove, my knuckles white against the wheel.

It wasn't until I got off at exit 42 on the Merritt Parkway that I knew what I was going to do. We'd been driving for hours in silence, growing increasingly uncomfortable. Anna must have known something was seriously wrong. If not, her suspicions grew when I pulled into a rest area that was just a parking lot and nothing more—no gas, no restaurant, and no mini-mart with a magazine rack.

At this late hour it was completely deserted. A couple of wall-mounted pole lights illuminated much of the area with a diffused white glow. I climbed out, my joints stiff and muscles aching. Above me a summer sky drenched in stars shimmered and glowed, stretching out to the infinite.

For a moment, I gazed up to the heavens and tried to picture where Max and Karen could be. Were they down here with me in spirit or somewhere else beyond the stars? Would they guide me through what I needed to do next? I reached my arms above my head, imagining I could take hold of their hands and we'd be joined together once more as a family of three.

Anna climbed out and came to stand beside me.

"Were your legs getting tired?" she asked, wrapping her arms around my shoulders in a hug. "Do you want me to drive?"

"No," I said. "I don't."

"What's wrong, Gage? Are you worried about Roy? Is there still a way he or someone else could hurt us?"

"Not anymore," I said. "That's not what it is."

"Tell me."

"I called Edward from the bathroom at the gas station," I said.

Anna broke off her embrace. She took several steps back.

"Why?" Her voice was shaky. "Why would you do that?"

I spun around to face her. Anna's eyes were wide as the full moon above. "Something you said in the car," I went on, "about being in the waiting room while Lily got her ultrasound. With all that happened, I just needed to be sure."

My voice was calm and even; I felt an unwavering determination. Calm as I seemed on the outside, I could feel the veins on my neck pulse with a steady rush of blood.

"Sure of what?" Anna's voice sounded fraught.

"Of you," I said. "I needed to be sure of you."

"Oh, Gage, no . . ." In a snap, her face turned taut and strained. "Tell me nothing has changed," she said. "Tell me you still love me."

That was when I looked down and saw the gun in Anna's hand. She must have taken it from the glove compartment.

"You lied to me," I said. "You lied about everything."

Anna raised the gun higher as she continued her cautious retreat. A shot could pierce my heart, but that organ was already broken and bleeding. All around us the sound of crickets and other night creatures saturated the air with their music while the steady thrum of traffic zooming down the Merritt beat a rhythm all its own.

"Please, Gage, don't do this."

"Are you going to kill me, Anna?" I took a step toward her, my feet scraping on the parking lot pavement. "Are you a liar *and* a killer?"

"Gage . . ."

Her hand shook like the petal of a flower in the wind. I dared another step.

"Do you have it in you to kill? Pull the trigger if you do."

Another step.

I felt impenetrable, and incapable of being hurt any more than I already had been. "Do it if you dare."

I took another step.

"Pull the trigger and become a killer," I said. "Prove to me you never loved me. Prove it by pulling the trigger. All it takes is five-point-five pounds of pressure, so do it if you don't care about me. Do it."

One more step closer, still.

Anna's hand was rigid, steady as steel. I braced myself because I thought I saw murder dancing in her moonlit eyes.

"Gage, I'm so sorry," Anna said. Her words were a whisper strangled by the memories of us. "I'm so sorry." She lowered the gun just a little.

I charged. Using my shoulder as a battering ram, I slammed into Anna's midsection, catching her completely by surprise. She grunted and cried out as the force of the impact threw her back against the side of the car. She tried to take aim with the gun again, but I reached up in time to grab her wrist. I used my strength to jerk her hand over her head. With my other hand, I seized her throat and began to squeeze. I could feel the veins pulse within my grasp.

Anna kicked and thrashed, but my grip was strong and I wasn't about to let go. Her skin color changed like a chameleon in a panic, going from pale to red to purple as I constricted her breathing even more. Her mouth opened. She wanted to scream but couldn't get enough air in her lungs to make any sound louder than a wheeze. She weakened, her legs giving way, her kicks becoming less frantic.

Taking advantage, I wrenched her arm down and twisted her wrist. The gun easily transferred from Anna's hand into mine, and I let go of her throat. She slumped to the pavement, body resting up against the car, shaking as she rubbed at the injury I'd inflicted to her neck. I saw marks where my fingers had been.

My face was flush with anger. I got down on my knees and pressed the gun underneath Anna's chin.

"Have you done this before, or was I your first?"

No response.

"Who is Lily?" I shouted. "Who is she?"

Anna tried to speak, but no words came out. My teeth stayed tightly clenched. I dug the barrel of the pistol harder into flesh underneath her chin and twisted it like a bore drilling into a tree.

"Answer me," I demanded. "Who is Lily?"

"She's . . . she's my half sister," Anna said.

CHAPTER 63

I pulled the gun away and stood. A sob broke from Anna's trembling lips as she buried her face in her hands. "I'm so sorry, Gage. I'm so sorry for everything."

I loomed over Anna, the gun dangling harmlessly at my side. Anger drained from my body as I watched her weep. I couldn't hate her. Residue of our life together lingered, enough at least to keep me from pulling the trigger or squeezing her throat once more.

"Tell me everything," I said. "Start from the beginning." I pointed the gun at her head.

Anna held up her hands, shielding her face, nodding her submission.

"I'll tell you . . . I'll tell you, Gage . . . please, don't hurt me, I'll tell you."

I gave Anna a moment. She took several readying breaths before she spoke.

"Lily came to visit me in California a few years ago," Anna began. She was speaking slowly, thoughtfully it seemed. "It was before I met you, before I agreed to be a part of this."

"What is this? What is Lily involved with?"

"She works for Roy."

"Roy. That's his real name?"

"One of them," Anna said.

"What does Roy do?"

"He calls himself an information retrieval specialist," Anna said in a raspy voice. She kept rubbing her injured throat. "He gets corporate secrets for people who can afford his services. He's paid millions of dollars for what he does, and he's been doing it for years."

"He's a con man," I said. "That's what he is."

"Yes and no. Roy specializes in retrieval without trails. At least that's what he calls it."

"Computer hacking," I said.

Anna shook her head. "No. The opposite. He gets the jobs computer hackers can't do on their own. He penetrates the most sophisticated computer security systems in the world and, yes, sometimes hacking is a part, but it's never the whole part.

"He won't resort to kidnapping. That creates too much of a police response. He never tries bribes. Those always backfire, he says. People get greedy and then they start demanding more, or threaten to talk. He keeps it stealthy, under the radar, and never links his work back to his employer. He operates from the inside out by making people believe him. He creates their reality to manipulate it, taking time to build trust. Sometimes a job lasts a few months. Sometimes it's a few years. He's got multiple jobs going at once, all at different stages of development. It's what he does, and he's very good at it."

"Jack Hutchinson? The Moreno brothers?"

"They work for Roy," Anna said. "He employs different people for different jobs. His network is extensive and highly secretive. Most of his associates have other jobs and businesses, but they can become anything Roy needs them to be. They're loyal and dependable."

"The stuff from the prison registry you printed out about Roy? Those documents your PI guy dug up?"

"Fake," Anna said. "That was all a forgery. I never hired any private investigator."

"And your job? Was that fake, too?"

Anna looked up at me through a glaze of tears. "I managed an art gallery in San Clemente before," she said. The tears were flowing freely. "I'm not a business consultant. I don't know anything but the buzz words Roy taught me. I didn't even paint those wall murals. It was someone else's work, someone with a lot more talent than I have. Roy thought if we each did something for sick kids, it would help you to fall for me."

"Oh, it did," I said, completely disgusted. "It sure did. So was it Lily who asked you to be a part of one of Roy's cons?"

Anna nodded. "She knew I was unhappy in my marriage to Edward. She knew I wanted to make a change, but I couldn't afford my lifestyle, not after the prenup I signed. I was trapped in this horrible, loveless life with a man I couldn't stand. I could have anything I wanted, so long as I lived with Edward. Those were his demands, and his divorce lawyers were prepared to leave me broke. To be honest, Gage, I was attached to the money," she said, sounding both ashamed and authentic. "Lily told me I could make over ten million for a couple years' work. That would be my cut. Ten million. That was the ticket to my new life."

"I was *work* to you? I was your *job?*" I couldn't believe the words coming out of my mouth.

"Gage, it's not like that. That's not what it became."

"And to do your *job*," I said, "all you needed to do

was get me to fall in love with you?" I paused, waiting for an answer. "Is that it, Anna? Smile at me enough. Show interest in me? Win my heart? And then what, pretend to want to start a family again? Pretend you understood what it felt like to lose a child? You lied about being a grieving mother? God, you're so sick, so cruel, to do what you did to me."

I was the one shaking as my anger returned. I kept talking because I couldn't stop.

"It was all to get Lily into our lives," I said. "We needed Lily to come live with us."

Anna nodded rather grimly.

"So she could make me crazy," I went on. "Everything: the present, the necklace, finding my Adderall, your missing folder, it was all staged. And you helped stage it."

"Yes."

"You kept turning the screws, knowing eventually I'd break. You lured me up to Lily's apartment. You knew I'd go there to get the folder. You gave Lily one of my condoms. You sick, twisted bitch—you gave Lily a condom full of my semen."

"We needed to corner you. Roy did all sorts of psychological profiling beforehand. He studied your e-mails and ran them through these programs he wrote, looking for keywords and other things I don't really understand. He knew with almost 100 percent certainty you'd offer up a payout to make them go away. You had to believe the stakes were high enough—that they'd tell me you and Lily slept together—only he wanted proof of an affair. You needed to think I'd believe whatever they told me. He recorded you offering him a bribe as the final piece to get your cooperation. It was all part of his design."

"But of course I wasn't going to have enough

money. Not for what Roy said he needed. But you knew that too, didn't you?"

"Roy knew everything. His psychological profile on you filled two massive binders. Gage, he knows you better than you know yourself."

I smiled, because Anna was wrong.

"No," I said. "He didn't know I wouldn't give him the real plans. He miscalculated there. I gave him useless information."

Anna responded only with a nod.

"But I have to admit, holy crap. This is some elaborate shit you guys pulled off," I said. "I go on a drug deal with Roy to make up the difference for what he needs, and in exchange they go away. Only the drug deal is staged to go horribly wrong and I end up shooting a man. What if I hadn't pulled the trigger?"

"There were all sorts of contingency plans in place," Anna said. "One way or another, you were going to fire that gun, even if Roy had to use your hand to pull the trigger."

"So he rigged some special effects bullshit. He made me believe we needed a million dollars or you would die."

"That's what he does, Gage. He makes you believe."

"What about the knife under your pillow?" I stopped because I got a sick feeling in my gut. "You put it there, didn't you? You put that knife under your own pillow."

Anna looked away.

"If you had given him the plans, nobody would ever have known. You would have kept it a secret from me because you killed a man, but eventually, and this was all part of the plan, I would have found out you had offered Lily a bribe to leave. Lily would have called me to clear her conscience, and then I would have left you. That's how it was supposed to go down."

I bowed my head and kept my eyes glued to the ground, trying to brace myself against the onslaught of information, this new reality, my sham of a life.

"Words fail me," I eventually managed to say. "I can call you heartless, horrible, but that isn't even close to describing you. Is Anna even your real name?"

"Yes . . . yes, it is." She tried to stand, but I pushed her back to the ground with my foot. Anna looked up at me with her big, sad eyes, resigned to staying where she sat. "We needed a real backstory in case you checked up on me," she said. "I needed to once be married to Edward Daggett from California. That couldn't be a lie."

"But I never did check up on your past, because you told me not to."

"Roy's profile on you was inconclusive there. We couldn't be sure you'd respect those wishes."

"I loved you," I said. "I loved you with every bit of my being. I was a shattered person, and you made me love you. Of course I was going to respect your wishes."

"At first I felt sick about what I was doing to you. I really did. But then I got to know you. It wasn't all an act, Gage. I really did come to love you."

"You used my son to get to me!" I screamed inches from her face, eyes wide and wild. "My *son!*"

Anna began to sob, her body wracked with spasms. As for me, I had to calm down and swallow past the brick-sized lump in my throat. My thoughts spun out of control while I tried to reconcile all the false bits and pieces of our life together.

"You were tied up when I found you," I said.

"When I heard you coming up the stairs with Roy, we quickly put on the restraints," Anna said, still sobbing. "We couldn't let you know."

"A little bit of Roy's contingency planning?"

Her tears stopped like a faucet turned off.

"Actually, that was my idea," Anna said. The crinkle of a smile soiled what had once been a pure and beautiful face. I caught a twinkle in her eyes, not reflected by moonlight, and heard a note of pride in her voice as well. I understood why Anna did what she had done. She had to keep up the charade.

"What else did you lie about?"

She returned an indifferent look. "I guess a lot of things."

"The miscarriage?" I asked.

Anna grimaced. "I never had one," she admitted.

"And the pregnancy test?"

Anna took a few readying breaths. "We got it from a pregnant girl, someone we recruited online, the same girl who took the ultrasound for us. We paid her."

"Your files? Your paperwork for your business?"

"Roy arranged all of that," Anna said. "Same as he did my backstory."

"Backstory . . . what else about your backstory did he arrange?"

The bite to my voice came because of a new suspicion I had, something that made me feel utterly sick. I couldn't believe Anna would be capable of doing this. But still . . .

"My business trips, mostly I went to see my family."

"Your family," I repeated.

"My mother, Gage."

Bile raced up my throat.

"Who . . . who was the woman we visited in the nursing home?"

"She's someone Roy picked. He got a job at the facility working as a janitor, doing reconnaissance work before we got started. He found an Alzheimer's patient, someone who didn't have any local family. Her kids never came to see her. Never. So I told the nursing home staff I was a close family friend and you were my husband. At least we provided her with some comfort. Nobody ever came to see her, Gage. Nobody."

"We provided her with comfort?" I said. "We provided her with lies!" I raised the gun and pointed it at Anna's head, my hand shaking. Anna cowered, shielding herself with her arms, while my whole body surged with a fresh rush of disgust. "That was why Bessie recognized Lily, isn't it? Isn't it! She'd seen her before with Roy."

Anna bit her lip and nodded.

"We were worried after that incident, but nothing came of it. I needed to have some family, something so you wouldn't be too suspicious of me. I couldn't have just shown up in town with no connections. Bessie was there to help you trust me. That's why we did it. It was all Roy's creation. Even my cousin Gladys, that was really Lily who you spoke with on the phone. The lie had to be perfect and utterly believable."

"And it was," I said. "It was perfect and utterly believable. What's your last name? Your real last name?"

"I changed it to Miller when we picked Bessie," Anna said.

"And before that?"

"I was Anna Daggett."

Every part of me felt ravaged by disease. "I just wonder why Brad couldn't see your aura," I said.

"Maybe because it wasn't all a lie," Anna whispered.

"What about Will Gaines? Our tenant?"

She shrugged—apparently he was just a bit player. "I paid him to leave. It didn't take much."

"And the pictures of Kevin, if that's really his name?"

"That's his name," Anna said, nodding. "But he's Edward's nephew, obviously not my son."

"And if I had looked up your son's death certificate?"

"Things would have gotten complicated," she said. "It was a bit of a risk, but I made sure you knew his life was private to me."

"That's why you never wanted Brad to connect you to Kevin."

Anna nodded. "And why I supposedly painted pottery on his birthday. You weren't going to suspect anything, and you didn't. I gave you no reason to check up on my story. You believed what I told you because I was your wife."

Again my stomach somersaulted.

"All those tears you cried?"

Anna thought about this. Then she did something truly surprising. She kind of laughed, as if she was impressed by something. "I was really good, wasn't I?"

"What?"

"I mean as it went along, I just got more and more into it. I really *became* this other person. Anna was quite something, a remarkable creation." I couldn't believe she spoke of herself in the third person, reverently, like a critic lavishing praise on a rising starlet. "Sometimes I would say things to you that I couldn't believe were coming out of my mouth. I really felt like Anna Miller, your wife, this woman who loved you, and it got so hard to tell the difference between reality and what I was doing. Like those cops who go so deep undercover they forget who they really are. That's what was happening to me. For the longest time I couldn't figure out why everything was feeling so real, and then it came to me."

"What did?"

"I must really love you, Gage. That was why. That's why I could be so good, so honest. You see, it wasn't all faked. I really did fall in love with you. I wasn't going to leave you, even though I told Lily and Roy I would. We were going to have so much money. A rich uncle of mine who died, that's where I was going to tell you it came from."

I nodded. "Yeah, more lies."

Anna began to cry into her hands—real tears or crocodile ones, who could tell?—while I went to my car and popped open the trunk. I took her bag out and dropped it at her feet.

"What are you going to do?" she asked, watching me through sad, red eyes glossed with salty tears. "What are you going to do with me?" Her expression pleaded for mercy or a change of heart.

"I'm going to leave you here, Anna," I said. "I'm going to leave you in the middle of nowhere without a wallet, or money, or an ID, or a phone. You'll have nothing because that's what you are. Nothing. I don't want to bother with police. What's that going to do? You conned me into giving garbage product plans to our competitor. I gave you nothing. No money ever exchanged hands. You'd do a couple years in prison, if that. And what then? I'd have to live with this story being told over and over again. I'd be confronted with reminders of how you defiled the memory of my son and my wife, my real wife, in every media channel across the country. I don't want to think of you. I don't want to give you any more of my time or energy."

"What . . . what am I going to do?"

"You'll figure something out, Anna. You're good at that."

I pushed her away from me, using my foot. I wanted to spit on her, I wanted to punch her, I wanted to put the gun in her mouth and pull the damn trigger, but instead I put the weapon back into the glove compartment and fired up the car's engine. I drove away, leaving Anna sitting on the pavement of a deserted parking lot somewhere in Connecticut. I'd toss her purse and wallet into some trash can once I got a few miles away.

In my rearview mirror I watched Anna get back to her feet. She stood in the middle of the empty space with her arms dangling at her sides, looking lost and alone.

Just like me.

CHAPTER 64

The man who called himself Roy Ripson—his name as flexible as his appearance—sat at an ornate, round metal table on the outside patio of a café in Sonoma, California, sipping from his cup of espresso. His fake tattoos had faded some in the month since everything went wrong, but they still served as a painful reminder of the only job he'd ever failed to complete.

With him were two women. The younger of the pair, a woman named Lily, drank from a bottle of Evian water while she checked her appearance in a compact mirror. She was grateful to have stopped eating all the garbage food that had helped her to gain weight. It would take some time to get back to her peak physical condition, but hours in the gym, coupled with a regular regiment of yoga and Pilates, would do the trick eventually.

Sitting beside Lily was a woman named Anna. Anna appeared removed, preoccupied, as though she had misplaced something of great value and was trying to recall where it might be. Her face was tired, and those who knew her best, but had not seen her for some time, would think she'd aged years in weeks.

Roy, by contrast, was looking far more relaxed than he had of late, his demeanor bordering on jubilant. He was a hunter who was back on the hunt again. While Lily needed time to rebuild her body, Roy feared it would take far longer to reclaim his tarnished reputation. He was accustomed to having a waiting list of clients, but word had spread among his associates of a failed attempt to steal the product plans for a revolutionary type of lithium ion battery.

In the aftermath of this debacle, Roy's client list had dried up as quickly as a pool of rainwater in the summer's heat. He knew those clients would return eventually—greed and power had always proved strong motivators—and those who knew and respected his ability would soon forget his only failure. But even Roy was surprised at how quickly this new opportunity had emerged. Maybe it was luck, maybe they didn't know about Lithio Systems; whatever the reason, Roy was grateful for the opportunity and committed to giving it his all. He was studying his sheets of paper carefully, only now bringing Lily and Anna up to speed on his research.

"His name is Andre Rosen. He's the CTO of a leading Nanoimprint Lithography company."

Lily showed her interest, but Anna remained distant.

"What's that?" Lily asked.

"It's the future of chip making, my sweet," Roy said. His accent was unremarkable, different from the one he used with Gage Dekker. His voice, same as his appearance, could change as often as he needed. "It's the gateway to ultrafast, ultracheap electronics and communications."

"Sounds pricey," Lily said.

Anna's gaze remained elsewhere.

"It's very pricey, and I do believe Mr. Rosen has access to the information our new client would like to purchase."

"Should we just ask him for it?" Lily inquired. Her pert mouth bowed into a sly smile. Of course they wouldn't ask.

Roy checked his papers once more.

"It would appear Mr. Rosen has a thing for expensive girls."

"Prostitutes," Lily said, her eyebrows arching.

Anna remained silent.

"Well, classier," Roy replied. "Which is why I believe he'll find you quite attractive, Lily, darling. But it will be a shame when you OD in his hotel room. Naturally, things could get ugly from there."

Roy thought back to his earliest days of his business. It had begun with something similar to what he was now planning for Mr. Rosen. A dead call girl in a hotel room; a payout demanded; sensitive information exchanging hands to salvage equally sensitive reputations. It was sad to think he was regressing, rehashing an old con he'd performed so many years ago like some pimped-out stage magician, a ragged mule barely a shadow of his former greatness. But Roy would not let himself be relegated to the equivalent of some eighties rock band, touring the country on the strength and merits of their past hits. Eventually, with time and determination, he would build back up to another opus like the one he had almost pulled off.

Almost . . .

As much as Roy loved the art of the con, he fed on the increasingly elaborate nature of his creations. Over the years, Roy had transformed himself into a master craftsman who took the "art" in "con artist" quite seriously. As his reputation and abilities grew, so did his appetite for the extravagant. It was not long before merely conning someone—just another information retrieval job—wasn't enough; it no longer satisfied. Roy felt a compulsion, a yearning need to penetrate the lives of his marks at the deepest of levels, to embed himself into the fabric of their souls. The more sophisticated, the better. The more complex, the more it satisfied. He was a vampire for whom common blood no longer satiated his constant, unyielding hunger. It had to be something truly special—like Gage Dekker—for it to be meaningful.

But Roy was a practical man as well as a cunning one, and he understood the need to retreat, recalibrate, and reengage. When the time was right, and he'd know when it was, Roy vowed to orchestrate a job that would put all his others to shame. It would be his crowning achievement, the stuff of legend.

"We haven't done the prostitute bit in quite a while," Lily said. "I'll tell you this much, I don't ever want to play pregnant again."

Roy knew she wouldn't have to but kept quiet about his intentions. In fact, if he was careful in planning, they could probably swing the Rosen job without having to hire extra help, though that would disappoint his many contacts—actors in his company—who had come to depend on Roy for part, if not all, of their livelihood.

Roy was protective of his troupe, as he'd taken to calling the players in his organization. He would not want to keep them on the sidelines for long, but he needed this time to lick his wounds. Roy took a mental note to thank one of his favorite troupe members with a hefty bonus. He would use the upfront money from the Lithio job—money his Chinese employers demanded he repay for his failure to deliver.

It was a lucky break Jack Hutchinson had been out

getting sandwiches when Gage Dekker made his daring assault. Hutchinson had been able to free Jorge and Lucas and get them all upstairs before the fire department showed, so when they did arrive, the only thing out of the ordinary was a busted window and a faulty boiler. Roy had heard from Hutchinson that the police had contacted him regarding a story Gage Dekker had told, but there was no evidence and no follow up. Still, Hutchinson was spooked. The money from the Chinese might go some way to smoothing things over.

Technically, Roy should have paid his client back part, if not all, of his fee when they discovered the fault in the plans. But Roy found it difficult to part with his hard-earned cash, and had enough evidence of illegal doings to hold his former client at bay. After all, he had done the hard work, the heavy lifting. He *had* pulled it off. The last part in Hutchinson's warehouse, a grand display of Roy's improvisational abilities, an adrenaline rush like no other, should have worked. It almost did.

Almost . . .

Anna stood up suddenly, but Lily pulled her back down.

"Don't be that way, Anna," Lily said.

"I'm not being any way. I just want to go."

"You still have feelings for him, don't you?" Roy said.

"I just don't want to do this anymore," Anna said.

Roy checked his papers.

"It appears Mr. Rosen prefers more than one girl at a time," he said, peering at Anna over the top of his sheets.

Anna sighed and stood once more.

"I'm not doing this again," she said to Lily.

Roy and Lily stood as well.

"If the numbers work out right," Roy said, "you won't have to."

Roy and Anna locked eyes. In his estimation, Anna was something special. She was a rare bird who equaled, if not bested, Lily's gifts. Perhaps Roy would take Anna as a lover, same as he had Lily. For now, he was satisfied just to admire her talents. But one thing was certain: Anna would never give up the rush. They were the same in that regard, both addicts who got high off telling lies. Anna thought she still loved Gage Dekker, but Roy knew that was nothing more than a lie she told herself.

Roy left a sizable tip—he was feeling quite optimistic—and the trio headed for the parking lot.

Three hundred yards away, Jian Wu stood on a nearby hillside overlooking the café. Watching. He was a short, solidly built man with jet-black hair and dark eyes focused on his targets. His wicked grin broadened as he saw them walk toward a cobalt-blue Tesla. His dossier held three pictures, and all three were together. What good fortune! He had inquired about a fourth individual, the inside man at Lithio Systems, but his employers had told him he was not to be touched. Jian didn't question why. It was not his place to question. He had a job to do.

And soon, very soon, his employer would be pleased with a job well done.

EPILOGUE

The field was a stretch of grass several hundred yards wide with sixty-foot pine trees lining the edge of an adjacent forest. It was early autumn and the perfect day for a rocket launch with cloudless skies and wind speeds of less than five miles per hour. There wasn't an airplane in sight as I inspected the circular launch pad a second time, looking for defects. I had taught Max to double-check his work prior to liftoff and felt satisfied it was constructed to a standard we both would have approved. Brad helped me set the rocket on the launch pad, while I made sure it was perfectly positioned. We stepped back to appraise it from a distance.

The Estes Cosmic Explorer Flying Model Rocket with laser-cut fins and waterslide decals looked powerful enough to leave the atmosphere. Max would have been calm, stoic even, as we prepared for liftoff. He would have been quiet and focused while we walked through our checklist.

Rocket attached to the launch pad? Check.

Launcher disarmed? Check.

Alligator clips attached to igniter leads? Check.

"We're ready for lift-off," I said to Brad.

I don't think I'd ever spent more time prepping a rocket for a launch. The box it came in was covered in dust when I pulled it out from under my bed. For several minutes I couldn't bring myself to open the lid. When I did, my breath caught. It was like taking a glimpse into my past, confronting a rush of painful memories coming at me faster than the Class IV rapids of the Kennebunk River we never got the chance to ride.

"Max, buddy," I said, gazing up at the sky to wherever he might be. "Remember that rocket we were building? Well, I'm going to launch it now. I think I'm finally ready to launch it. It doesn't mean I'm going to stop thinking about you any less. I promise, you're always in my thoughts. But I think it's about time we let this one rocket get its flight on. What do you say, buddy? Shouldn't we let her ride?"

My question was met with silence, but my heart knew the answer, and that answer was yes.

A gust of wind kicked up, and for a second I worried we might have to delay the launch. Quick as it came, it settled, and once again we were ready to send her skyward.

"Are you sure this is what you want to do?" Brad asked.

"I'm sure."

Brad knew how much this rocket meant to me, what it represented. Now it represented something else—a time for me to move on with my life.

It wasn't just the rocket I was letting go of. Before heading to the launch site, I had used a hammer to pulverize my entire supply of Adderall into a fine dust. As a final act of defiance, I covered the launch pad with the remnants of my addiction, until it looked like the entire surface area was coated in a thin dusting of snow.

Soon, a burst of flame from the rocket's fire would turn that dust into ash.

"I just wish Max were here to see it take off."

"I know you do," Brad answered, putting his arm around my shoulder.

I visualized the trajectory and felt confident the flight path would carry the rocket to someplace deep into the woods. I didn't know exactly where it would end up. The modifications I'd made were something I'd never tried before. Instead of a normal engine, I made the jump to E18-4 and added weight to the tip of the nose cone using epoxy and a few ball bearings. My eyes squinted against the sun's glare, taking in the rocket's shape.

It was perfect.

While I was changing the batteries in the ignition switch, Brad asked, "Have you decided where you're going?"

"I'm thinking about the Caribbean," I said. "I could use a little sun and sand to rejuvenate. I'll figure something out from there."

One thing was certain: I wasn't going back to Lithio Systems. I gave them my notice with not much of an explanation. Both Patrice and Peter offered to give me a reference, and each was open to the idea of my coming to work for them again if I changed my mind. But I wasn't going to change. I knew I'd land on my feet. I'd find something else to do. But I couldn't in good conscience keep working there, and I guess Matt Simons felt the same, because he resigned on my last day of work.

Neither in good conscience could I let Roy orchestrate another elaborate con, so after a bit of reflection, I went to the police with my story. By then Roy and the rest of his crew had vanished, including Jack Hutchinson, but at least they were on somebody's radar.

Brad and I spoke the countdown together, ten down to one. As soon as I hit the ignition switch, a loud *swoosh* filled the air as the engine caught fire. The coating of Adderall on the launch pad vanished within a billowy cloud of gray smoke. Shielding my eyes against the sun's glare, I craned my neck to watch the magnificent rocket cut an arcing trail across the sky.

For a moment, I felt sad that something this beautiful had spent so long collecting dust. I wondered if somebody walking through the forest would one day find the note I wrote to Max; if they would pull it out from the hollow tubular body, thinking they'd found something like a message in a bottle. I wondered what they would make of the Red Sox ticket stub I'd put in there.

Would they give the note a real good read? Would the words have meaning to them? I hoped so. I wanted the note to be a stark reminder that we aren't guaranteed anything in this amazing world we all share, and that we should love wholeheartedly and live each day filled with gratitude, because all anybody really has is right here and right now. The words I had written to Max were etched into my memory, and there they would stay. But maybe somebody else would find them, and maybe they would mean something.

This beautiful rocket had spent so long collecting dust, it felt good to watch it take flight. No, it felt great, liberating, as if part of my soul had truly been set free. Watching the rocket's smoky trail, I knew that I would rebuild my life—again. I would. Not for Karen or Max, but for me. My wounds will heal. I will go on, because the obligation of the living is to live.

Acknowledgments

At the end of every writing journey, it is a special pleasure to acknowledge the multitudes of talented people who have helped along the way. This work of fiction is no different than my previous in that I owe a debt of gratitude to those who assisted with its creation.

As a general disclaimer, I used experts for the many technical details depicted in this novel, and any shortcomings in accuracy are mine alone. I'd like to thank Peter George, Nelson Ronkin, and Brian Milas, for their insights into corporate data security systems. Thank you to Brian Noe for sharing his knowledge about firearms. Phil Redman, an expert in wireless communications, offered the inspiration for what eventually became Olympian, while Lee Chong directed me regarding the more technical aspects of lithium ion battery manufacturing.

As with all my books, they would not read as they do without the keen insights and editorial eyes of my early readers, Clair Lamb, and my mother, Judy Palmer. My father, Michael Palmer, contributed his time and energy to the manuscript as well.

I auctioned the chance to name two characters in *Desperate* to benefit Raising a Reader MA and I'd like to acknowledge Donna DiFillippo for her continued efforts to help families of young children (newborn to age five) develop, practice, and maintain habits of reading with their young children at home. The winners of the auction picked the names Matt Simons and Jack Hutchinson.

I'm fortunate to have a fantastic publishing team including Meg Ruley and Rebecca Scherer of the Jane Rotroson agency. I'd also like to acknowledge the dedicated efforts of the team at Kensington, Steve, John, Laurie, Lesleigh, and Adeola. I'm grateful for your support.

I'd also like to give a special thank you to Tory Veiga for his insights and talent.

Desperate is not a story about adoption, though adoption does play a pivotal role in the plot. It is my personal view that adoption is a beautiful way of bringing about the joy and blessing of adding a child to a family. I would like to acknowledge everyone involved in the process—from the lawyers, agencies, and social workers, to the families with adopted children, and birth mothers and birth fathers who help to make this blessing a possibility.

As Nat King Cole sang in his beautiful song, "Nature Boy": "The greatest thing you'll ever learn is just to love and be loved in return." To that end, I thank my wife and children who are there to reinforce this idea every day.

As always, I'd like to acknowledge my readers. Thank you for letting me entertain you for a while. It's truly my pleasure.

In Daniel Palmer's electrifying, brilliantly plotted new thriller, a private school campus becomes a battleground as a desperate father takes on a terrifying enemy. . . .

When Jake Dent's dreams of baseball glory fell apart in a drunk-driving incident, his marriage did, too. In those dark days, a popular survivalist blog helped to restore Jake's sense of control. He's become an avid doomsday prepper, raising his diabetic son, Andy, to be ready for any sudden catastrophe.

Andy, now a student at the prestigious Pepperell Academy, where Jake works as a custodian, has a secret—he's part of a computer club that redistributes money from the obscenely wealthy to the needy. Usually, their targets don't even realize they've been hacked. But this time, the club has stolen from the wrong people: a vicious drug cartel that is coming to get its money back. . . .

Staging a chemical truck spill as a distraction, the cartel infiltrates the Academy, taking Andy and his friends hostage one by one. Jake, hidden inside the school's abandoned tunnels, knows that soon the killing will start. With his training, and a stockpile of weapons and supplies, he's the last best hope these students—including his son—have of getting out alive. But survival is no longer an abstract concept. It's a violent, brutal struggle that will test Jake to the limit, where there are no rules and no second chances. . . .

Please turn the page for an exciting peek of Daniel Palmer's

CONSTANT FEAR

coming in June 2015 wherever print and e-books are sold!

CHAPTER 1

"*Death doesn't schedule an appointment.*"

Jake Dent had said this on many occasions, but wasn't certain the mantra had stuck in his son's teenage brain. Still, it was the truth. Death could show up at any hour, on any day, uninvited, unwelcomed.

Jake was dressed for the cool March weather; and much like a hunter, he wore three layers to protect him from the elements. The windproof fabric of his camouflage jacket was a four-color woodland pattern, designed to blend with the widest variety of western Massachusetts foliage.

It would help him evade the enemy.

At three o'clock in the morning, his son would be sound asleep. Sure enough, Jake could hear heavy breathing through the hollow-core door to Andy's bedroom. Jake could have upgraded that door to a more substantial model, but it would have been an unnecessary expense. Jake opted to invest his limited resources in products that could help him and his son stay alive. *Priorities.* For this reason, Jake kept everything to only essentials in the double-wide trailer he and Andy called home.

To reach safety, Jake and Andy would have to traverse several miles of rugged woodland in complete darkness. If anything went wrong en route to their destination, they'd carry enough provisions to make the forest their new home until it was safe to move again. Everything Jake needed to survive was stored neatly inside his GOOD (Get Out of Dodge) pack. The nylon camouflage bags mounted to an ALICE frame, standard issue for the U.S. military for some years, offered plenty of storage. Two zippers on the front of the bag allowed rapid access to the contents within.

Inside the bags, Jake had packed three liters of water—one liter per day per person—as well as a four-liter water-filtration system. The other contents of his pack were equally vital. If they couldn't reach their destination, the meals and energy bars would provide enough nutrition for several days. Jake prepared for the "ifs" as *if* they were certainties.

He had packed enough clothing for a weekend camping trip. Sturdy boots, long pants, long underwear, two shirts (good for layering), two socks (wool, not cotton), two hats, and a bandana. Bandanas had multitudes of uses, Jake had discovered over the years. A tent and ground tarp would provide some protection from the elements, and his down-filled sleeping bag was long and wide, perfect to cocoon his broad-shouldered, six-two frame. Jake had also packed three different ways to make fire, cooking gear, hygiene products, a first aid kit, and, perhaps the most important item of all, a .357-caliber SIG Sauer P226, carried by police officers and the military. Jake's SIG held fifteen 9mm rounds and was a durable weapon that could thrive in tough conditions.

Jake opened Andy's bedroom and sidestepped several piles of clothes strewn about like mini moguls.

Standing beside Andy's bed, Jake gazed at his son and watched him sleep. They should be moving, and quickly, but he couldn't resist the urge to stop and stare. Even though Andy was sixteen— *Sixteen? How did that happen?*—Jake could see the little boy lurking inside the young man. This was his son, the one person in life Jake most wanted to protect.

With his ruffled mop of curly dark hair and penetrating chocolate eyes, Andy would one day grow into a truly handsome man. But according to him, the girls at Pepperell Academy—popular, preppy, and loaded with cash—focused on Andy's braces, his nose (a bit too big for his face), a slight peppering of acne, and thin arms not yet muscular. While the awkward teenage years lingered, Andy would concentrate his energies on things other than dating.

Andy's cluttered room was typical of any teen. Posters on the walls showed characters from the hit television shows *Doctor Who, The Big Bang Theory,* and some cartoon that was apparently an Internet thing Jake didn't even pretend to understand. The most spectacular object in Andy's cramped but cozy bedroom was a desk he and his friends had built to look like a large-scale model of a TIE Fighter from the *Star Wars* movies. Andy and his pals from Pepperell Academy were self-proclaimed geeks, and damn proud of it.

Atop the TIE Fighter desk was the largest computer Jake had ever seen. Andy had built it piece by piece, and it looked to Jake like a sentient robot, with all the blinking lights and wires jutting out from the back. While Andy was a computer code maestro, writing apps that he and his buddies sold via iTunes, Jake's knowledge of the blasted machines was limited to e-mail, Google, and the occasional Microsoft Word document.

Jake shook Andy awake. The boy's bony shoulder fit

inside his palm like a baseball, and Jake's thoughts flitted back to days long gone. He closed his eyes and imagined the smell of fresh-cut grass, the feel, the texture of the pitcher's mound, and the roar of the crowd. How times had changed.

Andy's eyes fluttered open. He looked disoriented, but only for a moment.

"They're coming," Jake said, his voice calm and even. "We've got to go. Now. It's go time."

Andy swung his legs off the bed. A second later, he was on his feet, sturdy as if he'd been awake for hours. In the next instant, Andy had the accordion closet doors pulled open, grabbing the clothes he'd set aside for this very moment. They were the only clothes in his bedroom neatly folded and organized. His steel-toed hiking boots were intentionally unlaced, making them easy to slip on. Like his father, Andy dressed in layers, and wore a matching camouflage pattern.

Jake observed the rise and fall of Andy's chest. A push of adrenaline had turned his son's breathing visibly rapid. Adrenaline had its advantages. It would help Andy move faster through the woods, and might make him impervious to pain—should he fall or twist an ankle during the run. It had a downside, too. If stress and adrenaline induced insulin resistance, Andy could be in serious trouble, but his son knew best how to manage his diabetes.

Keeping Andy to a regular eating and sleeping schedule would have been ideal, but that was no longer an option. Andy must have shared his father's concern, because he took out his OneTouch UltraMini blood sugar monitor and a test strip. He held the lancing device against the side of his finger, pressed the release button, and didn't flinch when the needle broke the skin. A small drop of blood materialized with a slight squeeze of the finger. Andy placed the blood drop perfectly on the test strip. Practice, thousands of repetitions.

Andy didn't share the results with Jake. This was part of adolescence. Monitoring Andy's condition had been Jake's responsibility since his son was five. At some point, however, the baton had passed, and Andy took responsibility for his blood glucose levels without Jake's intervention. Like setting a curfew, Jake trusted that Andy would follow the rules and be diligent with his health. It was all part of building Andy's confidence and self-reliance.

When the levels weren't ideal, Jake had learned to avoid making accusations. As much as he wanted to shout, *"Why is your blood sugar so high? Did you eat something you weren't supposed to?"* he didn't. Jake believed in giving roots and wings, and he needed to show Andy that he trusted his judgment. He encouraged his son to make decisions for himself, offering praise whenever Andy made the right ones. It was what any parent of a teenager would do.

The glucose reading must have been fine, because no insulin injection followed. Andy slipped on his own GOOD pack. Inside were the same provisions Jake had brought, minus the SIG Sauer, as well as everything he needed to manage his diabetes.

Once his jacket was on, boots laced, pack secured, Andy got his night vision system in place. It was a tactical helmet, military issued, with an L4G30 mount from Wilcox. Secured to the swiveling J-arm was a PVS-14 night vision monocular, powered by a Gen 3 image intensifier. Jake had the same unit on his helmet.

For Andy's sixteenth birthday, Jake had bought his son an X-Bolt Micro Hunter rifle and helped him with the paperwork for his firearm identification card. It was a lighter-weight rifle with all the features of a full-sized X-Bolt. Jake had wanted Andy to have some way to protect himself for years, and now, legally, he could.

Andy slung his rifle over his shoulder and without a word headed for the trailer's back door. Jake fell into step behind his son, grabbed his own rifle by the door, and checked his watch. In five minutes, Andy had gone from being sound asleep to crunching dead leaves on his march through the woods.

His son was learning.

Through the night vision monocular, the world was an eerie shade of green, but the powerful optics made the forest come alive. They could see everything in pristine detail, from the smallest tree branches to the bumps and ridges on fallen leaves. The path they walked was a well-defined escape route that Jake meticulously maintained. It was far enough back from the road so they passed behind houses without being heard or seen, and wide enough in most places to let them walk side by side.

Both Jake and Andy were on the lookout for the slightest bit of movement that might betray the presence of the enemy. They refrained from talking, though Jake used preset hand signals to check in with Andy.

Andy kept his rifle slung over his shoulder, while Jake's was trained on the darkness. Both were on high alert, ready to pick up any noise—a snap of a twig or the rustle of some branches. Nothing. Not a sound. But that didn't mean they weren't out there somewhere. Eyes could be watching from the shadows. *Keep moving.* No other choice would do.

At some point, the path widened and became a road. Jake and Andy kept to the wood line and continued their march. Moonlight, which had powered the night vision optics, now provided enough illumination all by itself.

Eventually, the duo emerged from a copse and entered a vast hilly field, looking like a pair of soldiers returning from a scouting mission. They trekked another quarter mile before reaching a small fieldstone building situated directly behind the Groveland Gymnasium.

Built in the 1980s, the Groveland Gymnasium served the students and faculty of Pepperell Academy and housed an indoor hockey rink, squash and racquetball courts, swimming pool, basketball courts, weight-lifting area, and all manner of fitness amenities. It was best of breed, as was everything at "The Pep."

Jake lowered his night vision to scan the darkness once more. All clear. He took a moment to assess his son's condition anew. Sweat matted Andy's hair below the helmet, and his short, sharp breaths meant the adrenaline rush was still in effect. Through it all, Andy remained alert and focused. He was disciplined and well trained. Jake didn't like to brag, but he was proud that his son's body and mind were as strong as his character.

To the east of the fieldstone structure stood the other campus buildings of Pepperell Academy, Andy's school and Jake's place of employment for the past ten years. While Andy looked on, Jake removed a loose stone affixed to the side of the field house to reveal a hidden key. Through the unlocked door, Jake and Andy entered a room crammed with supplies—bags of ice melt, sand, cones, all sorts of maintenance equipment.

In the center of the room, Jake moved a pile of lightweight mats to reveal the outline of a two-by-two square cut into the wood of the floor. One side of the square had two hinges, and a rusting metal ring lay in the center. Jake pulled open the trapdoor to reveal a ladder to the level below.

Nearly all of the buildings of Pepperell Academy were connected by a series of tunnels, some of which were rumored to date back a century. Forward-thinking architects, long before Jake's tenure, had designed the tunnels to hide the infrastructure belowground. They understood the value of distributing services (water, gas, power, heat, steam, telecommunication, and even coal) around campus without impeding the pedestrian traffic or having to maintain unsightly sewer lines and utility poles aboveground. The effort created a labyrinth of passageways few had ever seen.

As head custodian and grounds manager for Pepperell Academy, Jake was one of the few employees with access to these secret passages. The kids and faculty, even other maintenance personnel, were not permitted to use them. That was one reason it made a perfect bug-out location (BOL).

With their packs still on, rifles slung over their shoulders, Jake and Andy descended the ladder to the underground passageway below. The corridor they traveled was in an older portion of the tunnel system, and they followed it to another locked door. The passageway included several rooms—most, but not all, unoccupied.

An ADEL Trinity-788 Heavy-Duty Biometric Fingerprint Door Lock secured entry to one of the rooms. Jake put his finger on the biometric scanner, and the door opened with a click. They entered the room and Andy turned on the light.

The room was a massive larder, well stocked with canned and dry food, sacks of rice, water, fuel, portable heaters, gardening tools, guns, knives, and ammo. Jake lowered his weapon and took out a stopwatch. He pushed the stop button and the tension left his body in a long exhale. Andy relaxed as well.

"That's three minutes faster than the last time," Jake said to his son. "We're doing well, but we can still do better."

Andy slumped to the floor. He needed a moment to regain his composure. Jake could see the stress of the trek had taken a significant physical and mental toll. Andy's eyes flared with anger, but he mustered enough restraint to keep his emotions in check. His son hated these drills, and had been vocal about it for some time. However, whenever he protested, Jake would say, "Death doesn't schedule an appointment."

CHAPTER 2

Few things in life brought Fausto Garza more enjoyment than causing pain. Looking at Eduardo, the bruised and battered man in front of him, gave Fausto a rush of pure pleasure. Eduardo was sitting on the trash-strewn floor of an old, abandoned warehouse and was tied up with rusty chains secured to a radiator. His left eye was swollen shut, but he still had some vision out of the right. Jagged cuts from Fausto's many rings marred both of Eduardo's cheeks, and dried blood stained the front of his torn guayabera. For a time, the open wounds had poured blood, enough so Fausto had to apply dirty rags to the skin to keep Eduardo from bleeding out. He needed his prey conscious.

The unmistakable scent of urine filled Fausto's nostrils and fired up more pleasure centers in his brain. He relished the smell of fear like a fine perfume. It even got him aroused. He'd seek a release for his pent-up desires as soon as he disposed of Eduardo. But first, Eduardo had some information to share.

Fausto crouched to get eye level with Eduardo. *"¿Dónde están las drogas que te robaste?"* ("Where are the drugs that you stole?")

Eduardo's eyes flared; but as he gazed into the face of death, his bravado retreated like a nervous paca vanishing into the forest underbrush.

"No le robé ningun drogas, Fausto," Eduardo said. *"Lo juro por la vida de mi madre."* ("I didn't steal any drugs, Fausto. I swear on my mother's life.")

Fausto, a natural-born skeptic, didn't believe him. "Where are the drugs you stole?"

"I took nothing from you. Please, you must believe me," Eduardo answered. His split lips could barely form the words and his speech came out slurred, as if he'd spent the night alone with a bottle of mescal.

"No es tan bravo el león como lo pintan." Fausto enjoyed taunting Eduardo. In most circles Eduardo *was* considered a fierce lion, but Durango, Eduardo's home, and home to a rival drug cartel, was more than six hundred kilometers from Chihuahua. Here, in Sangre Tierra territory, the man had no power.

"Sangre Tierra," or "blood earth." The cartel traced its origin and name to the day Arturo Bolivar Soto had ordered the execution of the leaders of the rival Torres cartel in a single, gruesome bloodbath. Ten bound and gagged men, all of them rich from drug money, had been tossed into a previously dug shallow grave near the Panteón La Colina. Standing at the edges of the pit were men from Soto's group, Fausto among them. They were armed with AK-47 assault rifles, and some even wielded Uzis.

"Be it known, today belongs to Soto."

Those were the last words those ten men ever heard.

Blood spilled from bullet-ravaged bodies, pooling beneath the corpses until the parched earth swallowed every last drop.

Sangre Tierra . . . Blood Earth.

Arturo Bolivar Soto was its first and only leader.

From that moment on, a terror worse than the Torres cartel reigned. Already-dug graves became a trademark of Sangre Tierra, and mass shootings a favorite method of compliance and control. Soto's ambitions were far larger than the territory currently under his authority. The balance was soon to tip in his favor. Sangre Tierra already had a growing presence in the United States, and from there had plans to extend its area of dominance well beyond the boundaries the Torres Cartel once controlled.

Poor Eduardo had interfered with those ambitions. For that, he would pay.

"I don't have what you seek."

Fausto appraised Eduardo anew and suppressed the urge to bend back Eduardo's fingers with pliers.

"I'm going to tell you a story," Fausto said, standing and using his pants to brush away the grime collected on his palms. Fausto had a long face, a prominent nose, deep-set eyes, and hair like the mane of a stallion, which he pulled back into a long ponytail that swept across his broad shoulders. He was fit, narrow at the waist, muscled and in perfect proportion. Women were drawn to Fausto, but he preferred the whores, who asked for nothing and never complained of his sexual proclivities.

"When I was a young boy, no more than thirteen," Fausto began, "I lived in Ciudad Juárez. It was there I met Soto's cousin, Carlos Guzman, who gave me a gun and ordered me to shoot a man he had tied up and dumped on the ground. Guzman was so drunk he didn't think he could hit the man at point-blank range. I didn't know what to say. I had never killed before. But what captured my imagination was Carlos's diamond-studded watch, the fancy clothes he wore, the pearl inlay on the pistol's handle. You see I came from nothing, Eduardo.

I was an orphan boy who escaped from an abusive master."

Here, Fausto could have elaborated on the sexual abuse he had endured, the endless rapes by the pervert who had taken him in under the auspices of hiring a young store clerk to stock shelves in his grocery store. *Store clerk!* His rapist wanted a victim, a plaything, and Fausto was too young, too inexperienced, too frightened, to find a way out.

"Why are you telling me this, Fausto?" Eduardo's voice snapped with fear.

"Shut up until I finish," Fausto barked.

Eduardo bowed his head sullenly.

"When I met Carlos Guzman," Fausto continued, "I had just recently escaped from my captor. I was living on the streets of Juárez, scrounging for food like an alley cat. I had experienced little but the darkest side of humanity for close to a decade. So when I pulled the trigger, blowing that helpless man's brains out his ears, I did so, hoping one day I, too, could have a pearl-inlaid pistol."

Fausto reached behind him. From the waistband of his jeans, he produced a pistol exactly like the one he had described. A pleased-with-himself grin creased the corners of his mouth as he put the gun away. The grin widened into a smile; for the first time since his abduction, Eduardo could see the ornately designed gold caps that covered each of Fausto's teeth. The caps were removable, but Fausto was considering having them affixed permanently. They sent a strong message of wealth and power, Fausto's two greatest loves.

"When Carlos sobered up and saw what I had done," Fausto continued, "he was so appreciative that he paid a visit to my so-called employer. The police found the grocery store owner's liver in one garbage can, his heart in another, and his head in another still. From that moment on, I became a part of something. Something I could believe in. Carlos raised me like a son. And Arturo Soto is a grandfather whom I treasure and adore. They trust me with the most important assignments. They respect me and my ability, and for that, I'm eternally grateful."

"Again, why are you telling me this, Fausto?"

"Why do I tell you this?" Fausto repeated. "Because you need to know that I view you like you're a rodent. Your life has that much meaning to me. I feel nothing for your suffering. And I would not be involved here unless this situation was indeed a very big deal."

Fausto went over to his toolbox, the only object on the warehouse floor aside from a busted wooden chair. He retrieved from within a cordless power drill, with a gleaming silver bit. With a push on the trigger, Fausto showed Eduardo that the drill's battery was fully charged.

"Now, then," Fausto said in a perfectly calm voice. "Let's talk again about the packages you took from us."

Fausto placed the drill on Eduardo's knee and squeezed the trigger. Eduardo's eyes burst with panic at the loud whirring sound. The angry metallic whine quickly dampened as the tip of the drill bored through the fabric of his soiled pants and penetrated the first layer of skin. Blood erupted from the puncture wound; the scream that followed was symphonic to Fausto's ears.

Fausto prepared to drill again. He had bet himself he could bore nine holes before Eduardo passed out from pain. Fausto steadied Eduardo's shaking leg in a vise-like grip. He set the drill tip on the other knee when his phone rang. Fausto exhaled a loud sigh and returned his attention to the drill, but the persistent ringing proved too much of a distraction. He glanced at the caller ID and sighed once more. Eduardo did not seem certain how to feel. The anticipation of pain was its own form of torture.

Fausto answered the call.

"¿Que quieres?" Fausto said. ("What do you want?")

Fausto kept the drill bit against Eduardo's knee, but he waited to pull the trigger. He didn't want to listen to the caller over Eduardo's screaming. Eduardo's blubbering was bothersome enough.

"Soto te quiere ver ahora mismo, Fausto," a man said. ("Soto wants to see you right away, Fausto.")

"I'm a little busy right now," Fausto answered in Spanish.

"It's urgent," said the man. "There's big trouble in America, someplace in Massachusetts. You need to leave immediately."

Fausto ended the call and turned his attention back to Eduardo. "Always something, eh?"

Eduardo looked like a man who'd been given a new lease on life.

"I'll have to finish with you later. In the meantime, let me leave you with something to remember me by."

Fausto pulled the trigger on the drill and wished he had more time to make Eduardo scream.

CHAPTER 1

It began, innocently enough, with a fall.

Beth Stillwell, a slight, thirty-five-year-old mother of three with kind eyes and an infectious laugh, was shopping at Thrifty Dollar Store with her kids in tow. She'd been stocking up on school supplies and home staples when she lost her balance and tumbled to the grimy linoleum floor. It was bad enough to have to shop at the dollar store, something new since her separation from her philandering husband of fifteen years. It was downright humiliating to be sprawled out on their floor, her leg bent in a painful angle beneath her.

Beth wasn't hurt, but as her six-year-old daughter Emily tried to help her stand, her left leg felt weak, almost rubbery. Leaning against a shelf stocked with cheap soap, Beth took a tentative step only to have the leg nearly buckle beneath her. She kept her balance, and after another awkward step, decided she could walk on it.

The strength in Beth's left leg mostly returned, but a slight stiffness and a disconcerting drag lingered for weeks. Beth's sister told her to see a doctor. Beth said she would, but it was an empty promise. Running a licensed day care out of her Jamaica Plain home, Beth was in charge of seven kids in addition to her own, and any downtime put tremendous strain on her limited finances. She rarely had time to make a phone call. But the leg was definitely a bother, and the lingering weakness was a constant worry. She occasionally stumbled, but the last straw was losing control of her urine while in charge of toddlers who could hold their bladders better than she could. That drove her to the doctor.

An MRI confirmed a parasagittal tumor originating from the meninges with all the telltale characteristics of a typical meningioma: a brain tumor. The tumor was already big enough to compress brain tissue, interrupting the normal complex communication from neuron to neuron and causing a moderate degree of edema, swelling from the pressure on the brain's blood vessels.

Beth would need surgery to have it removed.

Dr. Carrie Bryant stood in front of the viewbox, examining Beth Stillwell's MRI. A fourth-year neurosurgical resident rotating through Boston Community Hospital (BCH), she would be assisting chief resident Dr. Fred Michelson with Beth's surgery. The tumor pressed upon the top of the brain on the right side. Carrie could see exactly why Beth's left leg had gone into a focal seizure and why she'd lost control of her urine. It was not a particularly large mass, about walnut-sized, but its location was extremely problematic. If it were to grow, Beth would develop progressive spasticity in her leg and eventually lose bladder control completely.

Carrie absently rubbed her sore quadriceps while studying Beth's films. She had set a new personal best at yesterday's sprint distance triathlon, finally breaking the elusive ten-minute-mile pace during the run, and her body was letting her know she had pushed it too hard. Her swim and bike performance were shaky per usual, and all but guaranteed a finish in the bottom quartile for her age group—but at least she was out there, battling, doing her best to get her fitness level back to where it had been.

Carrie's choice to jump right into triathlons was perhaps not the wisest, but she never did anything half measure. She enjoyed pushing her body to new limits. She'd also used the race to raise more than a thousand dollars for BCH: a tiny fraction of what was needed, but every bit helped.

BCH served the poor and uninsured. Carrie felt proud to be a part of that mission, but lack of funding was a constant frustration. In her opinion, the omnipotent budgeting committee relied too heavily on cheap labor to fill the budget gap, which explained why fourth- and fifth-year residents basically ran the show whenever they rotated through BCH. Attending physicians, those docs who had finished residency, were supposed to provide oversight, but they had too much work and too few resources to do the job.

If the constant budget shortfalls had a silver lining, it could be summed up in a single word: experience. With each BCH rotation the hours would be long, the demands exhausting, but Carrie never groaned or complained. She was getting the best opportunity to hone her skills.

Thank goodness Chambers University did its part to fund the storied health-care institution, which had trained some of Boston's most famous doctors, including the feared but revered Dr. Stanley Metcalf, staff neurosurgeon at the iconic White Memorial Hospital. For now, the doors to BCH were open, the lights on, and people like Beth Stillwell could get exceptional medical care even without exceptional insurance.

So far, Beth had been a model patient. She'd spent two days in the hospital, and in that time Carrie had had the pleasure of meeting both her sister and her children. Carrie prepped for Beth's surgery wondering when having a family of her own would fit into her hectic life. At twenty-nine, she had thought it might happen with Ian, her boyfriend of two years, but apparently her dedication to residency did not jibe with his vision of the relationship. She should have known when Ian began referring to his apartment as Carrie's "on-call room" that their union was headed for rocky times.

At half past eleven, Carrie was on her way to scrub when Dr. Michelson stopped her in the hallway.

"Two cases of acute lead poisoning just rolled in," he announced.

Carrie smiled weakly at the dark humor: two gunshot victims needed the OR.

"We can do Miss Stillwell at five o'clock," Michelson said. It was not a request. Working at one of New England's busiest trauma hospitals meant that patients often got bumped for the crisis of the moment, and Dr. Michelson fully expected Carrie to accommodate him.

Carrie would have been fine with his request regardless. Her social calendar had been a long string of empty boxes ever since Ian called things off. During the relationship vortex, Carrie had evidently neglected her apartment as well as her friends, and it would take time to get everything back to pre-Ian levels. Carrie agreed to move Beth's surgery even though she had no real say in the matter.

The time change gave Carrie an opportunity to finish the rest of her rotations on the neurosurgical floor. She met with several different patients, and concluded her rounds with Leon Dixon, whom Dr. Metcalf had admitted as a private patient that morning. She would be assisting Dr. Metcalf with his surgery the next day.

Carrie entered Leon's hospital room after knocking, and found a handsome black man propped up in his adjustable bed, drinking water through a straw. Leon was watching *Antiques Roadshow* with his wife, who sat in a chair pushed up against the bed. They were holding hands. Leon was in his early fifties, with a kind but weathered face.

"Hi, Leon, I'm Dr. Carrie Bryant. I'll be assisting with your operation tomorrow. How you feeling today?"

"Pre—eh-eh-eh-eh."

"I'm Phyllis, Leon's wife. He's feeling pretty crappy, is what he's trying to say."

Carrie shook hands with the attractive woman who had gone from being a wife to a caregiver in a matter of weeks. The heavy makeup around Phyllis's tired eyes showed just how difficult those weeks had been. Carrie had yet to review Leon's films, but was not surprised about his speech problems; the chart said he'd presented aphasic. She doubted he'd stuttered before, but she was not going to embarrass him by asking.

"Leon, could you close your eyes and open your mouth for me?" Carrie asked.

Leon got his eyes shut, but his mouth stayed closed as well. Carrie sent a text message to Dr. Nugent in radiology. She wanted to look at his films, stat.

"He has a lot of trouble following instructions," Phyllis said as she brushed tears from her eyes. "Memory and temper problems, too."

Something is going on in Leon's left temporal lobe, Carrie thought. *Probably a tumor.*

Carrie observed other symptoms as well. The right side of Leon's face drooped slightly, and his right arm drifted down when he held out his arms in front of him with his eyes closed. His reflexes were heightened in the right arm and leg, and when Carrie scraped the sole of his right foot with the reflex hammer, his great toe extended up toward his face—a Babinski sign, indicating damage to the motor system represented on the left side of Leon's brain.

Carrie took hold of Leon's dry and calloused hand and looked him in the eye.

"Leon, we're going to do everything we can to make you feel better. I'm going to go look at your films now, and I'll see you tomorrow for your surgery." Carrie wrote her cell phone number on a piece of paper. Business cards were for after residency. "If you need anything, this is how to reach me," she said.

Carrie preferred not to cut the examination short, but a text from Dr. Robert Nugent said he'd delay his meeting for Carrie if she came now. Carrie was rushed herself. She needed to get to Beth Stillwell for her final pre-op consultation.

Dr. Nugent, a married father of two, was a competitive triathlete who had finished well ahead of Carrie in the last race they had done together. Over the years, Carrie had learned that it paid to be friends with the radiologists for situations just like this, and nothing fostered camaraderie quite like the race circuit.

The radiology department was located in the bowels of BCH, in a windowless section of the Glantz Wing, but somehow Dr. Nugent appeared perpetually tan, even after the brutal New England winter.

"Thanks for making some time for me, Bob," Carrie said. "Leon just materialized on my OR schedule and I haven't gotten any background on him from Dr. Metcalf yet."

Dr. Nugent shrugged. He knew all about Dr. Metcalf's surprise patients. "Yeah, from what I was told, Dixon's doctor is good friends with Metcalf."

"Let me guess: Leon has no health insurance."

"Bingo."

Carrie chuckled and said, "Why am I not surprised?"

It was unusual to see a private patient at Community. Just about every patient was admitted through the emergency department and assigned to resident staff. Dr. Metcalf was known for his philanthropy, and when he rotated through Community he often took on cases he could not handle at White Memorial because of insurance issues.

All the residents looked forward to working with Dr. Metcalf, and Carrie's peers had expressed jealousy more than once. Assisting Dr. Metcalf was the ultimate test of a resident's skill, grace under the most extreme pressure. Dr. Metcalf had earned a reputation for being exacting and demanding, even a bully at times, but his approach paid off. He taught technique, didn't assume total control, and was supremely patient with the less experienced surgeons. Like many world-class surgeons, Dr. Metcalf was sometimes tempestuous and always demanding, but Carrie was willing to take the bitter with the sweet if it helped with her career.

Dr. Nugent put Leon's MRI films up on the viewbox.

"It's most likely a grade three astrocytoma," he said.

The irregular mass was 1.5 by 2 centimeters in size, located deep in the left temporal lobe and associated with frondlike edema. No doubt this was the cause of Leon's aphasic speech and confused behavior.

"So Dr. Metcalf's scheduled to take this one out tomorrow," Dr. Nugent said.

"As much as he can, anyway."

Dr. Nugent agreed.

Carrie was about to ask Dr. Nugent a question when she noticed the time. She was going to be late for the final pre-op consultation with Beth. *Damn.* There were never enough hours in the day.

Carrie made it to Beth's hospital room at four thirty and found the anesthesiologist already there. By the end of Carrie's consult, Beth looked teary-eyed.

"You'll be holding your children again in no time, trust me," Carrie assured her.

Even with her head newly shaved, Beth was a strikingly beautiful woman, young and vivacious. Despite Carrie's words of comfort, Beth did not look convinced.

"Just make sure I'll be all right, Dr. Bryant," Beth said. "I have to see my kids grow up."

At quarter to five, Beth was taken from the patient holding area to OR 15. Carrie had her mask, gown, and head covering already donned, and was in the scrub room, three minutes into her timed five-minute anatomical scrub, when Dr. Michelson showed up.

"How would you feel about doing the Stillwell case on your own?" he asked. "The attending went home for the day, and I got a guy with a brain hemorrhage who's going to be ART if I don't evacuate the clot and decompress the skull."

Carrie rolled her eyes at Michelson. She was not a big fan of some of the medical slang that was tossed around, and ART, an especially callous term, was an acronym for "approaching room temperature," a.k.a. dead.

"No problem on Stillwell," Carrie said. Her heart jumped a little. She had never done an operation without the oversight of an attending or chief resident before.

Quick as the feeling came, Carrie's nerves settled.

She was an excellent surgeon with confidence in her abilities, and, if the hospital grapevine were to be believed, the staff's next chief resident. It would certainly be a nice feather in her surgical cap, and helpful in securing a fellowship at the Cleveland Clinic after residency.

"Unfortunately, I'm going to need OR fifteen. Everything else is already booked," Michelson said.

Carrie nodded. Par for the course at BCH. "Beth can wait," she said.

"I checked the schedule for you. OR six or nine should be open in a couple of hours."

Carrie did some quick calculations to make sure she could handle the Stillwell operation and still be rested enough to assist Dr. Metcalf with Leon's operation in the morning. *Three to four hours, tops,* Carrie thought, *and Beth will be back in recovery.*

"No problem," Carrie said. "I'll let you scrub down and save the day."

"Thanks, Doc Bryant," Michelson said. "But you're the real lifesaver here. I don't think there's another fourth year I'd trust with this operation."

"Your faith in me inspires."

Carrie did not mention the promise she'd made to Beth during her pre-op consultation. Michelson would not have approved. If one thing was certain about surgery, it was that nothing, no matter how routine or simple it seemed, was ever 100 percent guaranteed.

CHAPTER 2

Carrie had met Beth again in the preoperative area, this time accompanied by Rosemary, a certified registered nurse anesthetist. While Carrie had never worked with Rosemary before, watching her insert the IV into Beth's arm made Carrie confident in the CRNA's ability. Rosemary gave Beth a light dose of midazolam, which decreased anxiety and would mercifully bring about amnesia. Some things were best not remembered, brain surgery among them.

Once in the OR, Rosemary got Beth connected to the monitors that tracked vitals. She delivered a dose of propofol to induce general anesthesia, followed by a push of succinylcholine to bring on temporary muscle paralysis. From that moment on, the endotracheal tube would do all the breathing for Beth.

Dr. Saleem Badami, originally from Bangalore, India, and a highly regarded intern, was to assist with the operation. This was really a one-person show, so Dr. Badami was there primarily to monitor Beth's neurological status during surgery.

The circulating nurse had painstakingly prepared the necessary equipment, including the Midas Rex drill, which Carrie would use to penetrate the skull and turn the flap. Last on the team was Valerie, a scrub nurse born in Haiti. A longtime vet of BCH, Valerie was one of the best scrub nurses on staff. As usual, Valerie looked in total command of her craft as she prepped her station for the upcoming operation. It was Valerie who had introduced Carrie to the joys of listening to jazz while operating, and over the years the two had grown close.

If there was one drawback to working with Valerie, it was her unwavering commitment to finding Carrie a date. Beneath her surgical cap and scrubs, Carrie had luxurious brown hair down to her shoulders, almond-shaped brown eyes, enviably high cheekbones, and a body toned and muscled from hours of training. All that, combined with her intellect and outgoing personality, and Dr. Carrie Bryant was somebody's total package. Despite Carrie's repeated assurances that she was happily single, Valerie never failed to bring a list of eligible bachelors to surgery.

"His name is James, and he's some hotshot at a biotech startup in Cambridge. My mother knows his family."

"Thanks for the suggestion," Carrie said, checking over the equipment, "but today the only man I'm interested in is John Coltrane. Let's fire up the music, please."

Carrie waited for the first notes from "Out of this World," the first cut from *Coltrane (Deluxe Edition)*, to play before she picked up the scalpel and positioned it for the initial cut. The little stomach jitter that had been kicking around was gone. The first solo flight had to happen to everyone at some point, and today was her day.

You've got this, Doc. You trained hard.

Any and all distractions faded. Lingering thoughts

of her ex-boyfriend, Valerie's biotech guy, and tomorrow's surgery with Dr. Metcalf were just ghosts in her consciousness. Her focus was intense. She loved being in the zone; this level of concentration was a rush like no other. Prior to surgery, Carrie had managed sundry pro forma tasks, those checklist items requiring no thought or decision. Following standard procedure, she had used Mayfield pins to secure Beth's head in three fixation points.

It was time to operate.

Carrie made the first scalp incision, expertly cutting the shape of a large semicircle over the crown of Beth's shaved and immobilized skull. She paused to examine her work. It was a fine first cut, and Carrie was pleased with the results. The skin flap was certainly large enough.

The growth was sitting underneath the skull, originating from the meninges, the membrane that covers the brain. It was directly adjacent to the superior sagittal sinus, the major venous channel coursing between the brain's hemispheres. From what Carrie had seen in the MRI, the sinus appeared to be open. This was one of her chief concerns going in. If the tumor were adhering to the sinus, Carrie could do only a partial resection, which would mean Beth would need additional treatment, such as radiation.

Why did you make that promise?

It was probably seeing Beth's kids, especially little six-year-old Emily with her sweet toothy smile, that had clouded Carrie's better judgment. If the tumor were free from the sinus, the only treatment Beth would need would be careful follow-up to ensure no recurrence, and perhaps an anticonvulsant medication to reduce the risks of residual seizures.

Surgeons were not, in Carrie's opinion, like normal people. They were more like clutch shooters who took the ball with three seconds left and the basketball game on the line. Difficult times seemed to bring out the best in their cool. Sure, Carrie had sweated for just a bit at the start of the operation, but that was normal. Good, even. She was young, inexperienced, and it was smart for her to be cautious. Things could head south in a flash, but Carrie was not overly concerned. By the fourth year of residency, any surgeon who would cower in a decisive moment had been culled from the herd.

Carrie set to work placing the Raney clips around the margins of the retracted tissue to hold the scalp in place. The slim blue clips were atraumatic, designed to minimize injury and limit both bleeding and tissue damage.

Thirty minutes into surgery.

It took another fifteen minutes for Carrie to set all the clips in place. Now it was time for her to drill. Carrie held the high-speed stylus in her steady right hand and made four expertly placed burr holes on either side of the parasagittal sinus.

"Change the drill, please," Carrie said.

The circulating nurse handed Carrie a different high-speed pneumatic drill, and she used that one to cut through the skull between the burr holes. Carrie took in a breath as she lifted the bone flap over the dura. She carefully handed the bone flap to Valerie for safekeeping until she was ready to reconstitute the skull after removing the tumor.

Valerie, being Valerie, anticipated Carrie wanting bone wax to control bleeding from the exposed skull margins.

You've got a great team here, Carrie thought.

Pausing, Carrie examined the dura, a thick membrane that is the outermost of the three layers of the meninges surrounding the brain, for any signs of damage. Using her gloved fingers, she carefully palpated the hard, solid tumor beneath. She judged the location of the growth to be perfect for resection, and then used cotton pledgets to tamp down the margins of the exposed dura.

Carrie was exceedingly careful with the pledgets, because too much traction on the dura might cause tugging on critical veins over the surface of the brain, which could result in bleeding. When the pledgets were properly positioned, Carrie was ready for her next incision, keeping in mind that she would cut one centimeter away from the tumor.

One centimeter. Exact. Precise.

Done. After her perfect cut, Carrie used the coagulator and Gelfoam sponges judiciously to control hemostasis and limit bleeding. And there it was, the tumor, sitting on the top of the brain, pressing down on the cortex that controlled Beth Stillwell's leg and bladder. It was not too big, but it sure was ugly, and more vascular in appearance than she had expected from the MRI image. Thank goodness it was not adherent to the sinus! Carrie could resect it cleanly. Still, the vascular supply was far more complex than she had predicted.

"James is a heck of a lot better-looking than that nasty thing," Valerie said.

Carrie laughed lightly.

The time was 10:30 p.m. Beth had been in surgery for two and a half hours, a little bit longer than Carrie had anticipated, but not unusually long.

"Vitals?" Carrie asked.

"Looking fine," Rosemary said.

One hour and I'll be done, Carrie estimated.

Working with care, Carrie removed the tumor, along with the adherent patch of excised dura, which would be sent off to pathology for a frozen section. It did not appear malignant by gross inspection. She would want to be sure the margins were clean and there was no evidence of malignancy elsewhere. At this point, Carrie figured she could get to the on-call room by midnight and grab five or so hours of sleep before she needed to be back in the OR by seven o'clock the next morning for surgery with Dr. Metcalf.

Ah, the glorious life of a doctor. Her dad, an internist at Mass General, had warned Carrie about the rigors of residency, but his description paled in comparison with the real thing.

Carrie paused to examine her work once more. Something was beginning to bother her. The margins of the craniotomy looked to be oozing blood, much more than usual.

"More Gelfoam and four-by-fours." Carrie's voice sounded calm, but had a noticeable edge.

Valerie complied with speed. As Carrie dabbed away the bleeding, her whole body heated up beneath her surgical scrubs.

"Vitals?"

"Blood pressure stable at one hundred over seventy, normal sinus at ninety."

What the heck is happening?

Carrie did everything she could to stanch the bleeding, but the oozing persisted. She started to worry.

Why isn't Beth's blood clotting?

Her pre-op labs had showed a normal coagulation profile. She should not be having this problem during surgery. What is going on? Where is the bleeding coming from?

From the beginning of her residency, Carrie had been taught to think on her feet, but her mind was drawing blanks.

Think, dammit! Think!

As if Dr. Metcalf were whispering in her ear, Carrie got the germ of an idea. She recalled a case from back in her internship year. A seventy-year-old woman undergoing a craniotomy for an anaplastic meningioma lost blood pressure during surgery and at the same time developed significant skin hemorrhages.

The body normally regulates blood flow by clotting to heal breaks on blood vessel walls, and after the bleeding stops it dissolves those clots to allow for regular blood flow. But some conditions cause the same clotting factors to become overactive, leading to excessive bleeding, as in the case of that seventy-year-old woman. Carrie recalled the outcome grimly.

Could it be DIC—disseminated intravascular coagulation—causing Beth's bleeding? A tissue factor associated with the tumor could be triggering the cascade of proteins and enzymes that regulate clotting. It was a rare complication of meningiomas, but it did happen, especially if the tumors were highly vascular like Beth's.

"Vitals?" Carrie asked again.

"Stable, Carrie."

Victims of DIC often suffered effects of vascular clotting throughout the body. Once the clotting factors were all used up, patients began to bleed, and bleed profusely—the skin, the GI tract, the kidneys and urinary system. DIC could be sudden and catastrophic.

"Get me a pro time/INR, APTT, CBC with platelet count, and fibrin split products," Carrie ordered. "Saline, please. Rosemary, keep up her fluids."

In a perfect world, Carrie would get a hematology consult pronto, but at such a late hour, nobody would be available. Valerie entered the lab test orders into the OR computer.

"Blood pressure is down a bit to one hundred systolic," Rosemary said.

Carrie continued to control the bleeding at the tumor site as best she could. Now she was in the waiting game. Nobody spoke. Carrie asked Valerie to shut off the music, and the only sounds in the OR were the persistent noises of the monitors and the rhythmic breathing of the ventilator.

Fifteen minutes later Beth's labs came back. Carrie was sponging away a fresh ooze of blood as Valerie read the results off the OR computer.

"Pro time and APTT markedly elevated," Valerie said. "Platelets down to five thousand. Crit down to twenty-two percent—about half normal. Fibrin split products positive."

No doubt about it, Carrie thought, *this is DIC*. Beth had been typed and crossed prior to surgery. Carrie ordered FFP, fresh frozen plasma, and a transfusion of packed red blood cells.

"Carrie," Saleem said, his voice steeped in worry, "I'm seeing hemorrhagic lesions all over Beth's arms."

Carrie stopped sponging to examine Beth's extremities. Sure enough, blood was pooling underneath the skin, forming ugly bruises marred by bumpy raised patches that looked like charcoaled burn marks. Carrie bit her lip as she cleared beads of perspiration from her brow with the back of her hand.

On paper, she had made no missteps. There was no way for her to have predicted this rare complication of a meningioma surgery. It was just the nature of how the tissue itself could react and explode in the tightly regulated, complex coagulation homeostasis process. The body is finely tuned to form clots and dissolve them to keep blood flowing. One small tip of the scale could have been enough to send the entire well-balanced system into complete disarray. The reduced hematocrit meant that Beth was bleeding internally as well—within her GI and urinary tracts, perhaps elsewhere. Sure enough, the indwelling Foley collecting bag was filling with blood-tinged urine.

"Give me two liters of normal saline."

At this point, the FFP and PRBC were ready for transfusion.

"BP down to ninety over sixty. Pulse one twenty," Rosemary announced.

Carrie took in the information, but she remained calm.

I'm not going to let you die.

At one o'clock in the morning, Carrie had another decision to make. Should she treat Beth with heparin, too? The drug could dramatically worsen the bleeding because it was a blood thinner, but on the other hand, Carrie remembered from her rotation on the medical service that heparin could help by preventing the clotting that caused the consumption of coagulation factors. In some DIC cases, a blood thinner could actually promote clotting. It was a crapshoot. Carrie had been right to give Beth a traditional treatment thus far, but her condition was again deteriorating, and rapidly.

"I want a heparin infusion, now."

The words left Carrie's mouth before she realized she'd spoken them. Though her team was masked and gowned, Carrie had no trouble seeing the astonished looks on everyone's faces. Saleem hesitated, but Carrie barked the order again, and this time he jumped. Everyone held a collective breath as the drug was administered intravenously. Carrie kept a careful watch over the wound and continued to sponge away the bleeding. To her eye, the blood flow seemed to have lessened.

Still not out of the woods. Not even close.

All Carrie and her team could do now was contain

the bleeding, keep administering fluids, and pray the decision to use heparin was the right course of action.

At four o'clock in the morning, Beth finally seemed to be stabilizing. Her blood pressure had risen to 110/65. By that point, everyone in the OR was utterly exhausted, with Carrie in the worst shape of all. This was her patient—on her watch! Carrie's feet had swollen to the size of water balloons and her back strained against the tug of eight grueling hours spent standing.

Carrie ordered another set of labs. This time, while the FSP was still elevated, the PT and APTT were definitely showing signs of improvement. The bleeding looked better, too.

Valerie appeared stunned, as did Saleem.

"Carrie, whatever in the world inspired you to give this poor darling heparin?" Valerie asked.

Carrie was breathing as though she had just finished a sprint-distance tri. "Just a thought I had, I guess."

At five forty-five in the morning, Beth Stillwell was handed off from surgical to the medical and hematology teams in the ICU. Her DIC was still a problem and she would need much more intensive work to stabilize her, but the major bleeding seemed to be contained. Fifteen minutes later, Valerie and Beth were changing out of their bloodstained surgical scrubs in the women's locker room.

"She's going to make it because of you, because of what you did in there," Valerie said, brushing tears from her eyes.

Carrie had never seen Valerie cry before, and the sight set a lump in her throat. "But what's the quality of her survival going to be?" Carrie answered. "She bled a lot."

"Carrie Bryant, don't be so hard on yourself. If it had been any other doc in there, they wouldn't have ordered the heparin and we'd be having a very different conversation right now."

"Maybe."

Valerie turned fierce. "Don't you maybe me, Dr. Bryant! You diagnosed DIC quick as you did, and correctly at that. Then treating her with heparin? Girl, in my humble opinion, you are a hero here. Real and true, and I want to give you a hug."

Valerie opened her arms and Carrie fell into her embrace. The moment she did, the tears broke and would not stop for more than a minute. It had been such a long night. *I made a promise. . . .*

Carrie broke away from Valerie, but could not get the faces of Beth's young daughters out of her mind. She took a moment to regain her composure, then checked the time on her phone. It was six fifteen in the morning. She was due back in the OR for the astrocytoma surgery with Dr. Metcalf in forty-five minutes.

"I've got to go break the news to Beth's sister," Carrie said, her chest filling with a heavy sadness.

The conversation would be briefer than the family deserved, but she'd page Dr. Michelson and make sure he could be there for follow-up questions. At this point, Carrie only had time to take a quick shower and wolf down a peanut-butter-and-jelly sandwich with a black coffee chaser outside the OR.

That was all the time she ever seemed to have.